The Broygus

LAURENCE KERSHOOK

To Gill

With love

From

Laurence

xx

This edition published in the UK in 2022

Cover design by Caroline Goldsmith.

ISBN: 978-1-3999-2036-0

Also available as an ebook edition

For Stella and Pin.

With love, and apologies for the wait.

ONE

1976

It was Sam's most damaging kind of anger, he knew that: the short-lived kind that quickly morphed into deep misery. Slumped head in hands at the kitchen table, he gazed at Deborah's abandoned breakfast and wished he could rewind and start the day again. It was his assistant Eleni's morning to open the shop, so he could have stayed in bed for an extra hour trying to catch up on some sleep after another restless night. But he'd got up specially early to be with Deborah before she set out on her long day of guiding tourists around London in the midst of the freak July heatwave. Dishevelled, unshaven, happy to stay in his cotton bathrobe for as long as possible before needing to bathe and dress, he'd admired her poised coolness in her ultra-light summer business suit, her chestnut hair combed stylishly to fall to just above her shoulders, a hint of her perfume curling its way towards him through the aromas of toast and coffee. He'd shared in her happiness as she passed him the card yesterday's client had given her with a ten-pound note clipped inside it.

'Dear Deborah,' he read aloud, 'Thank you so much for showing us round Good Old London Town. A great day with a lovely little lady. If you ever come to Roseville, Minnesota, be sure to look us up. Happy trails, Shelby and Sandra Weaver.'

'That's a really nice message,' he said, handing it back. 'And a tenner on top of our fee! That's a bloody good tip.'

'They asked me to take them round again on Saturday,' she said. 'I had to say no, of course.'

'Why's that?' He knew the answer perfectly well.

'You need to ask? You know I won't work on Shobbus.'

He laughed. He saw her flinch and he knew she knew he was about to hurt her, but the demon had already taken charge. 'Not even for a day's wages and another tenner on top? Tell you what, you could do the job, then pop round the *shul* and split the tip fifty-fifty with the rabbi. He'd keep shtum, and that should get you off the hook with Hashem.'

So, who could blame her for calling him a cynical bastard and storming out? He felt angry with himself and sick with remorse. He wished that he'd tried to make it right before she left, but now he'd have to carry around his regret and self-inflicted misery for the whole of another long, mercilessly hot day. And, worse still, he could feel it threatening to bleed into the far more dangerous kind of emotion, the dull-grey one shading into black, the one he'd known since childhood; the one that tried to drag him into a dark pit and hold him there until he believed he'd never find the strength to fight his way out.

It took a while for the sound of the doorbell to filter through to his consciousness, but no sooner had it than he felt a renewed wave of anger kick in. It was a persistent, nagging ring; short repetitive stabs with precisely the same brief pause between each one, as if whoever was out there was taking a deliberate pleasure in mangling his overstretched nerves. Resting his elbows on the table and covering his ears with his hands, he waited for the noise to stop and the intruder to go away. After two more minutes of torture he jerked tight the belt of his robe, stomped across the flat's tiny hall and wrenched the door open, fired up to do battle.

A stocky, broad-shouldered man stood there, looking confident and perfectly relaxed in a pearl-grey linen suit with a matching trilby hat. He was carrying a leather briefcase with a shiny brass catch. The corners of his eyes creased as he smiled at Sam, revealing even white teeth and a flash of gold. As Sam studied the man, to his surprise he felt his fury ebb away to be replaced by a mixture of embarrassment and confusion. He felt all too aware of how he must appear in the man's eyes: wild-haired, sweaty, barefoot and no doubt looking slightly ridiculous, standing in the doorway clutching his robe around himself. The man seemed to be older him, maybe in his early forties, but he looked solidly built and unlike Sam he showed no sign of excess weight. His eyes were brown like Sam's. His hair, what could be seen of it under the trilby, was the same rich black but in contrast to Sam's it was cut short and neatly trimmed. For a moment the two men faced each other in silence. Sam was the first to speak. 'Look, this isn't a good—'

The man lifted a finger as if to deflect the dismissal and his smile widened a fraction. 'Mr Shaykin? Samuel Shaykin? Do I have the pleasure? Pleased to meet you. I'm Aaron Green. Call me Ron.' With a conjurer's deftness, he produced a visiting card and offered it to Sam. It read:

Hackney Jewish Aid. A registered charity. 103 Ashdown Drive, Gants Hill Essex. Tel. 554 0070. Aaron Green, Trustee.

So that was it. A charity collector, simple as that. He hadn't been anywhere near a shul for at least ten years, and still they'd managed to track him down. Well, the bloke had come to the wrong place – and definitely at the wrong time. He handed the card back. 'Sorry, I'm not giving. Goodbye.'

Unhurriedly, in the same confident voice, the man spoke to the closing door. 'Sam – I can call you Sam, you don't mind? – believe me, Sam, I don't want your money. I can see this isn't a good time. What can I say? For things like this there's never a good time. But, Sam, my word of honour I need to talk to you. And you need to hear me. Out here if you like. Inside would be *noch besser*.'

Perhaps it was the confidence of the man's demeanour, or the earnestness in his voice, or something – impossible to put a name to it – that made Sam instinctively believe in his sincerity, that made him stop short of shutting the door. Or perhaps he thought that having someone to talk to – anyone at all, even this unwelcome stranger – might help him to fight against sliding any further into that pit of depression. Whatever the reason, he opened the door wide and spoke to the man in a voice so calm that he surprised even himself. 'Yes, I'm Sam Shaykin. Come in.'

TWO

Sam showed Ron into the darkened living-room, drew back the curtains and opened the window. He winced as the bright sunlight hit him full in the face and bounced around the white-painted walls. The heatwave had lasted for three weeks now, and the motionless air smelled of car exhausts and dustbins. In the street two floors down, children shouted to each other as they kicked a ball around, the boys and the girls exchanging mocking obscenities with equal volume and in equal measure. Ron seemed not to notice any of this. He took off his trilby, revealing a black silk skullcap clipped to a head of wavy Brilliantined hair. He patted it into place, put his hat and briefcase on the coffee table and looked around, nodding and smiling.

Sam left him alone for just long enough to splash water on his face, put on a pair of jeans and a T-shirt and untangle his hair with his fingers. More in control of himself now, he felt torn between satisfying his curiosity and getting rid of Ron so that he could dress properly and get off to work.

In the living-room he found Ron scanning the bookshelves and thumbing through his LPs. He gave Sam a reassuring gold-flecked smile. 'You don't mind? Books. Records. Pictures. A wonderful thing, a man of culture.'

Sam's irritation welled up again. He gestured Ron to a chair and sat opposite him, fingers interlaced and his thumbs circling each other in jerky movements. 'Look, Ron, I've got a busy day, can we please make this short? What exactly do you want to say to me?'

Ron snapped open his briefcase and fished out a manila folder. 'I can see you're busy, so I'll get straight to the point.'

He leaned towards Sam and put a consoling hand on his knee. 'Boychick, I'm sorry, I bring sad news. Your Aunt Esther, long lost to your family because of some old broygus that goes back years and years, is very ill. In fact, she'll be standing before Hashem any time soon.'

Sam stared at Ron. He felt his irritation turn into disbelief, then into amusement, and finally into a spasm of uncontrollable laughter. Seeing Ron's expression change from compassion to bewilderment made him laugh even harder. 'It's okay, Ron,' he stuttered, catching his breath and wiping away the tears with his hand. 'You must think I'm a callous bastard. The thing is, though, you've come to the wrong place. You see, I've got no Aunt Esther.'

Tut-tutting and shaking his head, Ron patted his skullcap, bent over the file, licked his index finger and began anxiously flipping through the pages as if hoping to spot a mistake or any small fact that he might have overlooked. He went through every page a second time before giving up and fixing Sam with a pleading expression. 'You're sure, Sam? That's *emmess*? You're sure you haven't got an Auntie Esther?'

Sam raised his eyes to the ceiling. 'If I had an Aunt Esther, you don't think I'd know? Or maybe you think I might have forgotten?'

Ron was undeterred. 'A great-aunt, maybe?'

Sam shook his head. 'Definitely not. No Great-Aunt Esther, and no – what did you call it? – no broygus. What is that, by the way?'

Ron shut the manila file and glared at it as if it had done him a personal injury. 'You, a Yiddishe boy, you're telling me you never heard of a broygus?'

Sam laughed. 'Okay, I'll admit it. I think I've heard the word. You're talking about those stupid old family rows they used to have in the *shtetls* that they carried on for years and years, long after anyone could remember what started them in the first place. But that's not how we behave here. And it's got nothing to do with me.'

'If you say so,' said Ron. 'But, boychick, I don't know what to think, and that's a fact. Maybe if I tell you the whole *megillah*?' He held up the file. 'It's all here. You don't mind?'

Sam sighed. 'If you must. But is there any point?'

Ron ignored the question and cleared his throat. 'So. First, to explain. I run this charity, HJA. Hackney Jewish Aid. I don't take pay, I do it for the *mitzvahs*. By trade, Sam, I'm a bespoke tailor. Top quality. Savile Row. Only for *ganzer machers*, I make. Actors. Businessmen. Politicians. Gangsters.' He hurried on as Sam stirred with impatience. 'Anyway, long story short, we visit old Jewish people in hospitals. We bring fruit, we sit with them, we ask how are you, have you got anyone, what do you need? You get the picture?'

Sam glanced ostentatiously at his watch. Ron took the hint and hurried on. 'So, last week I get a call I should go and see this old Yiddishe woman in Hackney Hospital. She's thin like a rake and *fermisht* – maybe even a bit *meshuggah*. The doctor tells me she hasn't got long. She's got cancer and a bad heart, *nisht duggedacht!* She lives on her own, he says, so she should go to a place like a hospice, he says, until the end, God forbid. So I talk to her, but she says no, she's going home, no arguments. So I ask her, who in her family should I call? So she tells me she's got no family now. No children, no friends. She says there was a big broygus years and years ago. A terrible thing. The whole family turned her out. For *gournisht*! Slung her out on her ear! Told her never to come near them again! Now, she says, there's only one left who might want to know her. She says I should find him and tell him, come. A nephew. Name of Samuel Shaykin.'

The two men sat in silence for a moment while Sam thought over what he'd heard. He was sorry to disappoint Ron, in fact he was starting to take a bit of a liking to him, but it was time to bring this little episode to an end. He stood up, preparing to close the conversation and see him out. 'That's a sad—' A particularly loud outburst of shouting and shrieking from the street drowned his words. He waited until it subsided and began again. 'That's a sad story, Ron, but like I told you, she's not my aunt so it's got nothing to do with me. There must be another Sam Shaykin living somewhere in London.'

Ron nodded. 'I suppose so.' He sighed, put the papers back in his briefcase and stood up. 'Still, you're not the one, so I'll just have to keep looking.' He gave his skullcap a final pat and retrieved his hat. 'A pleasure to meet you, anyway.'

'And you,' said Sam. 'I'm sorry this was a waste of your time.'

Ron waved away the apology. 'I don't see it that way, boychick. You won't mind me asking, I know – are you *frum*?'

Sam stiffened. 'You mean, do I practice the religion? Do I pray? Do I go to *shul*? No. Not for years. I don't believe in that stuff. Why should that concern you?'

Ron looked contrite. 'I'm sorry. I asked in a clumsy way. Just—' He pointed to the silver symbol that hung by a slender chain over Sam's T-shirt. 'You wear that. It must mean something to you, then, being a Jew.'

Sam hadn't realised it was showing. He tucked it back in, out of sight against his chest where he always wore it. His face was hot and he could feel the sweat gathering in wet patches under his T-shirt. He regretted letting his guard down to Ron, allowing the conversation to take this unwelcome path. 'What it means to me is my business! Now, if that's all…'

Ron put a hand on his shoulder. 'Boychick, of course it's your own business. Every Jew finds his own way. So, please God I'm not putting my foot in it again, but if that's how you feel, why do you keep those close to you?' He was pointing to a shelf where he'd spotted an oval tray with two candlesticks and a silver *kiddush* cup.

'They're Deborah's. My – girlfriend. She's – that's to say, we've got different opinions about these things. She still likes doing the mumbo-jumbo.'

Ron took down the *kiddush* cup and studied the Hebrew

inscription engraved on it. 'Mumbo-jumbo? This is what you call it?'

Sam took the cup out of his hands and put it back on the shelf. 'It's a long story. I've got to see you out now. I've got things to do.'

Ron gave his skullcap a final tap, put his hat back on and picked up his briefcase. 'Goodbye, Sam. For upsetting you, and for wasting your time with this Esther business, again, I'm sorry. But – you won't mind me saying, I hope – maybe Hashem has brought us together for a reason.'

Just in time, Sam bit back his response. His temper had got him into enough trouble for one day.

Ron offered his business card again. 'Take it, just in case. You never know. My number's on the back. If you need anything, call me.'

Sam took the card and saw him to the door. 'Bye, Ron. I hope you find who you're looking for.'

Ron paused on the doorstep. 'I will, Sam. And when I do, I hope he's a *frum* man because then there'll be a family member to say the *kaddish* mourner's prayer for that poor lonely woman. Then we can say, like the *goyim* always say, Esther Symonds, you should rest in peace.'

Sam froze for a second. He kept his face expressionless, but in his head everything he'd heard from Ron was suddenly turned upside-down. 'This woman. Her name's Symonds, you said? Esther Symonds?'

'I didn't say before? Why's this, you know the name?'

Sam struggled to keep his expression casual. He needed time to think this through. 'No. It just sounded familiar for some reason.'

'That's all? I see,' said Ron. He eased his hat into place and made a deft adjustment to the brim. 'Shalom, boychick. Stay in touch.'

Deep in thought, Sam stood on the landing and watched until the top of Ron's trilby had bobbed out of sight.

THREE

Sam had made a special effort this morning; he'd put on his new lightweight chinos and a crisp blue cotton shirt, but he already felt as if he'd spent the night fully dressed in a sauna. And now that he'd re-checked the address Ron had given him, he could see that he'd parked on the wrong side of Cliften Common, a good half-mile from where he wanted to be. He wiped the sweat from his head and neck with a handkerchief and reached behind the seat for his A to Z. It was in his backpack, and also, stuffed in beside it, was Esther Symonds's handbag.

He rubbed his hands over his eyes. They were sore and stinging, partly as a result of driving in the harsh sunlight, but mainly because of the sleepless night he'd had, lying awake thinking about Ron's visit. He'd tried talking it over with Deborah, but she was still angry with him and after a long day's tour-guiding she was only interested in taking a bath and getting into bed. But by dawn he'd thought it through, and even though it made him feel sick and scared to think about it, he knew he had to find out for sure one way or the other.

Only when Ron had mentioned the name of the woman who claimed to be his aunt did he have the first inkling that this story might really have something to do with him. Symonds – he knew that was his mother's family name. And Esther – that, he knew, was the name of the grandmother he'd never met, because, as his parents had told him all his life, she was an evil, wicked woman who'd done unspeakable things going way back even before he was born. But two things made no sense to him: firstly, if it really was her, why had she said he was her nephew, not her grandson? Maybe she'd just got it mixed up in her head. After all, Ron had described her as ill, confused. 'A bit *fermisht*, even maybe a bit *meshuggah*,' he'd said. But secondly, and even more to the point, his parents had always told him that the wicked Esther Symonds was dead. So Ron Green's old woman couldn't possibly be his grandmother. She was someone else called Esther Symonds with a nephew who had the same name as his. Was that possible? Well, there was no other explanation.

Ron's mention of a broygus was what had clinched it for him. He wasn't sure exactly why, but he hadn't been straight with Ron. The word was all too familiar to him – so familiar that he couldn't even remember the first time he'd heard it. It was as if he'd always known it, had lived with it and grown up with it. He knew next to nothing about his family's broygus, only that it stretched back to long before he was born and that at its heart lurked this evil figure – his grandmother – whose very memory his parents still reviled. As a small child he'd often overheard snatches of conversations that, even though they were beyond his understanding, had been unsettling enough to haunt his imagination and trigger his night-time terrors. And growing up, he'd had to learn to live with his mother's dark moods and her cryptic references to the miserable experiences of her childhood. She never made clear exactly what she'd suffered, but he'd always been aware of the unspoken assumption – or even expectation – that just as his parents hated and feared this person's memory, so naturally would – should – he.

Despite all his doubts and misgivings, it was a mystery he was finding impossible to resist. In the early hours he'd watched the clock hands creep round until he thought it would be okay to call the number Ron had given him. By mid-morning he was leaving Ron's workshop – not, to his surprise, in Savile Row, but under a railway arch beside Hackney's run-down London Fields – entrusted with

Esther Symonds's address and the grimy leather handbag that she'd left behind when leaving the hospital.

Ron had given him the full guided tour as promised, and explained that, yes, he really was a Hackney-based Savile Row tailor. 'All these rich *ganzer machers,*' he'd explained with a straight face, 'you think they'd come here to Ron Green's *verkakteh* railway arch? No, they go to some fancy-shmancy tailor in Savile Row. A *mensch* in a suit measures them up, then he sends a boy down here with the measurements and we get busy. What they get is a top-quality Aaron Green Bespoke Garment that'll last them a lifetime, but it's got a Raffles of Savile Row label inside, and that's what makes them happy. So everyone wins.' He'd extended his right forefinger and laid it against the side of his nose. 'You see, boychick, in this world nothing is what it seems. Never forget that.'

He clicked open the glove compartment and dug around inside it, pushing aside cassette tapes, parking meter coins and petrol reward stamps, hoping to find a cigarette that had escaped his latest purge. There was a crumpled Gauloises packet with two left in it. The dark, rough-edged odour of Algerian tobacco spread through the car, offsetting the smell of sweat and evoking memories of happy student days spent exploring Paris with Claudette, his first love. With a luxurious feeling of relief blended with a tinge of guilt, he spaced out the puffs and exhaled through his mouth and nose as he sat watching the stream of rush-hour traffic crawling past in both directions, and thought about backing out and going home. What the hell was he doing here anyway? If this woman really was his grandmother, how come she was still living when she was supposed to be dead? And what if she turned out to be every inch as bad as his parents had always painted her? Plus, there were other things he hadn't thought of until now. She was dying of cancer – maybe he'd find her repulsive. She might be smelly, maybe worse. How would he cope with that? He'd never been near anyone in such a state and he had no idea what to expect, or what to do. And if he did go through with it, what then? He'd have to go to his parents and break the news to them. But then, no doubt, they'd produce a photo or some document that would prove to him with certainty that he'd been wrong, that his grandmother was definitely dead, that he'd made a fool of himself and betrayed and angered them by trespassing onto forbidden territory.

He flopped back in his seat, squinting into the sun's glare. The cigarette, his first in a month, gave his mouth a bitter taste and made his head swim. He threw it out of the window and followed it with a line of spit. He laughed out loud at his own stupidity. There was no point in being here, no point in going on with this. He fired up the engine, thought a moment, turned it off again and sat with his head in his hands.

The sound of an impatient car horn broke into his thoughts. The line of traffic passing his parking space had ground to a halt. Another horn, then another joined in until the noise of dozens of horns, all bleating together in impotent rage, became so loud that he had to wind up his windows, sending the temperature inside the car into orbit. He couldn't stand the noise and the heat a moment longer. He had to make his choice: drive off, go home, go back to work, forget the whole thing. Or overcome the fear that was bubbling up inside him, walk across the Common and do what he'd set out to do. He put his hands over his ears, closed his eyes and fought to come to the right decision.

FOUR

At the top of Keir Hardie Street he found four oddly out-of-place Victorian villas, looking almost self-conscious with their fresh paintwork and well-tended front gardens. Beyond them, spread along both sides of a road that sloped downhill until it ended at the derelict timber-yards beside the River Lea Canal, were six identical eight-storey blocks of flats. This far from the main road the traffic fumes competed for dominance with a range of pungent cooking aromas and the smells from overflowing rubbish hoppers rusting away behind broken metal shutters.

He found Henderson House halfway down on the left. On the ground floor, box-shaped balconies faced the street. On one, a woman was hanging out washing. She was thick-set, metallic blonde, red-lipped, pale-skinned. She wore cut-off jeans and a tight tie-dye T-shirt that rode up as she pegged the clothes on the line. He stopped at the edge of a patch of weeds bordering the balconies and hesitated, wondering if she'd be able to give him directions.

'Help you?' Her voice sounded suspicious, and just on the guarded side of hostile. He could understand why: a dishevelled wild-haired man dripping with sweat, standing there looking lost and gazing at her for no apparent reason.

'I'm looking for Mrs Symonds? Number 24?'

The woman looked at him more closely. 'You want Esther? What do you want with her?'

Until that moment he hadn't thought of how he'd explain himself. He stumbled over his words. 'I'm her – I mean—'

'You one of them Council people? Come to give her aggravation?'

So she'd had problems with the Council. Why would that be? He shook his head. 'No. No, I'm a – a friend.'

The woman's suspicious look didn't change. 'Oh yeah? I hope you are. She could do with a friend.' She picked up her washing basket and pointed with her chin. 'Fourth floor. That way.'

He nodded his thanks and walked away.

'Hey!' He stopped and looked back. The woman's face had softened slightly. 'You're really a friend?'

'Yes. Really.' Maybe he should have crossed his fingers when he said that. The woman gave him a smile with a tinge of warmth in it. 'Tell her Maisie says hello. And you watch yourself. There's some right bastards up there.'

'How do you mean?' he called back. The woman tugged down her T-shirt, went inside and closed her balcony door. It was getting far worse than he'd imagined. He felt alone and vulnerable. He could still, even now, cut his losses and walk away. He hovered a moment, then headed for the entrance marked *Henderson House. Flats 1–48.*

At his second knock, slender fingers opened the door an inch without releasing the security chain or showing a face. He looked at the fingers. Brown. Young. Not her, then.

'Yes?'

'I've come to see Esther Symonds. Is this the right address?'

'Mrs Symonds lives here. Can I ask who you are?' The voice was velvety, polite and neutral; neither warm nor hostile.

He took out the card Ron Green had given him and held it up like a talisman. 'I'm…my name's…Josh. Josh Silver.'

Josh Silver? Did he just say that? His mouth was dry and his left leg had developed a twitch.

'I work for – that is, I'm a volunteer for Hackney Jewish Aid. Ron Green asked me to look in. I've brought her handbag back. She left it at the hospital.' He fumbled in his backpack and held up the bag for the voice's owner to see.

'Oh, good. Just a minute.'

The woman closed the door, slid the chain off and half-opened it again, leaving him just enough room to follow her inside, then quickly shut it and slid the chain back into place. The dark, airless hall smelled of unwashed clothes and stale food. A black telephone sat on the floor on top of three thick London directories.

'I'm Anna Bijou, Esther's social worker,' she whispered and held out her hand. She had brown skin, tied-back hair just a shade darker than his own, and an open, friendly smile. She wore a cool-looking linen trouser-suit, a crisp white blouse and round, wire-framed glasses. He took her hand and caught a welcome whiff of her clean, floral-smelling perfume. Her handshake was business-like but warm. He instantly liked her. He ran his fingers through his hair and surreptitiously straightened his rumpled shirt.

'She's asleep,' said Anna, still whispering. 'Come in here.'

She led him into a cramped kitchen that smelled worse than the hall. The floor felt sticky under his shoes. Every surface was covered with dirty dishes and half-empty foil containers. They stood opposite each other in a space where their clothes were least likely to come into contact with anything greasy.

'The Council's supposed to send someone in,' she said, looking round and grimacing. 'This is disgusting. I'll sort something out when I get back to the office.' She smiled at him; a welcoming, sincere smile. 'So you're from the HJA? Esther will be pleased. I'm sure you'll get on well with her.' She looked at her watch. 'I haven't got long but I can give you a bit of background – if you think that would be helpful?'

Background? Social worker talk, he supposed. Probably nothing of value to him. Still, she seemed nice, and as long as he could keep her here he wouldn't be alone in the place with the old woman. 'Yes, it would be. Thanks.'

She gave him a searching look. 'You understand, Josh, that this is all confidential. I need to be sure that you—'

Sam raised a hand to stop her. 'I'm a colleague. Of course you can trust me.' He was Pinocchio; he could feel his nose growing. She smiled, reassured. 'In a nutshell, then, Esther's got heart disease and cancer. She's all alone, but she's determined to spend her last days at home rather than in the hospice. And it's getting harder for her all the time.'

'How long – I mean—'

'How long has she got? Doctors never give us a time. But I'd say not long. She's getting thinner by the day.' She gestured to the foil containers with their 'Meals on Wheels' labels. 'And she won't eat this stuff they send.'

The smell in the kitchen was making him feel sick again. His head was hurting and he longed to be back in the open air. But he found Anna's presence reassuring, and her evident concern touched him. Maybe, then, he'd go just a little further.

'Isn't there anyone to bring her proper food, or cook her a meal? Children, maybe? Or grandchildren?' He felt ashamed, as if he'd asked her a trick question.

She shook her head. 'Nobody. She's told me her life story. How many times have I heard it? Married at eighteen to an unstable man. Beaten so many times she could never have children, then abandoned. She's got a long history of mental illness so she's never kept a job for long. She's always got money problems. The Council's after her for rent and her phone's been cut off.'

So that explained the suspicious manner of the neighbour downstairs. He wished he'd asked her what her connection with Esther was. But more importantly, Esther's life story, as Anna was telling it, didn't fit at all. Unless, as he'd suspected, she was the wrong woman. Except, possibly, for one thing.

'She's mentally ill, you said? In what way?'

Anna smiled. 'Basically she's an ordinary nice old lady. Except that she sees imaginary people – talks to them, hears their voices. And sometimes she's aggressive. She starts arguments with people: the neighbours, for instance. Mind you, some of them are just—'

Her voice trailed off. She looked at her watch. 'Anyway, none of that's important any more. I'm afraid the truth is, she won't be with us for very much longer. I just thought it would help you to know. I'm sorry, I've really got to go.'

A wave of panic welled up. He didn't want her to leave yet. He couldn't do this on his own. He tried to think of something to say to make her stay longer. Nothing came to mind. 'Sure. No problem.'

He got the reward of a bright, reassuring smile that came as much from her eyes as from her lips. 'She should be awake soon. She'll be pleased to see someone from the HJA – and to get her bag back, of course.'

'Will I see you again?' He bit his lip as he realised how that must have sounded. But she handed him a card. 'Of course. Let's work on this together. Call me and let me know how you get on. Go slowly when she wakes up. She can be a bit cantankerous at—'

Anna broke off as the kitchen door was pushed open. Sam went rigid and stared at the bent, skeletal figure of the woman who stood in the doorway, gripping her wooden walking stick with a trembling hand. Sparse grey hair framed her face. Her fleshless cheeks had subsided to form deep crevices on each side of her nose. Her lips were clamped together, whether in pain or in anger he couldn't tell. Granite-coloured eyes glinted from behind huge tortoise-shell glasses. Threadbare slippers stuck out from beneath a food-stained pink candlewick dressing-gown. For a moment all three stood motionless; a frozen tableau. Sam forced a smile, but it faded away as the woman fixed him with a cold-eyed glare. Her voice, when she spoke, was croaky and sounded full of phlegm. 'Who are you?' She took an uncertain step towards him. 'I know you. Don't I?'

He was caught off guard. Not knowing how to reply, he said nothing, but taking the least dirty glass from the draining board, rinsed it three times, filled it with water and offered it to her. She fixed her eyes on him as she drank from it, twisting her mouth into an almost-lascivious smile as she handed it back.

'A nice-looking *mensch* you've brought me today, Annie. Who is he? Your boyfriend?'

Anna laughed. 'No, Esther. This is Josh. He's from the HJA. He's come to keep you company. To see if you need anything.'

Esther glared at him again. 'I don't need company, I need my health.' She pointed at the handbag that he was still holding. 'What are you doing with that? Give it back, you *gonif*!'

'You left it at the hospital, Esther,' said Anna. 'Josh has brought it back for you.'

Esther snatched it from him and fumbled to open the catch with her free hand.

'Let me help you,' he said. His hand brushed hers as he reached for the bag. It felt cold and scaly. When he looked down at it, it brought to mind the chickens' feet that he used to watch the kosher butcher chop off when his mother took him shopping for Friday night dinner.

'Let go! Don't you touch me!' She wailed the words so loudly and with such force, her face contorted with fear, that he sprang back in alarm. Esther clutched the bag to her chest, gazing at Sam with narrow-eyed malevolence.

'It's all right, Esther,' said Anna. To his relief her velvety voice had an immediate calming effect on the old woman. 'Josh won't hurt you. Why don't you go in the living-room and turn the TV on, and he'll bring you a nice cup of tea? And I'll drop in on you again tomorrow.'

'A nice cup of tea,' mimicked Esther. 'Like I'm an imbecile she talks to me. Okay, so go if you have to. And you, *mensch* – you bring me the tea. And make sure it's strong. Two sugars.'

She went into the living-room and slammed the door behind her. Anna mouthed 'Good luck', waved and went on her way.

He was alone, his last chance of turning tail gone. At least his leg had stopped twitching, but his head still hurt and the panic was mounting. He felt imprisoned in someone else's kitchen sink drama. He stood bewildered amongst the debris, then started searching through the cupboards.

The kettle on the gas stove reminded him of the one that his parents had when he was a child. Fitted over the spout was a dome-shaped whistle that let out a high-pitched screech when the water boiled. When no one was watching he used to take it off the spout and march round the kitchen blowing into it. He filled the kettle and found a box of matches to light the gas. He opened the fridge in search of milk and recoiled from the stench. Inside was a milk-bottle full of pungent solids and a half-packet of green sausages. He threw them away and made his decision. He knocked on Esther's door and opened it a crack.

'Esther, there's no—'

'What's this Esther business? It's Mrs Symonds to you.'

'Sorry – Mrs Symonds, there's—'

'What are you talking? Standing out there like a *schvantz*! Come in, will you!'

She was sitting in a high-backed armchair with her feet on a stool and her handbag on her lap. Beside her was a table with packets of pills, a water glass and a transistor radio. He glanced around. The curtain drawn across the closed single window was too thin to prevent the sun shining through it, highlighting the dust motes that hung in the hot, stale-smelling air. On a stand with spindly black legs was a small television set with a fuzzy picture and the sound turned down. Against one wall was an un-made bed; against another, a wardrobe and a chest of drawers. On the drawers he saw a china cat and a photo propped up against an empty vase.

'I need to go and get some milk,' he said. 'If you give me your key I'll let myself back in.'

Her eyes glinted behind her thick lenses. 'Two seconds he's here and my key he wants. What, you think I'm stupid? Why don't you just hit me over the head now and rob me?'

He felt his face redden. Who the hell did she think she was, talking to him like that? But he kept his voice even.

'Didn't Anna say you could trust me? Do you really think I'm a – a *gonif*? Do I look like one?'

The lascivious look again. Her laugh made him shiver. 'You're all *gonifs*. You're all *mamzers*. Specially the good-looking ones. You think I don't know? Come here.'

She beckoned him to come closer and bend down to her level. He let her grasp his chin and move his head from side to side. He tried not to pull away or reveal his revulsion as he felt her fetid breath on his face. For a brief moment their eyes locked together. He looked for some resemblance in her features to his mother, but saw none. Was that because illness and old age had erased any that there might have been? Or maybe because this woman and his mother weren't even related?

'Josh, eh? You…' Her voice trailed away into a mumble. She shook her head and let go of his chin, opened wide the gilt metal jaws of her handbag, upended it onto the table beside her and picked through its contents. He glimpsed a purse, a comb, a gold-painted powder compact, a lipstick, an assortment of crumpled papers and finally a key on a ring with a plastic fob in the shape of the Star of David. She took two folded pound notes and some loose change from the purse, counted the change, put the money back and held out the purse and the key to him.

'Get me some eggs and a TV Times and a bottle of Tizer. And a tin of tomato soup. And a Wonderloaf. And milk. I know how much is there, so no funny business.'

He was near his limit. Five minutes he'd been there, and the miserable old cow was giving him orders. Giving him a shopping list like he was there just to run errands for her – and even implying that he'd rip her off for a few bob! Suppressing an urge to tell her to go out and do her own bloody shopping, he took the purse and the key, and went off looking for the nearest convenience store.

Half an hour later, he was back from the local Co-op. He'd thought things through and calmed down. The panic had subsided, his headache had gone and he felt calmer and stronger. He had no idea where this was going, and for now he didn't care. He took her a cup of tea and some biscuits and gave her back the purse and the key. She put the key in her bag, emptied out the purse and counted the money. She shook her head and made clucking noises with her teeth.

'It's all here. What I gave you. So how come you get the shopping for nothing? You're a *gonif* after all?'

He smiled down at her. 'Call it a present from me, Mrs Symonds. To begin our friendship.'

'You think I'm a *schnorrer*?' she snapped, glaring at him. 'You think I need your money? Money I've got, believe me.'

Anger and resentment bubbled up again. His first clumsy attempt at a peace offering and she'd thrown it right back in his face. Well, after all, what else did he expect from this crabby old bitch?

She scooped the notes and change back into her purse. 'This time okay, but never again. Next time you buy for me, you take my money. *Fershteyt*?'

Fershteyt. One of his mother's most-used Yiddish words. Coincidence? 'Sure, *fershteyt*.' A deep breath and a rapid decision. 'You want me to come again?'

There was no change of expression. A silence, then: 'Come tomorrow. Bring a paper. And some boiled sweets. And Mister Kipling Cakes.'

Tomorrow? Not what he'd expected. And not convenient. There was work to go to. Still, maybe just for a couple of hours – 'Okay, that's a deal. See you tomorrow, then. I'll be going now, unless there's anything else I can do for you before I go?'

Later, telling Deborah about it, he tried to describe how he'd seen the smile flick off like a shutter coming down. How the light had gone from her eyes and they'd become chips of cold flint.

'Do for me? Yes. My kitchen's filthy. Clean it up.'

FIVE

It was late-afternoon by the time Sam got back to his car, and still the sun was blazing. By this time in mid-July the novelty of the heatwave had worn off. People were asking each other how long they thought it could go on for, and complaining of the sleepless nights, the daily torture of travelling in stifling buses and trains, and the miserable hours spent working in torrid shops and offices.

But for Sam and Deborah, the weather had worked to their advantage. They'd started their London Adventures tourism company a year ago, and now, in just its second summer season, it was doing well. At this rate, they'd soon be able to take on more guides and Sam could give up his job as manager of the little travel agency squeezed between a greengrocer's and a Turkish café on Hackney's traffic-choked Mare Street. Today, Deborah was leading a coachload of German visitors on their Summer Special Package: the Tower of London, a river trip to Greenwich and back, then dinner at The Spaghetti House in Soho and off to the Palace Theatre for a performance of Jesus Christ Superstar. Even after paying all the overheads it would make them a tidy profit. After the terrible years he'd lived through before meeting Deborah, it was all a very welcome change. Thanks to her, things were at last coming right and life was starting to be good. Now, he hoped, he'd be able to shake off the past and put an end to those dark moods and restless nights.

But right now, he wasn't feeling good at all. He was over-heated and thirsty. There was rancid grease under his fingernails and on his chinos. His new shirt had sticky splotches splattered all over it, and his head wouldn't stop itching. As he opened his car door the heat hit him like a punch in the face, and when he drove off the steering wheel was painful to the touch.

His first and last meeting with Esther Symonds had left him feeling sickened by her and disgusted with himself. She'd been everything he'd feared: crabby, rude, hostile, dirty. The whole place had stunk of piss and sickness and God knows what else.

On the way home he stopped at an off-licence and bought two bottles of R. White's lemonade and one of red wine. Once home, he threw his filthy clothes in a heap and ran a bath. Cooler in fresh clean clothes and starting to feel more relaxed, he opened the windows wide and put the lemonade and wine in the fridge. He'd learned in his teens that he coped badly with alcohol; after drinking two or three glasses of wine, or even a small whisky, he could expect to have a chronic headache all the next day. Today, though, after all he'd been through, he'd decided to allow himself a glass or two, even if it meant paying the price tomorrow. Through the rest of the afternoon and long into the evening he sat at the kitchen table sorting through his thoughts, hardly moving except to fill his glass from the fridge, alternating between the lemonade and the wine.

He was still there when dusk finally came and the street children's shouts died away as they straggled home for supper and TV. Going to the fridge for more wine, he crouched down by its open door and luxuriated for a moment in the cold air. Tantalising smells wafted in through the wide-open window and he could hear the sounds of people in the neighbouring flats enjoying their evening meal. His stomach felt gassy and acidy from the wine, made worse by the fact that he'd eaten nothing since breakfast. He found a bag of crisps in the cupboard and took it with his wine to the kitchen table.

Furious with himself as he was for letting Ron Green talk him into the encounter that had turned out so badly, a small part of him couldn't help seeing a grimly funny side. He smiled as he imagined what Deborah might say when he told her about it:

'Tell me again. You asked was there anything else you could do for her, and she came right out and said yes, you can clean up her kitchen? So you did? Just like that? How come? You never do that here. I didn't even know you knew how!'

It was true, he felt pretty stupid now. He didn't know why he hadn't just told her to poke it and left. It was as if she'd – he couldn't say exactly what it was.

The wine tasted bitter in his mouth and burned its way down into his stomach. He went over it again and again. What exactly was it about that woman? What was it about Ron's story that had so aroused his curiosity after all those years of certainty that his grandmother was dead and buried, and wouldn't be missed? And every time, he came back to the same answer. It had been the mention of a broygus. But as Ron had told it, Esther Symonds had been the blameless victim of the broygus. Which was strange, because from everything he'd ever managed to piece together, it was the other way round. His grandmother had been an outcast from the family since before his birth, and for his entire life he'd accepted that she'd brought this pariah status on herself. A madwoman, his parents called her. A wicked person. A monster. A *dreck*. A *mekashefeh*. Someone to be feared because of what she was, what she'd done to his mother, and what, even though dead, she might yet do. What was he to think? None of it made any sense. He gulped down the rest of the wine and shuddered as it pooled in his stomach.

By 10pm it was a little cooler, the occasional gust of wind through the window bringing some much-needed fresh air into the darkened kitchen. He'd drunk more than enough wine, so he topped up his glass with lemonade, rolled it against his cheek, squeezed his eyes closed and probed deep into his childhood memories. His grandpa, a kind, sickly old man who lived with him and his parents, had made up a hobgoblin character to scare him with, who he called Mad Hetty. 'You be a good boy, or Mad Hetty'll come and get you,' he'd say. And his parents would join in and laugh. They should have known that with his child's mind he took them seriously, that their talk of Mad Hetty was fuelling the fears and stoking the nightmares that had plagued him all through his childhood and still did even now. Only much later could he understand that Mad Hetty was Esther, his reviled grandma, who'd long ago been his Grandpa Ben's wife. But to the young Sam she was just a frightening figure who appeared in the night's shadows as he lay awake, taking all the grotesque forms his imagination could conjure up. Especially in the weeks and months after…

The noise from his neighbours' windows had died away. It was late now, and the people in the flats around him were settling down for the night. Leaving the window open, he pulled down the blind to make the room even darker. Going back in time was easier like that; the images more vivid.

He was five. In the old house where he'd lived since before he could remember, he was sitting at a green-topped card-table opposite his Grandpa Ben. They were playing draughts and he was winning, as usual. He could smell his grandpa's open bottle of cough mixture and the smoke from the coal fire. His dad was at work, his mum in the kitchen they shared with the Bronstein family upstairs. When a rash move of his grandpa's left him an opening he bounced on his chair, laughing happily as he zigzagged around the board, jumping over pieces and taking them for his own. His grandpa leaned over the table and kissed him on the forehead. '*A klug kind, kaynahorah*! No more draughts now. That's for babies. Tomorrow, *tatteleh*, I teach you to play chess.' With a pair of tongs he took two lumps of coal from the scuttle, put them on the fire and poked them until the flames caught. Sam was a small child again, frozen with fear as he saw his grandpa drop the tongs and clutch his chest, gasping for air, before falling to the floor almost in slow motion, banging his head on the brass fender, overturning the table and scattering the draughts pieces in all directions.

The thump of him hitting the linoleum and the sound of the pieces rolling across the floor rang again in Sam's ears. An angry woman's voice from a neighbouring flat, followed by a child's cry of anguish, jerked him back to the present. Sweat was pouring down his face and he was trembling. He went to the bathroom, drenched a towel with cold water and pressed it to his face, holding it there until the water ran down his neck and inside his shirt. Refreshed, he returned and switched back from lemonade to wine. The woman was still shouting at the wailing child.

His mother, too, had wailed, running in answer to his cries of alarm, finding her father on the floor, his eyes closed, one arm twisted under his body, blood gushing from the gash in his forehead. He was feeling again the panic he'd felt when he saw her trying to pull him into a sitting position. He didn't know what had happened to his grandpa. He didn't understand, until they explained later, that he'd died. But he knew something very bad was happening. And he'd never seen his mother like this. Her wails had turned to screams. She'd forgotten he was there. She was pulling Grandpa and shaking him. She was screaming, 'Come back! Come back!'

He took his chair to the window and raised the blind a few inches so that he could make the most of the cooler night air. He closed his eyes and rubbed them until waves of red and green danced around under the lids. It was like watching a film he'd been forced to watch dozens – hundreds – of times before, and hated every time. It was a memory he'd kept tightly locked away until finding the courage to talk to Kate about it. When he and Deborah had met two years ago he was still in a bad state after a bruising marriage break-up. She'd persuaded him to see a doctor, who'd put him onto Kate McGeehan. With Kate's help he'd begun to face up to the corrosive cocktail of anger and depression that had been eating away at him for so many years, and also to talk about the nightmares. Before her, he'd never told anyone about them.

'You see your grandfather die in the nightmares?' she'd asked.

'Yes. No. Yes, that and—'

'There's something else? Something else that you see?'

He'd nodded, reluctant to take the step.

'Can you tell me about it?'

He took a drink and pictured himself sitting opposite her in her consulting room, gathering the courage to go on, searching for the words. 'She was pulling Grandpa and shaking him. She was screaming, right in his ear, "Come back! Come back!" Then she – she – she sort of put her hands over his face, like this, and – and pushed his eyes open with her fingers. They looked right at me. I was looking right into them. They were cold, hard, like a dead fish's. There was no colour any more, they were whitish-grey. And they were looking straight at me. And I thought – I'd never seen him look at me like that before – so I thought he must be angry with me. So, what happened to Grandpa, it must be my fault. I made it happen. That's why he's angry with me.'

He pulled the blind down and sat back at the table, wetting his fingers with his tongue and gathering up the crumbs from the bottom of the crisp bag. He squeezed the bag into a ball, dropped it onto the table and watched it straighten itself out with a tiny rustling noise. He pushed his fists against his forehead and tried to force his scattered thoughts into order. On that day, when he'd stood by helpless, ignored and terrified for what seemed like hours while his mother sat rocking back and forth pouring out her misery, he'd heard her repeat again and again, in a high, strained voice that sounded to him like a prolonged shriek of pain, that it was his grandmother who'd killed his grandpa, *as sure as if she'd stuck a knife in him.*

At that, his terror had peaked. He'd be next. His grandmother would be back to kill him. And she'd be silent, invisible. He wouldn't even see her coming, just as he hadn't seen her when she'd come and killed his grandpa. So, when, just days later, his parents announced that from now on he was going to sleep on his own in Grandpa's old room – in Grandpa's old bed – he knew for certain that Grandma Esther would come and find him, and he'd be on his own, and she'd kill him.

His dad had laughed. 'Silly boy. She's gone away. She won't come back.'

'Where is she?'

His dad had laughed again but this time not like he thought it was funny. 'Don't you worry. You'll never see her. Not ever.'

A bitter feeling welled back up, one that he'd been trying for years to hold down and push away: anger at his parents for polluting his childhood by putting into his head those images of a nightmarish creature who might appear out of the dark in his room with murderous intent, while he lay alone and terrified in his grandfather's bed.

He pulled open each kitchen drawer in turn, hoping to find a forgotten cigarette. No luck this time. He settled for another glass of wine, fighting down the nausea. Eleven-thirty. Deborah was late. When she'd left this morning she was still angry with him. The thought drove home an additional spike of anguish. He needed to tell her how sorry he was, and how near the edge he was feeling. And he needed her to help him find the courage to lift the phone and get back in touch with Kate. She'd helped him through the worst of it, but maybe he'd stopped seeing her too soon. He thought of what she'd said to him when he'd told her he was okay now – that he wouldn't be coming to her any more: *It's your decision, Sam. We've made good progress together, but you've still got all that other stuff to deal with, haven't you?*

He pushed the glass away and slumped over the table, his head on his hands. Oh yes, there was plenty of other stuff.

There was his disastrous marriage. Five years of misery, ending with that day that he just couldn't put behind him. There were the other memories, the other half-buried resentments and conflicts. And now, of all possible things, this woman turns up who happens to be called Esther Symonds. He was certain now, it was all a mistake. How come he'd let himself be conned into visiting her and almost coming to believe that she was his dead grandmother – that she was Mad Hetty? No! It wasn't possible! Dad had promised him. 'You'll never see her,' he'd said. Which meant she was dead. Didn't it?

There was a steel clamp round his head and a bubbling clot of undigested fat in his stomach. He needed to decide what to do. He needed to make a choice. That's what Kate was always pulling him back to: the choices he made, and the ones he ran away from.

You've still got all that other stuff to deal with, haven't you?

'Other stuff?'

Do I need to remind you?

'You mean, what I did?'

Or maybe what you didn't do. You made a choice, an important one. Remember?

He pressed his hands against his ears, trying to stem the piercing pain of Kate's voice drilling into his brain.

'Did I? No, I don't remember.'

Do I need to remind you?

He pressed harder, setting off a roaring in his head that sounded like waves crashing on a stony seashore.

'You mean, what I did?'

Kate's voice cut through the noise of the waves, as relentless and insistent as ever.

What you did. Tell me how it felt.

'I told you.'

Tell me again. Tell me how it felt.

He hammered his fists against his temples. 'Leave me alone already! How many more times? Good! Good! It felt fucking good!'

Is that how you remember it? That it felt good?

'I don't know! I don't know! Stop asking me that!'

But you made a choice. You made the right choice.

'What choice? You call that a choice? I just stopped! I don't know why! That, you call a choice? Do me a favour!'

Kate sounded puzzled now. 'Sam, who are you shouting at? What's the matter? I could hear you from downstairs. I thought—'

He took his hands away from his eyes and focused his rage on the dimly lit shape in the doorway, then came the tears of relief as the light clicked on and Kate morphed into Deborah.

She sat opposite him at the table and took his hands in hers. 'You're shivering. What's wrong?'

'I've – something…' His voice came out as a sob. Deborah came around the table and took him in her arms. He clutched her like a small child, put his head on her chest and cried. She made shushing noises and stroked his hair. The reassuring feel of her body, the familiar smells of her hair and her perfume, gave him some comfort and calmed him a little. He raised his head and brushed his eyes with the palms of his hands. 'Deborah, I was a shit. I'm sorry, really I am.'

Deborah carried on stroking his hair. 'Yes, you were a shit. I'm glad you admit it.' She pulled away a little and cupped his face in her hands. 'But there's no need to get into such a state about it. Have you been having one of your bad days? Is that it?'

He felt a sharp pang of guilt at the thought of how much he loved and needed her, and how it would be his own fault if his stupid behaviour drove her away. He held onto her hands and spoke quietly, searching for the right words. 'It's hard to explain. I was just thinking over some – some things that happened a long time ago, and I – I kind of got upset, that's all. But also—'

He let go of her hands, pressed his fingertips into his eyes and rubbed them, groping his way back over the day's events, hoping even now to make some sort of sense of them, as much for his own sake as for hers.

SIX

By the time Sam reached the third floor of Henderson House with his four full shopping bags, he was out of breath, running with sweat and wishing that he'd taken the lift despite the litter and the smell of piss. With Deborah's help, he'd made a list of things to bring: fruit – pears and bananas, nothing her teeth couldn't manage – eggs, tins of soup, cereal, fresh vegetables, instant mashed potato, fruit juices. And sausages, butter and other things to replace the rotten food that he'd thrown away before washing the inside of her fridge. Also, a supply of cleaning materials. At the bottom of the fourth flight he put the bags down, mopped himself with his handkerchief, sat on a step and waited for the burn in his calf muscles to die away.

He and Deborah had talked far into the night. 'Let me get this right,' she'd said. 'This woman you saw: you're saying she might be your grandmother? The one you've told me about? I thought she was dead.'

He'd shrugged. 'Me too. That's what they've always told me. So I don't see how it can be her.'

'Wouldn't you like to be sure one way or the other? Will you go and see her again?'

He'd been so tired he could hardly think. He was slumped over the table in the darkened room, his head on his hands. 'I've got no reason to,' he mumbled. 'Anyway, it was horrible. And in any case, wouldn't my mum just love that? Her little *tatteleh,* walking right into the hands of the wicked old witch who made her life a misery, come to life again. She'd fucking freak. And I've had more than enough of that.'

She gently massaged his neck. 'This isn't about what your parents do or don't want you to do, is it? Come on, Sam. This is about you. Just you. Tell me what you want to do.'

That was the problem. After those hours of talking it round and round, he still didn't know. He turned his head to one side and squinted up at her. 'Search me. But one thing I do know. I'm sick and tired of my mum's tough time bollocks! This has been going on all my life! Her hang-ups, her miseries, she's handing them on to me like they're some kind of family curse.'

She laughed. 'You mean like in those Edgar Allen Poe stories? *The Curse of the House of Shaykin! Chapter one – The Broygus!'*

He couldn't help laughing. 'Okay, I can see the funny side. But maybe it's not so funny. This broygus thing is a real crock of shit.'

Deborah's eyes were starting to droop and she covered her mouth to conceal a yawn. 'One thing I'll say, though: doing that for her, cleaning up her kitchen like she asked, you did a real *mitzvah*.'

For once, he knew better than to let fly the angry retort that forced its way to his lips. This wasn't the moment to start another row. But when was she ever going to accept it? *Mitzvahs, kaddishes, yomtovs, Shabbos* – he'd given all that up long ago and all the mumbo-jumbo that went with it. What bloody use was religion – any religion – anyway? Stopping people from using their brains and making their own choices. Breeding contempt for people who don't believe the same things as them. And all those bloody silly do's and dont's! But Deborah still believed in it all – loved it all. If anything was going to drive them apart, he knew it would be that. And that scared him. But he had no idea what he could do about it.

Deborah had stood up and yawned again. 'Sorry, it's been a long day. I need some sleep. Why don't you go and see her again? Get to know her? See if she really is your dead grandmother? See if she's the monster they always told you she was.'

'And if she is? What then?'

She was already on her way to the bedroom. 'Sweetheart, that's for you to decide.'

At 5am he was lying beside her with his eyes shut, still hoping for a few hours of nightmare-free rest. He was thinking over the last thing she'd said before falling asleep: 'You know, I really think you need to be more understanding. I mean, you should cut your mother some slack. She must have had it hard as a kid.'

'Sure,' he'd said. 'I know that. But to hate her own mother so much that she carries it right through her life – can't get past it, even passes the hate on to me and tells me she's dead —it just doesn't make sense. There must be more. More than they've told me. What do you think?'

*

Arriving at Esther's door, he knocked loudly to make sure she'd hear him. There was no response. He waited two minutes then knocked again. Nothing. Maybe she was still asleep. Or maybe she was hard of hearing on top of all her other problems. Or worse, maybe during the night she—

'Joel?' The chained door had opened a crack. He wasn't sure what she'd said. Her voice was little more than a croak. He brought his face close to the opening so that she could see it.

'Hello, Esth— Mrs Symonds. It's Josh.'

There was no sign of recognition in her voice. 'Where's Joel? When's he coming?'

He didn't know what to say. Who the hell was this Joel? She probably didn't know herself. She was doolally, after all. Okay, just one more try before packing it in and fucking off. 'Er – I can't tell you exactly, Mrs Symonds. Can you let me in, please? I've brought you some shopping.'

Esther made no move to undo the chain and open the door. Her voice became less distinct. Sam guessed that she'd moved back into the gloom of the hallway.

'I don't buy at the door!' Her voice was louder again. Now he could see her flinty eyes peering at him through the crack. 'Where's Joel? Where's Annie? Go away! I'll call the police!'

The door slammed shut. He sighed deeply. Okay, if that was what she wanted – he picked up the bags, turned and walked away, stopped, turned round and walked back. He lifted the flap on her letterbox and called through it. 'Mrs Symonds, it's Josh. You remember? I came to see you yesterday.'

No reply. He tried again. 'I brought your handbag. I cleaned your kitchen like you wanted. You remember?'

Still nothing. He was close to giving up and walking away. Well, maybe just one more try. He lifted the flap again. 'I've brought you some nice things to eat.'

No sign of life at all. He sighed again. It was time to give up. He pushed open the letterbox for the last time. 'I'm going now. I'll leave your shopping here, by your door.'

He straightened up and backed away from the letterbox, almost colliding with two boys, one bigger and older-looking than the other, who were leaning against the landing wall, grinning at him. At first glance he thought they must be brothers. A second look explained the similarity. They were dressed the same: jeans with bottoms rolled up over boots; braces over check shirts; cropped hair that made them look almost bald and made their ears stick out.

'Shut you out, has she?' said the bigger of the two. 'Fancied a bit, did you? With that old Jew-moo? You dirty randy bastard!'

'No chance, Russell,' said the smaller one. 'This yid's a fuckin poof. Ooh look! She's got lovely girly shopping bags!'

Russell darted forward and made a grab for one of the bags. Sam smelled unwashed clothes and stale tobacco. Without thinking, he put out a hand to stop him. Russell jumped back and balled his fists. 'Oh, you want some, do you? C'mon, then.'

Cornered, Sam mustered all his willpower not to show any sign of the panic he was feeling. For what felt like minutes, but he knew was probably only seconds, the two of them stood glaring at him, clenching their teeth and breathing hard through their nostrils, like angry bulls about to charge. In place of his first fearful reaction, he felt an explosion of anger rising up inside him. So that was why Esther lived behind a chained and locked front door. How pathetic, that they got their kicks from persecuting a sick old woman. And how sickening to be reminded that this brand of hate went on and on, with no hope that it would ever change. Jew-moo. Yid. Kike. Just thirty years after the Holocaust, and here were these arseholes stomping around in big boots, their heads shaved, mouthing these obscenities. Their dad, if they had one, might well have been one of Mosley's blackshirt scumbags. This was a helpful reminder: it never, never goes away. And it never will, however much 'not a Jew; just Jew-ish' you think you are. The anger had taken him over, but in the form of a strangely detached calm, as if everything was happening to someone else, at another time and place. The rusty dryness in his mouth, the beating of his heart and the sense that everything had started happening like a film running in slow motion, silent except for the roaring in his ears, was just as he'd felt at the moment that his wife Libby had pushed him over the edge. He took a step forward. Courage, or the lack of it, was no longer an issue. To his relief, Russell retreated a step. He swallowed hard and focused on ensuring that when he spoke his voice would be firm and strong. Thank God, it was. He pointed to Esther's door. 'The woman who lives here – she's family. My family. You remember that. And you leave her alone. You want trouble with me, you'll get it. Now fuck off and don't come near her again.'

Another long stillness. A rigid triangle of hostility. His heart was beating fast but the roaring had stopped. He wanted to pant as if he'd just run a race, but he fought down the urge and did his best to stay looking calm and in control. The younger of the two boys broke the stalemate. 'C'mon, Russell, this fuckin kike's getting on my tits.' In a last gesture of bravado he pushed past Sam and swung a booted foot against the base of Esther's door, scarring the paint in a spot that bore the marks of previous attacks, then turned and strolled away along the landing. Russell spat on the floor at Sam's feet and sauntered after his accomplice.

As soon as Sam had seen them disappear into the stairwell he sank down with his back against Esther's door, his heart hammering and his body trembling. He only just managed to keep his balance and not fall inside as the door swung open.

'Those *mamzers*!' snarled Esther. 'You know what they do? *Dreck* they put through my letterbox. Filthy things on my doormat. The police? Feh! I call them, they do nothing. What do they care?'

She stretched out a trembling hand to him, in what might have been a vain attempt to help him up. Trying to look braver than he felt, he waved it aside and pulled himself to his feet. His head swam and his mouth felt dry and bitter.

'Bring that stuff in,' said Esther. 'Wipe your feet. Make me some tea. Make for yourself as well. Did you bring my Kipling cakes?'

Supporting herself on her stick she stumped back inside. Sam carried the shopping into the kitchen, gulped down a large glass of water and looked around, feeling an unexpected surge of pride at the fresh smell, the shining floor and clean surfaces while he waited for his head to clear. He put away the food, buttered two slices of bread, opened a tin of Heinz chicken soup, heated it in a saucepan until its aroma pervaded his gleaming kitchen, and poured half of it into a bowl. He carried the soup and bread on a tray into Esther's room, where she was sitting in her armchair peering at a grainy snowstorm on her television screen. He cleared a space on the table beside her chair and put the tray down. 'I've brought you—'

'What are you doing?' she shouted. 'Leave my things alone!' She pointed to the television. 'Get me the picture. Turn the aerial! I can't see anything!'

He held down the aerial's flimsy plastic base and wiggled its two telescopic prongs until a semblance of an image emerged from the snowstorm.

'Better?'

She craned her neck and gazed at the screen. 'No. It'll do. Leave it.'

The adrenalin rush brought on by his encounter with Russell and his friend had subsided, to be replaced by a return of his irritation at letting this smelly old woman push him around. He'd done some cleaning and brought her some shopping. So he'd helped out a bit. Now he could back out with a clear conscience. But first he'd see she got the soup down her. So far, she'd ignored the tray. Maybe he should have stuck a rose in a little vase on it for her. He'd have to try and remember that thought, so he could tell Deborah about it later. He inwardly rehearsed a patient tone before speaking. 'I brought you some chicken soup, Mrs Symonds. Shall I put the tray on your lap? Or do you want to come and eat it in the kitchen?'

She looked away from the television and glared at him. 'Chicken soup? From where?'

From where? What should she care? 'From Tesco. Try some. It'll do you good.'

'Put it here.' She gestured to him to put the tray on her lap. She filled a spoonful, sniffed at it, blew on it and drank it.

'Good?'

She screwed up her face. 'Ach! *Pishachs*! What – you call this soup?'

The nasty, ungrateful bitch! 'You don't like it? Something wrong with it?'

She let the spoon drop into the bowl. 'You call this chicken soup? If I had my strength I'd make you. Real chicken soup. With *lockshen* and giblets. Nectar, he used to say. Esther, your chicken soup—'

She faltered and looked up at Sam, studying him for a moment. He tried to read the look. It wasn't the glare he was getting accustomed to; it was more a look of curiosity. He thought she was about to say something, but she bent back to the soup and took another spoonful. 'It's not like mine but—' She began taking faster spoonfuls, then tore up a slice of bread with shaky hands and dropped the pieces into the bowl. She waited for the soup to soak into them, then spooned them up with loud sucking noises. The sounds made him cringe. His dad, although fastidious about his appearance and in every other way, was a notoriously noisy eater. As a child and teenager Sam had sat through countless family get-togethers, inwardly raging with embarrassment as his dad slurped and gurgled his way through his meal. But when Esther handed back the empty bowl, he was amazed to feel the same surge of pride that he'd felt when looking round her kitchen. He managed not to notice as she leaned sideways, farted, and settled back. He picked up the tray, headed back to the kitchen and heard her speak to his retreating back. 'You know what?'

He stopped, but didn't turn round. He was beginning to know her a little. Something in her tone of voice had put him on his guard. 'Yes?'

Her voice had a slight wheedling tone. 'I'm taking a liberty but maybe you can make a bit better for me in here? Some dusting, a bit tidying up? You don't mind?'

Oh, bloody hell! That was the limit. He wasn't going to

fall for it again. He sighed inwardly. Something he couldn't explain was going on. It was as if, now he'd started his involvement with this woman, he just couldn't put an end to it. It was like the dream that he had from time to time where he'd got on the wrong bus and it was going in the wrong direction, but too fast for him to jump off and no sign anywhere of a bus-stop. Yet again, he had the strange feeling that the words coming from his mouth were being spoken by someone else. 'Sure. No problem.'

He washed up the soup bowl and got started. As he went round the room tidying up, spraying polish on wooden furniture and wiping away dust from the worst-affected places, he took the chance to look more closely at Esther's knick-knacks. In particular he was drawn to the photo leaning against the empty vase. He looked across at her. She was staring at the television, muttering to herself and paying no attention to him. He picked up the photo and studied it. It was a faded sepia studio portrait. A handsome well-built man with thick black curly hair and a bushy beard and moustache stood in front of a painted Grecian temple backdrop, looking straight into the camera with a confident air. The eyes were those of a strong-willed man, so much so that Sam felt as if they were drilling into him through the layers of dust and the cracked glass. He wore an old-fashioned suit with braided edging on the jacket lapels, a shirt with a shiny collar and a broad, richly patterned cravat with a pin that gleamed under the studio light. In his right hand he held a heavy-looking black stick with an ornamental handle, the kind Sam had only ever seen in old films carried by men in top hats and evening clothes.

'Leave that alone! Put it down!'

He started as if he'd been caught in an illicit act. 'No harm done, Mrs Symonds. I was just dusting off your photo. Did you know the glass was cracked?'

'It wasn't,' said Esther. 'Nathan must have done it. Bring it here.'

Nathan, now. Not Joel any more? He remembered what Anna had told him. Of course, Esther was a couple of sandwiches short of a picnic. That would explain these people she talked about, who clearly existed only inside her head. He did as she asked and held out the photo to her. She snatched it from him, raised it to her lips and planted a kiss on it.

'Careful,' he said. 'Mind the cracked glass. You'll cut yourself.'

Ignoring him, she pulled a grubby corner of her cardigan over her hand, bunched it together with her fingers and began rubbing it over the glass. He saw her hand go close to the jagged edge and reached out to intercept it. He should have remembered. As soon as his hand touched hers she flinched and began screaming in wild-eyed panic. 'Don't touch me! Get away!' He stepped well back, holding his hands out palms forward in a gesture meant as an appeal for her to be calm and trust him. 'It's all right, Mrs Symonds. I won't touch – your photo.'

To his relief she stopped screaming, but she continued glaring at him, clasping the frame to her chest and folding her arms over it. 'You better not! Leave it alone!' Her voice was harsh and there was still a note of panic in it. 'Don't you touch it!'

He was still holding his hands out in the placating gesture. 'I won't, Mrs Symonds. Trust me.'

She unclasped her arms and held the photo close to her eyes. 'The glass is cracked.'

He was starting to feel like Alice down the rabbit hole. 'Yes, I can see that. I could get it fixed for you if you like.'

She shook her head and thrust it at him. 'No! Put it back. Put it back where you found it. Don't touch it again.' He went to take it from her, but as it was leaving her fingers she tightened her grip, pulled it back and cradled it in her arms again. Her voice was calmer now.

'You know who this is? My father.'

'He was a good-looking man. You kissed his picture. Do you miss him?'

She was still cradling the photo, rocking it slightly as if holding a child. 'Yes.'

He searched for something else to say. 'You must have loved him very much.'

Her violent outburst of laughter shook her thin frame and brought on a racking cough that made her writhe with pain and clutch her side with one hand while clinging to the photo with the other. He could only watch and wait until the laughter and the pain subsided and she was able to speak again. When she did, the strength of her voice took him by surprise.

'That *mamzer? Shteyner af zayne beyner*!'

He understood odd words of Yiddish. *Mamzer* was clear enough. She'd called her father a bastard. But the other words were new to him. Spat out like that, they seemed to be some kind of curse. He was perplexed. Her words and actions didn't match. Still cradling the photo she rocked back and forth, her eyes closed, muttering to herself. She seemed to be falling asleep. He waited. Her head fell forward. A bubble of saliva between her lips expanded and contracted in time with her laboured breathing. He pulled a chair out, taking care to make no noise. He sat and watched her. Five, then ten minutes passed.

Deborah would be waiting to hear how he'd got on, and to continue the thankless job of trying to help him understand what was going on inside his own head. 'I've got a feeling,' she'd said, as they cuddled up in bed, 'that you're getting more out of this than you'd bargained for.'

'You're dead right,' he'd mumbled, half-asleep. 'I'm getting a lot more aggravation than I'd bargained for.' But he had to admit to himself that this wasn't just about curiosity, or another way of settling old grudges against his parents. He was feeling something he had no words for. Certainly, the slight chance that she might be his own grandmother had something to do with it. But it wasn't just that. There was more. What, exactly, he still had to figure out.

Esther was snoring loudly now, her head slumped forward on her chest. He was unsure what to do. Leave her sleeping and creep away? No, he should at least say something.

'Mrs Symonds, I'll be going now,' he whispered. Her eyes shot open. She was wide awake. 'Why did you ask about my brothers?'

Brothers, now? She'd wrong-footed him again. 'I don't think I did, Mrs Symonds. I didn't know you had brothers.'

Her cardigan had fallen open. Beneath it was a blue Terylene blouse that looked as if it could do with a wash. She pulled the edges of her cardigan shut and held them together with a defensive gesture. 'You didn't know? Brothers, yes! Two! I've got two brothers!'

She was rambling. Talking about imaginary people. Maybe she thought they were in the room with her now. Best humour her. 'Really? Where do your brothers live?'

The question seemed to disturb her. 'Live? They – they come, they go. They—'

'What are their names?' She stared at him, then resumed rocking and muttering. He'd had as much as he could take for one day. Now it really was time to leave. 'I think you're tired. Maybe you want to sleep now.'

She nodded, closed her eyes, then opened them again. 'Enough with the questions! *Ferdreh mir nisht in kop mit* the questions! I should tell you everything I know? Go away now.'

He didn't need telling twice. He gathered up his empty shopping bags. She was dozing off as he crept away.

'Wait!'

Oh, shit, not again! He forced a friendly expression. 'Did you forget something?'

She pulled herself up on an elbow and pointed with her chin. 'Get me that photo. From the drawers.'

Now she was ordering him to bring her the photo she'd told him not to touch ever again. He would have liked to point that out to her, but he resisted the temptation, put his bags down and fetched it. His irritation rose almost to bursting point when she gave him one of her most cutting glares and pushed it away. '*Nudnik! Shmendrik!* Not that one! Did I say that one?'

She was getting worse. 'This is the only one. There isn't another—'

She waved him to silence. 'From the drawers! From the drawers! Top drawer. Look there. In a paper bag. Bring me the bag.'

The drawer was a jumble of cotton-reels, string, ribbon, scissors and Green Shield stamps. The paper bag was yellowed, crumpled and torn. He held it up.

'This one?'

Her face contorted with anger. 'Bring it! Bring it!'

Calling on his very last reserves of patience, he held out the bag to her, but she ignored the gesture. 'Look inside. Take it out.'

Flakes of the brittle paper floated to the floor as he used his forefinger and thumb to slide out an age-spotted ivory-coloured cardboard folder some six inches long and four wide. On the folder's cover was a logo in gold copperplate lettering: *Samson Rezler Photographic Studio, 6B Brick lane, E.* Below that, in smaller, plainer, black lettering, *A. Elfish & Sons, Monumental Masons*. He folded back the cover and saw, as he'd expected, another old photo. What he hadn't anticipated was that the subject would be a gravestone: tall and most likely made of marble, with many lines of inscription and a low barley twist shaped railing around it. He looked from the photo to Esther, waiting for an explanation.

'What do you think?' she said. 'You like it?'

Did he like her photo of a gravestone? What was he expected to say? 'Yes,' he tried, 'it's very nice.'

'Very nice?' she almost snarled. 'Very nice, he says! *Nudnik*! Look at it!'

He brought it close to his face and made a show of examining it more closely. The first line of the inscription was in Hebrew lettering. From his childhood studies he could make out some of the words but they made no sense to him. On the next line was carved the name 'Isaac Levinson'. The lines below that were too small to be readable.

He felt a stirring of curiosity. 'Who was Isaac Levinson?'

'Who? My father, is who!'

He pointed to the photo he'd just replaced on top of the chest of drawers. 'The man in that photo? This is his gravestone? Your father was called Isaac Levinson?'

'God rest his soul, yes.'

He was confused again. 'But didn't you just—' He bit back the rest of his question. 'Rest his soul?' So what was all that *mamzer* stuff, and the cursing? Best just to let it go. No way was he going to get a sane answer. He closed the cover and passed the photo back to her. 'Thanks for showing me that, Mrs Symonds. Very interesting.' He made a show of looking at his watch. 'Now, I really must —'

She put out a hand with surprising suddenness and grasped his wrist. He could feel every bone in her fingers. He was afraid that her yellow nails digging into his skin might draw blood. '*Matzevahs*,' she croaked, 'you think they grow on trees? Believe me, this one cost plenty. Who do you think paid for it?'

As gently as he could, he freed himself. 'I-I don't know. Who paid for it, Mrs Symonds?'

'Who?' she cackled. 'Me, who else? No one gave me *gournisht*! You know that? No one gave me *gournisht*. You know why not?'

He was completely lost now. He just wanted to get away. She cackled again. 'Because of the broygus! What else?'

Of course. The broygus. So she'd been mixed up in one. Another clue. At least it would be, if a family broygus was a rare thing, which of course it wasn't. Still…

'And another thing.'

'Yes, Mrs Symonds? And another thing?'

'What's with this Mrs Symonds schtick? Mrs Symonds this, Mrs Symonds that! What am I, an old woman?'

'I thought that's what you—'

'You call me Esther. *Fershteyt*? Esther!'

He looked at his watch again. He needed to get out while he had a shred of sanity left. 'Yes, of course. Esther. Fine. Esther from now on, then. Now I must be going.'

'So go!' she said. 'Who's stopping you? And take them. Bring them back next time.'

He was lost. 'Take what, Mrs – Esther?'

She made a long, rasping noise of impatience, a cross between a raspberry and a growl. 'My photos! What else? Get the glass fixed. And get me nice frames, both the same.'

Oh, if that was all – 'I'll do that for you, Esther.'

'Good. You want money? Take from my purse. Don't spend too much. And don't you try to catch me or run off with them. Bring them when you come again. Don't be a stranger. You got my number? Phone me up before you come.'

So she was saying she wanted him to come back. That should have pissed him off, but he felt strangely pleased. Her phone had been cut off, though. He'd have to sort that out. 'I'll bring them back soon, Esther,' he said. 'And I promise I won't catch you – or run off with them.'

He thought, just for a second, that he saw the bitterness leave her expression. And unless he'd imagined it, there was even a tiny hint of warmth in the granite eyes. 'I know. Go.'

He headed again for the door.

'Wait!'

Oh, fuck! 'Yes?'

She was holding a key. 'It's my spare. Keep it. Use it when you come back – Josh.'

SEVEN

1916

As the sunny spring day gave way to a warm evening, the uniformed concierge of the Rodrigues Club adjusted his military-style cap and took up his post at the street door, ready to greet the first of the evening's diners. The traffic in Leadenhall Street had come to a complete standstill and the fetid air rising from the road's mixture of mud and horse-dung was thick with the angry shouts of drivers and passengers. Stepping to the pavement's edge for a better view, he looked up the road in the direction of St Paul's where the drivers of an omnibus and a brewery waggon were facing each other off, neither wanting to take the trouble to climb down and coax his team of horses into reverse. Already, the soberly clad office workers heading for home were stopping to take sides and egg the two men on in the hope that there would be the spectacle of a street-brawl to compensate for the monotony of their day.

A sharp tap on the shoulder interrupted his absorption in the scene. Turning, he saw a thickset man in evening clothes complete with gloves and top hat, carrying a black walking stick with an ivory handle. The man's boots were highly polished, his shirt-front gleamed white and he wore a paisley-patterned silk cravat held in place with a diamond-studded stickpin. His luxurious beard was black streaked with grey, as was the hair that protruded from beneath his hat. The concierge touched his finger to the peak of his cap.

'Evening, sir. Help you?'

'Levinson. Isaac Levinson. I have an appointment with Mr Julius Shapiro. Kindly inform him of my arrival.'

The man's voice was deep, firm, authoritative. He was used to giving orders and being obeyed. His speech was well modulated and cultured, with just a trace of a foreign accent that was difficult to place. The concierge led him into the club's foyer, took his hat and invited him to make himself comfortable in a deep leather armchair. He sat with his back upright, both hands resting on the handle of his stick, eyes darting around the room, taking in every detail and working out his strategy. He was going to have to stay alert. These people wouldn't be giving him the time of day unless they wanted something. But what? He'd have to be patient. There was bound to be some schmooze before they got down to business.

Less than five minutes later, a smiling silver-haired man, also in evening dress, appeared and held out his hand. 'Mr Levinson, welcome! Julius Shapiro. Thank you so much for agreeing to meet me. Can we dispense with the formalities? Please call me Julius. May I call you Isaac?'

Isaac stood and shook hands. The older man, lean and clean-shaven, towered over him by at least three inches. Like Isaac, he wore a black silk skullcap. Isaac noted with distaste the man's light handshake, smooth palm and manicured fingernails. The hand of a man who had never grafted at a market stall or seen the inside of a sweatshop. 'Of course. An invitation from you is an honour, Julius.'

'Nonsense!' Julius replied. 'We're just two honest businessmen about to share a convivial dinner. I've heard many good things about you and I'm looking forward to getting to know you personally. Shall we go in now?'

He took Isaac by the elbow and led him through a double door into the club's oak-panelled dining room where the inviting smells of well-cooked food mingled with the toasty aromas of expensive cigars. The room was large enough for each of its tables to be at a comfortable distance from its neighbour. Waiters glided around the room with no clash of plates or clatter of cutlery, and the men at the four or five occupied tables spoke in low murmurs with their heads close together. At a sign from Julius, a waiter showed them to a table and brought menus. Isaac looked down at the silver cutlery, the gleaming wine glasses and the snow-white damask tablecloth, then ran his eyes over the other diners. All were in full evening dress, their ages appearing to range from twenties to seventies, and everyone wore a silk skullcap similar to his own. A City club full of rich Sephardim. What a sight. So what did they want from this *shtetl* Ashkenazi? For all their smiles and handshakes, he was all too well acquainted with their low opinion of his kind.

'A wonderful sight, isn't it?' said Julius. 'Yes, the Rodrigues is the City's only fully Jewish businessmen's club. We have stockbrokers, entrepreneurs, manufacturers, department store owners, hoteliers – and a few shady characters, no doubt!'

'Remarkable indeed,' said Isaac. 'An entirely Sephardic membership, I presume?'

'So far, yes. We've been here longer, we've had more time to get on our feet as a community. But some of you Ashkenazi chaps are giving us a run for our money these days. Remind me, please, when did your parents come over?'

So he wanted a pedigree. Well, he'd get one. 'My parents, God bless them, are living out their final days in peace – at least for the time being – in Smorgon, in Russian Poland where I was born. I wanted to bring them but they said no, the journey was too long; they wished me well, they chose to stay.'

'So you weren't born here? When did you come?'

'In 1890. I was twenty-nine.'

'But – forgive me – the way you speak—'

Isaac laughed. 'Not like an immigrant – not like a Whitechapel ghetto Jew, is that what you mean? Not like

Abraham the trouser-maker? No, I learned early on that you don't just get out of the *shtetl* by moving to another country. It takes more than that. You know I'm selling my goods now to the new West End stores, to Liberty, to Selfridges? You walk in there talking like a rabbi from Minsk and they'll throw you out on your ear!'

Julius seemed unsure whether or not to laugh. 'So – again, forgive me, how did you — ?

'How did I learn to speak your English language like a *goy*, or even – no offence – like a Sephardi? It's a long story. Do you really want to hear it?'

'Another time I'd love to,' said Julius. 'But for now shall we make our choices from this excellent, entirely kosher menu and get down to business?'

So far, it was going exactly as he'd expected. Now he was being softened up and, later, when he was supposed to feel he owed them something, would come the proposition. He was happy to go along with it for the time being. At the very least he'd get an excellent dinner. They both chose chicken soup for their first course. Isaac took a spoonful and nodded his approval. It was golden, aromatic, redolent of herbs and generously laced with vermicelli and small meat-filled dumplings.

'I should tell you,' began Julius between spoonfuls, 'that I represent a group of entrepreneurs on whose behalf I'm approaching you. We have a proposition that we are sure will interest you.'

That was a surprise. He was getting down to it sooner than expected. It revealed a lack of respect. They didn't think the *shtetl* Jew would understand the niceties of genteel business dealing. He slowly despatched another spoonful. 'Excellent soup. Please do continue.'

'I believe your business was originally one of manufacturing and selling leather goods?'

Ah. The first clue. So this was going to be about his factories. Time to spice up the story a little. Lay it on thick.

Make him feel even more superior. Before replying he finished off his soup, taking care to reinforce Julius' expectations of him by scraping up the last shreds of vermicelli, cleaning round the plate with a piece of bread and wiping his mouth with the back of his hand. 'Manufacturing is a big word for where I started from. I'm sure you know Smorgon is famous for its leather production. I was a leather worker. When we came, we had nothing. Not even money to buy materials to get started. I used to go round the Whitechapel sweatshops begging scraps of leather – even taking them out of rubbish bins. At night we made little things – purses, wallets, bracelets. Daytime we stood in Wentworth Street selling them from a tray. That's how I started.'

Julius nodded his admiration. 'And from there you acquired your first sweatshop, then a factory, two factories—'

He'd obviously done a lot of checking up. This was getting more and more interesting. He beamed at Julius. 'Four factories, as a matter of fact. Now I make and sell for the Bond Street shops, for the big stores. Shoes, coats, belts – and not just leather. Dresses, men's suits, everything.'

'And now you're a rich man,' said Julius. 'And you have influence. Your community looks up to you. Am I right?'

Ah, now the purpose was getting closer. 'If they do, it's because I never cheat anyone, not because I'm rich. I pay good wages, I look after my people. You know what they call me?'

'I do. They call you The Balaboss,' said Julius. 'The Lord, the man to respect.'

A waiter brought the second course: roast goose for Isaac; fried plaice for Julius.

'Naturally,' said Julius, 'you have contracts with your various clients?'

'Of course,' said Isaac, tearing off a hunk of bread and signalling to the waiter for more wine. 'For delivery of goods on time and to quality. And I always fulfil them.'

'We are asking you to terminate those contracts.'

Isaac paused with the bread halfway to his mouth and laughed out loud. 'What? Why on earth—'

'You're a rich man, Isaac,' said Julius. 'But you're not a millionaire – not yet, that is. How would you like to be a millionaire?'

The moment had come. Now he was about to find out why he was here. He put down his knife and fork, wiped his fingers on his beard to keep the illusion alive, and looked straight at Julius. 'Your proposal? I presume you have one?'

Julius swallowed the last mouthful of fish and pushed his plate aside. 'It's simple really. We have the offer of a gigantic contract worth a fortune. But we need someone like you; with the facilities, the skills, the contacts and the workforce, to help deliver it for us. Believe me, come in with us and your reward will be colossal.'

'And the commodity?'

Julius leaned conspiratorially towards Isaac and breathed a single word: 'Uniforms.'

'Uniforms?' Isaac guffawed so loudly that several diners turned and glared disapprovingly at him.

'It's no laughing matter,' said Julius. 'The Government is looking for a company to take on the manufacture of British Army uniforms and everything that goes with them: battledress, dress uniforms, shirts, belts, webbing, boots, harnesses, holsters, caps, badges – just think, the army is bigger than it's been in living memory, and the War Office just can't keep up with demand. It's a golden opportunity and an act of patriotism at the same time. Think about it.'

'But this is surely a bubble,' said Isaac. 'The war's already been going on for two years, and it can't last more than a few months longer.'

'I wish that were true,' sighed Julius. 'If the politicians and the newspapers were to tell the truth at this moment there would be a serious risk of public unrest. The truth is that we're bogged down in this war. Not just on the Western Front but in the Middle East, Africa – the whole thing's running out of hand. And in France the spring offensive's about to start. A gigantic army moving against this country's enemies. And those boys will need to be equipped.'

The waiter cleared their plates and offered the menu for desserts. Both men declined and ordered coffee and brandy. There was a pause in the conversation while they lit their cigars. Isaac was rapidly running rows of figures in his mind. Materials, workers, machines, foremen – yes, he could do it. But he'd been too long in business to look keen. This jumped-up Sephardi would certainly be hoping to get him cheap. He swirled his brandy around in the glass and took a sip. 'You should know that I have two sons in the army, in France as we speak. Nathan and Joel, just twenty-one and twenty-three. And Ben, the son of an old employee of mine from Smorgon. Just eighteen. And countless other boys from Whitechapel families who know me. Do you think I would like to be seen to be profiting from the misery of this war? Isn't that what the Gentiles say about Jews? That we make money from other people's misfortunes?'

Julius shrugged. 'True. But they'll say those things whatever we do. Nothing we do will ever make them like us any better. They'll always hate us, that's never going to change.' He leaned forward and jabbed his cigar at Isaac to emphasise his words. 'Our soldiers need those clothes and those uniforms. That's a fact. They have to come from somewhere. Why shouldn't they come from us? Will you at least think about it? Why don't we meet for dinner in a week from now? Then you can give me your answer. I tell you what, let's meet at The Savoy. We could bring our wives along, get to know each other better.'

Here was another surprise. The man was asking to meet Millie? Wasn't he afraid she'd turn up at The Savoy wearing an apron and carrying a basket of beigels? Or a couple of herrings, maybe? He'd been wise to stay wary. Something else was going on here. He beamed at Julius again. 'It would be a pleasure. No, an honour.'

'I look forward to meeting your wife,' said Julius. 'And I believe you have a daughter?'

Was that it? Was Julius on the lookout for a *shidduch* into the bargain? But something wasn't quite right. Why would he go shopping for a bride in Whitechapel? Why wasn't he looking for a rich Sephardi girl for his son? Unless maybe the son wasn't too marketable for some reason? Nevertheless, perhaps this too was an opportunity. 'Yes, my daughter Esther. The light of my life. Seventeen years old. And clever? *Kaynahora*!'

'And good-looking too, so I've heard.'

'That, without a doubt. But a little too fond of keeping up friendships with the children from the old *shtetl* families. Years ago, that was all well and good. But times change. She's a well-off young woman now. I want better for her. And she deserves better. Much better.'

'I understand perfectly,' said Julius. 'Maybe you and I can help each other in that direction too. Why don't you bring her along? I have a son, Elias. He would love to meet her. Another brandy?'

Isaac sat back and puffed on his cigar. 'Yes, Julius. Another brandy. Why not?'

EIGHT

1976

July was nearing its end and still the heatwave showed no signs of letting up. The grass in Cliften Square and in St James's Churchyard opposite had turned brown, then black, then shrivelled to nothing. As Sam left for work, looking forward to what lay ahead despite another night of broken sleep and fearful dreams, the temperature was already in the high seventies and forecast to climb another ten or more degrees by midday.

Managing the shabby Hackney branch of the SL Travel Company was all he'd managed to get in the bad time after his divorce, when he'd lost his high-up job with Bespoke Tours Europe. But it had the attraction of being just a five-minute walk from his home, and in just two years he'd built it up into a going concern and taken on an assistant, Eleni, who was young, bright, and eager to get on.

He stood on the pavement outside the shop for a moment, running an expert eye over the window display. Everything was in perfect order; Eleni always saw to that. Beside the neat racks of leaflets and stacks of colourful brochures, life-sized cut-outs of laughing women in bikinis and handsome men in bathing trunks sipped cocktails on sandy beaches. This was the busy time of the year when people came looking for bargains on charter flights to places like Rimini and Ibiza. A few more weeks, then all the holidays would have been booked and it would start to go quiet until the Christmas adverts came on TV and customers would start coming in to grab the new season's special offers.

Eleni, looking cool and fresh in an ultra-light lime-green business suit that would have coped with the most sweltering of Cyprus summers, was showing a brochure to a young couple with a baby in a pram when he arrived. He nodded a cold greeting to Gordon Platt, the London area manager, who sat at the counter polishing his glasses and running the tip of his tongue around his lips as he followed Eleni's every movement and gesture. With a jerk of his head he diverted Gordon's attention from Eleni and invited him into the kitchen, a small space separated from the shop by a glass partition. He sat across the table from Gordon and took in the cream linen suit, crocodile-skin slip-on shoes and red-framed designer glasses. Gordon was still in his late twenties but his rise through the company had been meteoric. He was bony, long-limbed and fair-skinned, with thinning pale-red hair.

He unfolded a handkerchief and wiped the perspiration from his forehead. 'She's a hell of a looker, your Eleni. These Cypriot girls, eh? Lovely little arse, she's got. And those tits – blimey, you don't get many of them to the pound! You must be very happy to have her. I would be, if you get my drift.'

Sam kept his disgust to himself. He knew Gordon of old; he hadn't expected any better from him. 'Thanks for offering to meet me here. I would have come to Head Office if you'd preferred.'

'No way, mate,' said Gordon, 'It's been ages since I came down here. It's a nice little set-up you've got. Considering.'

He had an idea what was coming. 'How do you mean?'

'Well, considering this is a poor district. And your clientele's – well you know – a bit mixed. Different skin shades and funny hats, if you get my drift.'

If Gordon had not been so self-obsessed, it would have been harder for Sam to conceal his contempt for the man. As it was, he was having to keep a close check on himself –

not let his temper get the better of him or say anything too insulting. He needed to get Gordon's agreement to what he was planning. Everything else was unimportant today. He had to keep this strictly business. 'Have you checked my accounts lately?'

Gordon uncoiled himself and took a sheet of paper from his inside pocket. He unfolded it and grinned at Sam. 'I certainly have, mate. This pie chart says it all. Size for size, this year and last year, yours has been the most profitable of our five London branches. Well done, you!'

Through the glass partition Sam saw the family leaving, the couple smiling and waving at Eleni. She'd no doubt proved her worth again. He turned his attention back to Gordon. 'Thanks. I do think we're a good team, me and Eleni.'

'I can see that, mate, if you get my drift.' Gordon sculpted an exaggerated female shape in the air with his hands. Sam ground his teeth and said nothing. If he gave himself the satisfaction of kicking the man's arse out of the door, everything – including his job – would be lost. So he controlled himself and waited.

Gordon took off his glasses, breathed on each lens in turn, polished them with his handkerchief and replaced them before continuing. 'So I was chuffed when you asked for a meeting, because I was just about to get on the blower to you.'

That was unexpected. 'You wanted to talk to me?'

Gordon grinned again. 'I did, yes. Because the guys upstairs have noticed your performance and I'm here to tell you… you're getting a bonus and a promotion. I told them how it's all down to me, how I personally trained you up and taught you everything I know. So now I'm going up the ladder again and you're getting my job.' He drew a name-plate shape in the air with his thumb and forefinger. 'Sam Shaykin, London area manager. How does that sound, mate?'

Still beaming and perspiring, Gordon offered a damp palm for a congratulatory handshake. Sam ignored it and looked down at the table, his thoughts racing. This was the last thing he'd expected. Talk about sod's law! At any other time he'd have grabbed the offer with both hands. A great career step, more money, a better future. But why did it have to come now? He thought rapidly. Maybe this was meant to be. Maybe this was a sign that he should abandon the plan that he'd called Gordon here to discuss. The thought made him laugh. It was that bloody Ron who'd started him off thinking about signs, along with his *mitzvahs* and Hashems. He saw that Gordon was looking at him oddly. He must have seemed strange, just suddenly bursting out laughing like that. He realised he had only seconds to choose which way to go: whether to stick to his plan, or to forget it and grab the job opportunity while it was on offer. Gordon was looking at him, still grinning, waiting for him to say something. He had to make his choice. Now.

'A bit sudden, was it?' Gordon's grin changed to a man-of-the-world smirk. 'You worried about Eleni? Don't worry, I'll personally see she's taken care of, if you get my drift. Or I suppose you could take her with you. As your PA, shall we say?' He bunched his fist and held it up in an obscene gesture.

Sam struggled to ward off the roaring in his ears. 'Let's get this straight, Gordon. Eleni's a looker, you think I haven't noticed? But she works for me, there's nothing more to it than that, and what's more she does it bloody well. So let's have a bit of respect, shall we? Let's not have any more of your silly tit-and-bum talk. Okay?'

Gordon raised both hands in surrender. 'Whoa there, mate! Whoa! That's a bit OTT, isn't it? I was just having my little joke.'

'No you weren't,' said Sam. 'You were saying I must be getting in her knickers. Which I'm not. And in case you're thinking of having a go on your own account, I'll warn you she's got a very big boyfriend. He's called Costas. He comes most evenings to drive her home. If you want to come back later, I'll introduce you.'

Gordon let his hands go limp and mopped his forehead again. 'Okay, mate. So I put my size tens in it that time. No need to throw your toys out the pram. Gordon Platt's never too big to know when he's out of line.' He put his hand out again, and this time Sam took it. 'Okay, Gordon, no hard feelings as long as we've got that clear. But about that other thing – the promotion – I'm grateful for the offer, but it's come at a bad time. I can't take a promotion right now. You see, I wanted to meet you to tell you I want to take some time off. Two weeks starting now. Maybe a month. Maybe even longer. It's a – family matter. A personal thing. So, thanks, Gordon, but please tell the – the guys upstairs – tell them no. Tell them I can't take the promotion. Not now, anyway.'

Gordon gave his glasses another vigorous polish. 'Blimey, that's a turn-up. You're passing up a big opportunity, mate. You're sure you want to do that? It might not come round again. And by the way, who do you think would run your branch if we let you go swanning off?'

That made no sense to Sam. He'd have had to be replaced if he'd accepted the job. But he'd been expecting the question and he had the answer ready. 'Eleni's more than capable, and she's ready for more responsibility. Why don't you ask her to stand in? I think she'd jump at the chance.'

'You really think she could do it?' said Gordon.

'I'm positive. And won't it impress the guys upstairs when they find out it was you who spotted her potential and gave her her break? Think about it, Gordon. I hope you'll back me up. I'm owed a week's holiday. I'll take the rest unpaid. Hopefully they won't sack me, but that's a chance I'm going to take. If you get my drift. Mate.'

Sam could see that the trump card he'd played had done the trick. Gordon stood up and gave him a man-to-man slap on the shoulder. 'Okay, okay, I get it. Something big's come up. Let's not have any more talk about sacking or unpaid leave. I'll talk to the guys upstairs and I'll make the arrangements. And I'll put in a word for your Eleni.' He held up both hands and crossed his fingers. 'Mind you, if I was you I'd hope she doesn't do too well. If she does, who knows, your job might not still be there when you want to come back. If you get my drift.'

The slimy bastard! He had to get one in before leaving. But Sam let it pass and saw him out, noting with satisfaction the respectful way in which he said goodbye to Eleni. Glad that the shop was empty of customers, he slumped into a chair behind the counter and put his head in his hands.

'What's up, Sam?' said Eleni. 'I didn't like the way he sat there staring at me while I was serving those people. Did I do something wrong?'

Sam looked up and smiled at her. 'No, quite the opposite. Let's just say you really impressed him. I might as well tell you right away. I'm going to take a bit of time off and I've recommended you to act as temporary manager.'

He'd never heard Eleni scream before. 'What? No way! That's fantastic! Thank you so much, Sam! But do you really think I can do it?'

'Of course you can. And you can always call me at home if you need to know anything.'

Sam watched, amused and pleased, as Eleni jumped up and down like an excited child. 'That's – it's – I don't know what – thank you, Sam! I know it's silly, but – can I phone my mum and tell her?'

He was still smiling. He felt her happiness rubbing off on him, raising his spirits a little. 'Sure. You go ahead.'

There was one thing left to do. He held the fort in the shop while Eleni made her call, then went into the kitchen, took Ron Green's card from his wallet and dialled the number.

'Aaron Green bespoke tailoring? Yes?'

The voice was curt and impersonal. In the background Sam could hear shouted conversations and the clatter of sewing machines. Maybe this was a bad time, or even a bad idea.

'Is – er – Ron Green…'

'Ron Green here. Who's this?'

Sam was wrong-footed. This wasn't the slick, persuasive Ron who'd visited him just a few days ago. 'Oh hello, Ron,' he stammered. 'This is Sam. Sam Shaykin. I hope I'm not—'

'Boychick!' Suddenly Ron's tone was warm and friendly. Sam's anxiety level dropped several notches. 'What a *mechayeh!* I thought you'd forgotten about me. So tell me, how's it going with – wait, let me see – Stella, wasn't it?'

'Esther. Esther Symonds'

'Oh, yes. *Fermisht* old lady. Not your auntie, as it turns out. Am I right?'

'Yes, but I think she might very poss—'

'So, you've been to see her like she wanted? Boychick, you've made my day! What a *mitzvah* you're doing!

The *mitzvahs* again! It seemed he was always having to explain to people how he felt about such things. He didn't want to offend Ron, but he had to make it clear. 'Ron, I don't —'

'Sure, sure, a *mensch* like this one, he's too modest to make a fuss, bless him. But let me tell you, boychick, whatever you say, Hashem will reward you for what you're doing.'

Sam bit his lip and decided not to argue the point. 'Ron, what I phoned to tell you is, I've seen her and I'll be doing what I can to make her —'

'Wonderful! Every word like diamonds to my ears! So the broygus is settled?'

He hesitated. 'It's complicated. It's not exactly sett—'

'Marvellous! Now, listen. The charity's got funds. Anything she needs, you call me. Any help you want, you call me. And if you want a new suit, you come and see me. I'll make you a good price. Any material you like. Waistcoat, second pair of trousers, the full *megillah*!'

Sam laughed. So, whatever else he was, Ron really was a salesman as he'd first suspected. 'Thanks, Ron, but I don't wear suits much. And anyway, I couldn't afford your Savile Row prices.'

Ron guffawed into the phone. 'Savile Row? Feh! You've been to my place. Drop in again some time. We'll have a glass of tea and I'll measure you up. What's to lose?'

Sam was starting to enjoy the conversation as he warmed to Ron's strange mixture of seriousness and humour. But, looking at his watch, he remembered that he needed to get away in time to collect Esther's photos before Mr Howarth closed for the day. 'Thanks, Ron. I'll bear that in mind. And thanks for your offer, but I'm OK for now. I just wanted to let you know what was happening, so—'

'Good boy, good boy! A real *mensch* we've got here! Keep in touch. What you're doing for that old lady, it's like gold on my heart. And you want to know the icing on the cake? It means that when, *nisht duggedacht*, the old lady passes, she'll have a close family member to say the mourner's *kaddish* for her.'

Sam's grip tightened around the receiver. 'Ron, please listen. I can't do that.'

'Don't worry, boychick. Lots of Jews these days can't read the Hebrew. We can get it written out in English letters for you.'

He felt himself breaking into a sweat. It was so clear to him, and yet it seemed so hard for Ron to accept. 'I can read the Hebrew well enough. At least, I could if I wanted to. But the thing is, I don't believe. I used to, but now I don't. And I'm not saying prayers – especially that one – that mean nothing to me. I'm sorry.'

For once Ron hadn't interrupted and didn't seem to have a ready answer. But his hesitation lasted no more than a few seconds. 'Boychick, now I know why Hashem saw to it that our paths would cross. Believe me, when the time comes, you'll find your way back. You'll say the *kaddish,* trust me. But now, I've got work to do. Stay in touch. Call if you need me.'

*

Eleni was bubbling with excitement for the rest of the day as customers came and went. Seeing her delight at the chance he'd given her raised his spirits just enough to damp down his frustration at Ron's stubborn refusal to take him seriously. But still, uncertainty nagged at him as he thought about the promotion he'd just thrown away. After all, he really didn't know why this crazy notion about Esther was threatening to come before everything else in his life. He'd just passed up a golden career opportunity for the sake of what he realised was becoming an obsession. He had no idea whether he'd made the right choice, or why he'd made it. It was sheer lunacy. But he'd done it, and there was no going back.

At four o'clock he left Eleni in charge and drove to Howarth's Photographic in Lauriston Road. Mister Howarth took Esther's photos from a drawer and placed them proudly on the counter. Sam was impressed. The two bright, fully restored and re-framed photos were hardly recognisable.

'Lovely old pieces, Mr Shaykin. They'll be family of yours, I take it? From the old country?'

'Possibly,' said Sam. 'Probably. But I can't be sure.'

Mister Howarth gave the new matching frames and glass a final polish with a soft yellow cloth.

'They've come up wonderfully. I've cleaned off the surface dirt – very carefully, so as not to damage the coating on the paper – and I've touched up the scratches and blemishes with a fine camel-hair brush. Not that I had to do much. Those old-fashioned glass-plate cameras were superbly efficient. Just look how sharp the inscription is on this tombstone.'

Sam bent down to the counter and looked more closely. Mister Howarth might well say the inscription was sharp, but that didn't change the fact that, except for the line of Hebrew at the top and the name of Esther's father beneath it, the secrets the words might reveal seemed to be mocking him by staying just out of his reach. He straightened up. 'It's still too small to read, though. Pity.'

Mr Howarth lifted his glasses onto his forehead and squinted at the inscription. 'I see what you mean.' He dropped his glasses back onto his nose. 'You know, I think we can put that right if I make a new negative and print an enlargement. I could have it ready for you tomorrow or the day after.' He must have read the disappointment in Sam's expression. 'Tell you what, though, there's a quicker way. We could take it through to my workshop now and put it under the big magnifying lens.' He picked up the photo and lifted the flap in the counter.

The smell of the workshop reminded Sam of the chemistry laboratory at his school. It was an Aladdin's cave of ancient and modern photographic equipment: cameras, tripods, enlargers, shelves of chemicals, boxes of film, studio lights, back-cloths and a dark-room. Mr Howarth slid the photo under a large lens mounted on a metal stand. He motioned Sam to look down into it and placed a notepad and pencil next to him. He pressed a switch and stood back. The words shone up at Sam through the lens, sharp and clear. He gazed down, studied the inscription and let out a shout of excitement. He grabbed the pad, scribbled down the words, checked to make sure that he'd copied them accurately, and straightened up. 'Thank you so much, Mr Howarth. That was fantastic!' was all he could think of to say.

Mister Howarth snapped the light off. 'You're welcome. I assume you're satisfied?'

Feeling even happier than if he'd won £75,000 on the Treble Chance – not that he ever did the football pools – Sam took Mister Howarth's hand in both of his and pumped it up and down. 'More than I can say,' he said. 'You just gave me a grandmother – and a great-grandfather as well.'

NINE

From the lightness in Deborah's voice as she called out and the tune she was humming as she dropped off her shoes in the bedroom, Sam knew that she'd had a successful day. She joined him in the living-room with a cold bottle of Chardonnay and two glasses, filled one for herself and poured a careful half-glass for him before flopping down on the sofa with a satisfied sigh. In what had become a ritual at the end of every working day, she reached up to the top of her head and pulled out the pin holding her thick dark hair so that it fell in torrents around her face and shoulders. There was something about that gesture that never failed to excite Sam. He ran his hand through her loose hair and lifted a lock to his face so that he could inhale its scent. 'Mm, that feels good. Smells good too. Is that a new perfume?'

'Yes, it is!' She took a small dispenser from a black satin pouch in her bag, sprayed a tiny amount onto her wrist and held it up for him to breathe in its woody aroma. 'It's Anaïs Anaïs. I bought it during our drop-in to Harrods this morning. I'm really pleased you noticed.'

He pretended to look offended. 'Meaning I don't usually take notice of you? Well, maybe. But today I'm noticing everything about you. Every single thing. And it's all fantastic!'

She laughed and put her arms around his neck. 'You're in a good mood. Any particular reason?

He pulled her closer to him. 'I've got some news. Good news. But first, why don't you tell me about your day?'

'My day?' She pushed him gently away and took a drink. 'I took a Japanese group round South Ken. You remember booking it? The V&A, the Natural History and Harrods, of course. I really enjoyed it.' She held out her glass and Sam re-filled it. 'Now, you said you've got news. Is it about your meeting with Gordon? Did it go well?'

He allowed himself a satisfied smile. 'Yes and no. He was acting the pillock as usual. Long story short, I let him get on my nerves and we had a bit of a ding-dong. Tell you the truth, I thought I'd gone too far and was wishing I'd kept my mouth shut, when out of the blue he offers me a promotion. London area manager. The last thing I expected.'

'Sam, that's fantastic!' said Deborah. 'When do you start?'

'I turned it down.' Saying it out loud was painful. It brought home to him what a ridiculous thing he'd done.

She stared at him. 'You're kidding! But why?'

He chose his words carefully, watching for her reaction. 'There are more important things in my life right now.'

She re-filled her glass. 'I see. This is about Esther, isn't it? Is that why you'd arranged to see him?'

He nodded. 'That's not all. I'm taking a few weeks off. So I can spend more time seeing to her.'

'Seeing to her? What does that mean exactly?'

He'd have liked to know what to tell her. He was painfully aware that he was acting entirely on instinct and gut feeling. 'I don't know exactly. Be with her. Talk to her. Listen to her. Try to get past the dying person and see the living one. Does any of that make sense?'

'It does to me,' said Deborah. 'But did you have to turn down a promotion and put your job on hold?'

'Maybe not. But it's what I did. And there's still the London Adventure work.'

'I'm glad you remembered. There's a load of new bookings coming in. A lot of work for both of us. I can't lead the tours and do the admin as well, I hope you haven't forgotten that.'

He took a small sip of wine, eking out his half-glass. 'Of course I haven't. But, like I said, there are other important things in my life right now.'

She put a hand on his arm. 'This Esther thing: it's that important to you?'

'Yes.' He took another sip while working out how to put his thoughts into clearer words. 'There's something about her. I can't say what, exactly. It's like she's trying to get back something of herself that she's maybe lost. And what gets me is – how can I say it? – nothing makes sense now. This harmless, dotty old woman's the ghost who scared me shitless all the time I was a kid? She's the monster my parents were – no, are – terrified of? She's "Mad Hetty?" For God's sake! It's all so…' He put his head in his hands and buried his fingers deep in his hair.

'Can I point one thing out? said Deborah. 'I understand what you're saying. But it would only make sense if you could be sure she's really who you think she is.'

He looked up at her and smiled. 'Of course. But I can be certain now. I'll show you.'

He took the two restored photos from a drawer and laid them side by side on the coffee table, eager with the excitement of sharing his discovery with her. 'These are Esther's. She asked me to get them fixed up for her. Now I know for sure I was right. Just look at this.' He pointed from one to the other. 'This is Esther's father. Isaac Levinson. And this is his gravestone. She's very proud of it. She told me she paid for it.'

Deborah affected a shudder. 'She keeps pictures of gravestones around the house? This isn't a bit weird?'

He laughed. 'She's weird in all sorts of ways. But just wait until you see this!' With a magician's flourish, he turned over the frame and handed it to Deborah. Glued to the back was a copy of the inscription that Mister Howarth's magnifier had revealed:

IN LOVING MEMORY OF

ISAAC LEVINSON

WHO DIED 14TH JANUARY 1942 AGED 81

DEEPLY MOURNED BY HIS DEVOTED DAUGHTER ESTHER

SON-IN-LAW BENJAMIN

AND GRANDDAUGHTER SADIE

He watched her, waiting for the change of expression when the significance of the inscription sank in. She studied it for just a few seconds before handing it back. 'So?'

He felt a sharp pang of disappointment. 'So, it's proof that Esther really is my grandmother.'

'How come?'

'"How come? How come?"' Her lack of enthusiasm irritated him. He jabbed at the photo. 'Look here. "Son-in-law Benjamin". My grandfather was called Ben. He was Esther's husband. The names match. It's proof. Don't you see?'

'Maybe,' said Deborah. 'I'm sorry, Sam, but there must be thousands of Jewish couples called Esther and Benjamin.'

He breathed a theatrical sigh of frustration and prodded the photo with his finger. 'Well, what about this name? His granddaughter – that would be Esther's daughter – is called Sadie. That's my mum's name.' If only she would see what to him was so bloody obvious! He tried again. 'This is the proof! This woman is definitely my grandmother! So now I can drop this Josh business and tell her who I really am!'

She took the photo back, stood up and walked with it to the window. It was gone seven in the evening, and still bright and warm outside. A group of teenage boys and girls had gathered on the pavement, smoking and talking. The smell of tobacco and the sound of their laughter rose up to the open window. Deborah held the photo up to the light, studied it again and turned it over to re-read the inscription. He watched and waited, twisting his fingers in his hair and forcing himself to be patient.

She turned from the window and sat beside him. 'I don't think you should do that just yet.' She handed the photo back to him. 'I know how much you want this, and I can see how it might be possible. But I'm just saying. These are common names. Plus, this "granddaughter Sadie" might not be your mother. Esther might have had brothers or sisters.'

He snorted his irritation. 'Brothers or sisters who also called their daughter Sadie? That would be a bloody big coincidence, wouldn't it?'

He saw her angry look and cursed his impatience. 'Sorry. I didn't mean to – you really think that's likely?'

'No,' said Deborah, 'but you've got to admit it's possible.'

He put both photos back on the table and spoke softly, taking care to keep himself under control. 'So, if Isaac had other children, Esther's brothers or sisters, why aren't their names here? Any ideas?'

She shook her head. 'No. No idea at all.'

They sat side by side, gazing silently at the photos. His elation had faded away. Of course she was right. All he had was a flimsy theory and a few commonplace names. Unless – he stood up and paced up and down the room, banging a fist repeatedly into his open palm, then sat back down next to Deborah. 'It's so simple, why didn't…' He took her hand. 'Okay, so these names don't prove anything. But what if we knew for certain that my real grandmother's maiden name was Levinson? That she was Esther Levinson before she was Esther Symonds? Would that do it, do you think?'

'I suppose it would,' she said. For the first time there was a note of excitement in her voice. 'In fact, it would make it almost a hundred percent certain!'

His feeling of triumph lasted just a few seconds. 'Sure, but how can we find that out? All we've got is a couple of names and a date of death. I suppose there might be some records somewhere, but we'd have to find out where they are, then spend God knows how long shlepping through old documents.' He turned both photos face downwards in a symbolic gesture of defeat. 'It's not worth the bother, and that's that.'

Deborah turned the photos back face upwards. 'There's a much quicker way, isn't there?'

'I don't follow.'

She laughed. 'It's so obvious. Ask your mother. She'll know, won't she?'

Sam shook his head. 'You know I can't do that.'

'Why not?'

'You know why. My parents have always told me she's dead. I don't want them to know I've found out the truth. Not yet, anyway. Not until I'm ready. Maybe not ever.'

'You don't have to tell them anything. You could just say – I don't know, maybe you could say you've taken up family history as a hobby, or something like that.'

He laughed. 'Oh yeah, I can see that working. Look, can we please leave it? I'm not saying a word to Mum and that's final.'

Deborah surrendered. 'Okay, but I can't see why not. One little question, that's all. And if the answer's no, that'll put an end to it for you. You could ask her tonight.'

He looked blankly at her. 'Tonight? What, you mean I should phone her up, out of the blue? And just ask her? Are you serious?'

It was her turn to laugh. 'You forgot, didn't you? We're having Friday night dinner with your parents. We're supposed to be there by eight.'

He shut his eyes and groaned. 'Oh shit, yes! Oh bloody hell!' He felt instantly tense. Friday night dinner with his parents was an unpredictable event at the best of times, and right now – 'I don't feel up to it, Deborah. Couldn't we just—'

'No we couldn't! It's half-seven now and Shobbus comes in at half-eight. They'll be pissed off if we miss the candles. We'd better get a move on.'

Leaving a trail of curses behind, Sam went to the bedroom and returned minutes later wearing a clean shirt and a jacket. 'We'd better get going, then. Get it over with.'

He headed for the door then did a double-take and turned back to look at Deborah. 'You've put your hair back up. Pity.'

TEN

'Ninety-eight, ninety-nine – a hundred!' Esther took her hands away from her eyes and looked around for likely hiding places amongst the trees, bushes, statues and lawns of Victoria Park. First she looked for spaces large enough for Joel and Nathan, who liked to hide together. Her best friend Eva and Eva's younger brother Ben preferred separating, so they favoured the smaller spots such as behind one of the larger trees or in the shadow of a statue's plinth. She shaded her eyes against the low late-afternoon sun while turning through a full circle and looking in every direction. Nothing moved. Her playmates were well hidden and today they were giving her no clues.

On her second circuit she saw a shrubbery surrounded by a low green railing, easy to step over and a likely hiding place. She walked towards it, hitched up the hem of her white cotton summer dress and searched amongst the foliage, breathing in the rich scents of earth and greenery. A movement caught her eye and she called out. 'Joel! Nathan! I can see you! You can come out now!' A squirrel squirmed from under a rhododendron bush, squatted on its haunches while nibbling at a titbit that it held between its front paws, and ran off.

She stepped back over the railing and looked around again. Victoria Park, just a two-mile bus ride from the crowded streets of Whitechapel, had been her playground for as long as she could remember. At first her mother Millie would bring her and push her around in her pram along with the other proud women and their new babies. As a small child she would run around the lawns with her brothers and her friends. Now that she was eighteen years old she, Joel and Nathan, Eva and Ben often came here together. They liked best to stroll along the paths and have tea and cake in the café by the lake, but sometimes, as today, they enjoyed re-living their childhood pleasures, racing each other across the grass or playing hide-and-seek. After all these years Esther and her friends knew every inch of the two-hundred-acre park and felt totally at home in it. Today, though, for some reason, she was beginning to feel uneasy. There was still no sign of her brothers or her friends. They should be coming out of their hiding places by now, laughing at her because they'd been so near and she hadn't been able to find them. Some of the landmarks around her were starting to look unfamiliar. There was a drinking fountain that she'd never seen before, and a building that looked like a miniature church steeple with a statue of a soldier holding a gun beside it.

'You lose again, little sister!' Esther sighed and laughed with relief as her beloved twenty-four- year-old brother, slim and handsome in his lieutenant's uniform, appeared as if from nowhere and put his arm around her waist.

'Nathan, thank God! I couldn't see you anywhere! Where's Joel? Was he with you?'

'I'm right behind you, idiot!' Joel, like his older brother, had appeared without her seeing where he'd been hiding.

A pair of hands covered her eyes from behind. 'Guess who?' She pulled the hands away and turned to see Ben and Eva.

'We were watching you all the time,' said Ben, 'from over there.' He pointed to a low, square concrete building that she'd missed.

'Ben! You're also in uniform now?' said Esther.

Ben shrugged. 'You think I want this? But anyone over eighteen, we have to go.'

Esther linked arms with Eva. 'You're all such *mensches* in your uniforms. Who's the handsomest, do you think, Eva?'

Eva pondered. 'Hmm, I think it must be my brother Ben. But only just!' They all laughed.

'So the game's over,' said Esther. 'Time for tea and cake.'

'The café's closed, remember?' said Nathan. 'The war. No one left to run it.'

'Anyway,' said Joel, 'we've only got a few hours left, then we're on the train to Arras to get ready for the big push.' He poked Nathan in the ribs with his elbow. 'My big brother's got himself a commission. Me, I'm still just a private. But I'll catch up with him, just give me a few more months.'

'How about you, Ben?' she asked.

He laughed. 'I'm plain Rifleman Benjamin Symonds. I told them I'm a tailor, but they said tailors we don't need. So now I'll have a gun. And a bayonet. Do they think I'll stick it in anyone? But what can I do? They say go, so I have to go.'

'But not for long,' said Eva. 'It's September now, and I read in the *JC* it'll be finished by Chanukah.'

Ben looked up to the sky. 'From your mouth to God's ears.'

Esther hardly made out his last words because of the low roaring sound that she suddenly realised had been growing steadily in volume and was now becoming overpowering.

'Zeppelin!' shouted Nathan. 'Lie flat! Cover your ears!' Esther threw herself to the ground, put her hands over her ears and screwed her eyes shut.

*

'Are you all right, dear? Can I help?'

Esther turned her head, opened an eye and saw a woman's face looking down at her. She caught a glimpse of flat shoes, a plain brown jacket, a skirt and a turban. Couldn't the woman see the danger? 'Zeppelin!' she screamed. 'Zeppelin! Get down! Cover your ears!'

A man's face appeared. There was something familiar about him. Black hair curling from under a wide-brimmed hat; a thick beard with ringlets beside the ears; a severe-looking black jacket and open-necked white shirt.

'*A meshuggeneh alte froy*. Leave her. Walk.' His voice was hard, unsympathetic. It made her shiver with fear.

'This by you is *tzedekah*?' snapped the woman. 'I won't leave her. Find a phone box. Call 999. Quick, go! *Geh geshvint*!'

The woman bent towards Esther and put the back of her hand on her forehead.

'Oy *gevalt*, she's burning up!' she muttered. 'If I hold you, can you sit up? My husband has gone to phone for help.'

'Zeppelins,' whispered Esther. 'Nathan, Joel. Eva, Ben. Where are they?'

The woman had her arm around Esther's shoulders, cradling her like a child. 'There's no one here, *bubeleh*. Just me. Don't be frightened. There are no zeppelins.'

The man was back.

'*Nu*?'

'So I told them, come. To help a mad woman they should come.'

The woman stroked Esther's hair. 'You should be ashamed! You told them where to come?'

'No! I told them, go to Krakow! What are you talking?'

'I don't trust you. What did you say? Exactly.'

'Exactly, come by a madwoman who sees zeppelins in 1976 on Cliften Common, Stamford Hill.'

Esther looked up in alarm. 'No! Tell them Victoria Park!'

Her mama smiled gently down at her. 'We're a long way from Victoria Park, *bubeleh*. Is that where you've been all day? Were you with Eva? Papa and I were worried.'

'I was with Nathan and Joel, Mama,' said Esther.

The man leaned down over her so that his beard dangled an inch from her face. She was looking directly into his angry eyes. She saw no hint of love or compassion in them. They were like chips of cold flint. How could she not have recognised him sooner? Tears poured down her face. She reached up and grabbed the man's wrist. 'Papa, they were here! Just now! Ben too! And Eva! They were here!'

The Hassid wrenched himself free. 'She's calling me Papa now? And you Mama? I told you, a *meshugenneh*.'

*

The phone rang just as Sam and Deborah were leaving for dinner at his parents'.

'Leave it,' said Deborah. 'We're late already.'

Sam opened the front door, then hesitated. 'I'll just be a minute.' He went back inside. 'Hello, Stamford Hill 4573.'

'Josh? This is Anna Bijou, social worker. I'm sorry to ring you at home, but—'

'Hello, Anna. What's happened?'

ELEVEN

Sam parked, switched off the engine and gazed at the dusty trees lining the street outside Frobisher Estate.

'I remember the day we moved into this place,' he said. 'I was nine. I cried my eyes out when I saw it. The pokey little flat high up in the air, no garden for me to play in, no friends, a playground with two swings and a load of big rough-looking boys.' He laughed. 'I told my mum and dad I didn't like it and I was going back to live in our half-a-house in Bell Street. My dad explained that the Council was pulling it down, that's why they gave us this place to live. I hated it for months – cried every night.' He laughed again. 'I remember asking my parents if Mad Hetty would follow us here, or if she'd still be in the house when they pulled it down.'

'We lived in a place like this in Edmonton,' said Deborah. 'I cried too, when I first saw it. I was fifteen. It was the most miserable day of my life. Just weeks before that, my parents told me our furniture business had gone bust. My dad's partner had done some dodgy deals on the side and we were deep in debt. So, suddenly, it all went. The house in Chigwell and everything in it. The Rover and the Triumph Herald. My education. My dad got a job in Rumbelow's selling washing machines, and my mum – well, she just had a nervous breakdown and went to bed for a year.'

Sam stared at her, amazed. 'I never knew any of that. I thought you were—'

'Brought up on the Sidney Sadler Estate, Edmonton? Well, now you know. You're not the only one with secrets.'

'How come you never told me before? How come your parents never said anything?'

'Pride. They made me promise never to talk about it. They still feel the shame. So do I. But I thought you should know.'

'So that's why—'

Deborah lifted a bunch of flowers and a bottle of wine from the back seat. 'Yes, that's why I work so bloody hard. That's why I'm ambitious. So as not to be poor and slip down the ladder. Never again. Now, let's go.'

Sam took several deep breaths. 'Bloody hell, that's a lot to take in!' He fumbled to pull the key out of the ignition, where it seemed to have jammed. The delay brought on a bout of anxiety. He knew the signs: the thumping heart, the rushing sounds in his ears. With a last effort he freed the key from the ignition and wound up his window. 'It'll be sunset soon. Let's go.'

The few brave birds in the courtyard's solitary tree were beginning their pre-dusk chorus, and the latest generation of boys shouted to each other as they kicked a ball around the playground.

Deborah slipped her hand into his. 'Are you okay? Do you feel up to asking them?'

'I'm not sure. I'm in no mood to put up with my mum if she starts getting up to her tricks.'

'Her tricks? What does that mean?'

'You know. Putting on the miseries. Getting at me.'

Deborah stopped walking. 'Sam, your mother doesn't deserve that. I thought we agreed you were going to cut her some slack. It really wouldn't hurt you to try and be a bit more patient with her. Especially if you want to find out —'

'Okay, okay! Enough! I heard you!' He saw the warning look in her eyes. 'Sorry, I shouldn't have – It's just that – I don't know, since this Esther thing started, all that stuff I thought I'd got sorted out – it feels like it's all being raked up again.'

'I can see that,' said Deborah. 'But you mustn't let it get on top of you again. Taking it out on your mum – or me –

will just make things worse for you. So, make a bit of an effort, or you'll be doing it without me. I mean it!'

He looked up at his parents' small balcony. As a child, he'd stand on tiptoe looking out from there, waiting for his father to come home from work. His father would appear round the corner and break into a smile at the sight of him, and they'd wave to each other. It was the most precious moment of his day. A daily dose of pure joy, the like of which he knew he could never again experience.

He dragged himself back to the present. 'I'll do it. What's the problem? Just one little question: "Mum, what was your mother's maiden name? Was it Levinson by any chance?" Piece of cake!' He could see she wasn't fooled.

*

'Sammy! My son and heir! Deborah, darling! Good Shobbus! Come in, come in! Your mother was starting to worry.'

Pinchas Shaykin – Jack, as he'd preferred to be called since his army days – was slim and fit-looking for his fifty-nine years, and smartly dressed as always. He welcomed his guests at the door with a peck on Deborah's cheek and a slap on his son's shoulder as he took the bottle of wine. The hall was rich with the smells of the Sabbath-eve dinner coming to its point of perfection. Sam's mood softened a touch as he breathed in the aroma of roasting chicken and envisaged all its accompaniments.

'Good Shobbus, Jack,' said Deborah. 'How are you keeping?'

'All the better for seeing you, darling,' said Jack, smiling. 'You're looking lovely as usual.'

He put his arm round her waist as he guided them towards the dining-room. 'Tell me,' he said in a mock whisper, glancing at Sam, 'is that *lobbus* behaving? Has he asked you to marry him yet? I tell him, what are you waiting for? A girl like that, she could get snapped up.'

'I'm working on it, Jack,' laughed Deborah. 'You'll be the first to know.'

Jack lowered his voice. 'Just a minute.' He looked over his shoulder at the closed kitchen door. 'Sammy, do me a favour, Son. We haven't seen so much of you lately, so let's try and have a nice evening. I know how it can be, with you and your mum. Just – please, if she says anything that—'

'I understand, Dad.' Sam glanced at Deborah. 'I'll behave myself.'

'Don't you worry, Jack,' said Deborah. 'I'll see to it.'

'Thank you, darling. I know you will.'

In the dining-room, Sam cast a cynical eye over the table. As a child he'd loved Friday nights. He'd been enchanted by the gleaming white tablecloth, the ornately embroidered blue-and-gold velvet square draped over the shiny challah bread, the silent movement of his mother's lips as she lit the candles, and the sip from the silver *kiddush* cup of heavily watered wine that he was allowed to take after his father had said the prayer. Now, all he saw were the trappings of a pointless ritual. He watched Deborah as she walked round the table, admiring every detail. To her, all this was still real and important. And that difference was the wedge between them that he knew could force them apart. He felt a sinking feeling in his stomach at the thought of losing her. Maybe he should grit his teeth and just go along with it. After all, it wouldn't hurt him to tolerate some mumbled words, a sip of wine, some candles, to make it easier between them. On the other hand, why the hell should he? None of it mattered to him any more, and he wouldn't be part of it at any price.

Sadie Shaykin bustled into the room. Just a year or two younger than her husband, she was no more than five feet tall, slightly built and a bundle of energy. She was wearing an apron over a two-piece outfit of a light material suited to the warm evening. She put her arms around Sam's neck, drew him down to her height and noisily kissed him several times on both cheeks. She and Deborah exchanged embraces and kisses, and Deborah handed her the flowers.

'Flowers for me? Thank you, darling.' She patted her permed hair, once brown as Sam remembered, now grey and dyed a shade of auburn. 'Good Shobbus! Everything's under control, don't worry! Sit a minute. A little late is no problem. Nothing will spoil, please God.'

Sam felt a metal band fastened around his head, tightening notch by notch.

'Can I help you, Sadie?' Deborah called after her as she headed back to the kitchen.

'No need, no need. Everything's done. Just sit. Jack, get things ready!'

They sat as invited, with Jack at the head of the table and Sam and Deborah opposite each other. Jack put on a black silk skullcap, took another one from his pocket and passed it to Sam. 'Here. Wear it for your mother's sake.' Sam was about to refuse when he caught Deborah's eye. He took it and put it on.

A moment later Sadie re-appeared without her apron. 'We're just in time, thank God. I'll do the candles now. Thank you for not coming any later.'

The metal band clicked up another notch.

Sadie lit the candles, drawing her hands three times around them in a circular motion then once towards her face, and said a short prayer in Hebrew. Deborah and Jack responded with a hearty '*amein*', while Sam pressed his lips together and kept his eyes fixed on the tablecloth. Sadie registered her disapproval with a shake of her head and a single click of her tongue. Jack uncovered the challah bread, tore a piece off and said another prayer to which Sam, prompted by the pressure of Deborah's foot against his, muttered a response. Jack tore off three more pieces and passed them round, then filled the *kiddush* cup with wine, said a third prayer and offered everyone a sip. The ritual completed, he beamed and declared: 'Good

Shobbus, everyone! Let's eat!' Sadie brought in a brimming china soup tureen and carefully lowered it onto the table. Delicious smells filled the room as she ladled out helpings of chicken soup, making sure that each plateful had a good share of chicken pieces, *lokshen,* carrot and *knaidlach.* Dipping his spoon into the golden liquid and raising it to his lips, Sam's thoughts wandered back to Esther and the call that he'd taken from Anna.

'A Mr Glick called 999. His wife came with her in the ambulance. The hospital called me. They've been checking her over. They want to admit her but she won't have it.'

'How is she?'

'There's no physical damage but she's very confused. She's still rambling.'

'What happens now?'

'I'll get her an ambulance home and I'll go with her. Any chance you could drop in tomorrow? It's my day off and I'm taking my mother shopping.'

'Of course I will. Tell her I'll be there, will you?'

'Thanks, Josh. You're sure it was okay to call you?'

'I'm grateful you did.'

*

'You don't like the soup, Sammy? There's something wrong with it?'

Sam jumped as his mother's voice broke into his thoughts. His first spoonful was still hovering halfway to his mouth and was tipping out of control. Before he could prevent it, the spoon's contents slid onto the tablecloth and settled into a greasy puddle. Sadie reacted with lightning speed. 'Never mind, never mind! It happens!' She rushed into the kitchen and emerged with a wet sponge and a red plastic bucket. She applied the sponge vigorously to the tablecloth, dropped the soup-soaked napkin into the bucket, took it back to the kitchen and returned seconds later with a clean cloth that she spread over the wet patch.

Sam could feel Deborah's eyes on him and realised she was urging him to make some kind of apology. A barely audible 'Sorry' was all he could manage. Sadie gave him a smile that went only as far as her lips. 'Sorry? What's to be sorry? You don't want my soup, no need to throw it on the floor. Just say, Mum I don't want!' Her voice had acquired the tell-tale tremor that was all too familiar to Sam. The band tightened another notch.

Sadie cleared Jack and Deborah's soup plates and stacked them on top of her own. She sat down next to Sam and pulled her chair close to his. He felt cornered, menaced. It was the old familiar scenario of his childhood. Love equals food. Food equals love. You won't eat, then maybe you don't love. He knew was at breaking point, despite the assurances he'd given.

'You're going to eat your soup now, Sammy?' said Sadie. 'We can wait. It's chicken next. And I did the roast potatoes just how you like them. Please God, nothing will spoil if we wait. I hope.'

He looked down at his plate, which seemed to be growing in size. As the soup cooled, globules of chicken fat were re-forming on its surface. He forced himself to take a mouthful, felt his gorge rise and put down the spoon. 'I don't want it.'

Sadie's smile became more fixed, the tremor in her voice more pronounced. 'I'll warm it up for you. It'll only take a minute.'

'I said I don't want it.'

Deborah shot him a warning look but he pretended not to see it. What with the prayers, and Deborah getting on at him, and his worry about Esther, and his mother trying to force food down him just like when he was a kid —

'I'll get you something else,' said Sadie. 'I've got some meatloaf —'

'Leave the boy alone, Sadie,' said Jack. 'He says he doesn't want, he doesn't want. Why force him? Leave him alone already.'

Sadie flinched at Jack's words as if she'd received a blow. Her lower lip trembled. 'What did I say that was so bad? Sammy, I'm not forcing you, am I? Tell me, am I forcing you?'

Aware of Deborah's threatening glances, Sam made a supreme effort to keep his voice steady. 'No, Mum, you're not forcing me. I'm just not hungry.'

Her expression changed from injured to indignant. 'What, you two ate before you came?'

He'd had enough. His stomach was churning and the pressure on his temples was unbearable. He let out a loud, deep sigh of exhausted patience. 'For God's sake!' A kick on the ankle stopped him from letting fly, but he spoke through clenched teeth. 'No, of course we didn't eat. I'm just not hungry. Is that so hard to understand?'

Sadie picked up a napkin, pressed it to her eyes, burst into tears and rushed into the kitchen. Deborah followed her and closed the door behind them.

Jack stood up from the table and pointed accusingly at his son. 'You know what – it breaks my heart, the way you get at your mother. And after you promised!'

'The way—' Sam decided not to argue the point. 'I shouldn't have let her wind me up, I know that.'

Jack poured himself a glass of wine. 'No, you shouldn't, Son. She's your mother, after all – and a bloody good one, never mind her funny ways. Thank God you've never had to go through what she had to. You should try understanding a bit.'

It always came back to that – what she'd been through. Sam bit back his reply and nodded contritely. From behind the kitchen door he could hear his mother's raised voice and Deborah's soothing tones. He might as well take advantage of the opportunity. 'I know, Dad. I do try.' He kept his voice as casual as possible. 'Dad, while we're alone, there's something I want to ask you.'

'Ask me?' said Jack. 'So ask. Is it trouble? That wife of yours is giving you aggravation again?'

'Ex-wife, thank God. No, nothing like that. That's all finished now. I just wondered if you knew —'

'Here we are, everybody!' Sadie sailed in from the kitchen, smile tightly in place, carrying a tray of heaped plates. They brought with them a cloud of aromas that Sam would normally have found irresistible, but now the smells made him feel nauseous.

Sadie put the plates down with a defiant flourish. She was smiling, the kind of rigid-lipped smile that he knew was meant to communicate that she was being very brave and trying hard not to cry. He'd seen a lot of it during the Libby period. '*Mahlzeit*, everyone. Good Shabbos!' she said in a trembling voice, and picked up her knife and fork.

'Thank God. At last!' said Jack. In a well-meaning effort to defuse the tension, he picked up his knife and fork and dug in, miming compliments and making appreciative noises.

Sam was losing the fight to retain control. His anger at his mother's single-minded determination to give him food boiled over. He pushed the plate away and stood up, knocking the chair over in his hurry. Sadie looked aghast and the tears flowed again. Deborah rushed to comfort her. He picked up the chair and put it back in its place. He felt his chest tightening. He wanted to be nice to his mother, to say he was sorry about the chair, for messing up her table, sorry for upsetting her, but anger and impatience had taken him over. 'Mum!' was all he could say, 'Will you for God's sake stop that crying!'

Jack put a hand on his arm. 'That's enough, Son! Such disrespect to your mother! And on *Erev* Shobbus as well!'

'Sam,' said Deborah, firmly, 'I think we should go. For your mother's sake. Look how upset she is.'

Without warning, Sadie turned on Deborah. 'That's right! You go! You take my son away from me! You think you're the first to try? You're not, believe me!'

Deborah's mouth opened but no words came out.

'Hold on, Sadie,' said Jack. 'The girl only said—'

'Now you're on her side?' wailed Sadie. 'Let them go! Haven't I had enough misery in my life?'

Despite his fury, Sam felt torn between frustration at his mother's behaviour and concern at her distress. He wondered if he'd really ever understood how badly the memories that she carried still weighed her down. But he had to speak up in Deborah's defence. 'Mum, that's so unfair. Deborah's just thinking of you. I am too. We'll go now, and maybe you should have a lie down.'

Sadie scrabbled in her pocket, found a screwed-up handkerchief, opened it out and rounded on Sam. 'Lie down? You talk to me like I'm an invalid? Or a *meshuggeneh*? You stroll in late, you spoil my dinner. You sit there like a dummy through the prayers. You soak my best tablecloth in soup—'

'What? For God's sake, it was one spoonful!'

'Oh sure,' said Sadie, 'you laugh at me. I deserve that.'

'I'm not laughing, just saying,' said Sam. He no longer cared about provoking his mother.

'Always he's got an answer! Always he's too clever for his mother!'

'Sadie, calm down!' Jack pleaded. 'You too, Sam. Please, will everybody please calm down!'

'Oh yes!' Sadie turned on her husband with a bitter, derisive laugh. 'You take their side, not mine!'

Sam had had enough. He summoned up a last shred of remorse. 'We're going now. Mum. Sorry about the soup. And sorry I didn't eat much. Maybe next time.' He leaned towards her to kiss her cheek, but she covered her face with her forearm. 'Don't kiss me! Go! You think I care? Go! Both of you!'

Sam's face and ears turned a deep shade of red as the last dregs of his self-control drained away. The time for understanding and remorse was over. Despite himself, he searched for something to say that would unbottle his anger and unleash it full force on his mother. It was easy to find. 'One thing before we go, Mum. Dad and I were talking just now. I was just going to ask him something. You want to know what about? Shall I tell you?'

Deborah shook her head at Sam, waving her finger frantically and silently mouthing 'Sam, no! Stop it!'

He ignored her and kept his eyes fixed on his mother. 'I've been visiting a woman. An old, sick woman. Getting to know her. Getting to like her. She's ill, she's a bit loopy. But she's no devil – no monster – no *mekasheyfah*. No murderer! And what's more, she's not dead! Shall I tell you her name? Shall I tell you who I think she is?'

Sadie was staring at him, the handkerchief forgotten. 'No! You wouldn't!'

'Esther Symonds. Her father's name was Isaac. Isaac Levinson. Does that mean anything to you, by any chance?'

TWELVE

On Sunday morning the heatwave came to an end with a massive thunderstorm that flooded the streets in ten minutes. It was the first day of August, but the sky was so overcast that it was as dark as night. People were rushing for any cover that they could find: shop doorways, bus shelters, even under trees despite the jolts of lightning that flashed at regular intervals. Deborah was out and about in London with a family from Cincinatti who had won a trip to Europe in a TV quiz show. Sam hoped she'd got them safe and dry somewhere. He'd been caught on his way home from the Co-op carrying milk, newspapers and a loaf. Just as he was turning from Mare Street into Cliften Square, a car passed too close to the kerb and covered him with a torrent of water, reducing the paper bag, the bread and the newspaper to a pulpy mass. There was no time to go back for replacements, so he dropped them into the gutter, lowered his head and ran the last few yards to St James's Mansions, where he found his father, immaculately dressed as always and bone-dry, waiting for him in the porch.

'Hello, Dad.'

'Hello, Son.'

The awkward formality in their greeting drove Sam close to tears. He knew that his father had good reason to be angry with him. He felt ashamed when he thought of how he'd lashed out at his mother. He wanted to admit that to his father, and to tell him he was sorry. He wanted Jack to put his arms around him and say, 'It's all right, Son, we all lose it sometimes,' but he was afraid of being rebuffed. He stepped inside the porch.

'Sorry I kept you waiting, Dad. I just popped out for a minute.'

'That's okay. I got here a bit early.'

There was a time – long ago, he couldn't remember when, but he was still very small – when he'd been so bad that his father had been angry, had shouted at him and – something that he hardly ever did – had smacked him. Exactly what he'd done, he'd forgotten. What he did remember was the moment when his father had forgiven him, picked him up and hugged him. He'd buried his face in his father's shoulder and sobbed with remorse, until finally his father had laughed and said, 'That's enough, now. You're making my shirt all wet.' He could remember the feeling of relief at knowing that his father's love for him was whole and undamaged. He wanted to have that feeling now. He wanted to be forgiven. He knew it was up to him to make the first move; to say something to make it happen.

'Good thing as it turned out. You missed the rain.'

'You'll be wanting to get those wet clothes off,' said Jack.

Sam looked down at himself. Water was running in rivulets from his hair and his clothes and starting to form a pool around his feet. 'I'm glad you called. Let's go up.'

Dried off and changed, Sam joined Jack in the living-room where he found him holding the photo of Isaac Levinson between thumb and forefinger. He thrust it at Sam, wrinkling his nose. 'Did she give you this?'

It took Sam a few seconds to realise the importance of what his father had said. 'You know who this is?'

'You don't know?' Jack growled. 'She didn't tell you? No? Well, let me tell you. It's Isaac Levinson. The Balaboss, people called him. Like he was a bigshot. Like he deserved respect. Some bigshot! He was a *mamzer* and a *dreck* and a lowlife, like all the other Levinsons before him and after him! Like his daughter, your new friend, God should forgive you!'

Never before had Sam known his father, a gentle, mild-mannered man, to tremble with rage or speak of anyone in such terms. At any other time he would have been horrified – would have wanted nothing more than to see him get over his anger – to hear him laugh and say a friendly word and be himself again. But now, he was filled with a rush of excitement that he had to struggle not to reveal. His father had recognised the face in the photo. He'd given Sam the proof that he'd been longing for. He'd have loved to shout his delight out loud, but with his relationship with his father on a knife-edge it was not the moment for an outpouring of joy. Keeping his expression serious, he put the photo down on the coffee table. 'Please sit down, Dad. Let's not row again. Friday night was bad enough.'

Outside, the rain was still coming down in torrents. The lightning had passed, but there was the occasional distant rumble of thunder. Jack waited, slumped on the sofa, while Sam went to the kitchen and brought cups of tea. Jack, calmer now, smiled his gratitude and spoke quietly, his voice sounding tired and hoarse. 'I kid you not, Son, Friday was a nightmare. Your mother nearly had a heart attack. I was up half the night with her. What got into you?'

If only Sam could admit how miserable he always ended up feeling after he'd let himself get out of control like that. He so much wanted to tell his father that. But as usual, the words eluded him. 'How is she now?'

'How should she be? Miserable. Angry. Frightened.'

Sam found the courage to put his arm round his father's shoulders. 'Dad, what I said – I mean, the way I said it – I didn't mean—'

Jack shrugged himself free. 'Is it true? You really dug up that old bitch? And you've been to see her? You're making her your friend? Why? You couldn't leave well alone? We did something bad to you, you want to throw it in our face?'

Sam jerked his arm away. 'Do you honestly believe that? You think I wanted this? You think I suddenly just got it in my head to go looking for her?'

Jack snorted. 'Feh! So explain to your stupid father! Why are you doing it?' He jabbed his finger at the photo. 'This – this bastard's daughter, your mum's mother, believe me, she was the biggest dreck of them all! And she will be, so long as she – so long as she lives!' Jack closed the space between them and brought his face close to Sam's. 'So tell me, how do you think we should feel, seeing you get mixed up with this – this – this *chazerei*?'

Chazerei – filth! He felt his face redden. How could anyone, his father least of all, talk of a human being in that way? With the gulf between them growing moment by moment, he bit his lip and tried his hardest to calm down. But the dam burst and he made no more effort to hide his feelings or spare his father's. 'That's what you call her! I call her my grandmother! Can't you understand that? Letting me believe all these years that she was dead! Lying to me! How could you do that?'

Jack's breathing was fast and shallow, his voice little more than a whisper. 'If only you knew!' He took a handkerchief from his top pocket, unfolded it and mopped the sweat that had broken out on his face.

'All I know,' said Sam, in a calmer voice, 'is what I've always heard. That she was wicked. That even though she was dead, I was supposed to hate her like you and Mum do. If I don't know any more, it's because that's all you two have ever told me. So why don't you tell me right now?'

Jack's voice had a pleading note. 'Sammy, please believe me, you don't want to know any more. Whatever you think, I'm telling you, alive or dead, it makes no difference. Either way she'd be evil.'

Sam laughed. 'Evil? What, you mean like the Devil? You want me to go for that?

'You don't think there's such a thing?' said Jack.

'No, I don't believe that people are evil.'

'You don't?' Jack's voice rose again as he ticked the names off on his fingers. 'What about the Nazis? What about Hitler? What about Josef Mengele, or Ilse Koch?'

Almost as if on cue, a clap of thunder followed by a flash of lightning drew an emphatic line under Jack's words. It had been so timely that neither of them could resist glancing upwards for a second.

'You don't believe those people were evil?' Jack continued. 'If only you'd seen the things I saw during the war!'

'Okay,' said Sam. 'That was evil, no question. So yes, that kind does exist. But you're telling me there's evil in ordinary people? In old women? In your own mother-in-law? What are you telling me? She was possessed? By a *dybbuk,* maybe? She still is? She's Mad Hetty, like in Grandpa's old stories? They believed in those things in the *shtetls,* but you're not telling me you do?'

Jack looked down at the floor and shook his head. 'You don't understand, do you?'

'Then why won't you explain it to me?'

Jack muttered his reply, his shoulders hunched. 'You should only know!'

Sam had no stomach for carrying on the argument. His father suddenly looked old and tired. Seeing him like that brought Sam close to tears. He sat next to him on the sofa and spoke as gently as he could. 'Dad, let me try to explain. When I was a kid, I wanted to have a grandma like the other kids – a *bubbeh* that all the family loved and respected.'

'You're talking rubbish,' said Jack. 'You had your *Bubbeh* Pessah.'

'Your mother? Sure, I remember her. But she died when I was – what – ten?'

'She loved you.'

'That's not the point.'

'So what is the point?'

'The point is, instead of the *bubbeh* I wanted, you and Mum gave me the ghost of a wicked woman from a fairy tale. Did you know I used to have nightmares about her?'

Jack raised his head and looked at Sam. 'What, you think we didn't know you had nightmares? Of course we did.'

'So you knew,' said Sam. 'But do you know they never went away? I still get them. So when, all these years later and out of the blue, I finally meet this – this terrible thing you made me so scared of – and I find she's—'

'She's what?' said Jack. 'Just an old *bubbeh*? Like the one you always wanted? A nice old lady? A bit dotty, maybe, but harmless?'

'Exactly.'

Jack smiled as if he'd laid down the winning hand in a poker game. 'So she's as cunning as ever. And you're falling for it. What are you telling me? We've lied to you all these years? For fun? You think that?'

Sam stared at the rain still streaming down the window. 'Well – of course not.'

'Maybe your mum was the bad one, then? Maybe your grandpa was. Is that it?'

The guilt trip again. He waved away the suggestion with a dismissive gesture. 'Now you're being ridiculous.'

Jack pulled himself to his feet. 'You're calling your father ridiculous?' He wiped his eyes with the back of his hand. 'Your mother and I would never have dreamed that that – that woman would ever come back and come between us and our son. This is what she wanted. She must have planned it for years. She's getting at us through you. She'll be laughing about it right now.'

'I can't believe this,' said Sam. 'You really think that?'

Jack's voice was firm again. 'Sam, I've listened to you, but I'm telling you now, this has got to stop. You don't know what you're doing. Promise me that you won't have anything more to do with that woman. For your mother's sake and mine.'

Sam could hardly believe what he was hearing. Yet again, his parents were trying to lay down the law about what he could and couldn't do, who he could and couldn't be with. Painful memories flooded back. 'No, Dad. I won't promise you that.'

Jack waited a long time before replying. He took off his glasses, polished them, put them back on. He fiddled with his tie-knot and cleared his throat. 'Sam, it kills me to say this to you, but your mum and I, we've talked this over, and we've decided we don't want to see you again until you can make that promise.'

Sam was so astounded that he laughed despite himself. 'You remember what century this is? You're giving me orders? Next you'll be cutting me off without a penny!'

'Don't make fun, Sam,' said Jack. 'This is serious.'

Things were spinning out of control, but Sam felt helpless to do anything about it. Far from regaining the closeness with his father as he'd hoped, now they were standing on opposite brinks of an abyss.

'Let me remind you, Dad,' – he spoke the words with coldness in his stomach – 'that you and Mum tried this once before, and look at the mess you caused.'

'You're talking about your marriage to Libby?' said Jack. 'The way things turned out, you can't say we were wrong, can you?'

Sam felt the heat rush to his face. This was the moment to say the things that had been too long left unsaid, however hard he knew it would be. 'Yes, Dad, I can say you were wrong. The way you and Mum suddenly changed your tune – for me, that was the real cause of the trouble.'

'Tune?' said Jack, 'What tune? I don't understand.'

'You don't?' said Sam. The words came easily. Not surprising, as he'd been honing them, rehearsing them in his mind for so many years. 'Let me try to explain. All my life you and Mum have kept on telling me how very broad-minded, how – liberal you are. About the religion, I mean. You've always been so proud of that.'

'Why not?' said Jack. 'What's so wrong about that?'

Sam smiled. 'Nothing at all, Dad. If you meant it.'

Jack stiffened. 'What! How can you —?'

Sam held up a hand. 'Please, let me go on. I remember when I was a kid, how you always used to tell me to be a good Jew, observe our laws, and so on. But at the same time, it was: "You should mix. Have *goyische* friends." As if I wouldn't, anyway! "We don't keep to ourselves any more," you used to say. "That's the old way. Nowadays people can see we're not different." You remember that, Dad?'

'I still don't get your point, Son,' said Jack.

'Don't you? He put a hand over his father's with what he meant to be a loving gesture, and made an effort to bring some gentleness into his voice. 'Always with the religion, Dad. We keep to the religion, but we don't want to live apart like the Hassids do, that's what you told me. I understand that. You and Mum were born here. You served in the army during the war. We're Jews, and we're English. Both. You remember when I got older, what you used to tell me? "Girlfriends," you used to say, "why not? Go out, enjoy yourself. But don't forget you're a Jew. You've got a girl? Not Jewish, this one? So bring her home. What harm? Times have changed. Nowadays we all get on. Long as you never forget who and what you are." And I fell for that. Believed it. Lived it. Right up to the day I brought Libby home.' His voice had risen and a sob was constricting his throat. 'Then suddenly it was a different story, wasn't it? Like I said, you changed your tune. And you wonder why I don't want anything more to do with your religion!'

'That's not fair, Son,' said Jack. 'We only ever wanted what was best for you.'

'Best?' Sam barked out the word, saw the look of alarm in Jack's face, made the effort to resume a calmer tone. 'Don't you remember the tears, the dramas? I do! Don't you remember you and mum telling me that I was breaking your hearts? Betraying my heritage?' He turned his back on Jack, walked to the window and stared out, brushing his hand over his eyes. 'My bloody heritage,' he muttered. 'My bloody heritage!'

Jack pulled himself out of the sofa, walked to the window and put a hand on his son's shoulder. 'If that's how you remember it, Son, you've got it wrong. We just didn't think she was right for you, that's all.'

Sam turned to face his father, shook his head and slashed the air in a gesture of rejection. 'No, Dad. Be honest. It was because you hated the idea of me – of me marrying out, as you'd call it.'

'Okay,' said Jack. I'll admit it, it wasn't what we wanted. But we were right, weren't we? Look how it turned out.'

Sam closed his eyes, looked upwards, gave a deep sigh, opened his eyes and looked his father squarely in the face. 'What do I have to do to get you to understand? It didn't go wrong because she wasn't a Jew! It went wrong because she was evil! Just like you tell me Isaac was, and Esther is!'

'Hah!' Jack laid down his second winning hand. 'My son, the clever one, with his university education and his three languages! A minute ago you mocked me for saying so. Now you're seeing it my way all of a sudden?'

The tension between them was momentarily broken as they laughed together.

'You've got me there, Dad,' said Sam. 'Okay, I shouldn't have said she was evil. But you know what? Deep down, right from the start, I knew we were never right for each other. But at that time I was so angry that all I could think of was that if I backed out, you and Mum would have thought you'd won. And I wasn't going to have that. So, what I'm trying to tell you is, if you'd kept your noses out and left well alone, I'd have most likely have called it off and we'd never have got married in the first place. And the rest would never have —'

Jack raised a finger. 'Hang on. So, what you're telling me is, you got married just to get back at us? You're telling me that?'

Sam's laugh had a harsh, bitter edge. 'Sounds stupid, doesn't it? But that's what it amounts to.'

Jack stayed perfectly still, his finger still raised, his forehead knitted, as if trying to make sense of what he'd been hearing. Slowly he lowered his hand and stood, a little stooped, gazing at Sam.

'I see. And you still hold this against us? Like a – a grudge?'

'If you want to put it like that, yes.'

As if he'd come to a decision, Jack adjusted his tie-knot and buttoned his jacket. 'I've got nothing more to say, then. I'm going now.'

Sam kissed his father's cheek. There was no response. 'I'll run you home.'

Jack shook his head. 'No need. Goodbye, Sam.'He stopped at the door. 'Oh, I nearly forgot. I've got something for you. It might help you understand how your mother feels about what you're doing.'

He handed Sam an envelope, the flap sealed.

'What is it?' Sam began tearing open the flap with his fingers.

Jack put a hand on his wrist. 'Don't open it yet. I don't want to be here when you look inside. And this is just between you and me. Your mother doesn't know I'm giving you this. She doesn't even know I've got it. She keeps it hidden away.'

'What's the big secret? said Sam. 'Why can't I look at it now, whatever it is?'

'Please, Son, do as I say – just this once, if it's not too much to ask?'

Sam gave in, dropped the envelope on the coffee table and saw his father to the door. He stood at the window watching him walk slowly towards Mare Street, his back stooped, turning every so often to look back before moving on again. He fancied he read sadness and regret in his father's retreating figure. He, too, felt deeply miserable that they'd parted with the differences between them not just unresolved but deepened, possibly beyond repair. But still, the fact remained that Jack had seen the photo of Esther's father and recognised and named him as Isaac Levinson. Which meant, he realised with a renewed rush of elation, that there was now no further doubt that Esther was his reputedly wicked, and allegedly dead, grandmother. So now, when he next saw her, he could confidently confess that he was the Samuel Shaykin she'd been asking for, and explain that although he wasn't her nephew he undoubtedly was her grandson. But that presented a new problem: how was he to explain to her that he'd sneaked into her life under false pretences, using a fake name? How would he explain it to Anna? What would they think of him? Maybe he should put off telling Esther the truth for now; wait until he'd thought through how best to do it and found the right moment.

It had stopped raining and the sky had begun to brighten. He thought about how he might spend the rest of the day. Maybe visit Esther again? As he'd anticipated, she'd been sleeping when he and Deborah had dropped in on their way home on Friday night. He'd returned the next day, while Deborah went to *shul* with her parents and then home with them for Shabbos lunch. Esther seemed to have completely forgotten about her Cliften Common episode, and as far as he could tell it had done her no lasting harm. If anything, she was a little brighter than usual. She'd asked him about Deborah, offered him one of her Mister Kipling cakes, drunk her tea with none of the usual complaints about its strength or temperature. It seemed to him that she was becoming a little more trusting; more at ease in his company.

He picked up Isaac Levinson's photo and gazed at it, wishing that the man could speak to him and tell him his story. A *mamzer – a dreck* – a lowlife, his father had called him. Even Esther, who'd said she missed him, had laughed when he asked her if she'd loved him. He put the photo back on the coffee table and closed his eyes, running back in his mind what had passed between him and his father. It still made no sense. His father had refused again to tell him why this was such a big deal for them. A horrifying thought came to him: what had just passed between him and his father might be the start of a new family broygus. He found the idea intolerable. Maybe he could prevent it by doing what his parents wanted. But no, that was out of the question. He sank back into the sofa. It was all crazy. If it wasn't so crazy it would be funny. If it wasn't so funny it would be tragic. He couldn't even work out what he was feeling. If only Deborah were here.

He opened his eyes and looked at the envelope. His dad had brought it without his mum knowing, he'd said. What was in it would help him understand his mum's feelings about what he was doing. More drama, more mysteries. He tore open the envelope and peered inside.

THIRTEEN

As the Brighton train pulled out of Victoria Station, the rain lashing against the dirty windows turned the outside world into a kaleidoscope of impressionist paintings. Sam unzipped his bag and took out his Walkman and headphones. The last time he'd taken this journey he must have been – what? Eight, maybe? Nine? Happy times those, when his parents would entrust him to his Great-Aunts Eva and Fanny and they'd take him on wonderful adventures. Sometimes he'd stay with them in their enormous flat over a greengrocery shop in Willesden, but best of all were the summer weekends when they went on the train to Brighton to stay with their widowed sister, his Great-Aunt Sarah.

He put on his headphones and pressed Play. Frank Zappa's 'Hot Rats': perfect for blocking out the noise and allowing him to focus his thoughts. Since the break with his parents the old bouts of depression had taken hold again, and Deborah being away made it ten times worse. A week leading the Snohomish Seniors of Seattle around the Cotswolds, followed by a second week in the Highlands of Scotland, was a job too good for them to pass up, and she'd been eager to lead it. But it only served to remind him what an important part she played in his life. The times they spent together, doing the things they both enjoyed, meeting friends, talking to each other about anything and everything, sharing their secrets and inner thoughts, were all precious to him. And there was no doubt that when times were rough for him, she was always there to help him through them. He was, he thought for the thousandth time, very lucky to have her.

He'd been visiting Esther regularly for a fortnight now, sometimes finding her asleep and staying for just a few minutes, sometimes staying for an hour or more, tidying up, making sure she'd eaten, chatting with her when she felt like it. Sometimes he'd catch the hint of a smile on her cracked lips, or a glimmer of warmth flickering in the granite eyes. Now and then she would even laugh at something he said, then they'd laugh together and momentarily he'd fancy he saw the younger Esther, the happier and more vibrant woman she must once have been. With every one of those moments he felt the bond between them steadily growing, and now he was becoming more certain than ever that whatever had happened in the past was in the past, and in time his parents would understand their folly, and there would be a reconciliation. For the time being, he could see no signs that her health was getting worse, although of course he knew that it inevitably would.

Thinking about going to see his great-aunts after all this time brought on the old familiar blend of fear and anxiety that made his heart thump in competition with the Zappa drummer. His Auntie Eva's voice on the phone had given him no clue as to how his visit would turn out – whether they would resent his long absence from their lives, and how they would feel about his involvement with the woman who'd been the family pariah for so many years. He wondered how he'd go about asking them to tell him what they knew about her, and what their reaction would be.

A woman in a green overall pushed a refreshments trolley along the aisle. He bought a coffee and a corned beef sandwich. The coffee tasted like nothing in particular. The sandwich was even worse. Back then he'd be tucking into the picnic his aunties – he never used the 'great' part – brought along: chicken sandwiches, potato latkes and the little cakes called *kichels* that his Auntie Fanny made. He'd been very fond of Fanny. She was a pale-looking, scrawny woman who'd suffered from poor health since childhood and had scraped a living sewing buttonholes and coat linings at home until her parents died, after which she'd gone to live with Eva and taken on the role of housekeeper, cook and general helper. She was dead now. Eva and Sarah were the only two left of the seven siblings, one of whom had been his Grandpa Ben.

The train slowed and pulled into East Croydon Station. A tall, lean man in a dripping plastic raincoat trod on his toes on the way to the empty seat next to his and grunted an apology. He replied with a weak smile and adjusted his headphones. He closed his eyes and thought back to the train journeys of his childhood: the compartments with sliding doors, bench seats and leather straps to open the windows, and corridors where you could stand and look out. Those carriages had smelled of coal-smoke, cinders, dust and tobacco. This open-plan compartment smelled of the wet clothes of the people who'd got on at East Croydon, the orange that the little girl in the seat opposite him was sucking, and the damp dog at his feet that belonged to a toothbrush-moustached man who was sitting on the other side of the aisle.

Everything had changed, and none of it for the better. The trains were still steam-driven in those days. Before getting on board he'd stand on the platform, looking with wonder at the huge gleaming engine as it stood powered-up, hissing and belching steam, the driver in his blue overalls leaning out of the cab and waving at him just like in *The Railway Children* on TV. His great-aunts would be standing by, wanting to hold his hand to make sure he didn't slip under the train's wheels but understanding that a grown-up boy wouldn't be seen holding hands with old ladies.

Eva, as he found out later, had been no ordinary old lady. In fact, back then she hadn't really been old at all. Neither had Fanny – not that old, anyway. Later, when he was fifteen, he'd snuggled up beside Eva in the living-room of her Willesden flat and listened, enthralled, to her life story. Back then she'd been the teenage Sam's hero. She was unlike anyone else in his family. Amidst all the tailors, dressmakers, pressers, stitchers, cutters, and purveyors of buttons and trimmings, she alone had escaped the constraints of Whitechapel life to go her own independent, free-spirited way. She talked to the young Sam about her 'affairs', and 'lovers' – exotic words that excited his imagination. From an early age she'd been an avid reader and a lover of play-acting. At twelve she'd started playing truant from the Jews' Free School and spent her days hanging around the Grand Palais Yiddish Theatre in Commercial Road. By the time she was thirteen she was being paid two shillings a week plus tips to run errands and take care of the actors' costumes and props.

'I had my first walk-on at fourteen, right at the start of World War One, as a page in a Yiddish-language *Hamlet*,' she'd told him, laughing. 'A week after my seventeenth birthday the theatre put on my first play, a fifteen-minute melodrama called *The Rebbetzin's Shameful Secret*. It was the first time they'd ever performed in English. Believe me, they took some persuading.' She laughed again. 'It was a disaster. It ran for two nights. Half the audience didn't understand a word of English, and neither did most of the cast. But the thrill of hearing my words spoken by actors – even actors like those – that was the first time and it's never left me.'

She had better luck later on. Around 1927 she'd sold a half-hour radio play to the BBC, and after that, two more. That was the start of her successful career. By her early fifties, when she was holding Sam's hand on the platform of Victoria Station, she had countless television scripts and two Rank UK screenplays to her credit.

Arriving at Brighton Central Station he felt a leap of elation as he rushed up the stairs of a green and cream double-decker bus and grabbed the vacant front seat. As if to order, the rain had stopped and the sun had come out. He heard his Auntie Fanny's voice: 'Nearly there. First one to say "I see the sea" wins!' He always won. The bus began its zig-zag downhill journey. When it turned into North Street for the final stretch and the sea came into view, he quietly said the old words to himself.

He got off the bus on the wind-blown promenade and lingered a moment to watch the green foamy waves curl over the pebbled beach. A five-minute walk brought him to Galaxy House, a smart 1930s art deco apartment building overlooking the sea. The brass-bound glass revolving doors made a nostalgic swishing sound as he pushed through them into the deeply carpeted lobby.

*

'Come in, Sam. Give your Auntie Eva a kiss.' He felt a rush of pleasure at seeing her again. In the warmth of her welcome there was no hint of the resentment he'd feared. She held him tight and kissed him several times on both cheeks. She still smelled of the heady, musky perfume that he used to watch her spraying on herself from a white china dispenser decorated with lacy gold patterns.

In his memory she'd been small and plump. Now she was thinner. Her hair was greyer, but still short and stylishly cut. A loose white silk shirt billowed over her dark green skirt. He tried not to stare at her. In the past she'd been his old great-aunt, an adult fixture in a child's life. She must be in her seventies by now, but he was looking at a woman who scrutinised him with compelling green-grey eyes he'd never before noticed and couldn't look away from.

Little had changed in the flat. The sofa – strangely much smaller now – that he'd slept on as a child, and its two companion armchairs; the eight-seater dining table; the walnut sideboard with its forest of family photos; the tall, wide window with its view over the sea and the dejected pavilions of the derelict West Pier. He thought back to when he was a child, sitting on the sofa and looking up through that enormous window, high into the sky where seagulls wheeled and screeched. And at night, when the sofa had become his bed, he'd lie awake in the dark, listening to the waves crashing onto the beach and dragging the stones back out in their undertow.

'Sarah's out on her morning walk,' said Eva. 'When I say walk – well, she gets pushed in a wheelchair these days. Her health isn't that good. She'll be home soon. Then we'll eat.'

She took his hand and led him to sit beside her on the sofa. 'I'm happy you're here. Last time I saw you was at Fanny's funeral. Five years ago now.'

He fumbled for something consoling to say. 'I remember Auntie Fanny was always in the kitchen. She loved cooking for everyone.'

Eva chuckled. 'She certainly did. And before I retired, she always had a good meal for me when I finished my day's work.'

'How long did you live together?'

'At least thirty years.' She lifted a hand to her necklace of black, glassy beads and twisted them in her fingers. 'On and off that is, between my – adventures. After she died I was on my own in that big flat. I was glad to leave it. Too many memories. Too much junk. I got rid of nearly everything.'

Here was an opening. An opportunity to ask her. Did she bring family heirlooms? Photo albums? Papers? Anything?

'How do you like living in Brighton?' Shit! He'd missed the moment. As always!

Her face broke into a smile. 'After Willesden? What's not to like? And with Sarah not being too well, me being here is doing us both a favour. But…' She pulled him closer to her. He felt the silkiness of her shirt, smelled her muskiness. No wonder she'd attracted so many men – women too, from hints she'd let drop. Even now, at past seventy…

'Now, I want you to tell me about the trouble you're in.'

So she knew. 'Mum's been in touch then?'

'She phoned me. She was in a state. I couldn't understand a word she was saying at first and I couldn't get a word in. You know what I mean?'

He nodded. He knew only too well what she was describing.

The cool green-grey eyes were looking into his. 'She says you've lost your mind – gone *meshuggah* were her exact words. Have you?'

He laughed despite himself. 'Not this time, no. But it's true things aren't good between us right now.'

She pushed him away and studied him at arm's length. 'I'm not surprised. She says you arrived late in a foul mood and wrecked her Friday night dinner – took the mickey out of the Shabbos prayers and threw her food on the floor. Then worst of all – Sam, can it be true what she told me? Look, I know my niece well enough. But this bombshell you're supposed to have dropped out of the blue – tell me, from where could she have got such an idea?'

Sam watched a flock of seagulls wheel in formation past the window as he struggled to put his thoughts in order. It felt as if he was about to confess to committing a crime. After all, in his mother's eyes he'd done exactly that. He breathed hard and plunged in.

'It's true that I—' He didn't know how to start. 'What exactly did Mum tell you?'

'Promise me you won't get angry,' said Eva. 'I'm only telling you what she said, you understand that?' He nodded. 'She said that you've suddenly turned against her. She said that just to spite her you took it in your head to track down her mother, make friends with her and side with her to do your mother some terrible mischief.'

From Eva's look of mild amusement, Sam could tell that her niece's account of the events sounded as ludicrous to her as it did to him. 'Do you believe that?'

She raised an eyebrow. 'That's what Sadie told me. You're saying I shouldn't believe her? Is it true? Or isn't it?'

Sam could see that she was playing with him. 'No!' He shook his head from side to side. 'How could I go looking for her when I didn't even know she was alive? The way it happened, it was just …' He sighed. 'I don't know what to tell you. It's hard to explain.'

Eva's eyes held his. 'Try.'

His head was starting to ache. He forced his words out. 'A charity worker came looking for me. To tell me about this woman who was dying. He wanted me to go and see her, and say the *kaddish* at her funeral. Not that I would have, you know how I feel about all that stuff.'

'Why did this man come to you?'

'She'd given him my name. Told him the family had cut her off years ago because of a broygus. That I was her only relative left.'

'Twisting things. Just like always,' Eva murmured.

'I didn't really believe it could be her,' he went on. 'I thought she'd died years and years ago. But I'm sure now. It really is her. She's alive. My parents have lied to me all these years. And I need to know why.'

She thought for a moment. 'She didn't mention your mother? Even when the woman's dying, she forgets she's got a daughter? That didn't tell you anything?'

Of course she was right. How come he hadn't thought of that? His face must have shown his dejection. Eva laughed softly. 'You know, this could be a plot for one of those old Yiddish Theatre dramas.' She drew a stage in the air with her hands. 'Act One: a messenger comes to your door. Your grandmother has come back from years in exile. You agree to meet her in secret. Your mother learns the truth. Does she thank you for reconciling her with her long-lost mother? No, she calls you disloyal and turns you out. And you turn for solace to your loving great-aunt!'

Sam felt his spirits lifting. He was happy to be in this place that held such fond memories for him, and grateful for Eva's light-hearted way of discussing serious things, so different from the high-tension combative manner of everyone else in his family. He felt as if he could safely share with her what was going on in his mind and in his life. Everyone else, with the possible exception of Deborah, made him feel as if his thoughts and actions were crimes, or at best, confessions of stupidity or disloyalty.

With a five-second rendition of the opening bars of the *Hatikvah*, a clock on the sideboard chimed the half-hour. 'Sarah's late,' said Eva. 'They must have been sheltering from the rain somewhere. Now the sun's out, she'll be on her way home. Are you hungry?'

Sam smiled. 'I had a terrible sandwich on the train. I've got to admit…'

'Come and sit at the table. I'll get you a little something.' She went to the kitchen and brought out a small plate of pumpernickel bread fingers spread with cream cheese and smoked salmon. 'Just a snack to keep you going. I don't want to spoil Sarah's lunch. She's looking forward to feeding you.'

'Wonderful,' Sam mumbled through his first bite. 'This brings back memories.'

Eva sat next to him at the table. 'Do you want to carry on talking about this?'

Sam nodded, starting on his third pumpernickel finger.

'Joking aside,' said Eva, 'be honest with me. Once you knew it was her, after all the bad things your parents have told you about her, why did you decide to get involved?'

He knew that searching look only too well. The things he'd only ever told Kate, and then Deborah – the fears, the nightmares, the resentment and the guilt – he hoped Eva would understand, or at least listen without judging. But he was far from sure. After all, his mother was her much-loved niece. Even he felt that his anger was some sort of betrayal, so it was likely that Eva would feel the same. He swallowed the last mouthful. 'Just curiosity, nothing else. After all, to have a grandmother you've never even met – who you thought was long dead – and then to get a chance to meet her – you understand that, don't you?'

Her face revealed nothing. 'And how did she take it when you turned up? Was she pleased to see you?'

He tried, but failed to reach the meaning he sensed was lurking behind her question.

'She doesn't know who I am. I made up a name. I don't know why I did; it was a spur of the moment thing, but now I'm stuck with it.'

'Really? She doesn't know?' The same sensation again. She didn't wait for his answer. 'So explain to me: after taking all that trouble to keep this from Sadie, why did you tell her? And why in such a hurtful way?'

He avoided eye contact with her, trying to find the right words.

'Because she got on my nerves. Going on and on about us being late, about me not joining in the prayers and not being hungry. She got more and more wound up and things went from bad to worse. In the end I just lost my temper and – I suppose I just let it out on her.'

Eva made clucking sounds of disapproval with her tongue. 'That was a very bad thing to do to your mother.'

There was a plain gold ring on the middle finger of her right hand. She always wore it. Once he'd asked her about it but her reply had made it clear that it was something she wasn't going to discuss. Now she was twisting it round and round, as he'd often seen her do when reading or in conversation. 'I was sorry as soon as I'd said it. But I couldn't un-say it. We left after that.'

'Have you tried to make it up with her?'

He shook his head. 'I didn't get a chance. Two days later, Dad comes round. I thought he'd come to smooth things over. But no. He starts in with the threats. He tells me to give up seeing Esther—'

Eva's eyes glittered and she twisted the ring faster. 'Esther? You're on first name terms?'

'Why not? Give up seeing her or they – how did he put it? They won't want to see me any more.' He took a bite from the remaining slice of bread.

'And?'

He dropped the bread onto the plate. 'And now they don't want to know me.'

There was a silence. His shoulders heaved. He would have liked to rest his head on her bosom as he did when he was a child.

She toyed with her ring. 'I don't think they'll keep that up for long. Do you?'

He shrugged.

She didn't wait for him to answer. 'I can see how you got dragged into this, thinking there was no harm in it. But what I don't understand is, knowing how your parents feel about Esther Symonds, how could you let her come between you and them?'

He looked up at her. 'Dad said the same thing. It's not what I wanted. But I didn't like being threatened like that. Or being told what I can and can't do. You'd be the same, wouldn't you?

Eva's expression gave him no hint of agreement or disapproval. 'Go on.'

'But also…' His heart was beating fast. There was a rushing sound in his ears. He had to say it. 'But also, I'm getting to know her. We've talked, she's shown me her old photos, I've done some odd jobs for her. She's bad-tempered and definitely more than a bit weird, but…' He paused. Eva was gazing at him. Waiting. Impassive. 'But I think she's pretty harmless. If she wasn't so ill she might even be – nice. I just wonder if those things I've always been told about her are maybe – I don't know – maybe exaggerated?'

Eva's expression still didn't change. 'Why do you think your parents would want to exaggerate?'

He chewed his lip. 'I've thought a lot about that. I just don't know. Maybe – just maybe – there were faults on both sides, but after the big break-up they started piling all the blame onto her, building it up in their minds, changing their memories of what happened, to make themselves feel better. You think that could be it?'

'So, what you're telling me,' said Eva, 'is that your mother didn't really have good cause to turn her back for her entire life on her own mother; that she did it lightly, after some disagreement, and afterwards made up reasons to justify what she'd done?'

Of course, she'd made the point perfectly. Her gentle tone hadn't changed, but he was reminded of the incisive mind working beneath the light-hearted manner. 'No, obviously I don't mean…'

Eva put both hands on the table and leaned towards him. Her necklace swung forward and he had a glimpse of cleavage beneath the silk shirt. 'Why do you think Esther directed the charity worker to you, and not to your mother?' she asked. 'Why didn't she even tell him she had a daughter? Didn't you wonder about that?'

He was feeling increasingly helpless. He shrugged again. 'I suppose I should have, but—'

Eva pressed home her argument: 'But you still believe your parents might be – what? Making the whole thing up? Making a fuss about nothing?'

'No, of course not!' said Sam. 'But…' He started to speak, stopped, started again. 'Okay, I'm going to say it. Sometimes I wonder if Mum hasn't gone a bit—'

'A bit what?'

'I don't know – a bit crazy? Look at this.' He took the envelope his father had given him from his pocket and offered it to Eva.

'What is it?'

'Dad gave it to me. He told me it would help me understand how Mum felt. She doesn't know I've got it.

She doesn't even know Dad knows about it.'

'What is it?' Eva said again.

Sam shook out eight photographs onto the table's polished surface and arranged them in a row. They were torn at the corners and spotted with age. Some were blurry snapshots taken on a seaside promenade. Others were sharper, more professional. Eva examined each photo in turn. 'I know these.' She pointed to the sideboard. 'We've got the same ones. But—' She drew in her breath as she understood. 'My God! Sadie did this?'

Sam nodded. 'See what I mean?'

'My God!' Eva said again.

'Am I right?' said Sam. 'About the woman in all these photos? Is she Esther Symonds?'

He didn't need Eva to identify the little girl in the photos. He knew from pictures he'd seen in his parents' old albums that she was his mother. In one photo she wore a party dress with a flower pinned on the shoulder and a bangle on her forearm. He also recognised his grandfather Ben, here a young man in a dark three-piece suit and bow tie, his thick black hair brushed straight back off his forehead and shiny with Brilliantine like Marlon Brando in *The Godfather*. There were later photos, of his mother as a good-looking young woman, probably in her twenties, in a matching jacket and skirt with her hair curled in the 1940s style he'd seen in old films. In two of them she was posing, grim-faced, beside one of the lions in Trafalgar Square. All of the photos had one thing in common. The woman with his mother had no head. In every one, the woman's head had been roughly scissored away, leaving an angry jagged hole.

Eva picked up each photo in turn and examined it closely. She went to the sideboard, made a selection from the forest of photos, and laid down a matching undamaged print beside every mutilated one. The woman Eva had restored to completeness looked disappointingly ordinary.

As a young woman she was slim and pretty, dressed in the 1920s style that reminded Sam of Faye Dunaway in *Bonnie and Clyde*. In the later Trafalgar Square photos she was thick-set and tight-lipped, with eyes that seemed to be glowering at the camera. Maybe, he thought, the street-photographer had by chance captured the grim-looking mother and daughter in the midst of a row. What about? he wondered. If only you could lip-read from photos.

'That's your grandmother.' said Eva. 'That's Esther Symonds. And what you've got here shows you the anger your mum was feeling when she did this. I don't suppose she feels any different now.' She looked at him more closely. 'Now you've seen these, are you starting to understand?'

Sam kept his eyes on the photos. 'But this was a long time ago. Okay, she might not have been the best of mothers back then, but after all this time, don't you think Mum would have got over it? Maybe thought about forgiving her?'

Eva collected up her photos and replaced them on the sideboard. 'You don't understand yet, do you?'

'That's what they keep telling me,' said Sam. 'What is it, that I don't understand?

Eva made some minute adjustments to the display and wiped away some specks of dust. 'I knew her,' she said, still looking at the photo collection. 'Did you know that?' She turned and sat back down with him. 'I knew her well. When we were young. For a while we were – we were very close.'

Sam was riveted. 'You were friends? I had no idea! Was that from when she and Grandpa got together?'

'No. From before that. At the start, our two families were like one.'

He didn't know what he'd expected from this visit, but he'd arrived at a moment he could hardly have hoped for. He tried to give his voice a touch of nonchalance. 'What was she like?'

Eva smiled and twisted her ring again. She looked far away, as if calling up images from the past. 'She was a little bit older than me. Pretty. Very self-assured. I looked up to her. We spent a lot of time together. But her father didn't want that.'

To hell with nonchalance. He wanted to hear it all. 'Why not? What else can you tell me? Please, tell me everything you know about her.'

Eva shook her head and seemed to come back to the present. She gazed at him, smiling in a way that told him she'd known the purpose of his visit all along. 'So that's why you're here. And I thought it was because you were missing your old aunties.'

He looked back at her and thought he saw no ill feeling, just gentle amusement at his discomfort. He needed to say something in his defence. 'Of course, it wasn't just—'

Eva waved him to silence. 'Does your mother know you've come to see us?'

'No.'

'I see. Would you want her to know you're asking these questions?'

'Probably not.'

'So you're expecting me to keep things from my niece? Go behind her back?'

'Didn't they keep things from me? Lied to me all these years? I think I've got a right.'

'Why do you want to know these things?'

'I'm curious.'

'That's all?'

'Yes.'

'No other reason?'

Of course, she knew there was more. But it was so hard to explain. Difficult as it was, he had to try. 'There's all sorts of reasons. I want to learn everything I can about my grandmother, and my parents won't tell me anything, except to say that she's bad through and through. Now that I've met her, I think they must have got that wrong. Okay, she wasn't a great mother, she did bad things. But to do what they did – cut her off from themselves and from me for life – that was just cruel. That old family broygus nonsense – people carrying bad feelings through whole lifetimes – I think it's just plain disgusting. Ever since I was a kid they've been trying to drag me into it, and I'm not having it. Now I've met her, I'm sorry I didn't know her until now. She's my grandmother whatever happened in the past, and I want to make up for lost time by knowing her, learning all about her. She can't tell me herself, because of the state she's in. My parents won't tell me anything. Which is why—'

'Which is why you came to me,' said Eva. 'You might not like what you find out, did you think of that?'

'It can't be that bad, can it?'

Eva went back to the sideboard and again stood with her eyes fixed on the forest of photos. She seemed to be deep in thought. He watched her and waited. She turned back to him. Her face was composed, her thoughts unfathomable. 'Not all of it, no. But I'll leave that for you to decide. Of course, I don't know the whole story. Who knows everything about someone's life?' She sat down on the sofa and patted the space next to her. 'All right, then. Where do you want me to start?'

His heart was beating so fast that he had trouble controlling his breathing. So he was going to get the story after all. Now that he was so near, he felt doubts crowding in. Eva had warned him that he might not like what he heard. What if she was right? What if his parents were right? What if he'd opened some sort of Pandora's box, and he was setting out on a path that would lead to him doing harm to himself and to them?

Eva was waiting and watching him, now twisting the beads of her necklace. The sky was still blue and the seagulls were still making their rounds. The room was becoming uncomfortably warm. He should have been pleased that he was getting what he'd come hoping for, but for some reason his feelings of panic were returning. Pushing them aside, he zipped open his backpack and took out the brand-new notebook he'd bought at Victoria Station. He opened it at the first page and sat beside Eva, pen raised over the blank sheet. 'You don't mind if I jot a few things down, do you? Just start wherever you like.'

FOURTEEN

A chilly September breeze blew along Brick Lane, carrying with it the smells of turmeric, paprika and garam masala from the homes and restaurants of Whitechapel's most recent arrivals. To Sam, the very names of the streets that he and Deborah had been walking conjured up a past golden era. It reminded him of when he'd first been to Paris, when just saying the names of places – Montmartre, Montparnasse, Bastille, Saint Michel – had excited him with their romantic reverberations. The word Whitechapel stirred his emotions in the same way. However starkly unromantic the place was in reality, he knew that in the memories of his parents, and all the older members of his family, it evoked visions of a close-knit community where everything was simple, and everyone, no matter how poor or oppressed, was happy.

On the corner of Brick Lane and Fournier Street they stopped to look at a large, imposing old building. White capitals on a bright-green background above the entrance proclaimed it the Jamme Masjid – the London Great Mosque. High on the wall of the mosque was a reminder of its former function: the two triangles of the Star of David entwined together in the stonework.

'The old Great Synagogue,' said Sam, 'where Eva told me most of the Levinsons and Symonds were married.'

'So this is where Esther married your grandfather,' said Deborah.

They stood aside to make room for a group of men who came down the mosque's steps into the street, deep in conversation.

'No. Eva said they didn't have a *shul* wedding. They were married in a registry office. Something to do with the war, I think she said. The first one, that is.' He opened his A to Z at a page he'd marked. 'Now I want to find Old Montague Street. That's where Eva and all the others lived. It must be near here.'

*

The Brick Lane of Eva's childhood, as she'd so vividly described it to him, had been the hub of the immigrant Jewish community. Now, as they passed the Bangladeshi shops and curry houses, there was hardly a remaining relic of those times. Sam wondered when Eva had last visited this place that she'd spoken of with so much affection. With each street they passed, images of the vanished life that she'd described rose up in his mind: Heneage Street with its hardware and tailoring shops; Chicksand Street with its fishmongers, slaughter-house and kosher butchers, and Fashion Street with its clothing sweatshops and its Moorish market. And the Russian Vapour Baths where her father and all the men in the family would go on Thursday nights. Everything was so different now, he wondered if she would even be able to get her bearings if she came back. Where had all the Jews gone? he wondered. Moved on to what they hoped would be a better life, maybe, once they'd got a foothold? Someone, he remembered reading, had described the Whitechapel of those days as a gateless ghetto. So where had the ghetto-dwellers gone? Hackney? Stoke Newington? Golders Green, maybe? Neighbourhoods where, from what he'd seen, they'd re-erected their imaginary gates around their new communities. No doubt these people would also get on their feet one day and follow the well-trodden path. So where would the Jews go next? And who would fill these streets with their shops, their cooking smells and their street signs, when the present occupants had vacated them?

Old Montague Street was the epicentre of the family's memories: the street name that he'd heard since childhood, so that its four magical syllables held an enchantment for him equal to that of the Marais or the Quai des Orfèvres. And Eva's stories, that he'd scribbled down in his notebook as best he could while she spoke, had taken him back there and made the place feel solid and real for him.

'They all lived in the same house early on, my family and the Levinsons,' she'd told him. 'When Isaac and his wife came – a few years before our parents, I think – they found a room in Old Montague Street. Number fifty-nine. That's where Esther was born, and her brothers, rest their souls, before her.'

'Rest their souls?' He'd been surprised to hear those words. He remembered Esther once mentioning brothers, but he'd written that off as one of her fantasies.

'She'd be talking about Nathan and Joel,' Eva had explained. 'A terrible thing. Both brothers killed in World War One. It broke their parents' hearts. Esther's as well. I don't think she ever got over it. So now she imagines they're still around? That's very sad.'

As they walked along Brick Lane, Sam traced their progress with his finger on the page. Everywhere, a bustle of stall-holders and shoppers, cafés and restaurants already busy, and shop-fronts wide open to the street despite the cold. It occurred to him that it wouldn't have been that different if they'd been walking along here seventy years earlier, except for the stream of cars along the narrow road, the different appearance of the people, the halal signs in place of the kosher ones, and the scatter of newer buildings where the World War Two bombing had done its work.

Eva's family and Esther's were from the same *shtetl*, she'd explained. She didn't know the name. When her parents came, Isaac had helped them get a room in number fifty-nine.

'We were all born there. I grew up there.'

'All seven of you?' he'd asked. 'Nine of you living in the one room?'

She'd laughed. 'No! Things were bad, but not that bad. When our father got a better job we took over more rooms. In the end we had three. And by the time Harry and Rachel were growing up, Sarah and I had moved out. Sarah got married and I – well, you know my story. Still, it was crowded. But you get used to it. For me, the worst thing was having just the one outside privy for the whole house. Specially in winter!'

*

He tapped the outside pocket of his backpack to make sure he'd brought the notebook with him so he could bring Deborah up to date as they walked. He'd never have remembered all the details otherwise. Seven children. Sarah, the eldest – eighty now according to Eva, so born in 1896. Then two years later his Grandpa Ben, and Eva herself in 1901. Fanny next, then much later came the three babies of the family, Harry, Sammy and Rachel.

'Funny,' Eva had mused, 'me and Sarah, we're the oldest, and we're the only two left. Tough old birds the pair of us must be.'

'This is it!' said Sam, 'Old Montague Street!'

His disappointment must have shown on his face. 'Is this what you were expecting?' asked Deborah.

'It's the right place all right,' said Sam, gazing round. 'We've just come too late. Much too late, I'd say.'

They were looking along a crooked, narrow street lined on each side by two-storey red-brick blocks of flats with small windows, and a few forlorn-looking shops. Newspapers and food wrappers blew along the road. No sign remained of the cavernous old tenement houses that Eva had described; no trace of the Gradzinki bakery, the synagogue, the dairy where Eva's mother used to send her with a jug to buy milk straight from the cow.

'And no way,' said Sam, 'of even getting an idea of where number fifty-nine would have been. It's all gone. If only

I'd...' He felt like bursting into tears. He was angry with himself for never caring about his family's past until now. He felt stupid for having expected the past to hang around for ever, waiting for him to start taking an interest in it.

'I know it's disappointing,' said Deborah, 'but from what you've told me, those old houses were in a pretty bad state even then. And that was nearly eighty years ago. If the bombs didn't finish them off, old age did. If they were still there they'd just be slums.'

Sam was still gazing about, almost convincing himself that if he concentrated hard enough the Old Montague Street of his family's memories would re-build itself and emerge like Atlantis rising from the waves. He was astonished, and a little ashamed, to find tears running down his cheeks. He felt cheated, deprived of his chance to go back in time and see, smell and touch the places where his family had gained their first precarious foothold in this country. Strange, he thought, that up to a short time ago he'd never given a shit about any of this; never considered it to have anything to do with him; dismissed the old stories as belonging to the *shtetl* mentality and values that he'd spent his life determined to escape.

Deborah broke into his thoughts. 'How many families did Eva say lived in that house?'

'You want to know exactly?' Sam stood with his back to the wind, took his notebook from the inside pocket of his coat and flicked over the pages. 'Twelve. Including two in the cellar and two families – can you believe this? – two families sharing one room in the attic. Can you imagine what that would have been like?'

Deborah shuddered. 'I don't want to. I've heard the same stories from my parents. We've come a long way, thank God.'

They walked the length of Old Montague Street and back, looking at the shop signs in the scripts they couldn't read, accepting a friendly invitation into a grocery shop where they'd stopped to admire the bins brimming with brilliantly multi-coloured spices, breathing in the cooking smells from the flats, and watching children playing and calling to each other in mixtures of English and other languages. If they could turn the clock back, thought Sam, they might be watching Eva and Esther playing in the street, effortlessly mixing together their Yiddish and English. Thinking about it, not so much had really changed.

He was finding the spicy cooking smells coming from the flats more and more enticing. He looked at his watch. 'Fancy some lunch?'

'Now you mention it, I could do with a little something,' said Deborah.

'Let's go, then. When in Rome…'

Back in Brick Lane they found an almost-empty café with just six Formica-topped tables and a simple menu pinned up over the counter in English and two other languages.

'How about saag aloo with dhal, and a naan to share?' suggested Deborah. Sam nodded his agreement. The waiter, a young dark-skinned man in jeans and a yellow paisley shirt, went into the kitchen to place their order. The food came quickly. The dishes of vegetables were hot and plentiful, the naan fluffy and flavoursome. Deborah tore off a corner of naan, dipped it into the garlic-laced lentils and bit into it. 'Mm, pretty good.' She spluttered as the unexpectedly hot chilli caught the back of her throat. An old woman in a sari and a woollen cardigan sitting nearby called across to the waiter with authority in her voice, and seconds later he brought them a jug of water and two glasses. Deborah smiled her thanks to the woman, who smiled back and made a gesture of friendship with steepled fingers.

'That was a let-down for you, wasn't it?' she said, when she'd regained her breath. 'Are you getting over it?'

Sam tucked into his lentils and reached for the spinach and potatoes. 'I suppose so. Stupid, I know, but I hadn't even thought the old house might not be there any more. It's so…' He groped for the right words. '…it's so vivid in Eva's memory, it's hard to believe it doesn't exist anywhere else.' He zipped open his backpack and took out the notebook again. 'There's one thing in particular I wanted to tell you. Something I've been puzzling over.' He showed Deborah a page where he'd turned down the corner. 'Eva told me that by the time her family's home in Old Montague Street had grown from one room to three, the Levinsons had gone.'

'Gone where?'

He rubbed at the page with his napkin where his fingers had left a smear of dhal. 'On and up. Just ten years after arriving without a pot to piss in, Isaac Levinson's a rich man.' He passed the spinach and potatoes to Deborah. 'You'd better take some of this before I eat it all.' He carried on talking while Deborah re-filled her plate. 'It's a great story. They all came here from the same *shtetl* in Russian Poland, as they called it then. Every family had a trade. The Levinsons were leather-workers. Millie—'

'His wife?'

'Yes. Millie was a seamstress. They were piss-poor when they came. Worked their way up from nothing.'

The old woman exchanged a few words of conversation with the waiter and paid her bill. She made the steepled fingers gesture to Deborah again, acknowledged Deborah's return of the courtesy, and left. For the moment they were the only customers. The waiter leaned against the counter, trying not to seem as if he was listening to their conversation.

Sam turned the page of his notebook. 'Eva told me the story as if it was one of those plays she used to write. She even divided it into scenes and mimed curtains opening and closing for me.' He cleared his throat and began, now and then turning a page. 'Like I said, ten years after arriving, Isaac's a rich man. He's got nice clothes, he walks about with this ivory-topped stick – the one he's holding in Esther's photo. I suppose it was some sort of status symbol. And he does what very few immigrants back then managed to do. He gets rid of the old *shtetl* ways and manners. He teaches himself to talk proper, Yiddish-free English. So, what with the clothes, and the stick, and the elegance that he's practised, he can go and do deals with the big new West End stores that have just opened – Liberty, Selfridges, all those.'

'He must have had a lot of chutzpah to pull that off,' said Deborah.

'Chutzpah, yes, and charm. He was a very charming man, according to Eva. Underneath that, she says, he was tough, like you had to be in those days to survive, let alone to get on. But he was respected as a fair employer – compared to other sweatshop owners, that is. And he was a strict husband and father. But that's how it was in those days. I suppose her father was the same.'

The waiter brought them a complimentary dish of sandesh sweets and glasses of sweet-smelling, cardamom-flavoured masala chai. Sam thanked him and consulted his notebook again. 'Anyway, he must have been bloody good at what he did, because just ten years after arriving in this country he leaves Old Montague Street and moves his family across Commercial Street to Spitalfields, which is a big step up in the world. To be exact, to...' The notebook again. 'To Elder Street. She can't remember the number. A big house, she said. A mansion, she called it.'

The waiter brought the bill and Sam counted out four one-pound notes. 'Shall we go and have a look?'

A fifteen-minute walk brought them to Elder Street. It was a miserable sight. Most of the houses had been abandoned and were boarded up. Some showed signs of life, but judging by the graffiti and the assortment of bell pushes on the peeling doorframes they'd deteriorated into over-crowded slums and squats. They shielded their eyes and looked up at the broken remains of the tall, wide windows that ran along the top floor of the houses; the legacy of the Huguenot silk workers who had come as refugees from religious persecution, two centuries before the arrival of Jews fleeing their homes in Eastern Europe as victims of the same evil.

'Look at the state of them now, though,' said Sam. 'It's a pity. They must have been beautiful places in Isaac's day.'

'Mansions, like Eva said,' Deborah agreed. 'Best street in the neighbourhood. That would have told everyone that he'd gone up in the world.'

'So that's where Esther grew up,' said Sam. 'While my grandfather's family still had their three rooms in Old Montague Street.' He struck a pose, pointed up at the nearest house with a sweeping theatrical gesture, and imitated his great-aunt's voice: '"And that, dear boy, is where the trouble started."' He put an arm round Deborah. 'That'll do me for one day. How about you? Shall we go home and warm up?'

She put an arm round him. 'Sure. But you're not leaving it there, are you? With Eva talking about trouble starting?'

Sam laughed. 'I've been telling it to you the way Eva told it to me. The funny thing is, when Sarah came home everything changed.'

FIFTEEN

'That'll do, Maria. Put the brake on and pass me my stick.' The door opened and there was Sarah, leaning her weight on a wooden walking stick and grunting as she pushed herself out of a wheelchair. A sturdy blond-haired woman, her yellow nylon anorak unzipped to reveal a body-hugging red tracksuit, stood behind her and watched with a solicitous smile, ready to give support if needed as she drew herself upright. They brought with them the clean smells of salty sea air and clothes damp from the rain.

Sarah fumbled for her glasses suspended from a gold chain, put them on and pinned Sam with a look that made him feel ten years old again. 'What, you're just going to stand there? Help me get this off!' With her free hand she began unwinding a long navy-blue scarf from over her head and round her neck. Sam stepped forward to help. Sarah, he remembered, was never one for demonstrative greetings. He was unwinding the third coil when she grabbed his wrist. Her hand was plump, the fingers stubby, her wedding and engagement rings pressing into the flesh. So different, he thought, from the feel of Esther's hand with its dry, bird-like fragility. She spoke, without turning, to the woman.

'You see this little *pisher* here, Maria? You know who he is? He's my brother's grandson. My brother Ben, *olev hashalom*. Hasn't been to see his Auntie Sarah in years.' She prodded Sam's chest and pointed. 'Sammy, this is my friend Maria. She pushes me up and down the front three times a week. Muscles like iron, she's got. And legs? Well, you can see for yourself. What do you think?'

Sam and Maria exchanged understanding looks. 'Pleased to meet you, Maria,' said Sam.

'And me to you,' said Maria. 'Your great-aunt is so happy that you come to her.'

'Rubbish!' snapped Sarah. 'The *pisher*'s ignored me for years. Still, he's here now, I suppose that's something.'

Maria gave Sam a look that he read as telling him that she sympathised. She helped Sarah out of her coat, hung it up and folded the wheelchair. 'You okay now, Mrs Markovich? Anything else I can do?'

'Nothing else thanks, Maria,' said Sarah. 'Same time day after tomorrow?'

Maria zipped up her anorak. 'Okay, Mrs Markovich. See you.'

'Wait! Just a minute!' said Sarah. She rummaged inside her black, bead-encrusted handbag and took two one-pound notes from a purse. 'Here's a bit extra. Get something for your little girl. Tell her it's from the old dragon you push around.'

Maria laughed. 'I will not say so. But thank you, Mrs Markovich. I come the day after tomorrow.' She kissed Sarah on the forehead and left.

Sam smiled nervously and fumbled for a greeting as Sarah turned her laser-like stare on him. 'Hello, Auntie Sarah. You're looking—'

'I'm looking old and ill!' barked Sarah. 'Don't try your shmooze with me!'

Leaning on her stick, Sarah limped to an armchair and sank into it. Eva helped her to unlace her shoes – brown leather brogues with a little heel, the same kind he always remembered her wearing – and brought her slippers. With her coat off, Sam could see that unlike Eva, who had grown thinner, she had become quite hefty, so that her bulk filled the armchair. 'Bring a chair,' she snapped. 'Come and sit here. Left side. In my right ear there's *gournisht*, even with this *ferkakteh* thing my Arnold bought me.' She raised her hand to her ear and twiddled a tiny wheel in her hearing aid, causing it to emit a high-pitched squeal. She carried on twiddling until the noise stopped. 'Feh! Such a big *mensch* my son is, he can't find five minutes to come here and show his mother how this piece of *dreck* works! Bring that chair!'

Sam did as he was told. Sarah sat deep in the armchair with her feet planted some way apart so that her dress rode up a few inches, revealing buff-coloured stockings. 'So,' she said, 'all this time you don't come and see your Auntie Sarah, and still you don't think of giving her a kiss? Why's that? I'm too old for you? I smell funny? What?'

Sarah had him off balance, as she had so many times in the past. She had a way of leaving him uneasy, not entirely sure if he should take her seriously, or if she expected him to know that she was joking and to respond in kind. He decided to play it safe. Give her cheek a peck, and think of a reply while doing it. He stood over her and bent down to kiss her. Unlike the miasma of sickness that emanated from Esther, Sarah's breath was pleasant and she smelled of washed clothes and clean hair, mixed with lavender and a lingering touch of sea salt. If, as Eva had suggested, Sarah's strength was declining, it must be merely from old age and not from any life-draining illness.

Sarah gave him another of her piercing looks. 'You think I don't know why you're here? Is it because you love your Auntie Sarah so much you couldn't keep away a minute longer?'

'I…' He wasn't doing well.

'It's because of your broygus with your parents, isn't it?'

'I—'

Sarah snorted and waved her stick. 'I! I! Talk some sense, will you? I heard some *meshuggas* about you sticking your nose in, acting like a *schlemiel,* digging up that bitch Esther Symonds. Is it true?'

'I don't—' He was starting to sweat. The room was over-heated and he was tongue-tied and embarrassed. He gave Eva a pleading look.

'Sarah,' Eva touched her sister's sleeve and discreetly rearranged her dress, 'why don't you give the boy a chance to speak?' She gave Sam a smile of encouragement and sat down again, twisting the glass beads of her necklace between her fingers.

Sarah looked at her sister and chuckled. Sam suspected that she was enjoying his discomfort, playing with him for her amusement. She used her stick to pull herself to her feet and with a smile and a crinkle of her eyes, magically changed her expression from fierce to affectionate. He felt as if he'd come through a form of initiation rite. She held her arms out to him. 'Come here, you *lobbus*. Give the old dragon a kiss. Help me to the table. Did you eat yet?'

'We were waiting for you,' said Eva, before he could answer. 'We've been talking about—'

'Look at the boy!' said Sarah. 'There's nothing of him! Eva, did you buy like I asked you?'

'What, you think I forgot? You said buy, so I bought!'

Eva winked at Sam. He knew that her lapse into the vernacular had been a joke for his benefit. Sarah rubbed her hands together. 'Good, I'm starving. First we eat, then we talk. You know me, I don't mix up the two!'

*

An hour later, when Sam had finally convinced his great-aunts that he really couldn't manage another portion of chopped liver, one more slice of smoked salmon, or even one last tiny gefilte fish ball, and had politely declined a slice of cheesecake, Eva brought tall glasses of lemon tea in metal holders. After the rain, the low afternoon sun was shining in through the window, and seagulls were screeching as they wheeled over the water.

'Now then,' began Sarah, 'I know what you've been up to. And I'm telling you, I don't like it.' She picked up her lemon tea glass and blew across the surface of the hot liquid. 'You've lived – how old are you now?'

He was the little boy again, being told off. Being reminded that, at his age, he should know better. 'Thirty.'

'Thirty years without bothering about that woman, so why start now? You know what happened between her and your mother—'

'No, I don't,' said Sam. 'That's the point. I know it was bad, but—'

Sarah banged her hand flat on the table. 'But! But! Don't but me! You know how upset your mother is?'

Sam squeezed his slice of lemon and stirred it round in the glass. 'Upset enough not to want to talk to me. Dad too. That's never happened before – ever. How do you think it makes me feel?'

'Never mind that! More important, how do you think it makes them feel?' She leaned closer to him. 'You listen to me. I want you should stop doing this. Stop hanging round that *mekasheyfah,* asking questions about her. Better you left her where she was – dead and buried. Now, it's over! *Shoyn*! Finished and done! You hear me?'

Sam found it hard not to be daunted by this fierce old woman, but he summoned his courage as best he could. 'I'm sorry, I'm not going to stop. It's a terrible thing they did, lying to me – telling me my grandmother was dead when she wasn't. So, now they owe me.'

Sarah raised her eyebrows. 'This I don't get. How come?'

He panicked inwardly. Deborah, his dad, Eva – every time he was asked to explain why, he got himself tangled in knots. He knew exactly why, but putting it into words that others could understand – that was the problem. Sarah had a hand curled around her good ear. She was waiting for a reply. 'It's what I've been trying to say to Auntie Eva,' he began. 'There's two things.' He counted them off on his fingers. 'First, believe me, I know bad things happened to Mum, I've heard about it all my life. But I'm fed up having all her past miseries dumped on me. And also, I've met Esth – my grandmother now, and honestly—' He hesitated, looked from Sarah to Eva and plunged in – 'honestly, I can't see what everyone's made such a fuss about all these years.'

Sam could see a kind of silent conversation passing between his great-aunts as they each raised their tea-glasses to their lips and looked at each other over them. The silence seemed to stretch out, while the seagulls carried on their own conversation. Sarah spoke first. 'Did you try telling your mother that?'

He shook his head. 'No point. She wouldn't understand. She wouldn't even listen. Specially not now, not when I've met the evil monster at long last. And all I've found is – well, just an ordinary, harmless old woman.'

He saw his great-aunts exchange another silent conversation. Eva twisted her necklace while Sarah fiddled with her hearing aid.

They seemed to have reached a silent agreement. 'Are you sure about that?' said Eva.

'I'm sure,' said Sam, 'I think maybe you've all got her wrong. Or maybe it got exaggerated over the years?'

Another silent exchange, a quick flick of the eyes, a nod.

'So you want to know about Esther Symonds, do you?' said Sarah. 'You might not like what you hear.'

'I've told him that,' said Eva.

'What else did you tell him?'

Sam opened his notebook. 'She told me about the house in Whitechapel – in Old Montague Street,' said Sam. 'And about Esther's family.'

'Show me that!' said Sarah. Sam handed her the book. She let her glasses dangle on their chain, took another pair from her handbag, put them on and scanned the pages. She snapped the book shut, handed it back and changed glasses again. 'So, another writer in the family, we've got? One's not enough? You couldn't think of something better to do with yourself?'

A very good question, he thought. He wished he knew the answer. But at this moment, Sarah would have to be placated. 'I'm not trying to be a writer, Auntie Sarah. I just thought it would be nice if, whatever you tell me—'

'If I tell you anything!'

'If you tell me anything, of course. If you tell me anything, I can write a few facts down so I'll remember them later on.'

The idea seemed to amuse Sarah. 'A second Eva Symonds we've got in the family now, *kaynahorah*! Or maybe better, a Yiddishe Dickens?' She shrugged. 'Still, what harm? A five-minute *meshuggas* this'll be.' She turned to Eva. 'Did you tell him Isaac went in ten years from a nothing to a Balaboss with a Buckingham Palace in Elder Street? Went round with his stick and his top hat, like a Rothschild?'

'Yes,' said Sam, 'she told me that.'

'Did she tell you how he did it?'

'He did it by working hard, of course,' said Eva. 'That, and using his head.'

'Sure,' snorted Sarah, 'and his fists and his boots when it suited him.'

Eva put her hand over her mouth. 'Sarah! How can you say that?'

'I'm telling you!' said Sarah. 'He had a bunch of lowlifes used to run round after him. His *shtarkers*, we used to call them.'

'What are you talking about?' said Eva. 'I know he was a tough businessman and a hard employer, but that was normal in those days. That's what our father used to say, isn't it?'

Sarah retrieved an overlooked gefilte fish ball and bit into it. 'My sister, the *ganzer k'nakker* clever writer. She knows a lot about a lot of things, but not so much as she thinks.' She waved the remainder of the fish ball for emphasis. 'I left school at fourteen. Went to work for a cap-maker when she's still a *pisher* of nine. So naturally our parents tell me things they're going to keep from a kid.'

'There's five years between us and she talks as if she's my grandma!' said Eva. 'What about him helping our parents get a room when they came? Lending Papa money to get started? Was that bad?'

'And putting him to work in one of his sweatshops, eleven hours a day for twopence-halfpenny a week!' retorted Sarah. 'By you, this is helping a friend?' She popped the rest of the fish ball into her mouth.

Sam looked from one to the other. The sisters drained their tea-glasses, staring at each other so fiercely that Sam might have thought they were seriously angry with one another if he hadn't known them better. He felt excited. He could never have hoped for his visit to go so well. Listening to them arguing was almost as good as having the past re-lived for his benefit. 'So, Isaac Levinson and your father were friends?' he asked. They turned and looked at him, eyebrows raised as if his question had reminded them of his presence.

'You didn't know?' said Sarah. 'To start with, yes. In the *shtetl*, the two families were close. So when they came, our parents knew to find Isaac. But the minute Isaac gets on and goes to Elder Street, *mitten drinnen*, he's too good for us. Now Isaac's a *macher*, and our father's not his friend any more. Now he treats him like *dreck*, just like he treats all his other workers.'

Sam could see that Eva was bursting with impatience to respond. 'Sarah, how can that be? Our mother and Millie stayed good friends.'

Sarah rocked back and forth in her excitement. 'Sure, but he didn't like it. He tried to stop it. So she used to come and see Mama behind his back. Especially after he started walloping her.'

Eva stared. 'You're making that up!'

Sarah laughed out loud. 'You think so? Or did you

forget? You were never there when she came to Mama with lumps on her face?'

The two women were so engrossed in their to-and-fro that Sam almost felt as if another question would be an intrusion. But he was too intrigued by what he was hearing to stay silent. 'Did that happen a lot?'

Sarah nodded. 'He was a big man. And a temper? Terrible! He got nasty if he didn't get his own way.'

'But not with Esther,' said Eva. 'He wouldn't harm a hair of her head.'

Sarah gave a raucous laugh. 'What? She got her fair share of back-handers, I can tell you! And worse!'

Eva shook her head. 'No. Surely not. You're wrong. She would have told me.'

'You thought the sun shone out of your friend Esther's *tuchas*, said Sarah. 'But there's a lot she never told you.'

'I don't believe it,' said Eva, putting a handkerchief to her eyes, 'I won't.'

Sarah gave Eva a withering, pitying look. 'My sister! She's still living in her happy made-up world, just like she always did.'

Sam said nothing, sat still, watching the constantly changing sky through the window. As the day had progressed, the sky had turned from grey to blue, and now as early evening approached it was suffused with a deep-orange glow. He took care to make no movement or gesture that either great-aunt might interpret as him believing her version of events rather than her sister's. For the moment, neither of them seemed inclined to pursue the argument. He felt he needed to say something. But what? He thought hard before speaking. 'Auntie Sarah, you're saying Isaac was a violent man? Are you sure about that?'

Sarah directed her words to him, but kept her gaze on Eva, who still had the handkerchief to her eyes. 'I told you. Boots. Fists. Threats. *Shtarkers*. She knows it's true. Don't you, Eva? Talk, already!'

Eva stayed silent. Sam was thinking back to the things his father had said about Isaac. So it wasn't, after all, the simple story of a hardworking businessman making his way in his adopted country. He summoned up the courage to go on questioning. 'You called him the Balaboss. That's a mark of respect, isn't it?'

Sarah gave another of her snorts and banged her stick on the floor. The plates on the table jumped and rattled. 'It's a mark of everyone was scared of him! I'm telling you, you got on the wrong side of Isaac Levinson, you lost your living. Simple. So yes, the workers licked his arse, just like he went round licking the Selfridges buyers' arses, *shtipping* them to get the contracts, and sucking up to the Shapiros and the Montefiores and the other *macher* families.'

'What are you talking about?' protested Eva, twisting her beads to near breaking point, 'Isaac wasn't a saint, I'll admit, but he was never a sycophant, that's for sure.'

'Hark at my sister with the big words!' snapped Sarah. 'Arse-licker's not good enough for her. But that's what he was.' She spoke directly to Sam. 'You know why he licked so many arses? You know what he wanted most of all? You want to guess?'

Looking at Eva's face, Sam could see that she knew what her sister was going to say, but he had no idea what it would be.

'Give up?' said Sarah. 'To be a proper upper-class Jew – that's all he lived for. To be more than the *ganzer macher* of the ghetto. He dreamed of sitting with the best people in the Bevis Marks on Shobbus and the high holidays with a silk *tallis* round his shoulders and a top hat on his head. To mix with the rich Sephardis. Maybe get into politics even. Be a bigshot. A second Disraeli. And he had a plan. He had a secret weapon. You know what it was?'

Sam shook his head and waited. Another pause. Sarah turned to Eva. 'She knows what I'm talking about. She'll tell you!'

Sam watched Eva as she hesitated, licked her lips, ran her hand over her hair. She dabbed her eyes again and spoke quietly: 'Esther, Sam. Esther was his secret weapon.'

'That's right,' said Sarah. 'And he started early. She's twelve, thirteen, already she's up for sale.'

Sam's jaw dropped. 'You mean he was—'

Sarah laughed at Sam's horror-stricken expression.'What, make his daughter a *courveh*? No, even he wouldn't do that. But what he did wasn't much better.'

It might have been the effect of the setting sun's rays shining into the room, but it seemed to Sam that Sarah's eyes were glinting even more than usual. 'She's twelve, maybe thirteen,' she went on, 'and already he's in with those hoity-toity Jews and he's shlepping her round with him. A dinner here, a party there. Dressing her up like a film star. Making sure the goods are on display so the buyers can see what's—'

'Sarah! That's going too far!' protested Eva.

Sarah wasn't backing down. 'You think so? She was a pretty little thing, no? With nice clothes, no? He saw to that. A nice figure? Nice hair? Nice little titties?'

'Sarah!'

Sarah cackled with delight at her sister's discomfort. 'These Sephardis, they need good *shidduchs* so their kids can have more kids and keep the family businesses going. Am I wrong?' She didn't wait for an answer. 'And here's a rich man with a lovely daughter all ready to go on the market—' she looked sideways at Eva – 'the *shidduch* market, what else should I mean?'

Sam wondered what revelation would emerge next. His great-aunts seemed to have forgotten him as they'd become ever more tightly locked in their competition of conflicting recollections. He'd been reduced to the sidelines, looking in turn from one to the other as if watching a tennis match. But there was something he didn't understand – something too important for him just to stay a spectator.

'So how come she ended up marrying my grandfather?'

It was as if they'd suddenly remembered he was there. Both heads swivelled towards him and they seemed to freeze. Their stern expressions made him fear that his question had somehow offended them.

Eva was the first to recover. 'Esther was my friend. Whatever my sister here tells you, she liked me to come to her house, even though I knew her father didn't want me to. Luckily he wasn't there most of the time. Her mother liked me to come. She knew Esther needed her old friends. I didn't know all that *shidduch* business was going on. She never talked to me about anything like that. I was just a kid. I enjoyed going to see her in that lovely big house, and going for walks in Victoria Park.'

Sam waited again. Was Eva getting round to answering his question, or was she deliberately avoiding it?

'Ben was my big brother. Three years older than me, and just a little bit older than Esther. So the three of us were friends together. From when we were kids, right up to the start of the war.'

'But by the time the war came along,' broke in Sarah, 'they weren't kids any more. And they'd fallen for each other. You know, no *shtupping*, all lovey-dovey, like in the pictures. Esther had a lot more *seichel* than Ben. She knew what Isaac wanted from her, and she wouldn't dare stand up to him, so she must have known it was never going to come to anything. But that didn't stop her enjoying herself with Ben. And who knows? Maybe she really did hope it would turn out okay for them.'

Sam was more confused than ever. 'But it did last,' he said. 'They got married, didn't they? What happened? Did they persuade Isaac to change his mind?'

Another look passed between the sisters. 'Change his mind, that *mamzer*?' snorted Sarah. 'Esther knew what her father would do if he found out about her and Ben, so she tried to keep it a secret from him. But in the East End everyone knew your *gesheft*, and that *mamzer*, he had *arsch-leckers* everywhere, telling him *maisehs* for pennies. So one night Isaac, that piece of *dreck*, he comes to our house and he makes a big *geschrei*. He's red in the *punim*, he's waving that stick of his, he's shouting at our father, he's making threats what he'll do if Ben goes near his precious goods ever again.'

'I remember that,' said Eva. 'Funny, all those years ago and it's only now come back to me.'

'Sure,' said Sarah. 'Now she remembers!' She leaned across the table and cut herself a hefty wedge of cheesecake. 'Such a lovely generous man, your Balaboss Isaac Levinson.' She spoke looking first at Eva, then at Sam, then back to Eva. 'You know what he said? He told Papa he should keep Ben away from sniffing round Esther. Or else he'll sack them both and he'll make sure no other guv'nor gives work to either of them – not ever again. We'll be out on the street. We'll be in the gutter. The whole family. *Shoyn*! Finished and done! That's your wonderful Balaboss!' Her jaws clamped down on the cheesecake and she chewed out her anger.

SIXTEEN

Autumn had come early to Keir Hardie Street. The leaves on the big old plane trees were turning brown and some had started to fall. A wind was blowing up the street, bringing with it the smell of rotting vegetation and discarded rubbish from the River Lea. Sam walked with his coat collar turned up, hoping that Russell and the other vermin of Henderson House would be focusing their attentions elsewhere today.

The day had started badly. He'd upset Deborah yet again, by making some crass remark when she told him they were invited to dinner with her parents on the eve of *Rosh Hashanah*. He had no idea why he'd done it. They'd been getting on so well lately. All she'd asked was for him to go with her to spend an evening in Edmonton with Sandra and Michael Levine, participate in their Jewish-lite version of high holiday observance and enjoy the dinner, which he knew would be no hardship, because Deborah's mother was an excellent cook. Conversation with them was always lively, and their interpretation of the rituals and observances of Judaism, although extremely important to them, were on the extreme liberal end of the spectrum.

Deborah was furious with him. 'So, what's your problem?' she'd asked. 'As if I don't know! If it was a plain invitation on any old evening you'd have jumped at it. But just because it's for *Rosh Hashanah* your bloody principles kick in and you start taking the piss out of it – which, as you know only too well, is the same as taking the piss out of me! I warn you, I'm not going to put up with this for much longer!'

Yet again he was sunk into a deep trough of depression and regret. Lousy as he felt, though, and furious with himself for having yet again behaved callously to Deborah, he had important things to do today, so he was forcing himself to get a grip. In his backpack he had Esther's two photos, restored and re-framed. The man in the photo was no longer a stranger to him. Thanks to everything he'd learned from his great-aunts, he felt as if he knew his great-grandfather Isaac Levinson as well as it was possible to know anyone who'd been dead for almost forty years. He'd thought about little else since his trip to Brighton. On the train home he'd read through everything that he'd managed to write down, and scribbled some extra details that he'd remembered later.

He knew that when he saw his grandmother today, she would have been curiously transformed in his eyes. The sick, demented old woman would still be there. But beyond that, in a series of endless overlapping images, he'd be seeing the pampered child, the beautiful young woman exploited as marriage bait, and, above all, the bereaved sister having to come to terms with the violent death of both of her brothers. So much made sense now: the names, Joel and Nathan, that had meant nothing to him; the way she'd spoken of her brothers as if they were still with her; the feelings of hatred mixed with love that she'd expressed when looking at her father's photo.

He stopped at the Co-op to buy her some Mr Kipling cakes and a bunch of brightly coloured flowers. He wanted to please her, there was no point in trying to deny that to himself. He was looking forward to giving her the flowers and showing her the photos. Knowing the things he now knew about her, he was going to try harder to be more understanding of her behaviour and manner. And, who knows, she might be persuaded to fill in some of the gaps for him. He was still no nearer to understanding why his parents hated and feared her. Even his great-aunts, knowing as they did what hardships she'd suffered, seemed to feel no sympathy for her. And as for the other great mystery, why she'd ended up marrying his penniless Grandpa Ben rather than one of the rich young men that her father had lined up for her, that too remained – well, just that – a mystery. He was sure his great-aunts knew the answer, but they showed no signs of wanting to share it with him.

Arriving at the entrance to Henderson House, he looked at the blond woman's balcony. She hadn't actually said she was Esther's friend, but she'd implied it. And she'd warned him about Russell and his kind. He thought of knocking on her door to talk to her, but shrugged the idea off. Another time, maybe. He hefted his backpack and went inside.

There were fresh scars on the paint of Esther's front door, and the wood had begun to splinter in places. Sam let himself in and held his breath to stop himself from gagging while he cleared the doormat of leaflets and circulars, chip-papers laced with ketchup, a half-eaten hamburger and a used condom. As quietly as possible, he dropped everything into the kitchen bin and washed his hands. From behind the closed living-room door came the sound of the television with the volume turned up high. No one could sleep for long through that, but she might be dozing. Not wanting to startle her, he eased the door open a fraction. 'Esther?'

The room was dark except for the flickering blue light from the television screen. The curtains were closed and there was a musty, airless smell. Esther was nowhere to be seen. The toilet, maybe? He turned down the television, sat in the armchair and waited a few minutes. Nothing. With the curtains drawn and the television on, the room had a Marie Celeste feel, as if Esther had left suddenly and in a hurry. But she couldn't have done that on her own, not in her condition. So what could have happened? He felt a sense of panic. Maybe she'd taken a turn for the worse. Called an ambulance. Or called Anna. Of course – she'd had a bad turn and called Anna, and Anna had seen her back into the hospital. But why hadn't she rung to let him know? He shivered. Maybe it was worse than that. Maybe she was—

Out of the corner of his eye he caught a minute movement of the old-fashioned green eiderdown on her bed, followed by a low noise part-way between a whine and a whimper. He crept towards the bed and took the eiderdown between his thumb and forefinger. A high-pitched wail came from under the cover, followed by a cascade of jagged screeches. He dropped it and jumped back.

'Get away! Please please please! Get away! No no no no! It hurts! Please please! Don't! Don't!'

From under the covers he could hear Esther's laboured breathing, a cacophony of wheezing and whistling like a broken pipe-organ. He leaned down to where he judged her face would be, and whispered as gently as he could, 'Esther, it's all right. It's me, Sam.'

Oh fuck. Well, it was too late now. Anyhow, in the state she was in she wouldn't have noticed. At least she'd stopped that screaming. He wasn't sure what to do. Pull the eiderdown back a bit more, or wait? He watched the covers moving up and down in time with her breathing. The wheezing continued, interspersed with bouts of coughing. He hesitated, then crouched down and placed a hand lightly on what he hoped was her shoulder. He was shit scared. He'd never done anything like this before. As gently as he could, he stroked the shape under the covers in a gesture that he hoped she'd find comforting. She responded with a low moan. He desperately wished Deborah was here, or Anna. He put his mouth close to the eiderdown and whispered. 'Esther, its…it's me. Shall I pull back this cover a little bit? It must be hard for you to breathe under there.'

A brief whimper in reply gave him some encouragement, and a few seconds to think of what to say next.

'Esther, don't be scared. It's just me. Come out and look at your photos. I've had them beautifully—'

'Who did you say?' The voice was hoarse, almost indistinct.

He closed his eyes and bit his lip. 'It's me. Josh. I've brought your photos back. They're lovely. All cleaned up. With new frames. And I've brought you some Mr Kipling cakes. And some flowers. Do you want to see?'

Esther's bony hand clutched the edge of the cover and pulled it back to reveal a face that was more gaunt than ever, with staring red eyes that sent tears in rivulets down its furrows. Her outpouring of terror, whatever its cause, had subsided. She pushed the cover back further, her eyes still fixed on him. Grunting with the pain and effort, she eased her body near enough to the edge of the bed to swing her legs over and sit up. He noticed that she was wearing clean, warm-looking flannel pyjamas. Anna must have made a fuss and got the home-help arrangements working. Another coughing fit racked her body. He crouched beside the bed, waiting.

'Show me.' Her voice was calmer now, weak but with a harsh edge like the sound of tearing paper.

'The photos? Here.' He changed from a crouch to a kneeling position, unwrapped the photo of her father and passed it to her. She held it up close to her eyes.

'The other one.'

He put the photo of Isaac Levinson's gravestone into her hands. Another minute perusal.

'You brought flowers? For me? Thank you.' She seemed far away. 'Bring them. Please.'

Thank you? Please? This was a first. He fetched them from the hall and held them out to her. She took them from his hands with a brief smile that he thought made her look, for a miniscule moment, almost girlish.

'Esther, I —'

'Get my stick, Sam.'

So she had noticed. Never mind. In her state, names couldn't mean much to her. She was so mixed up, she probably couldn't even remember him from visit to visit. And even if she did think his name was Sam, it wouldn't mean anything to her.

'Help me.'

Leaning on him, she shuffled to her armchair. Her breath was as acrid as ever but now he didn't want to hurt her feelings by turning his face away. The effort of making the move brought on another coughing fit. He waited until it subsided, helped her to settle down, turned the television volume back up and set about tidying the room.

She banged her stick on the floor to get his attention. 'Stop that. Turn that thing off. Come here.'

She beckoned to him and lifted a quivering hand towards his face. Understanding what she wanted, he crouched down beside her. The eyes that looked at him were watery labyrinths of red veins surrounding pin-like pupils. They were searching his, and he had no doubt that they knew what – and who – they were seeing. She grasped his chin and turned his face from side to side. He wondered if she remembered doing the same thing on his first visit. Maybe she'd seen something – suspected something – even then. He felt every bone in her fingers but her touch was light and he moved with it. She dropped her hand into her lap, then raised it again and gestured to him to hold it. It was dry and feather-light, the skin parchment-like to his touch.

'So. Sam Shaykin.'

There was no point denying it. This moment had to come sooner or later. 'When did you know?'

'I look at you, I'm seeing Jack.' Their faces were close together, her eyes still fixed on his. 'What's with the Josh business?'

'I suppose I was scared of you. At first.'

The laugh rattled in her dry throat. 'Scared of me? Why? Because I'm old? Ugly? Now, maybe. But once—' She stopped in mid-sentence. He waited for her to go on but she let go his hand and closed her eyes. He watched her for a while, not wanting to move in case he disturbed her. Perhaps she'd drifted off to sleep again. But he'd been crouching for too long; his legs were starting to hurt. He unfolded himself and stood up.

She opened her eyes. 'Will she come and see me? Sadie – will she come?'

Another surprise. She knew about her daughter, his mother, after all. So, had she lied at the hospital? Or was it that the mists in her mind had momentarily cleared and a fragment of memory had drifted back? Either way, he had no doubt about the answer. He shook his head. 'She doesn't even want me to be here.'

Another silence. Outside he heard sounds – loud, swaggering voices of teenage boys walking along the landing, growing louder as they came nearer. He tensed, bracing himself to make his presence felt the moment the first boot hit the door. The footsteps passed by, the voices retreated. He tried to calm himself again.

'She told you about me?' said Esther.

'Yes.'

She raised a shaky hand and reached again for his, but she seemed to change her mind, or perhaps the effort was too great, and the hand dropped back into her lap.

'Did she tell you what I did?'

'I think so. Not exactly. But I still don't understand why they—'

She held up a trembling hand again, this time in a gesture that told him to stop talking. 'Enough. Get me up. Give me my stick.'

Leaning on her stick and on his arm, stopping midway while another coughing fit passed, she managed to cover the few feet between her armchair and her wardrobe. She hooked her fingers under the handle and pulled the door open. Sour-smelling clothes tumbled out in a tangled heap onto the floor. Turning his head away and doing his best to hold his breath, he picked some up and began folding and re-hanging them.

'What are you doing?' she snapped. 'Leave that!' The softness had gone. The nasty, irritable edge to her manner, that had so often brought him close to telling her to poke it and walking out, had returned in full force. She pointed with her stick to a bundle of clothes still in the bottom of the wardrobe. 'Under there. Get it. I can't bend.'

What did she want him to dig for under that foul heap? A stash of gold sovereigns, perhaps? Love letters from his grandpa tied in a pink ribbon? Holding his breath as best he could, he fumbled under the clothes, touched what felt like a book and pulled it out. He might have guessed. More photos. This time, a whole album with pages of stiff black paper held between crumbling cardboard covers. He offered it to Esther but she waved it away. 'Look in it. With me.'

He helped her back to her chair, sat beside her and opened the album at the first page. In front of a painted back-cloth of a country garden in full bloom, a pretty little girl stood between a man and a woman. She wore a frilly party dress, a ribbon in her hair, white knee-length socks and shiny black shoes with buckles on the front. The man was Isaac Levinson. He wore a suit with tails and gripped the familiar stick in his right hand. The woman, who looked younger than Isaac, wore a sequinned dress and a necklace and earrings that gleamed under the studio lights.

'This is you?' asked Sam.

'I was ten.'

'And this must be your mother? She's a beautiful woman.'

He saw the cracks in her dry lips as she tried to smile. 'I get it from her. Turn over.'

He turned to the next page. Here were the same people, again dressed in their finery, but the little girl was now a lovely young woman. Her lacy dress had three-quarter-length sleeves and a plunging neckline that set off the upward swell of her breasts. She wore a necklace with a gem-stone pendant, a bracelet that might have been gold and a bangle on her left forearm. She was looking into the camera with her lips parted in a smile that was demure yet bordering on the provocative. He looked at Esther. She was watching him, waiting for his reaction. He knew he had just one chance to make the right comment, ask the right question – not say anything that would send her back into her shell and ruin his chance of learning more about her. He drew a breath. 'How old are you here?'

'Fifteen.'

So far, so good. She still had the expectant expression.

'You like me? You like the dress?' She tilted her head a fraction, assuming for a second a coyness that gave Sam a hint of the woman she must once have been, and the power she must once have possessed.

Now he had to be very careful. She really had been beautiful, his great-aunts had been right about that. But fifteen? Surely not. With a neckline like that, and the expensive-looking jewellery? She must have got it wrong. Or maybe it proved that Sarah had been right.

'When was this?'

She screwed her eyes up as if trying to remember. 'Papa gave me the dress. On my birthday. For the party.'

Inch by inch. Careful question by careful question. Don't upset her. 'You wore it for your fifteenth birthday party?'

Again the screwed-up eyes. 'No. He – his friend.'

'What friend?'

She snorted with exasperation. Shit! he'd been clumsy. 'I should know? A party's a party! Rich people. Jewish people, but not like us.'

'Sephardim?'

She looked puzzled. 'Who knows? Lord Dunnabunk. Lady Muck. What do I know?'

'Do you remember the party? Was it at someone's house?'

She glowered at him. 'I should know from where! Some sprauncy place. What difference?'

'Was it a nice party? What do you remember?'

With surprising force she snatched the album from him, banged it shut and thrust it back at him. 'Enough! *Ferdray mir nisht in kop* with the questions! Put it away! Go away! Go on, go!'

He took the album from her. 'Shall I put it where it was? Under the clothes?'

'Yes – no.' She gestured towards her lap. 'Put it back here.'

A group of girls this time, walking past her door. He heard giggling, one or two shrieks of laughter and a snatch of song.

Her abrupt changes of mind and mood no longer surprised him. He put the album on her lap and watched her trembling hand leaf through it. She stopped five or six pages further on and gestured him to look. Two people stood side by side. A slightly older and even more alluring Esther in a different party dress with a necklace and tiara. Beside her, his fists clenched with protruding thumbs pressed hard against his trouser-legs, was a thin, stooped young man with large ears, a prominent chin and a toothy but uncertain smile. He wore a tailcoat with a carnation in his buttonhole.

'Who's that with you?' Sam asked.

'You don't remember? You came to our wedding.'

She must be getting tired. Confused again. He wasn't going to get any further. Bring her back gently. 'I don't think so, Esther.'

She looked puzzled. 'You're sure? Maybe you forgot?'

He wasn't going to argue the point. He reached for the album. 'Can I have a closer look?'

Something was puzzling him. Maybe he'd made a mistake. No, he was sure. 'Our wedding,' she'd said. But the man with her wasn't his grandfather. He needed to go carefully now. She was getting more confused. He really shouldn't ask her any more questions, but he couldn't leave it there. 'This was your husband, you said?'

She looked puzzled. 'Who said?'

She was losing the thread. Or maybe he was? He wasn't sure any more. 'I thought you did. Just now. You said I went to your wedding.'

'You said you didn't.'

Ever deeper into the rabbit hole. 'I know, but – I don't understand. This isn't Grandpa.'

'Who? Whose grandpa?'

'My grandfather. Your husband, Ben. This isn't him.'

'No? Who is it then?'

And deeper. 'I don't know. Can you tell me?' He knew he'd pushed it too far and made her confused. She snatched the album back and pressed it with both hands shield-like against her thin body. 'What do you want? Don't touch me! Get away! Go! Who are you?' Another coughing fit shook her. She gestured to the table with a clutching motion. 'Blue pills! There!'

She swallowed the pills and drank some water. They seemed to calm her and her eyes closed. Lately, he thought, every day had been full of surprises. Now he could do things that not long ago he would have shied away from in horror. With an expertise that surprised even him, as she slept he tucked a blanket from the bed over her knees and under the hands that still clutched the photo album. He sat for a while watching her sleep and listening to her laboured breathing. She mumbled some unintelligible words and gave a short laugh. Her hands relaxed their grip on the album and it began to slide from her lap. He reached out and caught it before it hit the floor. She mumbled again and shifted her position. He sat motionless until she'd settled again, then opened the album at the photo she'd shown him. He was certain now. People can change a lot over time, but this was definitely not his Grandpa Ben. Glancing at Esther to make sure she was asleep, he gently prised the photo from the slots in the page and turned it over. The handwriting in faded ink was neat and clear. The signature was underlined twice and under it were two small kisses:

Sunday 18th February 1917. To my beloved Esther on the occasion of our engagement. From your loving husband-to-be,

Elias xx

SEVENTEEN

'For fuck's sake! Arsehole!' Sam slammed on the brakes as a Range Rover moved forward a calculated inch, preventing him from joining the nose-to-tail line of traffic that was fumbling its way round the Elephant and Castle Gyratory. He sighed with disgust as the driver wound down his window and made a 'wanker' gesture at him. He eased into the space left for him by a bus driver and waved his thanks. It had been hard going this morning. An hour gone and ahead of them still lay the dense traffic of Brixton and Streatham, then the outer suburbs. After that it usually got easier as the road to Brighton wound its way through open countryside and eventually past places with names like Pease Pottage and Pyecombe. For now, though, the soothing strains of *Coltrane for Lovers* on the cassette player were doing very little to offset his irritation at the slow progress they were making.

He was glad that Deborah was free and had wanted to come with him. They'd decided to stay a couple of nights at the Golden Hind, a quiet hotel in a street of former fishermen's cottages in the Lanes. Things had been a bit strained between them since last week's row over her parents' dinner invitation. She'd made no bones about telling him how she felt about it, and he'd had to admit again she was right and tell her again how sorry he was. He knew that he'd been giving so much thought and time to what she'd started calling his Esther Quest, that he'd been even more inconsiderate to her than usual, and that she was coming to the end of her patience. Maybe these few days, when they could pursue the Quest together and also spend time just relaxing, seeing the sights of Brighton and enjoying the sea air, would help to bring them back closer together. That, in any case, was his hope. And also, there was the latest mystery to pursue: who was this Elias, who had described himself as Esther's husband-to-be? He thought again about Sarah's cryptic response when he'd phoned to ask her if she knew: 'Come. Come and we'll talk.'

Half an hour later they'd left the London suburbs behind and Sam could relax a little. He turned the cassette over and pushed it back in, but before he could press Play Deborah reached over and ejected it. 'There's something I want to talk to you about. To be honest I've been putting it off, but this is as good a time as any.'

He immediately tensed. He could tell from her voice that she was going to say something he'd rather not hear. He tightened his grip on the steering wheel and risked a sideways glance. 'That sounds serious. I'm all ears.'

'It is serious,' said Deborah. 'Can we stop for a while?'

A mile on, he pulled into the car park of a roadside café. 'Shall we go in?'

'No,' said Deborah, 'We can talk here.' She took a Thermos flask from her bag and poured tea into plastic cups. Her hand was shaking slightly as she handed him one. He tried to anticipate what she wanted to tell him. Was she pregnant? Was there someone else? He sipped his tea and waited, feeling his anxiety level rise. He needed to get the conversation started. 'So, what's this all about?'

It came out in a rush. 'I'd like us to wind up London Adventure for a while.'

He shifted in his seat to face her, feeling as if he'd been punched in the stomach. 'But why? Just when we're building—'

'I know. The summer season's done well for us, but it's tailing off a bit now. I'm just asking if we can put it on hold for a few months.' She clutched Sam's arm. 'Sam, I'm exhausted! I'm surprised you haven't noticed. I've been taking the tours out, then coming home and doing all the bookings and the admin. It's been like that since Esther came on the scene.'

Sam stared through the windscreen, focusing on nothing in particular, feeling numb. 'It's true, I've been selfish. I've piled too much on you. I'm sorry. I wish you'd said sooner. Soon as we get back I'll start—'

She put a finger gently on his lips. 'No, Sam. I've made up my mind.' She hesitated for a moment. 'I've been offered a job. In Barcelona.'

He spoke automatically, as if detaching himself from the reality of the moment. 'What kind of a job?'

'Tour guide, of course. I've been polishing up my A-level Spanish for a while. They're giving me a base in Barcelona and I'll be taking groups on tours all over Spain. They're paying very good wages.'

'They?'

'Breakaway Tours Europe. It's a new company.' She tried to draw him closer to her. He resisted the pressure and avoided making eye contact. 'It's a fantastic opportunity, Sam. I want you to be happy for me.'

There was a lead weight in his stomach. This was all his fault. If only he'd— 'No, I mean, yes, I'm pleased for you. It's just so… How long will you be away?'

'It depends. Three months at first, but if I do well it could become six. And…' She took a deep breath. 'And it could be even longer. People are starting to want winter holidays—'

'I do know that. I'm a travel agent, remember?'

'Of course. Sorry. So there's talk of moving me on to Switzerland.' She squeezed his arm tighter. He kept it unresponsive, wanting to punish her with his icy manner. 'What can I say, Sam? I know this is a difficult time for you.'

He retrieved his arm and gripped the steering wheel with unnecessary force. 'When do you leave?'

'In a week's time.'

'That soon?'

'I'm afraid so.'

'This is definite? You've made up your mind?'

She nodded. 'I might not get another chance like this. And I think it'll be good for both of us.'

He started the engine. 'We'd better get going.'

For the rest of the journey there was an uncomfortable silence. Sam responded with grunts whenever she tried to start a conversation. It was a relief to them both when they'd reached Brighton, signed into their hotel and were being greeted by Maria at Sarah's door.

'Is that them? Bring them in,' called Sarah.

'She's on her own,' whispered Maria, 'waiting and waiting for you. Eva is on big trip. Come.' She saw them into the living-room and left.

Sarah was sitting in her wheelchair with her coat buttoned up and her scarf wound round her neck. 'So at last, this is Deborah Levine. I thought you were hiding her from us. A *shayner maidel* you've found, Sammy. Come here, Deborah.'

Deborah leaned down and kissed Sarah. 'I'm so pleased to meet you. Sam talks about you so much I feel I know you already.'

'Levine,' said Sarah. 'We had a Levine family three doors from us in Fieldgate Street. What are your parents called?'

'Harold and Deana.'

'Is your *zayda* alive?'

'Yes, he's—'

'Herschel Levine? Butcher? Had a shop in Flower and Dean Street?'

'That's amazing!' said Deborah. 'How did you know that?'

Sarah laughed with delight. 'And your *bubbeh*? Malka Levine?'

Deborah joined in Sarah's laughter. 'That's right. How—?'

'I knew them,' said Sarah, like a magician basking in an audience's astonishment. 'You tell your *zayda* and *bubbeh*,

Sarah Markovich says hello. They'll remember me.' She heaved a deep sigh. 'Everyone knew everyone in the East End. Happy days, eh? That's all gone now. And when we're gone – but I'm still here, thank God, so let's go.'

'Wait,' said Sam, 'Maria said Eva's on a trip? I'm sorry we've missed her. Where's she gone? Will she be back later?'

'She's gone with the *shul* ladies' club on a trip to Israel. Tel Aviv, Jerusalem, the Dead Sea and God knows where else. Not my cup of tea. I told her she should bring me back a falaffel and a camel. Come on, let's go.'

'Where are we going?' said Sam.

'I gave Maria the day off. You're taking me for my walk. We can talk when we stop.'

Following Sarah's instructions, they manoeuvred her wheelchair through the revolving doors out of Galaxy House. There was a cold wind, slightly relieved by a few optimistic rays of sunshine. Sarah pointed with her stick to a seafront shelter on the opposite side of the road. 'Over there to start with.'

'I'll do the pushing, Sam,' said Deborah. She grasped the chair's handles, watched for a gap in the busy midday traffic and ran across the road so fast that Sarah laughed with pleasure, while Sam ran alongside waving thanks at the cars that slowed to let them pass.

'Which way now?' Deborah asked.

'That way,' said Sarah, 'towards Hove.'

For fifteen minutes they took turns at pushing her chair along the wide promenade. Their earlier conversation for the moment set aside, their mood lifted as they walked along enjoying the sight of the sea, the smell of salty air, the wind in their faces and the sound of seagulls.

'Stop here,' said Sarah. They'd arrived at a shelter, one of the many battered relics of Brighton's better days that they'd seen spaced out along the promenade. This one retained some vestiges of elegance beneath its chipped green paintwork, and looked sturdy enough to resist stormy weather and provide shade from the summer sun. They eased Sarah out of her chair, settled her on a bench and sat each side of her. She took off her glasses, cleaned off the sea salt and put them back on.

'Now, what do you want to know?'

Sam was relieved. He'd been wondering how to raise the subject and not at all certain that she would. 'I saw this photo—'

'One of that woman's?

'Yes. And there was a—'

'So you're still seeing her? Does Sadie know?'

He suppressed a sigh. He hadn't expected this to be easy, but Sarah seemed determined to divert him away from what he wanted to find out. 'I haven't seen Mum or Dad for a while.'

'They've still got the needle? But still you want to see that woman?'

'Yes,' said Sam. 'And she doesn't seem that bad to me. I Just don't understand what you've all got against her.'

'Thank God you don't!' said Sarah.

'What does that mean?'

'Never mind. You might find out one day. But now, you want to ask me something.'

'Yes, I do,' said Sam, 'I saw a photo of Esther and a man, and on the back there was a message from someone named Elias, calling himself Esther's husband-to-be. Do you know who this Elias is?'

'Was.'

'So you know? But he's dead?'

'Help me sit up.'

Sarah was slipping down on the bench. Sam and Deborah helped her into a more comfortable sitting position.

'What was he like in the picture?' said Sarah. 'Funny-looking? Skinny and bony? A bit of a *nebbish*? Big ears, poppy eyes?'

'That's him,' said Sam.

'Elias Shapiro,' said Sarah. 'Son of a rich *ganzer macher*, but the family *schlemiel*.'

An extra-large wave crashed against the sea wall and licked over it, reaching almost to their feet before retreating.

'You knew him?' asked Deborah.

'Knew him, no. I saw him maybe two, three times after they got engaged.' She laughed. 'A *shmendrik* like you never saw in your life, he was!'

'But Esther was going to marry him?' Sam asked. 'And then she ended up marrying Grandpa instead? How come?'

The sky had started to darken. Three waves in succession broke with a loud crash onto the sea wall. With each one they watched the spray hang in the air before dissolving into foam on the promenade.

Sarah beckoned them to sit closer to her. 'What I'm telling you, only I know now. I'm the last one. Not even Eva knows. Thank God she was too young, they kept it from her. And, Sam, listen to me: you must never tell your mother this. Or Eva. Or anyone. *Fershteyt*?'

'What about me?' said Deborah. 'I'd understand if you don't want to share this with me. I could go for a walk if you like – leave you two alone for a while?'

'You stay where you are,' said Sarah. 'If I can't trust Herschel Levine's granddaughter, who's left in the world to trust?'

'You can trust me,' said Deborah, 'I promise.'

'I know, *bubeleh*,' said Sarah, giving her arm a squeeze. 'You've got a good one here, Sam. Make sure you hold on to her.'

Sam looked at Deborah but she avoided his eyes. He turned back to Sarah. 'So what happened to Elias?'

'He ran off. Ran a mile from Esther. Broke off the engagement. The *mamzer*! If only he'd married her, my poor brother would never have ended up like he did.'

'Why did he break it off?' asked Sam.

Sarah thought for a while. 'His father was Julius Shapiro. A big man. An old Sephardi family. Rich. Businesses. Clothing, furniture – everything. Good connections. A *frum* man. Money every year for the Bevis Marks and the Jews' Free School. Even politics he was in. Come 1914, the war, from his friends he gets contracts with the government. Uniforms for soldiers. Boots. Helmets. Gas masks, tents, blankets, pots and pans – everything. So big he can't do it all. So he goes looking for lay-offs. And he finds Isaac Levinson. A Whitechapel Jew with already sweatshops, factories, workers – and big ideas and money to put in. A gift from God. So soon he's Isaac's best friend and Isaac, he's on his way to being a millionaire.'

'I'm starting to get the picture,' said Sam. 'And Julius has got a son he's trying to marry off.'

'Such a son!' said Sarah. 'Elias, he's a *nebbish*, the family dope. So Julius tells Isaac – he uses nice words but this is what he's telling him – you get the big contract after your Esther marries my Elias.'

'And as a bonus,' cut in Deborah, 'Isaac gets to be related by marriage to that family.'

'Smart girl,' said Sarah. She was starting to look uncomfortable. 'This bench is getting cold on my *tuchas*. Let's walk a bit more.'

They helped her back into her wheelchair and walked on, the sounds of the sea and the wind making conversation, for the time being, impossible. The sky had clouded over and the seagulls were hovering in flocks, uttering their shrill cries. The waves that crashed into the sea wall were bigger and more frequent.

Beside an iron-work bandstand with a pagoda-like roof was another shelter. 'This one,' said Sarah, 'Stop here.'

The weather was changing by the hour. Now, in mid-afternoon, the sky started to clear and there was a little warmth from the sun. The tide was turning and the waves spent their force on the beach rather than against the sea wall. Sarah had guided them to a shelter on the section of the promenade where iron steps led down to a lower terrace with kiosks selling souvenirs and snacks.

'You know what?' she said, 'I fancy a little something. How about you two?'

Sam realised that they hadn't eaten since breakfast. 'That's a great idea, Sarah. How about you, Deborah?'

'I'm pretty peckish,' said Deborah. 'Shall we start walking back or do you want to sit here for a while first?'

Sam guessed from Sarah's mischievous expression that she had another trick up her sleeve. 'No need to go anywhere,' she said. She pointed to the steps. 'Sam, you go down there to Neptune's Nook and you tell Neptune, Sarah Markovitch is here.'

Sam looked at the steps, bewildered.

'Neptune?'

'What did I say?'

If this was Sarah's idea of a joke, he was prepared to go along with it. A small price to pay for keeping her happy so that she'd tell the rest of her story. 'Okay. Don't go away.' He disappeared down the iron steps, returning five minutes later with a short, red-faced man wearing a white overall, white wellingtons and a green plastic crown, puffing up behind him. Holding his crown in place, the man made a ceremonial bow. '*Shalom*, Sarah. Neptune greets you. I see you have company today. *Mishpoche*, I presume?'

Sarah returned Neptune's bow with a mock regal wave. 'This is Sam, my brother Ben's grandson. And this is his young lady, Deborah.' Neptune bowed in Deborah's direction and she played along with a curtsey. 'Deborah Levine,' added Sarah. 'The Levines of Fieldgate Street. Herschel the butcher, you remember?' She pointed to Neptune. 'This is Bernie Jacobs. I knew his parents. They had a fish and chip shop—'

'In Whitechapel?' said Sam.

Bernie grinned. 'How did you guess? In Wentworth Street. My dad, rest his soul, moved us here after the war. I've made my living from that hole in the wall for the last thirty years.'

'You look well on it,' said Deborah.

Bernie beamed at her. 'Who should have a life like mine? A beach-side business, nice customers in all weathers, regulars like your Auntie Sarah.'

It was a day for magic tricks. As if from nowhere, Bernie produced a brightly coloured menu in the shape of a fish. 'Now, what can I get you today? Cod and chips? Or I make you up a nice tray of sandwiches? I've got some smoked salmon in the fridge – not on the menu, only for special customers. And a little boiled egg chopped up with spring onion in my Ginnie's own mayonnaise?'

'We'll have the sandwiches,' said Sarah, without consulting Sam and Deborah. 'And cups of tea.'

Bernie clutched his crown and bowed again. 'Neptune will provide the bounty of the sea.' He scuttled back to the steps and the crown disappeared from sight.

Sam and Deborah were helpless with laughter. 'What a character!' said Sam.

'One of the last, bless him,' said Sarah. 'Years ago, weekends here it was like Whitechapel On Sea. Now it's all Benidorm and Eilat. Times have changed. There's just a few of us *alte kackers* left now.'

Soon the tip of the crown re-appeared, and underneath it Bernie, panting up the steps carrying a laden wooden tray.

'Neptune returns,' he said, setting down the tray on the bench beside them. 'Tea, sandwiches, serviettes. Eat in good health.'

'Thanks, Bernie,' said Sam, taking out his wallet. 'How much do I—'

Bernie stopped him with a smile and a raised hand. 'My treat today, boychick. So that you remember old Neptune of Wentworth Street.' He leaned closer to Sam and spoke in a mock whisper. 'In case you don't know it, your Auntie Sarah, bless her, she's an angel. In the war, when our shop got bombed out and we had no money coming in—'

'Enough with the *maisehs*, Bernie!' snapped Sarah. 'Leave us in peace already so we can eat!' As Neptune descended back to his domain, Sam watched the crinkle in the corners of Sarah's eyes.

The sandwiches were delicious, the tea warming. Sam took the tray back down to Bernie and they exchanged a few friendly words. From the top of the steps he saw Sarah and Deborah deep in conversation, their heads bent together. Both women turned to him and smiled. 'Do you want to walk on now?' he asked.

'No,' said Sarah. 'We can stay here for a bit.' She signalled to Deborah to help her loosen her scarf a little. 'Where did I stop?'

'You were telling us about Elias,' said Sam.

'Elias, I'll come to,' said Sarah. 'First you should know what else was going on.' She took off her glasses, polished the lenses on her scarf, put them back on and cleared her throat. 'The middle of the war, my Arnold's born. Twelfth of May 1916. Sixty this year he is, *kaynahorah*. The same year, the fifteenth of June, your grandfather Ben turns eighteen. So the call-up letter comes for him to join the army, and a month later he's in France. Eighteen years old and he's a soldier. Who'd have dreamed? My husband, thank God they don't take because he had TB when he was a boy. They send him to do war work in a factory in Enfield. Isaac's two boys, they already went and joined the army a year before. Volunteered. Isaac, that schmuck, he was proud, like it was him did something clever, like he should take the credit. Went round boasting about it and showing everyone pictures of his boys looking handsome in their uniforms.'

'That was Joel and Nathan?' asked Sam.

'Don't interrupt!' snapped Sarah. 'Yes, that was them.' She gazed into mid-air as if collecting her thoughts and shifted her weight on the bench. 'So now I'm married, and my Arnold, bless him, he's still a baby. And Eva, she's still at home with our parents but she leaves school and starts working for pennies in that *ferkakteh* Yiddish theatre. Even in those days she's got her big ideas about being a big-shot writer. Once, maybe twice a week she comes to see me, plays with the baby, tells me the gossip. So one day she comes and she tells me there's trouble. Isaac's got Esther a *shidduch*. It's this Elias. And Esther doesn't want to know. "He's a *klutz*," she says to Eva. "And a *nebbish*. He's such a *nebbish*," she says, "even the army won't have him."'

'You're saying Elias wasn't fit enough for the army?' Sam asked. 'Even in wartime?'

Sarah gave one of her most magnificent snorts. 'Fit? A walking corpse as well as a *klutz*, that boy! Flat feet that turned out when he walked, big thick glasses, knock knees – much use he'd have been. The army didn't want him, and Esther didn't want him.'

A young couple came along the promenade, laughing, hand in hand. They stopped at the shelter and began unbuttoning their coats. Sarah glared at them, and to Sam's astonishment let out a low growl. The couple buttoned up again and walked on. Sarah's face relaxed and she gave Sam and Deborah a conspiratorial wink. 'Where were we? Oh, yes. The *nudnik* Elias. Isaac isn't used to people saying no to him. Not even his own daughter. And he wants this *shidduch*. It's good for him and good for his business. So there's big rows, and Esther's running out of the house and running to Eva, who's her only friend now Ben's gone away. Isaac's told her to stay away from Eva, but she goes anyway.'

'He was okay with her doing that, was he?' asked Deborah.

'Okay? He'd have taken the strap to her if he found out.'

'He did that? He beat her?' said Sam.

'Didn't I already tell you that? Eva says different, but

you can believe me. Enough with the questions now. Or I'll get it all *fermisht*.'

'Sorry,' said Sam. 'No more interruptions, I promise.'

Sarah took out her handkerchief and blew her nose. 'What Eva doesn't know, but our mother does, and she tells me – never mind Isaac would give Millie such a clout if he found out she's been coming round and talking – is this: Isaac's locking Esther in her room, hitting her on the *tuchas* with his belt, and doing God knows what else to her, to make her say okay, she'll marry Elias.'

'Oh my God! The poor girl!' said Deborah, with tears in her eyes.

This time there was no reprimand. Sarah nodded her understanding. 'In the end, Esther gives in. She says yes, enough already, she'll marry Elias. Isaac makes quick a big engagement party. At The Savoy, *noch*!

'Were you at it?' asked Sam.

Sarah laughed. 'Me? No! Isaac's too good for us now. After that he keeps her away from Eva, and Eva doesn't dare go to Elder Street. Once in a while Millie gets out to see our mother, but Isaac catches her once and gives her a black eye.'

'I had no idea!' said Sam. 'What a shit that man was! Oh, sorry—'

Sarah gave him a grim smile. 'It gets worse. You want to hear or not?'

'If you're not too tired.'

'I'll go on for a bit,' said Sarah. 'But I'll need the Ladies soon. So anyway – a year Ben's been away in the war. In that time we get four, maybe five letters. No one knows what's happening. Every day more boys dying. Then our parents get the letter. Ben's been wounded. He's in a hospital somewhere. They don't say where. France, maybe. Or Belgium, who knows? Serious, it says. "What does serious mean?" my parents are asking me. "Is he dying? Where is he?" We don't know. Nobody knows from *gournisht*. Then comes worse. Another letter. This time to Isaac. And then another one. In the same week, maybe the same day even, both Esther's brothers are killed.'

She lifted her glasses and wiped the back of her hand across her eyes.

'Time to go. Never mind the Ladies. I can wait till I'm home. Then I'll tell you the rest.'

EIGHTEEN

Shabbos morning it came. The 8th of September 1917. The letter nobody wanted. The one with Ministry of Defence printed on the envelope. She heard the postman come. She heard Mama scream and she heard her send the maid, Bessie, to bring Papa home from the *shul*. She went downstairs and found Mama in the sitting-room with the unopened letter screwed up tight in her hands. When Papa came he unbent Mama's fingers, took the letter from her and went into his private room. They waited. Mama knocked on his door but no reply. No one ever dared go in without his permission. They waited. An hour. More. Papa came out. His eyes dry, his voice calm. His fists clenched tight. 'Joel has been – Joel is – may God rest his soul. My son has been killed in this war.'

He sat down and put his face in his hands. She and Mama started sobbing. Papa pulled them both to him and put his arms round them. Then he sobbed too. 'It must be what God meant for us,' he said. 'Now we must pray for our son Nathan to come home safe.' Papa wasn't really *frum*, she knew that. He went to *shul* so people would see him there. But now she was glad he was praying and sobbing and she sobbed and prayed with him.

She was wearing one of her beautiful dresses. Lace and ribbons and lovely bright colours. Mama took her upstairs to her bedroom and helped her find something darker. Something to cover her up more. 'No need for black,' she said. 'We don't have to do that.' She had another room, a sitting-room where she kept her treasures and books and had tea in the afternoons. Mama helped her cover up the mirrors there and the one in her bedroom.

Downstairs, Papa had called someone to come and cover the mirrors. She watched him open his jacket and dig his penknife into his beautiful silk waistcoat and make a big tear in it.

Soon the house was full of men who'd come to pay their respects to the Balaboss and make a *minyan* for *kaddish*. They too were missing sons and brothers, but for the Balaboss they knew it was more important. The rabbi came and Papa sent her and Mama out, and the men said prayers. Then the rabbi left and she and Mama went back in. Papa was sitting like before with his head in his hands. They sat with him. It was quiet. She listened for a long time to the big clock on the mantlepiece ticking. She was floating in no time. It seemed like days ago, weeks ago that Papa had opened the letter. She didn't want to eat anything. She went to bed and dreamed of walking in the park with her friends and with her brothers.

That was the first time they came to her. Joel and Nathan both. 'Don't be sad, little sister,' Joel said to her. 'It's not like they say. It's not so bad. We're with you.'

Next day, she knew. She knew the postman would bring the second letter. She waited by the door. She wanted to be the one to take it to Papa and Mama so she could say, 'Don't be sad. Nathan is with Joel. And they're both with me.'

Papa, may God forgive him, tore the letter from her and pushed her away so hard she fell down and banged her head on the corner of a table. The blood ran out. She screamed. He took no notice. He was also screaming. She'd never heard Papa make a noise like this, a howl like once when she saw the coal-man's cart run over a dog in their street. She'd held her Mama's hand and watched the dog twitching and howling, saw the blood pump out from its crushed skull until it lay still and died. Was it like that for her brothers? Did their blood pump out? Did they make that noise that Papa was making now?

Mama came running. She saw the blood, she saw Papa's bent-over body and she saw the letter screwed up in the trembling fists that he was pressing into his eyes. And she knew.

The rabbi came again with his *minyan* and he sent her and Mama away while he calmed Papa and said a *kaddish* for both her brothers. The rabbi and his *minyan* left and she and Mama went back to be with Papa. He wasn't howling now. But he was sobbing. Something she'd never seen him do before yesterday, not her papa, the big strong Balaboss. Great big sobs. She and Mama put their arms round him. 'My sons. My sons, dead,' he kept saying. 'My sons dead. This war. For what? For who? Better we never came. Better the Cossacks and the pogroms. At least – at least…'

Only she knew. Only she, no one else, knew that someone had made a mistake. The men came back, they sent her away, and in her sitting-room there was Joel and here was Nathan.

Now, she came and went without Mama and Papa seeing or caring. The rabbi and his *minyan* brought low chairs and people brought food and drink and the house sat *shivah* and said *kaddish* for a week. Papa, always so handsome with his clothes and his stick and his silk waistcoats, didn't shave or comb his hair. Now she came and went un-noticed, and Joel and Nathan came and went with her.

The fourth day of the *shivah* was her eighteenth birthday. No one remembered. No one except her brothers and her friend Eva Symonds, and Ben, Eva's big brother. When the *minyan* came for *kaddish* she went out and no one noticed. Eva was waiting for her. They walked two miles through the dirty Whitechapel and Shoreditch streets to the sweet-smelling green freedom of Victoria Park. Her brothers and Ben walked with them. Ben, a year older than her and so handsome in his uniform that his mother had had to look away, say '*kaynahorah*' and spit three times to ward off the evil eye, liked her very much. And she liked Ben. Very much.

In Victoria Park on her eighteenth birthday she ran with her brothers and her friends over grass and along pathways. She drank tea with them in the café by the lake. She played hide-and-seek around the fountains and statues. Eva sang Happy Birthday, and Ben, Nathan and Joel joined in. Only she knew. Only she knew they were all there with her. But sing they all did.

When she went home and slipped back inside, still no-one noticed. When Julius and Elias Shapiro came to pay their respects to Isaac and Millie and to wish them long life, she took Elias to her sitting-room and Bessie brought them tea and cakes. Then Elias joined his father, the rabbi and the *minyan* for the prayers and *kaddish,* and she slipped away again to join her brothers and Ben. They weren't waiting for her, as they'd promised, in the shadows cast by the tall merchant weavers' houses of Elder Street. But she heard their voices whispering from doorways and basement steps, loving voices luring her into their game of hide-and-seek. 'Come and find us, little sister,' whispered Joel. 'Seek me and find me, in front or behind me,' whispered Ben. Happy to escape for a while from the black cloak of misery that had wrapped itself around her home, she followed their voices to the end of Elder Street and along the dark canyon between the Folgate Street mansions, only to lose track of them in the unfamiliar noise and bustle of Spitalfields.

Then, suddenly, she caught sight of Joel. He was standing at a fruit and vegetable stall, tumbling potatoes from a scale pan into a shopping-bag held open by a thin woman in a black dress and hat and black lace-up boots. She crept up behind him and tapped his shoulder. 'Joel! I found you. I've won! You're It now.' The stallholder gave her a brief glance, shrugged and turned back to his customer. 'Soft in the head, I expect. Shame. Nice-looking kid as well. That's fourpence halfpenny, love. Ta very much.'

She wiped away a disappointed tear, squeezed her lace-edged handkerchief into a ball and looked around, searching for a clue. And all at once, there was Nathan. Standing by the stall. Gazing at her and smiling. Tall and handsome in his uniform. Coal-black hair curling from underneath the cap pushed to the back of his head. Smoke rising from the cigarette he held lazily in his lips.

'You're looking for Joel? I know where he is. Come with me.'

'That's not fair, Nathan.' she said. 'I've found you, you're It now.'

'Nathan, eh? Yeah, that's me. The game's over, sweetheart. You want to find Joel, don't you?'

'And Ben? Will I find him?'

'The whole bleeding East Surrey Regiment if you can handle it, darling.'

'I beg your pardon?'

'Never mind. Just my joke. Come on.'

Smiling, he reached out his hand and happily she took it. She kept hold of it as he led her on an exciting dance through the rumbling, honking ranks of omnibuses, goods-carts, taxi cabs and lorries that flowed non-stop along Commercial Street, and brought her, laughing, to the other side. He led her on and she followed. A sign on a wall – black capitals with Hebrew letters underneath – said Brick Lane. Ben and Eva sometimes brought her here. She'd been to their house – or rather to the three rooms in it that were theirs. She'd met their mother and their sister Fanny. Nice people. But poor. Papa didn't like her having poor people as friends.

'Why not, Papa? I like Eva. I like Ben.'

'I've got plans for you. Their father's one of my workers. No one to respect. A nobody. Boys like that, they're not for you.'

Where was that house? Without them to show her, she had no idea. Brick Lane was muddy underfoot. Narrow to start with, and with most of the street taken up by food-carts, market stalls and piles of rubbish, there was little room for the shoppers who jostled past them in both directions. A boy in ragged clothes and boots gaping open at the toes grabbed her arm, held out his hand and asked for money. Nathan pushed him aside and walked on. She followed, still holding his hand. At a table in front of a butcher's shop a man pulled a fistful of entrails from a chicken, separated the last strands from the carcass with a flash of his knife, and threw them on top of a steaming pile in the gutter. The smell clogged her nostrils as Nathan led her on. Past stalls with fish on slabs, past open-fronted grocery shops where women sank their arms into barrels and pulled out shiny cucumbers and glistening herrings; past bakeries, clothing stalls, fried food shops, shops with pots and pans, and public houses. Everywhere, on walls and hoardings, in windows and hung on stalls, were placards, notices, adverts – the lettering here only in Hebrew, even where the words were English.

'In here.' They'd turned off Brick Lane into an alley. It was no more than a few yards long, closed off by the back yards of houses running across it at the end. She was still holding his hand. A low ceiling, a gaslight, a man behind a counter with bottles on it. Two tables with men sitting at them and more bottles. A ripple of interest as she and Nathan arrived. Nathan went over to the man at the counter and whispered in his ear. Heads turned towards her and there were grins. Nathan, Joel and Ben knew so many friendly people.

'This way, sweetheart. Not long now. Hold my hand, it's dark here.' He led her up a flight of stairs.

'Are Joel and Ben here?'

'They'll be coming. After I have, that is.'

Nathan laughs at his own joke. She laughs with him. He opens the door, holds tightly onto her arm and drags her into the room. Three more men follow. She doesn't know any of them. Nathan's scaring her now. He's pulling, tearing at her clothes. She can smell his breath – hot, stinking. See his brown teeth. He's saying nasty things to her, words she's never heard him say before.

Keep still. Put a fuckin sock in it, you fuckin Jew slag.

Look at them tits. Who wants a feel?

Ben, stop them! Ben! Please!

Jew bitch. Show us your cunt. How many fingers?

The other men laughing. Hands on her body.

Don't! Joel!

Shaddup. Put a fuckin sock in it I said. This'll shut you up.

A bottle pushed against her teeth, forcing her mouth open, something that burns running down her throat.

Feel this. Nice? Big, innit?

My turn. Get out the way.

Wait yer turn, I found her. Come on have another swig, it'll go in easier.

Come on, open up. Open it up. That's it. All the way in.

Jew bitch. Jew slag. Jew cunt—

*

Sarah's voice had become hoarse. She drank some tea and dabbed her lips with a handkerchief.

'Four days and nights she was gone. Isaac and Millie were frantic. You can imagine. Isaac called the hospitals, then the police. And he sent his *shtarkers* out to find her. Bad men, they were, who knew all the bad places, all the bad people. Who to talk to and what questions to ask. Nothing. He offered a big reward. Nothing. He even goes to the mortuary and checks the bodies they shlep out of the river. Nothing, thank God. And then they find her wandering round Brick Lane. Filthy dirty and her clothes in shreds, looking like she's got no idea where she is or what day it is.'

It was early evening. A wind was blowing in from the sea, bringing with it a heavy rain that drummed against the windows of Galaxy House. Sarah looked far away, thought Sam, as if still re-running in her mind the story that a distraught Millie Levinson had confided to her mother all those years ago. With an effort he took his eyes off her and looked at Deborah. Tears were streaming down her cheeks. He too felt an overwhelming need to cry, which he tried to resist for a few seconds before understanding that there was no point, and he felt a sense of great relief as he let the tears flow.

Sarah emptied her cup and cleared her throat. 'They bring her home to Isaac and Millie looking like a beggar, like a street-urchin. She's got bruises and she's filthy and there's blood on her clothes. But the worst thing, what they can't understand, she's got a big smile on her face – like she's really happy. How can this be? Millie holds out her arms and Esther runs to her, puts her arms round her. But Isaac, he lets out a *geschrei* and he goes *meshuggeh*. He takes Esther's arms and he drags her away from Millie and he shouts, "Where have you been? Tell me!" And Esther, all calm, standing there like a princess in her dirty torn clothes with the big smile, she looks at him and says, "I've been with Joel and Nathan and Ben." Isaac goes like a madman. He slaps her so hard in the face her nose bleeds and she falls down. He shouts at her: "Your brothers are dead and you run off and you come back and you tell me filthy lies. What are you? A madwoman? A *courveh*? You're not my daughter!" Millie thinks he's going to hit her again. She holds on to his arm and he gives her a backhander so she bleeds as well. The man's out of his mind. Millie takes Esther quick out of the room, she gives her a bath and puts her to bed, she locks herself and Esther in her bedroom. Isaac comes and bangs on the door, Millie's too scared to open it. She shouts to him he should get his daughter a doctor. Isaac calms down a bit, he calls the doctor. The doctor comes and checks her over, and he tells Isaac and Millie what they already know.'

She faltered. Her eyes too were full of tears. She pushed up her glasses and brushed them away.

'Sixty years I've kept this to myself. Even now…' She composed herself and went on. 'Millie says Isaac should call the police, but he says no. You know why? Because the lowlife's only worried about his big plans. About getting

Esther married to the Shapiro *nudnik*. And about his business deal. If they find out what happened to Esther, there's no more *shidduch*. *Shoyn!* Finished and done! And no *shidduch* means no contract. And no more Isaac the bigshot with a seat in the Bevis Marks. So he tells Millie they won't call the police. "I'll see to this," he says, "but we've got to keep shtum. That's the main thing. So I'll tell you what we're going to do."'

As Sarah paused to draw breath, Sam and Deborah exchanged glances, silently sharing their astonishment at the story that was unfolding.

'So the *mamzer* thinks up a plan there and then. He tells Millie he's going to stick Esther in one of those sprauncy country clinics they had in those days. Places where if you've got the money they'll lock a girl up for you, no questions asked, and they'll do whatever you want – treat her like she's a madwoman, do the business if she's pregnant – you know what I'm talking about. Millie argues and begs, but the *dreck*'s made up his mind and she can't change it. "I'll tell the Shapiros she's got TB or something," he says. "I'll say we've sent her away to recover. Then we'll wait and see. If she's pregnant they can get rid of it. If not, so all well and good. Four or five months later she comes home like new, no one knows she's spoiled goods, she marries the Shapiro *klutz* and everybody's happy."'

Nobody spoke. In the silence, the rain beat even more fiercely against the window. Sam sat with his head on his chest, eyes shut, clenching and unclenching his fists. Opening his eyes and looking at Deborah, he caught her look of shock and disbelief. Sarah, too, was clearly affected by the memories she'd revived. Her breathing was laboured and her glasses were dangling on their chain while she rubbed her eyes with her handkerchief.

Deborah was the first to speak. 'Sam, I think we should let Sarah rest now. She looks very tired.'

Sarah gave her a weak smile. 'The girl's right, Sam. I need my sleep now. Go.'

NINETEEN

The lobby of Galaxy House was a portal between two worlds. Inside all was hushed, carpeted warmth, but as the revolving doors ejected Sam and Deborah onto the Brighton seafront a vindictive wind assaulted them with needles of rain that drove into their faces and bodies. Leaving Sam's car parked for the night they held hands, lowered their heads and ran, splashing through puddles and rivulets, along the seafront to the Golden Hind Hotel.

Later, after drying off beside a huge log fire in the Golden Hind's bistro and enjoying locally caught fish and chips, they navigated the narrow creaky staircase to their bedroom. It had a comforting smell of furniture polish and newly laundered bed linen, and roof-beams that sloped almost to the floor. A sea-breeze blew in through the open casement window, carrying the soothing sound of waves breaking on the stony beach, but making the room feel chilly. Sam reached up to close it.

'Leave it open,' said Deborah. 'I like hearing the sea.' She opened her travel bag and unpacked, then began to undress. Sam took out his notebook, read over the snatches of Sarah's account that he'd managed to get down and jotted a few more lines, but he wasn't able to concentrate. Half-undressed, her face flushed from sitting close to the log fire over dinner, and her hair still showing the effects of the wind and rain, Deborah looked more beautiful than he'd ever seen her. Or perhaps, faced with the reality that he was about to lose her, he was looking at her as he'd never done before. Knowing that their time together was limited, he was thinking of her differently. She'd been so patient and loyal, standing by him as he toiled his way through his depressions and his Esther obsession, and what had she got in return? Far from enough, he had to admit. So, he realised, this wasn't just about a job offer coming out of the blue, a golden opportunity that she couldn't possibly pass up. This was her finally coming to her senses and wanting – needing – to get away from him for a while. Or possibly, even for good. The thought chilled him.

He closed the notebook and put it away. She was naked now, shivering as she slipped under the sheets and pulled the bedding up to her neck. 'Come on, get in,' she said, between exaggerated chattering of her teeth. 'If we huddle together for warmth we'll be okay.'

Maybe it wasn't too late. Maybe if he could reassure her – and himself – that he didn't just need her, he really, really loved her for her own sake – maybe she'd change her mind and not leave him? He undressed quickly and slipped in beside her. They laughed as they wriggled to offset the chill of the sheets against their bodies, but soon they were wound around each other and making love to the rhythm of the tide and the flapping of the curtains in the breeze.

He woke two hours later to find Deborah lying across his chest, her breasts pressing into him and his arm around her shoulders. Without the sounds of people or cars, the noises of the sea came through the ozone-scented air more clearly than ever, punctuated by the cries of seagulls.

He lay with his eyes half open, going over all that Sarah had told them. Picturing what Esther had suffered was unbearably painful, but it explained so much. In all likelihood she'd never recovered from that horrific experience, and was perhaps even now, as her life was drawing to an end, unable to come to terms with the memories. Maybe here was the root of all her strange behaviour, of her bitterness and her terrors. And perhaps it explained the unhappiness his mother had experienced in her early life; the reason why Esther hadn't been able to give her daughter the love that—

'Oh, fuck! Oh, fuck! Oh, no!' He drew his arm from under Deborah's body and sat on the edge of the bed, wishing desperately that he could have just one cigarette.

Deborah opened her eyes. 'What's wrong?'

'Hold on.' He was trying to put together a jigsaw puzzle in his head. On hooks behind the door were two white hotel bathrobes. He got out of bed, slipped one on, opened his notebook and rifled through the pages. 'If I'm right – Oh, God, it's true! Come and look at this!'

'What is it?' Deborah put on the other robe and they sat side by side on the edge of the bed.

'Here it is!' He held the page up for her to see. 'I don't know if we can believe everything Sarah told us – after all, she's an old woman and all this happened a long time ago. But look – I wrote it down as she said it – she said that Esther's brothers were killed in September 1917. And she said that – wait a minute, I've got it here – *The fourth day of the shivah was her eighteenth birthday.* And that's when she was – you know.'

'Raped,' said Deborah.

He took a deep breath as he searched for the right words. 'Can you help me, here? If one of those bastards had – had got Esther pregnant, and if she'd had the baby, that would have happened when?'

Deborah did a quick mental calculation. 'Nine months from September, that would be—' She stared at him. 'Oh, my God, Sam! Isn't your mother's birthday in—?'

'June. The 21st. Midsummer's day. My dad always jokes that even he can't forget a date like that.'

She hesitated as if unwilling to ask the question. 'Sam, do you know how old your mother is?'

He knew perfectly well. He almost wished he didn't. He shut his notebook. 'You remember we took them out to dinner on her last birthday? To that restaurant they like in Soho?'

'Of course,' said Deborah. 'And she kept going on about how—'

'About how she couldn't believe she was going to be sixty in just two years' time,' Sam interrupted. 'She even said it to the waiter! At least three times!'

'Which means—'

Sam nodded, biting his lower lip. 'Exactly. She's fifty-eight. So she was born in 1918.' He sat with his head in his hands, trying to absorb the idea and hoping that he could think of a way out.

'You're absolutely sure?' said Deborah. 'There's no chance that…'

Sam shook his head, unable to speak.

Deborah hesitated. 'It's a horrible thing for you to find out, but it can't make any—'

'No! I'm not having that!' Sam jumped up from the bed and walked to the window. The early morning lull had passed and another stormy day was looming. He watched the dark clouds blowing along and heard the angry booming of the sea. He leaned out, took several deep breaths and forced himself to be calm. He brightened as another possibility struck him. 'Maybe she was already – I mean, what if she and my grandfather had already—'

'I'm afraid that's not possible,' said Deborah. 'If Sarah got it right, Ben had been away in the army for about a year, and he was in a hospital somewhere at that time, badly wounded.'

He felt stupid for not thinking of that. But he wasn't ready to give up yet. 'Maybe Sarah got the dates wrong. Who knows? Maybe she made up the whole story. Maybe she's just a dotty old lady who watches too many soaps.'

'Do you honestly believe that?' said Deborah, quietly. 'You're clutching at straws, aren't you?'

He knew she was right, but while there was a single straw left – 'There's another possibility. Maybe Esther had already got it together with Elias Shapiro before this happened. So maybe he's my…' He began to laugh, almost hysterically. 'Maybe Elias, the – what did Sarah call him? The family *schlemiel*? Maybe the Shapiro family *schlemiel* is my real grandfather!'

Deborah gripped both his hands. 'You could hold on to that. At least it would be better than the other possibility.'

He nodded. 'You're right. Because if not him, then my mother's real father – my real grandfather – was one of those scumbags who raped Esther.' He shuddered. 'God! Just the thought makes me feel dirty!'

They sat side by side, hand in hand, the room becoming ever dimmer as the clouds darkened in anticipation of the storm breaking. When Deborah spoke, it was almost as if she'd read his thoughts. 'Do you think Sarah knows this?'

'She must know. After all, how long did it take us to work it out?'

They sat in silence again. Suddenly Sam slapped his forehead. 'My God! If my mum ever found out she's the – the product of a rape, or even the daughter of this Elias schmuck, I don't know what that would do to her. And if she knew that my Grandpa Ben, who she idolised, wasn't her real father—'

'And Eva and Sarah aren't really your great-aunts,' said Deborah.

'And so on,' sighed Sam. 'What a bloody mess!'

'You're sure she doesn't know?' said Deborah. 'You're sure no one ever told her?'

'I'll bet my life on it,' said Sam. 'She doesn't know.'

With a gigantic clap of thunder the storm broke and the rain came down in sheets, hammering against the roof and blowing in the window. Deborah slammed it shut and locked it.

'And she never will,' said Sam. 'Not now there's only you, me and Sarah who know.'

As the first impact of the shock started to pass, he began to think more clearly again. 'I need to know all of it – how everything turned out. I need to find out what happened to Elias. And how come Esther ended up marrying my gra — marrying Ben.'

'Any theories?' said Deborah.

He shrugged. 'Just some guesses.' He looked over his notes again. 'Isaac wanted that marriage because his big money-making plans depended on it. And if we believe Sarah, he had Esther shut away to keep what happened a secret and keep the Shapiros on the hook.'

'So they shut her up in a place no better than a prison,' said Deborah, her voice full of disgust. 'After all she'd been through! That was so cruel! Did she have any choice? Did she even understand what was happening to her? Imagine the state she must have been in!'

'And all for nothing,' said Sam, checking his notes again. 'Because Elias, Sarah said, *broke off the engagement and ran a mile from Esther*. And she ended up marrying piss-poor, war-wounded Ben Symonds. How the hell did that happen?'

'We'll have to ask Sarah,' said Deborah. 'One thing's for sure: in the end, the great Balaboss didn't get his way. And you know what? Serves the bastard right!'

TWENTY

1917

Despite nearing the end of its third year, the ravages of The Great War had made no impact on the luxury of the Rodrigues Club. In its lounge the leather of the sofas was just as supple, the woodwork and brass just as well-polished, the mingled aromas of brandy and cigars just as inviting. Immaculately dressed in evening clothes, his ivory-topped stick as always at his side, Isaac Levinson occupied an armchair in a discreet corner. He instructed an attendant to draw two more armchairs close to his, ordered a balloon of cognac and checked his pocket-watch. 6.50. He smoothed his beard, drawing his hand down both cheeks and under his chin. Julius Shapiro and his son were due in ten minutes and he knew that Julius, at least, was a man who was always on time. The same could not be said for Elias; indeed, little or nothing could be said for Elias. He sipped his cognac. He knew that he must be completely composed when they arrived if he were to get what he wanted. He felt confident. After all, he always got what he wanted.

They arrived on the stroke of seven. Smiling broadly, he rose and greeted them both with a warm, firm handshake. 'Julius, Elias. What a pleasure. It's far too long since we met. Still, these are busy times, eh? Work to be done. For king and country. Money to be made.'

'A pleasure as always to see you,' said Julius, returning the handshake. 'Isaac Levinson – my good friend, my business colleague, and soon to be my relation by marriage. I could not be happier. And neither could you, Elias, eh? Elias!'

Elias had been gazing around the room, his mouth slightly open and the clutched-together fingers of one hand tugging at his lower lip. 'No, Papa, never happier.'

'Come,' said Julius, putting his arm round Isaac's shoulders, 'Let's sit, then you can tell us what's on your mind. Another business proposition I'll be bound!'

Isaac looked from Julius to Elias, and back to Julius. It was hard to believe that they were father and son. The father, friendly and smiling, clearly suspected something and was alert beneath his relaxed exterior. The idiot son was incapable of suspecting anything. Isaac ordered brandy, offered cigars and waited for the completion of the clipping and lighting. 'Now, gentlemen, before we get down to business—'

'How is my fiancée? How is Esther?' interrupted Elias. 'Recovering, I hope? When can I visit?'

Julius put a hand on his son's. 'My apologies, Isaac. In his eagerness to hear news of your dear daughter's recovery he forgets his manners. Please do continue.'

Isaac waved the apology aside and stroked his beard. To have a son like that was nothing short of an affliction. Far better to have no son at all, than one like him. The thought caused him a momentary stab of pain, which he was careful to conceal. 'Please: I understand the impetuosity of youth.' An opening had presented itself. 'And on the subject of impetuosity, I'm afraid I must turn our conversation to an indelicate topic.'

'A necessary one, I presume,' said Julius. 'Please continue.'

Isaac caught an almost imperceptible tensing in Julius' amiable facade, a minute narrowing of his eyes. The man had sensed something and was on his guard. He flicked a quarter-inch of ash from his cigar. 'I need not remind you that some months ago my wife and I sustained a tragic loss.'

Julius nodded gravely and placed a hand over his heart. 'Your dear sons, *olehem hasholom* – may they rest in peace. Heroes and patriots, both.'

'Thank you. And – forgive me – you recall the evening when you and Elias here came to my house to join the *minyan* for prayers?'

'Of course. A *mitzvah* and an honour.'

'Indeed. And you, young man: do you recall my daughter Esther – how shall I put it – entertaining you on that sad occasion?'

Elias fidgeted, shuffled his feet, looked at the carpet and said nothing. Julius replied for him. 'I believe your daughter invited my son to take some refreshment with her in her sitting-room. You're referring to that?'

'I'm referring to that. Yes.' Isaac watched Julius. The man looked perplexed, as he'd hoped. He'd be starting to suspect where this was leading, but he wouldn't believe his son capable of anything of the kind. It was time for his opening gambit. 'I'm sorry to tell you, Julius, that I haven't been entirely honest with you.'

With a flick of the finger Julius signalled to a waiter for brandy refills. 'Really?'

'Julius, this will pain you.'

'Go on.'

Much as Isaac disliked Julius, he had to admire how still and composed he was being, calmly drawing on his cigar, patiently waiting for his adversary's next move. Hopefully this would be the one to shake him out of his near-supercilious serenity. 'My daughter does not have tuberculosis. I arranged for her to be – confined – because she underwent a distressing experience from which she has not yet recovered.'

'Not tuberculosis, then?' said Elias, 'Well, that's jolly good news.'

Julius waved his son to silence and sat still, relaxed, waiting. It was the moment for Isaac to go on the attack. He leaned towards Julius and lowered his voice to a murmur. 'There are no ladies here, so I can be plain. I have to tell you, Julius, that on that occasion, while men were at the very same moment saying *kaddish* for my dear sons downstairs, your son here – how shall I say? – insinuated himself on my daughter.'

'What? I did what?' Elias jumped to his feet. He had gone white and he was trembling. His glass fell to the floor and the brandy pooled onto the carpet. A waiter rushed forward with a cloth but Isaac waved him away.

'Papa, I didn't – I couldn't—'

'You couldn't?' said Julius. He stayed seated and his expression was unchanged. 'But evidently you did.' He emptied his glass. Isaac waited for the inevitable question. 'Exactly what is your daughter's – condition at present?'

He silently shook his head.

'I see.' Julius drew on his cigar, put his head back and blew a slow stream of smoke towards the ceiling, his face still expressionless. Isaac could almost see his mind working.

'Papa,' said Elias, I didn't—'

'Shut up! Not another word!' It was a whispered snarl that carried no further than the necessary few inches. 'You bloody fool! You've let this immigr—' He overcame his momentary loss of control. 'Get out! Go home! Now!'

Elias was in tears as he left. He was shaking so violently that he could hardly walk. Club members turned, tut-tutted and returned to their huddles. Isaac watched him go, stroking his beard and concealing his satisfaction. It was going even better than he'd hoped.

As soon as they were alone, Julius leaned forward in his armchair and gestured to Isaac to do the same, so that their faces were just a few inches from each other. 'Your daughter's pregnant? There's no doubt?'

'No doubt at all,' said Isaac. 'If you want a doctor's confirmation—'

'Pah!' Julius waved away the suggestion. 'But Elias? My son? Are you sure?'

Julius had left a perfect opening for Isaac to become indignant and ask him what precisely he was insinuating, but he decided to hold that in reserve. He sipped his brandy and took a leisurely puff of his cigar. 'It takes ten men for a *minyan*. I hardly need tell you that. As I recall there were at least twenty on that day. So, twenty men saw my daughter and your son mount the stairs in my house. Twenty witnesses, Julius.'

Julius nodded, his face unruffled. He was proving to be a tough adversary, thought Isaac – very nearly a real English gentleman, although unfortunately for him a circumcised one.

'So, Isaac. What do you want?'

The moment of getting down to business had come, as Isaac had known it would. Now was a good time to become indignant. 'Want? Want? Kindly explain yourself!'

Julius inched forward so that the two men's noses were almost touching. 'Let's not waste time, Isaac. What do you want?'

He could smell Julius's perspiration and see the slight sheen on his skin. So he was less composed than he was pretending. He looked directly into Julius' eyes. 'I want your son to marry my daughter.'

Julius laughed, still in an undertone. 'You heard my son deny responsibility for your daughter's – condition?'

He was glad he had held on to the retort. Now was the moment to use it. 'Precisely what are you insinuating? Of course your son denies it! When a child's misdemeanour is discovered, his first thought is always to deny it. And the father's first thought is always to defend him. Especially where family honour is at stake.'

'True,' said Julius. 'Elias is still in many ways a child, and not a handsome or gifted one at that. In a sense I should be relieved to learn that he has such capabilities. But to marry my family to yours in these circumstances? Out of the question.'

Not a bad move, thought Isaac, but he was obviously bluffing – and clumsily. They were still nose-to-nose and speaking in the merest whispers. 'Two questions for you, Julius, if I may?'

Julius raised an expectant eyebrow.

Isaac lifted a forefinger. 'One: where would you hope to find a rich wife for a clumsy fool like your son amongst your own class? Especially when everyone learns what he did to my daughter.' He lifted his thumb. 'Two: how do you hope to deliver the huge contract that you've signed, complete with crippling penalty clauses – oh, yes, I know about those – without someone who has the factories, the cheap workforce and the skills all ready to hand? For both of those, you've had to hold your nose and come to – what did you just call me? – the immigrant. Do you think you can do without the immigrant now?'

Isaac sat back in his armchair, stroking his beard, waiting for Julius' move, confidently anticipating the proximity of check mate. Julius too leaned back, his expression still implacable. To an observer they would have looked like any two club members luxuriating in their deep leather armchairs, smoking their cigars, discussing business and perhaps planning to dine together. Isaac allowed himself a complacent smile. Who would end up clearing the board: the smooth, pseudo-English gentleman Jew, or the rough Whitechapel immigrant? He had no doubt of the outcome. He was confident who would get the upper hand.

The grandfather clock in the vestibule struck eight. From the dining-room came the aromas of the evening's chicken, beef, lamb and fish dishes. The first few members were starting to leave their conversations and their newspapers and go in to dinner. Julius was sunk in his armchair with his eyes closed and his hands palm down on his thighs, immobile except for a minute drumming of his fingertips. Tired of waiting and starting to feel stiff from sitting for so long, Isaac stood up and stretched. Julius's eyes sprang open and he too stood up. Without looking at Isaac he signalled to an attendant to bring his hat, coat and stick. Only when he had put them on did he turn to face Isaac. He seemed in no hurry to speak. Isaac luxuriated in the wait. The man knew he was beaten. He just didn't know how to say it. The silence between the two men stretched out. Isaac was the first to lose patience. 'Well?'

Without taking his gaze from Isaac, Julius slowly pulled on his gloves. 'No.'

Isaac narrowed his eyes. This was not — 'What – no?'

Julius patted his skullcap and put his hat on over it. 'Elias won't marry your daughter. I don't believe for one moment that he would have had the courage to touch her. I'm sure he doesn't even know how it's done. So, no. I suggest you find the real perpetrator and make the same proposition to him – if you know which one it was.'

'*Vas? Du ferkakteh mamzer!*' The blood rushed into Isaac's eyes. He took a step towards Julius and raised his stick. Julius did not flinch. His voice did not tremor. 'If you do that, you'll be blackballed for life. You'll never set foot in here again. Look around you, Isaac. Look at my twenty witnesses.'

Isaac lowered the stick. He had to regain control of the situation. 'And when I tell your friends what Elias did? What reputation will he have left? Or you?'

Julius strolled towards the door. The concierge opened it for him. 'And if you do that, what reputation will your daughter have left? No, I don't think you'll try that. Good night.' Isaac tasted bile in his mouth. His heart was racing. Everything was slipping away. 'And the contract?' he called after Julius's retreating back, 'Don't forget you still need me for that!'

'Perhaps. Perhaps not,' said Julius without turning, 'We'll see.' The concierge closed the door behind him.

TWENTY-ONE

At eight o'clock on a cold, wet November evening, Mendel Symonds, head cutter and foreman at Koslov Fashions in Greatorex Street,wished his machinists and pressers good night in vulgarity-peppered Whitechapel Yiddish, checked that the gaslights were out and double-locked the doors. In Brick Lane the shops were closing up and the stall-holders were selling the last of their wares by the light of guttering paraffin lamps. Mendel was tired and hungry. With this terrible war now well into its third year, prices were rising all the time and often there were shortages. Yesterday, when his wife Anna had bought a chicken, and not a very big one at that, Krafchik the poultryman had charged her so much that she could only afford eight eggs in place of the usual dozen. Still, Anna was a genius at making a chicken and a few vegetables stretch to feed the whole family, so he was sure there'd be a good dinner waiting for him.

It had been a long day, but no longer than he was used to. The two-room sweatshop that was Koslov Fashions had given him a living of sorts for more than twenty years, since he and Anna had first arrived in London. Isaac Levinson had given him his first job there and later put him in charge. Mendel wasn't a man to nurse a grudge, but the bitterness welled up in him when he remembered how Isaac, his friend from the old country, had started looking down on him as soon as he'd made a little money. He clenched his fists as he thought of the night Isaac had come to his house and humiliated him in front of his wife and children. Threatened him. With sacking. With eviction. With blackballing. Threatened his son. 'So what,' he'd tried to tell him, 'so what if my Ben and your Esther like each other? Ben's a good boy. Where's the harm?' But no, Isaac talked about his Ben like he was some kind of farm animal. As if Ben needed just a sniff of his precious Esther and straight away he'd start *shtupping* her. 'Keep him away from her,' Isaac had said, 'or else.' Or else! A few quid and a top hat, and he's a changed man. Dead inside. A golem.

Mendel uttered a minor curse under his breath and walked on, still lost in his thoughts. At least – he raised his eyes skyward – at least thank God his Ben had come home to him. And Isaac's sons, they never would. Whatever he was, Mendel pitied the man for that. But he wanted no more trouble for his family. Please God, now his Ben was home, Isaac should keep his daughter Esther far away from Ben and he'd keep Ben just as far from her. Between the Symonds and the Levinsons there was nothing any more. It was finished for good.

Anna Symonds, small, grey-haired and dark-eyed, was waiting for him in front of the closed door of their living-room. The delicious smell of chicken soup pervaded the landing. His mood lifted as he put his arms round her and kissed her on the lips. 'Anna Lohmann, after twenty-five years and all we've lived through, I love you just like when we first kissed on the banks of the Villya.'

She smiled and returned the kiss, but he sensed the tension in her. 'What is it? Is it Ben? How was it at the hospital today? Has he been bleeding again?'

She smoothed her hair and straightened her apron. 'No, thank God. The doctor said the wound's closing up. But three more months at least it needs, maybe more. With bayonets, he said, there's the *kishkas* to think about. For them it takes longer.'

'God willing, he'll get better in time,' said Mendel. 'Shall we go inside now? Are Eva and Fanny home? I'm hungry. Is dinner ready?'

He moved to open the door, but Anna stood in his way. 'We have to talk.'

'So talk, I'm listening,' said Mendel, smiling. 'Then can we eat?'

'Isaac Levinson was here.'

Mendel's smile froze. 'When?'

'An hour ago.'

'Did he make trouble? Was he rude to you? What did he want?'

'He was polite. Respectful. He wants to see you.'

Mendel started taking off his coat. 'He can see me any day at the workshop. What's so special, he has to come here where he knows he's not welcome?'

Anna clutched his lapels. 'He wants to see you at his house. Tonight, he said. As soon as you get home. "Ask him please to come," he said. "As my guest."'

Mendel burst out laughing. 'Anna, is this Purim? Is this a joke you're playing? That *mamzer* said please? As his guest? Never in his life!'

'On my life, Mendel. No joke. Something to discuss, he said.'

The laugh died. He smacked his hand against his forehead. 'God in heaven, he's going to sack me! He's going to throw us out! Just like he threatened!' He slid down the wall and sat on the floor, his hat pushed back and his head in his hands. 'Not like a *mensch* he can't come to my work and tell me to my face. He wants me to go crawling to his house. Well, I won't go. Let him come to me.'

Anna sat down next to him and stroked his hair. 'Mendel, you should go. Stand up to him. Show him who's the real *mensch*. We'll manage. Eva's earning a little bit at that theatre. Fanny's fourteen now. She can leave school and look for work. I've got my sewing. You go. Stand up to him. Then come home and we'll have chicken soup. With *lokshen*. And with the giblets in, just how you like it.'

Mendel kissed Anna's cheek and stood up. 'You're a

wonderful woman. I'll go, and I'll tell him what I think of him.' He turned back at the top of the staircase. 'Did you say, with giblets?'

'Naturally, with giblets.'

'And matzoh balls?'

'Chicken soup without matzoh balls? God forbid.'

*

Delaying only long enough to wash his hands and face and put on a clean shirt, Mendel set out along Brick Lane, down Hanbury Street and across Commercial Street, to Elder Street where the Levinson family lived. He felt a new surge of anger as he looked up at the house. Two floors with three beautiful big windows on each one, a basement underneath, and sitting on top an attic with even more windows. Twelve families – more – could live in such a house and they wouldn't even have to look at each other. There were that many families living at 59 Old Montague Street, a house less than half this size with one privy in the yard and one tap on each landing. That was how his family lived, after twenty-three years breaking his back in this wonderful new country. And now he was going to be sacked. Well, before leaving tonight he was going to have his say.

On the panelled front door was a brass knocker in the shape of a lion's head. He knocked twice and tried his hardest to control the anger that was surging through him. A woman in a grey dress and a grey headscarf opened the door.

'You'll be Mr Symonds? This way, please.'

God in heaven, the man had servants! He wondered how many.

The woman led him across a parquet-floored hall, knocked on a door and motioned him to go in. The room was high-ceilinged, warm and deeply carpeted, and it smelled of cigars. Facing him was a writing-desk in front of a tall window hung with maroon velvet curtains. Isaac Levinson stood with his back to a coal fire, stroking his beard. Above the fireplace was a photographic portrait of a younger, black-haired and black-bearded Isaac, posing in front of a painted Grecian temple and holding the familiar ivory-handled stick.

Isaac approached Mendel with a broad smile, his hand outstretched.

'Mendel! My friend! Do come in. Tell me, how long is it since we've sat down together and talked over old times?'

His friend? Old times? Mendel kept his hands by his sides, his fists clenched. 'You said come. So I came.'

'Of course, of course. And I'm grateful. Please, sit. Be at home. A brandy? A cigar, maybe?'

'Brandy. No cigar.' Mendel sat on the edge of a chair, his anger mounting. The *mamzer* was playing with him, the cat tormenting the mouse before the kill. Any minute now he'd end the game and kick him out jobless. Well, the sooner that happened, the sooner he could say his piece and go home to his family and his supper.

'Tell me,' said Isaac, 'how is your son Ben? You must be overjoyed to have him back with you. Are those wounds healing nicely?'

Ben, who Isaac had threatened to have beaten and blackballed? This man was more than a *mamzer*. He was pure shit. 'He's doing well, *kaynahorah*. They sent him home a month ago. Discharged from the army. He won't have to go back, thank God.'

'God is good. To some,' murmured Isaac.

Despite everything, Mendel felt some compassion. The man was a *dreck*, yes, but still he was human. Two sons within a few days? *Nisht duggedacht*! 'I know. I should have wished you long life. A tragic loss for you. And for your poor Millie also.'

Isaac sighed. 'God's will. What can we do?' He turned away and brushed a hand over his eyes. Mendel waited, looking at the portrait over the fireplace. The photographer had posed Isaac to look like a lord in his manor. To Mendel it was a picture of the jumped-up Balaboss gloating over his ghetto kingdom.

Isaac turned back to Mendel. 'Mendel my friend, I believe I owe you an apology.'

An apology, *noch*? Mendel said nothing. He sipped his brandy and waited.

'Two years ago I came to your house and I behaved disgracefully. Do you remember?'

Remember? It was burned into his memory. 'I must have forgotten, Isaac. Can you remind me?'

Isaac stroked his beard and seemed to be deciding how to proceed. Mendel gripped the stem of his enormous brandy glass, the contents as yet untouched. There was a tap on the door and the woman who had shown him in scurried to the fireplace with a coal scuttle. The two men sat silently while she topped up the fire, poked it into flames and left, closing the door softly behind her. Isaac topped up his brandy glass from a decanter and drank most of it off in one go. Mendel watched and took note. Isaac had many faults, but heavy drinking had never been one of them. Something was troubling him. Surely he wouldn't need Dutch courage to sack a common worker, a nobody?

Isaac drew his chair closer to Mendel. 'Old friend, I'm telling you that I feel shame for my behaviour, and I want to know how I can make amends.' He drained his glass and re-filled it. 'But first, your son Ben – how are his injuries mending?'

How cruel this man was, using Ben's injuries as a tool in his cat-and-mouse game. Well, if he really wanted to know – 'Mending? A bayonet deep in the belly. Damage to his *kishkas*. Infection that nearly killed him. A month in a Belgian hospital, three in an English one. Stitches in him, God knows how many, and bandages my wife, bless her, changes three times every day. But at least he's not bleeding so much lately, thank God.'

'Thank God,' repeated Isaac. 'So he won't be able to work for some time?'

The axe was about to fall. 'No, Isaac. There's only my money coming into the house, with the little bit Eva can bring in, and Fanny too if she can find work.' It sickened him to beg, but he had to try for his family's sake. He felt the bile rising up. He fought it down and drank a mouthful of brandy. 'Isaac, please, I need to keep that—'

Isaac laughed. 'Mendel, I want to help you!'

What was this, another cruel game? Isaac was watching him, his expression serious. He drank another mouthful and took comfort in the heat of the brandy. 'Help me? Don't make me—'

'Your son will need money so he can keep himself until he's well enough to work again. I'll see to that.'

Mendel shook his head. He wasn't going to give Isaac the satisfaction of falling for his trickery. 'It's my family, it's my resp—'

'And with what I've been paying you, it must be hard for you to make ends meet. I'm expecting a new contract. Not as big as I had hoped, but big nevertheless. It will mean more work for you. Better work. And of course, more money.'

Mendel could feel the brandy mingling with the juices in his empty stomach. He thought furiously. There must be a catch, but he couldn't see it. Maybe, who knows, the loss of his sons had changed the man – made him want to do *mitzvahs* so God wouldn't punish him any more. Isaac held out the decanter to Mendel with a raised eyebrow. He nodded and drank from the re-filled glass, staying alert, waiting.

'As I said, Mendel, on that occasion I behaved disgracefully. Foolishly, I disapproved of the bond of affection that had grown up between Esther and Ben. I had, shall we say, intentions for her that did me no credit.

Esther has helped me to see that I did wrong to her, to Ben and to you. I want to make amends.'

Mendel's head was starting to spin and the brandy was burning in his stomach. 'Isaac, what are you telling me? You're not giving me the sack?'

With a guffaw, Isaac slapped Mendel on the back. 'Give you the sack? I'm offering you a better job, better wages, and a sum of money – call it a loan if it makes you feel better – to tide Ben over until he can start working again. And, above all, I won't stand in the way of our children's friendship. In fact, I'll encourage it.'

Isaac re-filled both glasses again, stood up and switched from English to the Yiddish dialect of Smorgon. 'Come, old friend. Let's say *lechaim*. If everything goes to plan, you and your family have a happy future to look forward to. I'll see to that.'

With great difficulty, Mendel stood up to drink the toast. His stomach was on fire and his head was floating on a sea of brandy and confusion. God had opened the door to a better future for him and his family. And God had chosen the most unlikely of messengers to do his work. Tears of gratitude came to his eyes. But as Isaac's words sank in, he was suddenly on his guard again. 'To plan, Isaac? To what plan, exactly?'

Isaac waved an unsteady hand. 'Did I say to plan? What I mean to say is…' He took another gulp of brandy. 'Mendel, I want nothing more than to see those two young people married.'

No! No! This was some sort of wicked joke. Mendel looked into Isaac's eyes but he saw no hint of humour there, just the familiar coldness. Like two chips of flint, he thought. 'You mean a *shidduch*? Are you telling me we make a *shidduch* for our children, like in the old country? Is that what's happening?'

'Call it that – a *shidduch*,' said Isaac. His speech was starting to slur, but his eyes were still sharp and cold. He put an arm around Mendel's shoulders, the smell of cologne and cigars a reminder of the distance between them and the need for him to keep looking for the trap. 'Once Ben's my son-in-law he'll never have to worry about money again. And neither will you. Your family will have a good life. Your daughters will make good marriages. How does that sound?'

Mendel sank back into his chair. So there was no catch! The man was serious after all! 'Isaac, how can I ever thank you?'

Isaac sat down, looked at Mendel and stroked his beard. 'Mendel, to be honest, there is one small thing.'

TWENTY-TWO

Ben Symonds was not in the mood for good manners. He hammered repeatedly on the lion-headed knocker until Isaac Levinson, wearing slippers and a purple silk dressing-gown, opened the door a few inches.

'Ben Symonds. Good morning. We're still at breakfast but come in.'

'I want to talk to you.' Ben shoved the door open, causing Isaac to stagger backwards, and pushed past him into the hall. He stopped and bent slightly forward, pressing his hand hard against his stomach as a jagged pain shot through him.

Isaac righted himself and adjusted his skullcap. 'The army has made a man of you, Ben. How is your recovery coming along?'

'Never mind that. You gave my father the sack. You had no business to do that! I want you to give him his job back.'

'Come into my study and sit down,' said Isaac. 'We'll talk there.'

Ben followed Isaac into the room and sat facing him across his desk. On it was a silver tray with pens and an inkwell, a supply of notepaper and a small handbell. Three silver picture frames faced towards Isaac.

'Now,' said Isaac. 'What brings you here, so early and so angry?'

Ben tried to keep his temper under control. He had to be firm with this man he despised so much, while not forgetting that he was powerful and could even be dangerous. So far, he had to admit, the man had at least been polite. 'Twenty years, my father works for you. Twenty years! Then you sack him like he's a nothing!'

'Does he know you've come here?' asked Isaac.

'No. He's a proud man.'

'He didn't tell you why I sacked him?'

'What difference? You did it because you're the *ganzer macher*. The Balaboss.'

Isaac leaned across the desk. 'Yes, I'm the Balaboss. But Mendel Symonds is better off than me. He has a son. I have no sons.' He turned two frames to face Ben.

Ben shrugged. 'So? Some of us came back, some didn't. That's not my fault.'

'No, not your fault,' said Isaac. He turned the photos back. 'He really didn't tell you why I sacked him? Shall I tell you?'

Ben shook his head. 'Don't bother. Just put it right and I'll go.'

'I might do that,' said Isaac, smiling. 'You could make me.'

Ben saw neither warmth nor sincerity in the smile. He tried to keep the contempt from his voice. 'So do it. Don't play games with me.'

Isaac sat back and put his hands behind his head. 'First, let me ask you something. Last night, before I sacked your father, I offered him a better job, more money, and help for you until you could work again. He turned me down. Threw it back in my face. That's why I sacked him. Did he tell you that?'

Ben jumped to his feet and slammed his fist on the desk. 'You bloody liar!' The pain sliced through him again and he doubled up.

Isaac gestured Ben to sit back down. 'You learned those manners in the trenches, I suppose. No, I'm not lying to you. It's the truth. Why don't you go home and ask him?'

Ben stared at Isaac, struggling to make sense of what he'd heard.

'Don't you want to know why your papa did that?' asked Isaac. 'Said no to everything I wanted to do for him?'

Ben clenched his teeth to fight off a growing feeling of nausea. 'I'm listening.'

'I'll be direct with you, Ben. I have a problem. I asked your papa to help me solve it, but he didn't feel that he could. If you help me solve it, your papa will get his job back and everything I offered.'

Ben laughed. 'Me, fix a problem for you? In my state? You've got your *shtarkers,* haven't you?'

'That's true. But it's not that sort of problem.' Isaac turned the third photo frame towards Ben. He stared at the image. For sure, it was Esther standing between her parents, but dressed like he'd never seen her. A bit of nothing with short sleeves and lots of lace, and showing nearly everything she'd got. He felt his face and ears redden. They had pictures of girls like that in the trenches. He'd been a couple of times with his mates to those places in Arras. But Esther?

Isaac pushed the photo closer towards him. 'She was fifteen then. And already beautiful, no? She's eighteen now. You should see her now.'

Ben tore his eyes from the photo and looked straight into Isaac's. 'But I won't, will I? You said what you'll do if I go near her again.'

Isaac put his hand on his heart and bent his head in supplication. 'I know. A terrible thing, I did. I was wrong. Last night I told your papa I was sorry. I asked him to forgive me. Ben, will you forgive me?'

Ben stared at Isaac. Losing his sons must have made the man go mad. On top of being a *mamzer* and a crook, now he was a lunatic. But still, maybe that would help. It was worth a try.

'If I say I forgive you, you'll give Papa back his job? Just like that?'

'Just like that.'

'Good. So I forgive you.' He stood up. 'I'll go home and tell Papa the news.'

'Wait,' said Isaac. 'Wait just a minute.' He took the handbell from his desk and rang it. 'Please sit down. Just for a minute.'

Another minute, what difference? Even now, he found it impossible to read anything in Isaac's eyes. He seemed to have a way of hardening them; of shielding them so that they were opaque, like the birds of prey that he'd seen picking at carcasses in no-man's land.

The study door opened and there stood Esther, nicely dressed now and looking more beautiful than he'd ever dreamed. In the trenches, and later in the hospitals, he'd tried again and again to bring her face to mind, to hold it behind his closed eyes where he could keep it safe. As time passed, it had become ever fainter, so that he'd had to re-imagine it over and over again. He'd never told her, or anyone else, how much he loved her. He'd been sure he'd never see her again. He was most likely going to die, and even if he didn't, Isaac had made it plain: he had plans for her, and poor Whitechapel boys like him had no place in them. But now Isaac was smiling and nodding at the two of them. It must be his imagination. That would explain it. He was delirious, still lying on a stretcher in that bombed-out church somewhere on the Menin Bridge Road near Ypres, clinging onto his last shred of life.

'Hello, Ben.'

It really was her. Glossy dark hair down to her shoulders, beautiful brown eyes, and a smile that made you feel like you were the only person in the world that mattered to her. She held out her hand in greeting, but as he stood up and took it in his, she moved closer and offered her cheek for a kiss. He glanced at Isaac, who carried on smiling and nodding, and shyly brushed his lips against her cheek.

'Come and sit down again, Ben,' said Isaac. 'You too, Esther.' He sat back behind the desk. Ben looked sideways at Esther and she smiled back at him. He felt a momentary shiver. It must have been his imagination, but he thought he'd seen the light in her eyes shut off for a second, and something else take its place. He wasn't sure what it was, or if he'd really seen it. He turned his attention to Isaac, and when he looked again she was smiling at him as brightly as before.

'Ben,' began Isaac, 'I know you are very fond of Esther. Am I right?'

He sensed danger. 'I didn't come here to—'

'And you, Esther, you've made me understand how wrong I've been to try to keep you two apart. Am I right?'

'Yes, Papa.' Esther slid her hand into his and before realising it he'd automatically closed his fingers over hers.

'Ben, you know that I've lost my boys. I need a son and heir. It would please me to see you and Esther marry. You'll have my blessing. Esther has told me that nothing would make her happier. Haven't you, Esther?'

'Yes, Papa.'

He felt her squeezing his hand, but he'd had this fantasy so many times before, he couldn't be sure what was real and what wasn't. Maybe the stretcher-bearers had given him too much morphine. It must be that. But it felt real enough. So maybe – just maybe she really had always loved him, and with Joel and Nathan killed, the old *mamzer* had softened up and given in to her. But something he saw, or thought he saw, troubled him. Minute glances kept passing between her and her father. Her eyes flicked towards her father each time she spoke, and now and again there was a tiny signal in response; a movement of the head, a flutter of an eyebrow. He shook off the feeling of unease. Because of what he'd been through, he saw enemies and evil intentions everywhere. But there was none of that here. His life was about to change for the better. 'You really mean we could get married?' he said. Again, he intercepted the momentary silent exchange.

'That is what I want. And it's also what Esther wants,' boomed Isaac. 'You both have my blessing.'

'And Papa gets his job back?'

'That, and much more,' said Isaac. 'That is what I offered him last night, and that is what he refused. But now that you've agreed to the match yourself—'

'The match?' Suddenly Ben understood. 'You tried to agree a *shidduch* with my father? In return for his job? He knew that was wrong, so he turned you down! So you sacked him – is that it?' His laughter set off another agonising jolt of pain. 'For God's sake, this is 1917! You're in England! You think you're still in some stinking *shtetl* where you can play God?'

Something passed again between Isaac and Esther, and this time Ben thought he caught the meaning. 'Put it right', the look was saying. 'Calm him down.'

'Don't be angry, Ben,' said Esther. 'Papa wants to help us, that's all.'

His head swam. She was winning him over. He regretted his outburst. But still, something wasn't right. He looked at Isaac, watching him, stroking his beard. Maybe the old *gonif* was just being honest for once in his life. But he wasn't just giving in, he was falling over himself to get them together. Why? It didn't make sense. And why hadn't Papa told him or Mama the reason for Isaac sacking him?

Isaac was still watching him, still stroking his beard. 'Come on, Ben. Why hesitate?'

Isaac was right. Why hesitate? He loved Esther, Papa would be well-off and so would he. He'd have this *dreck* as a father-in-law, but how would that be so terrible? 'Esther,' he said, 'do you really want this?'

'Yes, Ben.' She smiled, first at her father and only then at him. This time he knew what he'd seen, but it made no sense. He'd seen fear in men's eyes often enough. Just for a moment, watching her, he thought – but outside, it was an unusually bright November morning, and the light from the window was shining straight in at him. He shrugged the feeling off. Before he could say anything else Esther gently took her hand from his, and as if by some pre-arranged signal slipped out of the room.

'Come over to the fire,' said Isaac. 'Take a chair. We have to discuss some details.' He left his desk and sat down in one of the fireside armchairs. Ben followed his example and looked up at the portrait on the chimney breast.

'You like it?' asked Isaac. 'A fiftieth birthday present from my wife.'

'Very nice,' said Ben. 'I didn't know they made photos that big.'

'These days everything is possible,' said Isaac. 'I'll have a miniature copy made for you as an engagement present.'

A photo of Isaac Levinson to shlep round. Such a present he could do without. 'Thank you, I'd like that.'

'Good. I'll see to it.' Again, Ben saw his eyes become opaque. He thought again about the birds of prey. He'd watched one pecking out the eyes of a dead soldier caught on the wire.

Isaac opened a glass-fronted cabinet and took out a box of cigars. He selected one and held out the open box to Ben. He shook his head and waited while Isaac clipped the cigar, lit it, and took the first few puffs.

'There is something you need to know,' said Isaac softly, almost gently. Ben knew that tone of voice. It was the one the officers used when they told you to write to your mother and your sweetheart before going over the top. 'So tell me.'

'About Esther.'

'Go on.'

Isaac took out a handkerchief and held it close to his eyes. 'I know now that it was wrong, but I was thinking of her. I – introduced her to the son of a business friend – a rich one.'

'So?'

'They became engaged to be married. It was a terrible mistake. Neither of us liked him very much. But she thought she was doing it for me, and I thought it was what she really wanted.'

'Was this when I was away? In the army?'

'Yes.'

'So, what happened?'

There was a knock on the door and the servant appeared with the coal scuttle. 'Get out!' snapped Isaac. The door closed behind her.

'So, what happened?' repeated Ben.

Isaac looked down at the floor, up at Ben and back down at the floor. 'The man took advantage of my daughter's innocence. He came here, to my house, and – insinuated himself on her. And then he broke off the engagement.' He looked directly into Ben's eyes. 'I thought you should know this. I have Esther's permission.'

So that was it. He'd known there was something. A man had had her. But so what? In his parents' time, a terrible thing. But these days – he hesitated. 'Was it just the once?'

Isaac nodded. 'Yes. Just the once.'

Ben pressed down on his midriff as he pulled himself out of the armchair and offered Isaac his hand. 'That doesn't change anything. I'm so happy, I can't start to – I'll go home now and tell my parents all the news. They'll be—'

Isaac interrupted him with a raised hand. 'Not yet. Our conversation isn't quite over. There is another – detail, an important one, to settle before my business with you is concluded. Please sit down again.'

'Your business with me?' Suddenly Ben understood. He freed his hand from Isaac's grip. 'From that one time – she's pregnant, isn't she?'

Isaac nodded.

Ben felt an overwhelming wish to put his hands around Isaac's neck. The urge to kill, instilled in him by means of brutal, rigorous training, was threatening to return. He fought the feeling away before it could control his actions and jabbed an angry finger at Isaac as he spoke. 'Of course! Now I see it! No more posh husband for her, not now she's up the spout! But the Balaboss can't be having a bastard on his hands for everyone to see. No, not him! So he's got to get her married, and bloody quick. And never mind who to! Any poor bastard'll do, so long as he needs the money and he'll keep his mouth shut! Me, for instance!'

He felt a different kind of pain as the truth hit him with a jolt. 'And she – she went along with it! She was…all the time…when I thought…but only after you gave her a few good hidings, I'll bet! Am I right?'

Isaac sat motionless, his eyes as cold as ever.

Ben strode to the door and wrenched it open. 'You lowlife! So that's why suddenly I'm good enough for you! You really think I'll go along with that? Marry her and pretend to be the father, just to help you out? After you threatened to take away my father's job and my family's living?'

Isaac studied the glowing tip of his cigar. 'Yes, I think you'll go along with it. Think of it as a business deal. A good one. You'll do well out of it, I'll see to that. What do you say?'

Ben stood in the open doorway, looking out to the hall where the servant was on her reddened knees in a puddle of soapy water, sleeves rolled up, scrubbing the floor. He looked back over his shoulder at Isaac sitting at his desk in his silk dressing-gown, savouring his cigar. The pain from his wound was more intense than ever. He held onto the door for support and uttered a low moan. The servant looked up at him and for a few seconds their eyes met before he turned and walked back into the room.

TWENTY-THREE

1976

Deborah had gone. They'd enjoyed a loving last few weeks, and there had been a tender parting that they'd assured each other was temporary. Sam was sad to see her go, but her presence would still be all around him. She'd taken one suitcase and left everything else in place, just as if she'd gone out for the day. She wasn't there, but it was still their home – at least for now. He did his best to stave off his feelings of utter misery, desperate to believe that she'd come back but having to face up to the likelihood that she never would.

The day after she left, he looked in on Eleni and found that she had everything perfectly under control and was more than happy to spin out her temporary promotion, so he called Gordon and got him to agree to extend his time off by another fortnight. He took to organising his days around the time he spent with Esther, bringing her titbits to tempt her appetite and making sure that she was as comfortable as possible. She showed him no more photographs and he asked her no more questions about her past, for fear of stirring up painful memories. Her temper was as short, her manner as cantankerous as ever. But in those welcome moments when she'd grip his hand, or smile at him when he'd straighten a pillow or tell her about incidents in his daily life, he felt that a definite bond was growing up between them. Now he looked forward to the part of each day when he could spend time with her. Despite the pain of seeing her decline he experienced a sense of pleasure when he was with her, as with a new-found friend.

Sometimes his drop-ins coincided with visits from Anna. Occasionally they'd leave together and go for a coffee and chat for half an hour. During these times she'd be friendly and relax her professional manner a little. He enjoyed her company. At her suggestion they went together to meet Esther's district nurse, who confirmed what he'd already known: there was very little time left. Now she should be in a hospice so that she could be properly cared for, but she was still refusing to go.

The rest of the time he stayed home, playing his LPs and working on the journal he'd started, going back to when Ron Green had dropped from nowhere into his life. He tried to put into order every detail he'd written in his notebook and held in his memory, hoping to piece together an account of all that he'd learned about his grandmother and the world she'd lived in. It was a frustrating task, like trying to do a jigsaw with half the pieces missing. Every time he sat down to write, memories, fragments and images that defied being ordered crowded into his mind. Time and again the words would run away and hide from him, or refuse to make sense. In time a picture started to emerge, but it was still an unreliable story with shaky foundations, an uncertain beginning and an unknowable end.

He hadn't seen his parents or been in touch with them for a month or more. What with that, and with Deborah gone, despite his growing attachment to Esther he'd never in his whole life felt so totally alone – not even in the worst of times. He was struggling to prevent himself from slipping into the kind of deep depression that he knew of old. He could recognise the warning symptoms only too well: the anxiety, the feelings of panic, the dark thoughts that prevented sleep from coming – the endless revisiting of all the things he'd messed up in his life: the mistakes, the betrayals, the failures, the misjudgements and wrong choices. And when sleep did come, so did the old familiar nightmares. He was missing Deborah terribly. In desperation he reached into his mind, trying to hear her voice. He knew she'd have been able to tell him what he should do.

*

He counted twelve rings and still no one answered. Now he knew what it meant, to say your heart was in your mouth. After the seventeenth ring he heard his mother's voice.

'Mum?' Silence. 'Mum, it's me.'

'So it's you. Hello, stranger.'

Be like Deborah. Be calm. Be direct. 'I know you've been broygus with me, Mum, and I'm sorry. Could I come and see you? Would that be okay?'

'Me? Broygus? Who says so? Who've you been talking to?'

He should have known. Sadie Shaykin would always keep you guessing. His heart rate started to slow. 'So I can come and see you? And Dad?'

'Sam, are you *meshuggeh*? It's your mother you're talking to. Are you at work?'

'No, I've taken some time off.'

'So come today. Come this afternoon.' Some rustling, muttering, a chair scraping. 'Your father wants to talk to you.'

Jack Shaykin's voice came on the line. 'Son? Are you coming?'

'Yes, Dad. A couple of hours from now, would that be okay?

'To see your father you've got to make an appointment now? Since when?'

*

Sadie's welcoming hug and cheek-kisses were more prolonged than usual. 'Your father's in the lounge,' she said. 'I'll make tea.'

Jack turned off the television, grasped Sam's shoulder and shook his hand. 'Hello, Son. Come and sit down.'

Sam had always liked this room. For him, everything in it was a tribute to his parents' years of hard work and thrift, and their rock-solid determination to use their meagre income to build a good life for themselves and for him. Aside from a few TV upgrades, nothing had changed since his childhood. A Dansette record-player and a row of LPs occupied two shelves of a G-Plan wall-unit. On a third shelf were the family photos, with pride of place given to the twenty-year-old Sam looking solemn in his graduation cap and gown. He picked up the familiar sepia-tinted photo next to his own and looked at it with new interest. It was his grandfather Ben, looking into the camera with an expression that Sam tried to fathom: quizzical, possibly; a little guarded, perhaps. As if he was looking back at his grandson, knowing that he'd learned his secrets. The severely brushed-back hair and the wide-lapelled three-piece suit gave him an air of maturity, but the eyes were those of a younger man. Gentle, Sam thought. And tired. And hurt.

His father was watching him. As a child, when he was trying to hide or deny some naughtiness, his father would say, 'Son, I can read you like a book.' If he knew what he was thinking right now, he thought, he'd have a heart attack. The questions that he'd been turning over in his mind for days and sleepless nights started their round again: would he tell them what he knew? Should he? Or would knowing it hurt them so much that he should keep silent? Was it right to know such things about your own mother and keep them secret from her? His throat was dry and his heart was racing. He knew the symptoms. A panic attack was looming.

'Are you all right, Son?' said Jack, 'you've come over pale.'

'I'm fine, Dad. Just a bit of indigestion. Takeaway curry last night.'

Jack laughed. 'Serves you right. Don't let your mother know you eat that *pishachs*.'

Sam put the photo back in its place and picked up a favourite of his: a younger Jack and Sadie taken at a family wedding. They were smartly dressed and smiling happily, raising full wine glasses towards the camera.

'Here we are.' Sadie brought in tea and cake on a tray and sat beside Jack on the plumb-coloured sofa. Sam took an armchair and sat facing them.

'Are you warm enough, Sadie?' asked Jack. 'Shall I put the gas fire on?'

'I'm warm enough,' said Sadie. 'Are you warm enough, Sammy?'

Sam nodded. There was a silence. Jack bit into a slice of cake, drank some of his tea and cleared his throat. 'So, how do you think the Arsenal are doing this—?'

Sadie started with impatience and poked him with her elbow. 'Jack! Talk to him already!'

Jack sighed, put his cup down and took his wife's hand. 'Son, your mother and me, we want to know. What you said. About – that woman – we don't understand why you—'

'Dad,' Sam interrupted, 'I've already told you. What happened that night, how I behaved, I'm sorry. I was having—'

His father raised a hand. 'Never mind about that. What you said, about…' He looked sideways at Sadie, who had balled up a handkerchief and was pushing it against her mouth. '…about Esther Symonds—' Sam saw his mother shudder and push the handkerchief up under her glasses. 'And what you told me – about you finding her, going to see her, asking questions – you should know what this is doing to your mother – to us.'

Jack put his arm round Sadie while her tears flowed. He patted her hand for a minute, then gently took the wet, crumpled handkerchief from her fingers and gave her his own. She dried her eyes, blew her nose and gazed at Sam. 'You think your mother's *meshuggeh,* you think I don't know? Those things you said to your father, how I stopped you having a *bubbeh,* how I made up stories about…about my…is that what you believe?'

Sam shook his head. 'Mum, I don't know what to believe, and that's the truth.'

Sadie seemed to be making a huge effort to speak. She was clutching Jack's hand and trembling.

'When you were little I told you things when maybe better I should keep *shtum.* I see that now. But how come you think you're so hard done by? I've spoiled your life with my *kvetches,* you have to go running to that woman? Is that it?'

'It's not like that, Mum,' said Sam. 'I didn't go looking for her. How could I, when I didn't even know she was alive? Let me tell you how it happened.'

'Don't bother with that,' said Jack. 'It's done now. Your mother and me, we talked about it, and we know we should never have let you think she was dead. We see now that was wrong. Don't we, Sadie?'

Sadie gave the slightest of nods.

'And we've decided there are things you should know,' Jack went on. 'So that, please God, then you'll understand.'

Outside, darkness was falling. It was getting to the time of year when the cold could penetrate the windowpanes. Sadie put her teacup on the tray and stood up to draw the curtains. She sat back close to Jack and took his hand again. Sam watched as she closed her eyes, as if conjuring up pictures in her mind's eye.

'I want you should know…should understand…what it was like for me. So you won't think I'm just a – a – a neurotic, or something.'

'Mum, that thought never—'

Sadie silenced him with a look. 'What I remember from a little girl, is the rows. A temper that woman had on her! I was so scared I used to hide and cover my ears. Under my bed sometimes, or there was a wardrobe in the hall, so big I could get inside. This is how your mother grew up.'

The handkerchief again. Sam could see the effort that telling the story was going to cost her. 'What were the rows about? Do you know?'

She thought for a moment. 'Everything. Anything. Money. There was never enough for her. She used to shout at my father, rest his soul, he was useless because they had no money.'

Sam was surprised. She must have got that wrong. 'But you were well-off, weren't you?'

Her laugh caught in her throat and ended in a burst of coughing. 'Where did you get that idea? We had two rooms and a kitchen in Alie Street. My father, rest his soul, was a machinist. There was a slump in the trade. Every day he went out looking for a day's work. And sometimes he was too ill to work because of his war wounds.'

'But – your grandfa—' he bit the words back, but too late. Sadie narrowed her eyes. 'Isaac, that *mamzer*? What do you know about him?'

'Nothing,' said Sam. 'Only, your…she…my… She showed me a photo. Of her father. He looked okay for money. I just thought—' It sounded lame, even to him.

'He was a *ganzer macher* once,' said Jack, 'but after the war, in the twenties, what with the slump and the strikes and everything, he went bust. Lost everything. Serves him bloody right as well!'

So Sarah hadn't finished the story, thought Sam. That part was news to him. 'Did you know him, Dad?'

'Only from that picture and by his lousy reputation,' said Jack. 'I never met him, thank God.'

'How about you, Mum?' said Sam. 'What do you remember?'

Sadie bent down and fiddled with the cups on the tray, straightening each one on its saucer. Without looking up, she replied in a hesitant whisper as if warding off the pain of the memory as she spoke. 'Just once, when I was a little girl, my – she took me to his house. He scared me. He kept looking at me like he could kill me. Then they started shouting – no, screaming at each other. I remember crying, I was so frightened. I remember us leaving, her dragging me along by the hand so I had to run to keep up. That was the only time, thank God. There was a broygus between them. As far as I know, they weren't even talking, right up to when he died.'

'Why was that?'

Sadie shrugged. 'Who knows? She had a broygus with everyone. But he was as bad as her. Worse. I never knew anyone who had a good word for him.'

'So why did she pay —?'

Sadie's head jerked up. 'She told you that old story, did she? About how no one in her father's family wanted to pay for his stone? How she couldn't sleep for thinking about him lying in the ground with no *matzevah*? How she ended up paying for it all by herself?' She snorted. 'Oh, yes! A thousand times she told me that *megillah*. And, years later, I found out it was all lies!' She started to shiver. 'Jack, turn the fire on. I'm freezing here.'

Jack turned a dial on the gas fire and held it until the spark caught and the flames began dancing over the fake logs.

Sadie pulled her cardigan more tightly around her. 'The worst thing was, I never knew what was coming. One minute she's happy and loving, then suddenly she goes *meshuggah*. From nothing! So all the time, I'm frightened. I'm hoping maybe there won't be a next time. But there always was.'

'What was it like for Grandpa?' Sam asked. 'What did he do when she was like that?

Sadie thought for a moment, then sighed and made an arms-spread-wide shrugging gesture. 'What could he do? He was a lovely quiet man, my father, rest his soul. She…'

Her words faltered as she burst into tears. Jack put his arms round her. 'That's enough now, Sadie. Sam's got the idea. You don't need to go on.'

Sadie pulled away from Jack and dried her eyes with her sleeve. 'No, Jack. The boy must know what he's got himself into.' She turned to Sam. 'Once, I'll never forget…' She stopped, drew her sleeve across her eyes again. 'Once, we're having dinner. Something – who knows what? – sets her off, and a whole pot of soup from the table she picks up and throws. I can see it now. Over the walls, the floor, the furniture – everywhere. And she's screaming like a madwoman. Like yesterday I can see it.'

A sharp pain and a taste of blood made Sam aware that he was biting his lower lip. 'What did Grandpa do?' he asked. 'Do you remember?'

Sadie nodded. 'Times like that, he used to say nothing, just pick me up and take me out.'

'Where to?'

'Anywhere. Out. Sometimes to Fieldgate Street, to his sister, Auntie Sarah.'

She broke off her story and began slowly rocking back and forth, hugging herself. Jack looked anxiously at Sam. 'Sadie, you're upsetting yourself too much. That's enough now.'

With a visible effort of will, she pulled herself together and turned back to Sam. 'So, with the soup. After a couple of hours my father takes me back home. I'm hiding behind him, holding his hand. He opens the door, no sign of her. So we go in. It's not the same room. Everything's cleaned up and the broken stuff's gone. She comes in from the kitchen, she's sweet and nice like nothing's happened. She's done her hair and put on a nice dress. She kisses me, she kisses my father, she puts food on the table. Like nothing ever happened.'

She didn't go on. Keeping her head turned away from Sam, she busied herself re-arranging the tray and brushing away the loose cake-crumbs. Jack stood up to help but she waved him away and took the tray into the kitchen. It was dark outside now. Jack switched on the main light and a standard lamp beside the sofa. He and Sam sat in silence, waiting until Sadie was ready to come back. She bustled in two or three minutes later, a brave smile fixed on her face, took her seat and gazed into mid-air, while Sam waited, not wanting to break into her thoughts, and Jack watched her with a silent expression of love and concern.

With a rapid shake of her head she came out of her dream state and carried on speaking as if there had been no break. 'And this goes on for years. All the while I'm growing up. I never know what's coming. She rows with my father day after day for weeks, then *mitten drinnen* she's sweetness and light again. And to me…'

She clamped her mouth shut and sucked in her breath as if determined to stop herself from crying. Sam felt afraid for her. He felt responsible. Only because of him was she letting herself unlock these dreadful memories. He wanted to tell her to stop, but she seemed determined to go on. He exchanged glances with his father, who replied with a slight shake of the head that he read as a sign to stay silent and keep listening.

'And to me,' she continued, 'she was always just – cold. I had food, I had clothes. But she never…' She looked first at Jack, then at Sam. 'I knew from very young that she didn't love me. Always she was cold. Like ice. Never a – I don't know how to say it, never anything a mother should feel for her child. Like what I feel for you, Sammy.'

He'd never heard his mother talk so candidly of what he meant to her, and of what she herself had missed as a child. It moved him and made him feel guilty when he thought of all the ways that she'd angered and irritated him over the years. This might be the moment to tell her what he'd discovered. But what would be the point? What good could it do? And what harm might it do?

Sadie straightened the sofa cushions and puffed them up before beginning again. 'I remember one day, I'm maybe twelve, thirteen. We're out shopping in Hessel Street and I see a boy I know from school. Alfie Tillovitch. He says hello, I say hello back. She gives him a smile. He smiles back. That's all. Soon as we get home she starts shouting at me. Calling me a *courveh*. And worse. And then she takes me by the shoulders, and she shakes me, and she says, "You, you're not mine. You're a – a horrible thing. You come from dirt. I didn't want you." Then she gets like a – like a crazy person. Slapping me, scratching me. And I've got my hands over my face, like this.' Sadie crouched down beside Jack and hunched her shoulders, holding her arms crossed in front of her face. Jack put his cheek against hers and stroked her back, making soft soothing noises.

She pulled herself away and sat up. 'Then she picks up a cup from the table and she throws it at me. I run into my bedroom for a handkerchief and I hold it up to my face. Blood everywhere. Look!' She rubbed the makeup from her left cheek. There was a small, faint scar that Sam had never seen before.

She turned to Sam again. 'Sammy, all I wanted was a mother who loved me like other people's mothers loved them. All I ever wanted was to hear her say she loved me, but she never did. When she went *meshuggah* at me or my father, I always hoped this was for the last time. For him it must have been the same. But it happened again and again.'

'Did she ever…' Sam couldn't get the words out. He closed his eyes for a moment and swallowed hard. 'Did she ever attack you again?'

Sadie shook her head. 'No. Not until…' He saw his parents exchange glances. 'No. But the cold, the nastiness, that never stopped. Thank God when I was fourteen I could leave school and get a job. Two years in a dress factory, I swept up and made tea. Then two more years on the sewing-machine. After that I got work in a shop in Commercial Street. Much better than the factory. Anshell Fashions, it was called. People to talk to, a nice class of customer.' She laughed as the memories came back. 'The manageress, Mrs Margolies, a real bitch, pardon my French. God forbid you ever should let a customer walk out without you made a sale. A proper post-mortem, she'd make. "Why this? Why that? She didn't want silk? Why didn't you show her the rayon? What was wrong with the voile? She didn't like the blue? Did you show her the green?" Anyway, I made friends with a girl called Sally. She told me about this place she goes, the Oxford and St George's Jewish Youth Club in Berners Street. I can go with, if I want.' She put her hand into Jack's and they smiled at each other. 'I met your father there. Summer 1937. I was nineteen. He was the best-looking boy in the place – and such a *mensch*! We went together more than a year before I plucked up courage to take him home to my parents.'

TWENTY-FOUR

1938

A gust of cold wind blew along Alie Street, mingling dead leaves with the rubbish left behind by market stall-holders. On the top step of number 24, Jack Shaykin laid down his bunch of flowers, drew the lapels of his overcoat together and checked his watch. 6.20. Not quite time. He stood on one leg and polished an already immaculate right shoe against his left calf, changed legs and repeated the action. He straightened his tie and ran a comb through his hair. Pulling back the cuff of his overcoat, he checked the time again. 6.25. Two small boys came along the street, pushing an old pram with a crude dummy stuffed into it. The boys caught his eye and shouted to him: 'Penny for the guy, mister?' He tossed them two pennies, checked his watch again and picked up the flowers. It was time to do or die. He rang the bell.

Sadie Symonds opened the door, took his hand and drew him inside. The dimly lit hall had chocolate-brown walls and smelled of carbolic soap and floor polish. He kissed her on the cheek and held out the flowers.

'Not me,' she whispered with a giggle, 'give them to Mum like we said.'

She helped him out of his coat, then stood on tiptoe and adjusted his tie. He hoped she'd see how much effort he'd put in to making a good first impression. He'd pressed his double-breasted suit and bought a new white shirt.

He looked at her. 'You're – I mean you look…' he stammered. His face felt hot and he was sure that his heart was beating loudly enough for Sadie to hear. He loved her so very much. She was less than five feet tall and her dark, glossy hair curled upwards from shoulder-length to form waves at each side of her face and above her forehead. He wondered if he should remark on the unusual simplicity of her appearance this evening. Her light-grey dress was high-necked and calf-length, and she wore no jewellery, just a wristwatch with a brown leather strap. But she looked beautiful nonetheless, and he wouldn't want her to think he was criticising her.

'No need to worry, she's in a good mood tonight,' whispered Sadie. She smiled bravely, but he could see that she was just as nervous as him. 'She's made a lovely table. Make sure you admire it. Eat everything she offers. And say nice things about the food.'

'You told me all this already,' Jack whispered back. He swallowed hard and tried to bring some moisture past the lump in his throat.

'Daddy's there. Come on. Mind you don't trip up, there are some holes in the lino.'

Holding his hand, Sadie led him up one flight and then up three more steps to a section built onto the back of the house, not visible from the street. Here was another small landing and off it three closed doors. She opened the middle one and he followed her in. His ears were burning and he was trying hard to control a tremor in one leg. Two shaded lightbulbs hung from the ceiling and a coal fire cast the shadows of its flames over the walls. Most of the space was taken up by a table laid with a white cloth and four place settings. Every inch of the table was covered with dishes of food of all kinds that filled the air with a variety of delicious smells.

Sadie's parents rose together to greet him. Her mother reached him first and grasped his hand. Her father gave him a small smile and returned to his chair.

'So this is Jack, at last. Pleased to meet you.'

He gave Mrs Symonds what he hoped was a fetching smile and offered her his bouquet. She took it with a simper and passed it to Sadie without taking her eyes from him.

'Flowers for me? Thank you!' Holding his hand in both of hers, she drew it to rest for a second against her body, just above the v-shaped neckline of her dress. In the second before she returned it to him he glimpsed her cleavage, felt the heat of her skin and smelled her heady perfume. The tremor in his leg was almost out of control. He could see the resemblance with Sadie, although her mother was some inches taller and more amply-built – not surprising, he thought, as she must be at least in her forties. She was wearing a floral silk dress held in at the waist by a narrow belt. Her lipstick was bright red and she wore a gold necklace with a matching bracelet.

'I know what you're thinking,' said Mrs Symonds. Jack started guiltily and he felt his ears turn from pink to red. He very much hoped that she didn't.

'You're thinking is this a joke Sadie's playing? Am I right?'

'Er, no, Mrs Symonds. That is, I'm not sure what…' he stammered.

She laughed and fixed him with her eyes. One was slightly closed, as if she were looking at him down the barrel of a gun.

'You're thinking, how can this be Sadie's mother? This can't be. Her sister maybe. But her mother, never. A woman so young! Isn't that what you're thinking?'

From the corner of his eye he saw Sadie making tiny nodding signs. Mr Symonds sat quite still, watching the encounter with an expression that revealed nothing.

'That's – that's right. You guessed.'

Mrs Symonds laughed with delight. 'I don't blame you. All Sadie's friends, when they see me they think I'm her sister.'

He searched for an answer. None came. He nodded.

'I knew it. So now you can call me Esther. Like a sister. Or who knows what else?'

Jack was aware of his mouth working but no words were coming out. Sadie's father stood up and grasped his hand. His handshake was firm and warm. Tired eyes looked into his own. Jack thought he saw something apologetic in his expression.

'Pleased to meet you, Son. I'm Sadie's father.' He glanced at his wife. 'You can call me Ben.'

Jack held onto Ben's hand as if to a lifebelt. 'Pleased to meet you, er, Ben.'

'Jack, eh?' said Ben. 'What's that short for? Jacob?'

Jack smiled. 'No, my name's really Pinchas, but I never use it.'

'Why not?'

Jack shrugged. 'It's too foreign for my liking.'

Ben laughed. 'We're all foreigners here. My parents came from Poland. A town called Smorgon. In the part they call Russian Poland. Yours?

'Also Poland. Lodz.'

Ben nodded. 'Where does your family live now?'

'Langdale Mansions, Cable Street. Corner of Christian Street.'

'So you were right in the middle of it two years ago? You were involved?'

'The Battle of Cable Street?' He laughed. 'That's a date I couldn't forget. The 4th of October 1936, my nineteenth birthday. What a way to spend it! The barricade was right outside our buildings. I was there with my brother Harry and all our mates.'

'I was there too,' said Ben. 'We gave that Mosley bastard and his lousy blackshirts a kick up the arse they won't forget, eh? Bloody little Hitlers! Trying on over here what they're doing in—'

Esther's voice sliced into their conversation. 'Nice language, Ben! Enough with the politics.' Jack concealed a shiver as he caught the look that she gave her husband and heard the coldness in her voice when she spoke to him. She turned to Jack and took his hand in hers. Her expression and tone of voice changed in an instant. 'Come and sit down at the table, Jack.' She led him to a place and sat next to him. Ben and Sadie sat opposite. Sadie caught his eye and made small head movements to the table and to her mother. He remembered just in time.

'What a lovely spread, Mrs— Esther. Mm, it all looks good enough to…er —'

'Help yourself,' said Esther, taking his plate and starting to pile it with food from every serving dish. 'You like fish? It's plaice. I fry my own. Potato salad? I'll put some on the side here. Pickled cucumber?'

Jack forced a smile and started working his way through the pile.

'So, Jack, tell me,' said Esther, 'how old are you?'

'Twenty-one,' said Jack between mouthfuls, 'and a month.'

'And how long have you and Sadie been walking out?'

'We've known each other for quite a while, Mum,' said Sadie. 'We met at the Oxford and St George's.'

'It's a nice place. Respectable,' said Jack. 'It's a club for young Jewish people in—'

'I know what it is,' snapped Esther.

Jack and Sadie exchanged nervous glances. As she'd warned him, he was going to have to tread very carefully. He put a forkful of potato salad into his mouth and ate slowly to play for time.

'I asked how long you and my Sadie have been walking out.' Esther's voice had a steely tone. Jack swallowed and put down his fork. 'Well, we've been…that is…we're—' He could feel Esther's gaze drilling into him.

'Jack and I are going together, Mum,' cut in Sadie. 'We're – serious.'

'I see.' The voice had changed again. Esther spoke with

her lips set so tightly together that they formed a vertical cupid's bow in the centre. 'And what do you do for a living, Jack?'

'I'm a trousers cutter. I work for Felsenstein Fashions in Commercial Street.' He couldn't tell from her face what impression his answer had made.

'I'm a machinist at Krakauer's,' said Ben. 'I might have sewn up some of your trousers.'

This time she openly glared at her husband, before turning back to Jack and giving him a smile so glacial that he had to control another shiver. 'So we'll be seeing more of you.' She selected a slice of fried plaice from a serving dish, slid it onto his plate, patted the back of his hand and looked him directly in the eyes. 'Do you like dancing?'

Jack's throat was dry again. He fumbled for his water glass, hoping to think of an answer that would please her. 'Sometimes, yes,' was all he could manage.

Still fixing him with her eyes, she took the glass from him and put it down on the table. 'Good. I like dancing. Sadie, tell your boyfriend how much your mother likes dancing.'

Sadie stared at the tablecloth. 'That's right, Jack. Mum likes dancing.'

Jack tried not to flinch as Esther gave him another of her cold humourless smiles. 'So maybe you'll take me to a dance at the Oxford and St George's one Sunday, eh, Jack? Maybe find your sister a nice boy to dance with?'

Jack flicked his eyes at Ben, hoping for a word of support, but he too was staring down at his plate. 'Yes, we can do that,' he mumbled. 'Some time. Why not?'

Esther gave him another chilly smile. Her eyes made him think of some hard stone – granite, maybe, or flint. 'That'll be nice, won't it? I'll dress up. You'll dance with me, won't you, Jack? Now then, eat more. There's plenty left.'

*

'Was it really as bad as that?' said Sam, 'you're not exaggerating?'

It was dark outside, and drizzling. The gas fire was turned fully up and Sadie had plugged the gap between the door and the floor with a brown corduroy draught-excluder in the shape of a sausage dog. The dog's face seemed to Sam to be looking up at him, waiting for him to recover from the surprise of the story his parents had just told him.

Jack put his hand over his heart. 'Word of honour, Son. And I haven't told you the half of it. Mum had warned me about how she could behave but this was worse than we'd expected. To this day I don't know how we got through it.'

'What about Grandpa? Didn't he say anything at all?'

'Now and then he did,' said Sadie, 'but she was just too much for him. I told you, his health was never good. She wore him down to nothing.'

The sausage dog was doing its job too well. Sam took off his sweater and spread it over the back of the armchair. 'And from then on, Dad? How was she with you?'

'Like your mum's told you,' said Jack, 'with her you never knew where you were from one day to the next. One minute she's all over me, the next she's that cold bitch again. Or it'd be the other way round. I've never known anything like it. In the end I stayed away as much as I could.'

'Jack,' said Sadie, 'turn the fire down a bit. I'm *schvitzing* here.' Jack did as directed. The flame shrank to two small tongues that danced coyly above the sham logs.

'She was always dead against us getting married,' said Sadie. 'She kept saying I was too young. That she'd hate being a grandmother and people would think she was an old woman.'

Jack and Sadie looked at each other and laughed. Sam was glad to see that. He knew how hard it had been for his mother to talk to him about her childhood, but now their mood had lifted. They seemed to have been able to look back on the night of his father's first meeting with Esther with a sort of grim humour, even though it must have been terrible at the time.

'But she couldn't stop us,' said Jack. 'Ben, bless him, stood up to her and stuck up for us, and my family was all for it.'

'So we got engaged and started saving up,' said Sadie. 'In those days you waited. Till you could afford things – a three-piece suite, crockery, bedding, stuff like that. So you could start your married life like *mensches*, with a proper home.'

'But then the war came,' said Jack, 'and I got called up like everyone else. I did my basic training in Aldershot, then we got word we were shipping out in three days' time. So I phoned up your mum and we decided to get married right away. October 1940, that was. I got a special twenty-four-hour pass. The Blitz had already started. German bombers were coming over night after night…'

Sam was relieved to see his parents' mood lightening as his father launched into one of their favourite stories, one that he'd heard hundreds of times before but always enjoyed.

'The train stops half a mile from Kings Cross,' Jack went on. 'There's a barrier across the line so we get off the train and walk. In the station it's a shit-storm – sorry, love.'

Sadie acknowledged the apology, but her face said that she too was enjoying the reminiscence.

'It was a doodlebug,' Jack continued. A direct hit. It's chaos. Everywhere there's soldiers and firemen. Me and half a dozen other boys get pulled over by a Redcap sergeant. "Youse lot put your kitbags down and get on firefighting duty," he says. "But, Sarge," I tell him, "I'm on my way to my wedding." "Fuck your wedding, lad," says the Redcap—'

'Jack, please! Very nice language!' protested Sadie – as she always did at that point in the story.

Jack winked at Sam. '"F– your wedding," says the Redcap. "You get on and fight that effin' fire or you're on an effin' charge." I've got no choice. So in my best uniform and my specially polished boots I spend the next four hours with the firemen. When they let me go there's no buses or trains, so I have to run all the way to Whitechapel. But when I get to Philpot Street there's no *shul*, no hall, just a bloody great bomb crater. And your mum and my family and hers, standing there next to it.'

'Blimey!' said Sam. 'Was anyone killed?' Of course, he knew the answer.

'No, thank God. The air raids were always at night, so no one was in the building.'

This was the point at which Sadie liked to take up the story. 'So there I am, standing in the street in my wedding dress, with my family and your father's family and our friends, and suddenly here he comes. Wet and filthy dirty. Stinking of smoke. The bottoms of his trousers all burned off. But in one piece, thank God. It was just like in the pictures. We threw ourselves into each other's arms just like in *Gone With the Wind*.'

The next bit was the one Sam liked best. 'So then the rabbi,' said Jack, 'he's an old man with a foreign accent so thick you can cut it with a knife, he says four people should hold up his *tallis*, one at each corner, to make a *chuppah*, and he'll marry us right there in the middle of Philpot Street. Our guests, and people who just happened to be there – Jews, not-Jews, kids, a policeman, soldiers on leave, an ARP warden – everyone stood round and watched. And when I stamped on the glass and kissed your mother they all gave a big cheer. Then some of us went off to a caff and had sandwiches and cups of tea. Me and your mum had about an hour on our own before I had to start walking back to Kings Cross so I could get to Aldershot before my pass ran out.'

Sadie brushed away a tear but she was smiling. 'And that was the last I saw of your father for the next five years.'

'Five years,' said Jack. 'Think of that. Three days later, I'm on a troop ship to Alexandria. I didn't see your mum again until 1945.'

Sam felt a mixture of emotions. He was relieved that, despite their earlier ill-thought-out ultimatum, his parents were now welcoming him back into the fold. He also felt elated, knowing that the picture was growing, the story filling out, the jigsaw pieces slotting into place. He wanted to be home so that he could write down what his parents had told him. But also, he felt the pain of realising that he'd made a terrible life-long mistake. He'd always believed that his mother had exaggerated her stories of a miserable childhood to make him feel sorry for her. He'd resented her loading her misery onto him. What she'd said was true – he'd thought she was neurotic. Or worse. He'd only thought of his own feelings. He hadn't understood how much she'd wanted to get him to understand the dead weight of unhappiness she carried. He'd certainly learned a lot more about Esther today, and none of it was good. Knowing what he now knew, what reason could he have for going on? If he'd ever suspected that his parents had no good reason for that much anger, he was having to think again. But even so, to cut her out of their lives for ever – that was a hell of a choice to make. However much they'd told him, he was sure they must still be holding something back.

'Son, you're looking peaky again,' said Jack, glancing at Sadie, 'Is it the you-know-what again?' He patted his stomach.

Sam collected himself. 'Something like that, Dad.' He desperately needed to go away, to dig down deep inside himself and try to work things out. He stood up. 'I'll be getting along now.' He kissed Sadie and gave Jack a brief hug. 'Thanks for everything you've told me. I understand a lot more now. I only wish—'

'I'm just glad that we're not broygus with each other,' said Jack. 'So does that mean that you won't be—?'

'Shall we leave it there for now, Dad?' said Sam. He wanted to go, but something was nagging at him: some detail that he'd missed from their stories. 'Tell me again, will you? You were married in 1940, you said?'

'That's right, 13th of October,' said Sadie. 'Thirty-six years we've been married now.'

'And Dad, you were abroad until 1945?'

'Like I told you.'

'So, Mum, where were you for those five years?'

His parents exchanged looks and Jack nodded to Sadie.

'I lived with my parents,' she said. 'In that flat in Alie Street. Until your father came home. I had no choice. I had nowhere else to go.'

'And was your mother…did she ever…?'

'Like always,' said Sadie. 'Chalk and cheese. For weeks, months it's good, then suddenly, from nowhere she's *meshuggah* again.'

'And Grandpa? When she was – did he protect you?

'He did his best. Sometimes, like I said, we went to his sister's, but they had their own problems, what with the bombs and the rationing, so we never stayed too long.'

If he let this moment pass, the opportunity might not come again. They were never going to tell him. Not unless he had the courage to ask. And he desperately wanted to know – to understand. 'So, Mum, you were there until Dad came home from the war?'

There was no reply. He understood the 'yes'.

'So, when exactly did – did you see your mother for the last time?'

Sadie and Jack exchanged looks again. 'It was when – I mean, it was after your father came home,' Sadie whispered.

His mouth was suddenly dry. He swallowed hard to summon some saliva and un-stick his tongue. He forced the words out before he could change his mind. 'So, what made you decide that you never wanted to see her again?

Did you talk it over and decide together, because of how she'd treated you all those years? Or did something happen that made up your minds?'

He saw the look of alarm in his mother's eyes and the slight shake of her head. His father gave an exaggerated yawn and flexed his shoulders. 'We're all tired, Son. Let's pack it in for tonight.' He walked to the door and held it open. It was clearly a cue for Sam to leave, but he was determined to get his answer. 'Something happened, didn't it? Something that decided you to break with Esther —' He saw them both start angrily at his use of her first name – 'to break with your mother for good. Am I right? Will you tell me what it was?'

Sadie's mouth was set in a straight, firm line, the lips pressed together as though a dam of emotion was trying to burst out from behind it. Neither parent spoke. Sam felt that he'd gone too far, pushed too hard. He tried without success to think of something to say to put it right. The dam broke. Sadie burst into tears. 'Tell him, Jack. Tell the boy what he's so keen to know.' She turned to Sam. 'Then, at last, please God you'll understand.'

TWENTY-FIVE

1946

On a sunny afternoon in mid-April, Trooper Jack Shaykin sat waiting on a bench amidst the cluster of camouflage-painted Nissen huts that housed the London Military Dispersal Centre. Any time now, Trooper Shaykin would be gone for ever, and he'd be plain Jack Shaykin again; busting to get stuck into Civvy Street and married life. He knew it was going to be hard. There was a job to get, and a place to find for him and Sadie and the baby to live. Never mind about that, though. He couldn't remember the last time he'd been so excited. After six long years here he was, going back to take up where he'd left off. Not, he thought, that anything could be the same after what he'd been through and the things he'd seen.

'Not long now, eh, Jack? Here, have a swig.' Jim Murphy, regimental heavyweight boxing champion and his crew's radio operator for the past three years, passed him a bottle of brown ale. He wiped his hand over the top and drank a mouthful. 'Thanks, mate. Today's the day, eh? The one we always talked about in the desert? What we'd do when it was all over?'

Mick Burns, the crew's Geordie gunner, poked Jack in the ribs and took the bottle from him. 'All you ever talked about was going home to that wife of yours.' He winked at Jim. 'What was her name again? Sally, was it? Or Susie?'

'Sadie,' said Jack. 'And in a month there'll be our kid as well.'

Jim and Mick made a pantomime of counting on their fingers and burst out laughing.

'Blimey, said Mick, 'you didn't waste any time. We only got back to Blighty last August. You must have got right down to it.' The men laughed harder as Jack's face and ears went red.

'Got off the boat, got his leave ticket and rushed straight down to London and give her one, he did!' said Jim between guffaws.

'Give her more than one, I'll bet,' laughed Mick.

'Leave it out now, will you?' Jack knew his mates didn't mean any harm, but they'd taken the joke a bit too far for his liking.

'Never mind us,' said Jim. 'It's just your mates taking the piss a bit. You're a lucky man to have a wife and a kid to go home to.' His face darkened. 'Luckier than me, anyway.'

Jack nodded and passed round his cigarettes. 'I know, mate. I'm sorry. I hope things work out for you.'

'Yeah, me too,' said Jim. 'Three bloody weeks! Three bloody weeks before we're coming home, and she writes and tells me I've got no home to come to. She's met this lovely man, she says. Got his own business. Sodding protected occupation. He can give her a better life than I can. Better prospects for the nipper, she says. She's sold our furniture, give the keys back to the landlord, and fucked off with this bastard.'

He threw his cigarette down and ground it under the toe of his boot. 'Six sodding years and I come home to fuck-all.'

'That's well out of order,' said Mick. 'You want to find that prick and give him a kicking. Still, look on the bright side. You're home, you've got your arms and legs and your wedding tackle, and tomorrow morning we'll all be waking up in Civvy Street.'

On a parade ground the size of four football pitches, men were clustered round in groups like this one, saying their farewells to their mates, swapping stories and addresses, passing out cigarettes and downing illicit drinks. Throughout the day they'd been shuffling along the benches until it was their turn to go into a hut, be processed and paid off, and come out a civilian. All day long, buses full of happy men shuttled between the dispersal centre and the main London railway stations.

By the time it was Jack's turn it was after five o'clock. A lieutenant with Brylcreemed hair and a toothbrush moustache sat behind a green metal desk holding a mug of tea while a clerk stood beside a row of filing cabinets awaiting instructions. Jack stood to attention, saluted and ran an experienced eye over the officer. He was about thirty and well-fed. His neatly pressed tunic was devoid of campaign ribbons. He must have had an easy war. He'd probably spent it behind that desk.

Jack watched the officer studying him with an affected expression of boredom. He had a good idea what he was thinking. Desk-jockeys like him couldn't look at a row of campaign ribbons without concealing their jealousy. And this one was sizing him up with the look that he'd come to know only too well.

'Name?'

'Shaykin, Sir. 7907261. Trooper P.'

The clerk located the drawer and took out a file. He opened the manila cover and placed it in front of the officer.

'Forty-fourth Royal Tank Regiment, eh? Called up March the seventh 1940. One of the first lot, then.' He closed the file, slid it aside and looked again at Jack. 'That's quite a row of ribbons you've got there. No wonder you're not wearing your demob suit. Looking to impress the girls back home are we, old chap?'

Jack didn't think a reply was needed. The officer opened the file again.

'Let's see now. 1939–45 star, Africa star, Italy star, defence medal and war medal. And you came through all that without a scratch?'

The officer hadn't bothered to tell Jack to stand at ease. He could feel his muscles tensing as he knew for sure what was coming.

'Almost, sir. Small-arms wound in the leg in Italy.'

'Good show. Still, you people always were good at keeping your heads down, what?'

He'd guessed right. 'You people.' Well, he'd been called a lot worse. Oh yes, his 'people' knew how to keep their heads down all right. Izzy Goldberg, for instance, his tank commander who'd stuck his head out of the turret at Alamein and got it blown off. He'd dropped back down into the tank and squirted his blood out over the whole crew. They'd fought for seven hours with Izzy's headless body under their feet. Benny Woolf, half his body burned to a crisp in Libya. Sid Kravitz, Eddie Samuels – if he wasn't going home to his Sadie he'd happily plaster this bastard all over the wall. It would be worth a bit of jankers to see him shit himself.

The officer motioned to the clerk. 'Right, let's get on with it. Release book, cigarette ration, travel voucher. Pay book with balance in cash to get you started in Civvy Street, twenty-five pounds thirteen and four. Don't count it, it's all there. That's all. Dismiss.'

Jack picked up the documents and the money from the desk and put them away in his battledress pockets. He tucked the round tin of a hundred Player's cigarettes into his haversack, turned casually without saluting and strolled away. In his first moment of being plain Mister Jack Shaykin again, he held the door wide open, raised two fingers in a leisurely V-sign, yelled, 'Stick it up your arse, you fucking bastard!' at the officer, and walked away to the accompaniment of hoots of laughter, whistles and cheers from the men waiting their turn on the benches.

An hour later he was walking through a very different King's Cross Station from the one he'd seen six years ago, kitbag over his shoulder and a cigarette between his lips. A free man at last, going home alive and well and in one piece, unlike so many of the boys he'd grown up with and the men he'd fought alongside.

It was seven o'clock now and he was impatient to get home. Home? Funny, he'd been married six years and he didn't have a home. But he had his demob money and he'd find a place to live first thing. Then it would just be the three of them. Him, Sadie and their kid. It was going to be – perfect!

From the top deck of the bus he watched peace-time London putting itself back together. Bomb-sites were being cleared and new buildings starting to go up. But not, it seemed to him, in the East End, and definitely not in Whitechapel. They must be putting all the effort and money into sorting out the West End and the posher parts of town. His thoughts turned to the welcome-home dinner that Sadie had told him she was organising. She'd invited his parents and his brother Harry, also just demobbed, and Harry's wife Ruth. Ben had promised her he'd make sure Esther behaved herself. He hoped Ben would really be able to do that. But still, not even Esther could spoil things for him tonight. A couple of drinks and a good blow-out, then an early cuddle-up with his Sadie, and he'd be the happiest bloke in the world.

He got off the bus at Aldgate Station and bought a cheerful bunch of red and yellow flowers from a stall, then crossed the road to Mansell Street and turned into Alie Street. There was a deep trench in front of number 24. He read the sign: a gas main repair, thank God, not one of those unexploded Nazi bombs. He walked over the planks laid across the pavement, put his kitbag down on the doorstep, held the bunch of flowers at the ready, rang the bell and waited for Sadie to open the door and throw herself into his arms.

'Jack! What a surprise!'

Oh, well. Sadie was probably busy in the kitchen. He picked up his kitbag and stepped inside.

'Hello, Esther. A surprise? What, you forgot I was coming?'

He'd meant it as a joke, but her eyes narrowed and she jutted out her jaw. 'Forgot? Forgot what? Enough with the riddles! What do you want?'

Oh, bloody hell! She was having one of her bad spells. Tonight of all nights. And what did she look like? She was wearing slippers and a floral housecoat, unevenly buttoned and gaping open at the top. Her hair was twisted and tangled, as if her ironed-in waves had suddenly collapsed. Her face was plastered with powder and her lips were bright red, making her look like a child's doll.

'Give me a kiss, then.' She closed her eyes and presented a cheek. He approached her for a polite peck, but at the last second she twisted her head round and kissed him hard on the lips. He recoiled and wiped his mouth with the back of his hand. She stared at him with round eyes. 'What are you doing? You naughty boy!'

His mouth was filled with the cloying taste of her lipstick. The air between them was full of a sickeningly musky perfume that reminded him of the women in the bars he and his mates went to when on leave in Cairo. Anger filled him. He was used to her bouts of strange behaviour, but this was his big night and already she was turning it sour. He hefted his kitbag onto his shoulder, keeping as far away from her as possible in the narrow hall. 'Let's go upstairs now. Is everybody here?'

He headed for the stairs but she blocked his path and took hold of his sleeve.

'Yes, they're – no. Don't go up yet. Stay down here. Wait – a bit – wait here.'

He stepped back and pulled his arm away. 'Why?'

'She's – it's – a surprise. For you. Don't go up there. Yet.' She smiled at him. The joyless, near-lascivious smile that reminded him of their first meeting. 'Stay here with me.'

He'd hoped never again to need the instinct that warned soldiers in battle of an approaching danger, or the bitter rush of adrenalin that followed on its heels. But that instinct was warning him now. Something was very wrong.

'I'm going upstairs now, Esther. Get out of my way, please.'

Slowly, she let go of him and stepped aside. He was halfway up the first flight before she called to him. 'She's not there. There's no one there. I didn't do it. I didn't mean it.'

He went cold. He stopped and turned back. She was standing on the bottom step, her fingers fiddling with the buttons of her housecoat.

'Where is she?'

She grinned up at him but gave no reply. He went back down the stairs and took her gently by the shoulders, using all his self-restraint to stay calm. 'Esther, where is Sadie? Where's Ben? Has something happened?'

She let herself go limp and fell forward into his arms. He caught her instinctively. She rested her head on his chest and croaked a travesty of a flirtatious giggle. He pushed her away and held her at arm's length. He wanted to slap her. He resisted the urge and forced his voice to stay even. 'It's all right, Esther. Just tell me. What's happened. Where's Sadie? Where's Ben?'

Her eyes were unfocused and she was mumbling to herself. She reminded him of the shell-shocked men he'd seen. Andy Maxwell, his crew's nineteen-year-old gunner before Mick, had got so bad that every time he heard a bang, even an engine backfire, he'd burst into tears and piss himself. LMF – Lack of Moral Fibre, the Army called it. They put Andy on a charge. LMF in the face of the enemy. He got a spell of punishment then they transferred him. He was lucky. In World War One he'd have got the firing squad.

'Where is she?'

Esther smiled. 'Nathan. I found you. You're It.'

For fuck's sake! He could easily have strangled her. Fighting now to keep his self-control, he took her face in his hands as gently as he could and looked directly into her eyes.

'Esther! Talk to me! What happened? Where is she? Is Ben with her?'

'Not here. Gone.'

'Gone where?'

'The hospital.'

'Which hospital? What happened? Is she ill?'

'No. She fell.'

'Fell? How? Where?'

It was hopeless. Esther was mumbling, giggling, shivering. He took her by the shoulders again, making a massive effort to speak quietly to her.

'It's all right, Esther. Calm down. Now tell me, where did Sadie fall? And which hospital is she in?'

'London Hospital. She fell out there.' Esther pointed with her chin to the front of the house.

My God. Not the steps. 'She fell there? Down the steps?'

'No. Down the hole.'

Jack felt his body go rigid. Sadie must have slipped on the planks over the trench. A long fall. And with the baby due any time.

'How bad is she hurt? How's the baby?'

Esther shrugged. 'My bastard baby? Was it you? You seem too nice.'

He pushed her aside. He needed to get to the London Hospital and be with Sadie. At a run he could be there in ten minutes. He dumped his kitbag and set off. He'd only just reached the street when Esther called after him.

'Jack! Jack!'

He looked back. She was standing by the street door, one hand leaning against the doorframe and the other twisting her hair.

'I didn't push her. I didn't mean to.'

'What?' He went back and grabbed her wrists. He didn't care any more about trying to be gentle. 'Listen to me! Listen! What did you do?'

She was wide-eyed, trying to struggle free from him. 'I didn't push her. Don't believe her. She's a liar. Always was. She's not mine, you know. The *dreck* she came from —'

His heart was thumping. He didn't want to believe it. She giggled again, then burst into tears. 'Let go! Don't you touch me! Papa, you're hurting me! It hurts! Stop it! Please!'

He shoved her away and ran back along Alie Street, full pelt towards the London Hospital.

*

'It felt like hours until I found the ward where they'd taken your mum,' said Jack. 'Grandpa was there holding her hand. She had a broken arm and a broken ankle. She was covered in cuts and bruises. The baby, the nurse told me, thank God was going to be okay. Grandpa told me what happened. They'd kept him late working overtime. He could hear the shouting from the front door. By the time he got upstairs Esther was already attacking your mum – slapping, scratching, kicking, God knows what.'

Sam had no idea what to say. He was paralysed with horror. Anything he could think of saying would sound hollow, stupid. He could only think of one thing, the obvious question. 'Do you know what started her off?'

Sadie shrugged, her arms spread wide. 'It was from nothing, like always. How long to cook the *kneidlach*, something stupid like that. She said it should be like this, I said no, it should be like that.' She laughed. 'I should have known better. I should have known to keep shtum. But your father was coming home, I was excited, I wasn't careful like you had to be with her. Suddenly she's screaming at me, she's calling me these names, terrible names I can't even tell you now. And then she starts with the hitting and the kicking. And I'm screaming, trying to get away from her. I'm thinking any minute she'll pick up a knife. But thank God, at least not that.'

'Grandpa told me he tried to calm Esther down,' said Jack, 'but she'd gone *meshuggeh*. The worst he'd ever seen her, he said.'

'That's right,' said Sadie. 'Believe me, all those years you were away it was hard, but I never saw her as bad as that before.' She focused back on Sam. 'I'm running away from her and I start getting bad pains. Here.' She put her hand on her midriff. 'I thought I was going into labour. Grandpa said I needed the hospital and he ran to the phone box and called for an ambulance. And she's standing there laughing. Like it's a big joke.'

She stopped, pressed her lips together and took several deep breaths. Sam could see that she was determined to go on, whatever effort it would cost her. Jack, too, seemed to understand this, and made no move to support or comfort his wife. She spoke again, her voice quiet but firm. 'He comes back, he helps me downstairs. We're standing at the door, waiting for the ambulance. Next thing I feel this shove in my back and I'm falling. I'm lying in this hole and she's there looking down at me. I can't move. Grandpa's trying to pull her away but she's strong like a madwoman and she keeps looking down and she's shouting, but I can't hear what she's saying.' She paused, then let out a deep sigh. 'Next thing I know, I wake up in hospital.'

Sam could think of nothing to say. His mother was telling her story bravely, calmly now, without any outward show of emotion – almost as if it was someone else's story she was telling.

Jack took up the account. 'Grandpa told me, thank God someone called the police, and they got there before the ambulance. It took two big policemen to hold on to Esther.

Then thank God the ambulance came. They got your mum up and put her on a stretcher. And then – if I hadn't heard it from your mum and from Grandpa, I'd never believe it was true…'

Sadie spoke to Jack but she was looking directly at Sam. Her voice was clear and strong. 'Tell him, Jack,' she said. 'Tell him what his new friend, that he likes so much, tell him what she did.'

Jack took his son's hand, held it tightly and looked him in the eyes. 'They're putting her in the ambulance. Two big policemen are holding the woman's arms, and still she's struggling and screaming. And you know what she's screaming, over and over at your mother?'

'I'll tell him,' said Sadie, her eyes locked onto Sam's so that he could almost feel their burning intensity. 'She's screaming, "I hope I never see you again! Please God you should both die in childbirth!"'

The tears streamed down Jack's face as he gripped Sam's hand. 'This is what your mum has to live with. That's you, Son. That's you, who your grandmother wanted dead before you were even born.'

TWENTY-SIX

The phone had started ringing again. For three, maybe four days – nights too, he couldn't say exactly how many — Sam had been in bed. He'd slept most of the time, occasionally waking to take another pill and go for a piss, or sometimes to knock together a sandwich from some old cheese and the remains of a stale loaf. He'd ignored the phone and the doorbell. The post and the junk-mail had mounted up on the doormat. At one point he'd started on the bottle of cider someone had brought round last Christmas. It had made him puke. He'd tried to clean it up, but most of it was still on the bathroom floor.

The phone went on ringing. He got out of bed, scratched and yawned, went to the bathroom for another piss, stuck his tongue out and recoiled at his reflection. He went to the kitchen, filled the kettle and scraped loose the last spoonful of Maxwell House from the bottom of the jar. The milk smelled as bad as the bottle he'd found in Esther's fridge. He held it at arm's length and poured it away, ignoring the congealed lumps that gathered around the plughole. He remembered seeing a tin of baked beans somewhere. But where? All he had to do was ask Deborah. She'd do that comic eye-rolling thing and say something like, 'second shelf up where it always is'. Maybe it was her ringing. He'd have liked to talk to her but that wasn't likely. He couldn't find things under his nose in the kitchen, but he could read between the lines. Her last letter. Job going great. Lovely flat just off Las Ramblas. Management very pleased. Colleague, Jordi. Guess what, Sephardi Jew! Helping her brush up her Spanish, showing her the ropes. Oh yeah, good old Jordi. Showing her the ropes, I'll bet. What about: love you, Sam; miss you, Sam? Where was that? He was such a dick! Why should he think — Why didn't he—

The phone carried on ringing. For fuck's sake, why couldn't those people leave him alone? He took a mug out of the sink, spooned the coffee into it and poured boiling water over the table. Some splashed onto his bare feet. Fuck! That stung!

Was that phone never going to stop ringing? Why had he given the old bitch his number? It'd be her, the sly cow, wondering why he hadn't been round. Wanting to give him more orders. Clean this, fix that, get the other. Crabby, bad-tempered, two-faced murderous old lunatic. Right! Now was the time to tell her that he knew all about her and put an end to it. She had her social worker and her district nurse to tell her lies to, so she wouldn't miss him. All that bollocks she'd told Anna – husband who beat her up, couldn't have kids – he should have seen through her right away. But of course he didn't. That's how he was – Stupid Sam Shaykin. Put Up With Anything Sam, who'll just stand there with his finger up his arse while anyone who wants to can piss all over him any time they feel like it. Like Libby did. Five years! Five years he stood for her sulks and her taunts and her bloody tantrums!

The phone was still ringing. It was an opportunity. If it was her, he could fuck her off once and for all. And if it was Ron, he'd tell him to take his nice old ladies and his broyguses and shove them right up his own charitable arsehole.

His feet still stinging, he lurched into the hall and picked up the receiver, dropped it, picked it up again. 'Hello. Is that you, Granny? Is that my dear, sweet, harmless little granny? This is your Sammy. Remember me? The one you tried to abort? The one you wanted dead? 1946? May? Ring a bell?'

'Sam, what are you talking about?'

His head was swimming. He knew the voice but he couldn't place it.

'Sam, it's Kate. You've been leaving me messages. You sound like you could do with some help.'

Tears of relief came to his eyes. He pictured Kate's calm consulting room, the soothing taste of mint tea. He sank down the wall to the floor, the phone between his knees and the receiver against his chin. He was shivering. 'Kate, I don't know…I'm just—'

'Sam, I can't hear you. You're mumbling. Talk into the mouthpiece!'

He brought the receiver closer. 'Kate – I need you.' It had come out wrong. But those were all the words he could manage. Maybe it was the pills.

'You're having a bad spell? Did it just come on, or has something happened?' There was something wrong with the phone. Her voice had a strange, tinny echo. Or was it his own? He made an effort to put a sentence together, to tell her what was wrong.

'Some – something.'

'Do you want to give me an idea, or do you want to come over and we'll take it from there?'

The tears gushed. 'Can I come? Now?'

'Hold on.' A pause. 'Can you come at five?'

'What time is it now?'

'You don't know?'

'No.'

'Why not?'

'Lost my watch. What day is it?'

'It's Wednesday. Ten in the morning. You remember where to come?'

'Yeah.'

'I'll see you at five, then. Find your watch and try to calm down. Will you be driving?'

'Yeah.'

'You're sure you'll be okay to drive?'

'Yeah.'

'Be careful, then. See you. And look – don't let yourself get into that downward spiral. And don't take any pills. You remember what I told you? Whatever it is, we can talk it out. You know that, don't you?'

Sam said nothing.

'Sam!'

'Yeah. Thanks, Kate. See you.'

*

Nothing had changed since Sam had last sat in this room in Kate McGeehan's Victorian terraced house in Highgate. The two prints of Picasso line drawings still hung on the otherwise plain pale-blue walls, and the bronze Hindu god Shiva still danced on the low glass-topped table. She wore her familiar trouser-suit, silk scarf and embroidered slippers, and her grey hair with its remaining wisps of red formed the same stylishly unruly cloud around her head. While he drank his mint tea she seemed deep in thought, her thumb and forefinger lightly holding her lowered chin.

She lifted her head and her eyes re-engaged his. 'I'll ask you the obvious question. Why do you think that what your parents told you has affected you so badly?'

He fiddled with his watch bracelet. 'I don't know. It's just – I'm so sick of myself. I got everything wrong, just like I always do. I thought they were being stupid, making a big fuss about nothing. I didn't listen and look where it got me. I've pissed them off and I've fucked up my relationship with Deborah.' He put his head in his hands. 'And on top of everything else…' He didn't finish the sentence.

'Go on.'

He spoke to the dancing Shiva. 'On top of everything else I find out that I nearly wasn't born. If that woman had had her way I'd have been – well, just nothing.'

'And that thought makes you feel – what?' said Kate.

He sighed. Always the same question. How did it make him feel? If only he knew, he wouldn't need to be there. 'I've been turning it over and over in my mind.' He hesitated. Would it sound too ridiculous? Maybe, but... 'Sometimes I do this thing when I think about all the time before I was born – the millions of years – before I was anybody. Before I existed.'

'And?'

'Well, what I think is, obviously I couldn't care that I hadn't been born yet, because there was no me to care. I just – wasn't. Wasn't anything. I wasn't sorry, or sad, I didn't feel that I'd lost anything, because – well, because there was no me. So how come—' He paused, searching for words. Kate waited with her look of patient interest. 'So how come, when I think about dying – it should be the same, shouldn't it? I mean, there'll be no me, not for millions of more years, so I won't be sorry I'm not alive, just like before I was born. The trouble is – it's not the same.'

Kate made a minute adjustment to her scarf. 'I see. So you're saying it's dying that you're worried about? You think being dead is different from not being born? Is that what you're saying?'

'Yes, of course it's different. Once you've had life, you can think about not having it. Before you have it, you – well, you know what I mean. And then to find out that my own grandmother tried to stop me ever having a life – tried to kill me before I was born—'

Kate crossed her legs and sat back in her chair. 'How do you feel about Esther now?'

The question took him off guard. He thought for a moment. 'Angry. Bloody angry. Not just with her. With Ron Green for getting me into this. With my parents for lying to me about her. With myself for being so stupid, so – gullible.'

'Will you see her again?'

He shot back his reply. 'No! Never!'

Kate remained silent, unmoving except for a slight raising and lowering of her crossed-over foot. The silence seemed to drag out as she kept her eyes fixed on him, waiting for him to speak again.

'I don't know. Maybe. To tell her what I think of her.'

She uncrossed her legs and leaned forward. 'What do you think of her?'

It came out in a flood. 'I think she's evil. She made my mother's life a misery. Why? Because she was raped? How the fuck could she blame my mother for that? Then she tried to kill her – and me as well!' He ripped a tissue from the box. 'What a fucking idiot I am! She conned me into believing she was a harmless old woman. Into thinking bad things about my parents. She even got me starting to like her!'

'So, you might want to see her,' said Kate, 'if only to punish her. To abuse her for the hurt she's caused you and your mother. Is that right?'

'No. I wouldn't see her again, not even for that. And I don't like those words.'

'Those words?'

'Your words. Punish. Abuse. I couldn't – she's an old woman. She's dying.'

'Yes, so you've said.' Kate closed her eyes and steepled her fingers, their tips touching her lips. 'Let's think again about the incident your parents described to you. The one that's giving you so much distress. Can we do that?'

He folded his arms. 'Okay.'

'You say she wanted to stop you having a life – to see you aborted in fact, or to be stillborn?'

'Yes.'

'How can you be sure?'

He unfolded his arms. 'Kate, she pushed my mother down a hole and shouted that she wanted us both dead. What's not to be sure about?'

'Do you think she meant it?'

His jaw dropped and he laughed, pulling himself up short as he saw no change in Kate's expression. 'How can you ask me that? What do you think?'

'It isn't about what I think, Sam. I'm asking you if you really think she meant it.'

He stood up. 'I need the loo.'

'Sure. Let's take ten minutes. You want another mint tea? I'm having one.'

He nodded his thanks and headed for the toilet.

*

Kate blew gently across the surface of her tea. 'Let's go back a bit. You've told me how, after you first met Esther, you put a massive effort into finding out all about her. You had long talks with your great-aunts. You pieced together her life from her childhood onwards. You told me that it became an obsession for you. Is that right?'

He put his cup down. 'I wouldn't call it an obsession.'

'What would you call it?'

'I suppose I was just curious. I suddenly realised that I grew up taking all this for granted. My mother hated her mother. That's just how it was. It was as natural as – as my mother loving me and me loving her. Only, when I met Esther, that started me thinking. She was a terrible mother, I always knew that. But there are things I just don't understand. For instance, how could she not realise how much she was making my mum suffer? And if she did realise, how did she feel about it? Did she like it? Hate it? Could she have changed if she wanted to? Or was it something she couldn't control? Maybe she even knew exactly what she was doing, and got pleasure from doing it. I mean, was it really the rape that made her hate my mum so much? Or was she just, like I've been saying, just plain evil? And if she was, or even still is, how does that happen? How does someone get to be evil? Is it something you're born with, like some kind of deformity?'

'What do you think?' said Kate.

He put his middle finger under his watch bracelet, pulled it out and let it ping back. 'I don't know. But I've told you, I found out all sorts of stuff. She had a lot of bad things happen in her life.'

'So you've said,' said Kate. 'You've built up a picture of her. A woman who's led a troubled life and who, I suspect, may well have had a congenital mental illness even before it was aggravated by her experiences. Which is why I asked you, when she said those things, do you think she really meant them?' She raised a hand as Sam's incredulous look returned. 'Don't say the first thing that comes into your head. I'm not denying she meant those words at the moment she said them. But what I'm asking you is, how might she have felt about them a minute later? Or a week? Or a year? Or longer? Did you ever wonder about that?'

He shook his head. 'No.'

'Would you like to think about it now?'

'No.' He picked up his cup and swallowed the rest of his mint tea. Kate took several small sips from hers. 'Remind me: how long was it between that day, when all contact ended between your mother and Esther, and the day you stepped into her life?'

'That was just before I was born,' said Sam. 'So, just over thirty years.'

'What became of Esther during those thirty years?'

'No idea.'

'You haven't tried to find out?'

'No.'

'You're not curious?'

He fiddled with his watch again. His fingers moved to the winder and he turned it a few notches. 'No. Couldn't care less.'

'So your interest in her stops from the time of your birth. Is that right?'

'Yes. No. Yes, I suppose so. But I don't—'

Kate leaned forward again. He could feel her eyes holding his. 'So this woman who fascinates you so much – there's thirty years of her life that don't interest you at all?'

He couldn't see what she was getting at. But she was right. 'Put it like that, yes.'

'Any idea why that is?'

She was going too far. Attacking him. Trying to make him feel guilty. His voice rose. 'I don't know what you mean. Why should I give a shit what happened to her?'

Kate pushed the tissue box closer to him and waited a moment before continuing. 'Bear with me. And try to stay calm. You trust me, don't you?' She glanced down at her notes. 'You told me your grandfather left her after that night? And never went back?'

'That's right. He lived with his sister for a while, then he came to us. He lived with us until he died.' He faltered. 'I saw him die. I was just a kid. It's one of my earliest memories.'

'I know,' said Kate. 'You shared that memory with me once before. Does it still trouble you?'

He nodded.

'Do you want to talk about it now?'

'No.'

'Okay, we can come back to that. So, back to Esther. After Ben leaves, she's alone as far as we know. No husband, no daughter, no grandchild. Do you think she regretted things turning out like that?'

He folded his arms again. 'Dunno. Why would I care?'

'I'm asking you what you think. Do you think she thought about that night? Thought about what she did? Why she did it? What she said? Do you think she ever felt sorry? Wondered if she could put it right? Wanted to make amends with her daughter? Wished she could see her grandson grow up? Have you thought about those things?'

'No.'

'Would you think about them now?'

'No.'

'Why not?'

'Because—' He jumped to his feet and ground the words out. 'Because she tried to kill me! Because she tried to kill my mother! Because she's insane! For God's sake, isn't that clear enough for you?' He sank back into his chair, in tears. 'I'm sorry, Kate. I didn't mean it. I'm so stressed, I lost control—'

He saw Kate smile and nod as he realised what he'd said. 'People can lose control, can't they? And regret it later? I think you've experienced that yourself, before now, haven't you?'

There was a long silence while he sat with his chin on his chest and his eyes shut, opening them now and then to see Kate waiting, immobile except for the occasional crossing and uncrossing of her legs and dangling of her slippers. He knew where she was leading him, because they'd talked about it before, but the memories were still unbearably painful. Memories of Libby. Disgust at not seeing soon enough how it was going to be. Anger at himself for letting five years pass, always believing, or at least trying to convince himself, that things would get better. Anger at himself for keeping quiet. And finally, revulsion at the thought of the act that he'd let her drive him to.

Memories of Kev, the genial, blond-bearded PE teacher who came to live next door with his widowed mum after his wife left him. Kev, who talked Libby into joining his Tuesday night keep-fit class in the local church hall. Kev, who took to coming back with her after the class for a couple of drinks. And finally, as she announced to Sam one evening in the clipped animal-trainer voice she'd lately affected when speaking to him, Kev who was leaving his mum and moving in with her.

'We're finished,' she said. 'But I'm not leaving. You are. I want you to pack up and piss off. You're a useless fucker. And you always were. So, get your stuff and sod off!'

She'd let fly at him many times before, but this time she'd crossed a line. It was a memory still so raw that he'd only ever been able to tell Kate about it. He looked at her, still immobile, waiting. He knew that she had no intention of saying anything else until he did.

'Yes, I lost control that time. But only ever that once. And you know how bad I still feel about it.'

'Do I?' Kate said. 'Tell me again. How did it feel?'

'How did what feel?'

'You know. Do you want me to say it? How did it feel when—'

'When I put my hands round her neck? When I started choking her?' He put his face in his hands. 'I can't.'

'Try.'

He took a tissue and dried his eyes. 'I was fucking angry. Angrier than I've ever been, before or since. Five years of anger, all saved up. I just lost control. I – I put my hands round her neck. And I started squeezing. She sort of fell to her knees. She was making these funny sounds. I was looking at her and – well, just in time I realised what I was doing and I let go. She fell on the floor and I left her there and I went out. I felt sick. I drove around for hours. I don't know where, nowhere in particular. When I went back, she'd gone.'

'Remind me, what were your thoughts,' Kate asked, 'at the precise moment when you realised what you were about to do?'

'My thoughts? I don't know. All I know is, I was looking at her and I felt—'

'Go on.'

'I don't want to say it.'

'Say it. You're safe here.'

She never reacted, never judged. He felt he could tell

her anything. 'Wonderful! It felt fucking marvellous! I was loving it! That was the terrible thing. I was enjoying seeing her pain. I remember thinking, all I had to do was squeeze a little bit more and she'd—'

'Say it. She'd—'

'I don't want to.'

'Say it.'

'All I had to do was keep squeezing and she'd – she'd die.'

'And that thought pleased you?'

'Yes.'

'Does it please you now?'

'No, of course not. Except – Yes. Sometimes, yes.'

'And then?'

He shrugged. 'I let go.'

'Do you know why you made that choice?'

'I had to. I couldn't kill anyone. Not even her. You've got to be insane to kill. Or even to want to.'

'Have you?'

'Have I what?'

'Have you got to be insane to want to kill?'

'Haven't you?'

'You tell me. Tell me what you think "insane" really means.'

He understood. He clasped his hands together and stared long and hard at the bronze statue, until the Hindu god seemed actually to be dancing inside his circle of fire, and he fancied he could feel the heat of the flames licking at the dancer's feet.

'You're telling me I should go back? See her again? Knowing what I know?'

She smiled and shook her head. 'You know I don't tell you what to do. It's for you to decide. Do you think you might?'

He shrugged. 'Maybe.'

'To tell her how angry you are with her? To make her feel your anger?'

'She gave my mother a lifetime of grief, and I nearly never existed. You're telling me I'm wrong to be angry with her?'

She shook her head. 'There's no right or wrong. We're talking about your anger. I'm asking what you intend doing with it.'

He screwed his eyes shut and pressed his fingers to his forehead. He could feel a pulse throbbing in his temple. 'I know what you're saying. But no, I don't want to see her again. Just the thought of her – it disgusts me. It wouldn't do any good anyway. She wouldn't know what I was talking about. She might not even recognise me. Most of the time she's freaked out. She told them in the hospital that she had no family. She told her social worker she had no children. She mumbles. She talks to her dead brothers. A while ago she knew me, and she asked if my mother—' He stopped mid-sentence and slapped his forehead with his open hand.

'What is it?' said Kate. 'You've remembered something?'

He chewed his lip. 'Something she said. She asked me if Mum had told me what she did. I didn't know what she meant. Not then. So she does remember!'

'Or maybe she did for just that moment,' said Kate. 'That does happen. Either way, would you want to talk to her about it?'

'No.' He'd had enough. He felt exhausted. He wanted to go home and get back into bed. He stood up to end his visit. 'Thanks for seeing me, Kate. I feel a lot better now. You've helped me make up my mind. I've finished with that evil old lunatic once and for all.'

Kate stayed sitting, her head tilted as if she knew he had more to say. He sat down again. 'You have to understand, the family broygus is still a big deal for my parents. They told me all this so I'd put an end to my – my interest in Esther. So, supposing I did see her again, I'd have to do it behind their backs. Which I won't do. Never again.'

'Could you talk to them? Help them understand what finding Esther has meant to you?'

He laughed. 'I've tried. Waste of time. But…' He hesitated. 'There's this other thing I can't decide about.'

'Other thing?'

'What I told you. What I found out about my mum. Do you think I should tell her?'

'You're asking my advice? You know I don't—'

'Maybe just this once?'

Kate thought for a moment. 'Tell me, when you found out about this, did it change how you felt about your grandfather?'

'No, of course not. I still remember how much I loved him. And now I think even more of him for what he did for Esther – or tried to do, until it just got too much for him.'

'Go on.'

She'd made her point. 'So, even if my mother knew she was…you know…what happened to her – even if she found that out, it wouldn't change how she felt about him?'

'Exactly.' It was Kate's turn to stand up and signal that the session was over. 'Good luck, Sam. I'm glad you felt you could come back to me. Stay in touch.'

He gripped the hand that she held out to him. He liked the feeling. Her eyes seemed larger, bluer and gentler than he'd noticed before. She smelled good. Warm, comforting. He'd have loved to put his arms round her, but he kept the impulse to himself and maintained a respectful distance.

She prolonged the handshake. 'Maybe your mother already knows, did you think of that? If she does, it's understandable that she's kept it a secret from you, isn't it?'

He hadn't thought of that. 'I'm sure she doesn't know. I can't ask her, though, so I'll never known for certain, will I?'

She gave his hand a final squeeze before releasing it. 'No, Sam, you'll never know for certain.'

TWENTY-SEVEN

'Sam! Welcome back! How are you? How are – things?'

It felt like a return to normality after the months of anxiety and uncertainty. He was happy to be back at work with Eleni. She looked immaculate as ever in her autumn outfit, and she had a more confident air now; the businesswoman in charge of her own patch. More – what was it? More grown-up. He wondered how she'd feel about him coming back to take over again. 'Everything's fine now, thanks, Eleni. I can't thank you enough for taking this on. I had some things to sort out and, without you here, I couldn't have done it. So, thanks. If there's anything I can do for you—'

'No need to thank me,' said Eleni. 'I've loved it. I've made some changes. To the records and the accounting. And I've changed round the window display and I've got some ideas lined up for publicity events and special offers. You know, book by Christmas and kids go free, that sort of thing...'

With Kate's help he'd managed to pull himself out of the hole he'd dug himself into, but only just. Deborah's absence was still an ache that made his whole body throb with hopelessness and regret. The knowledge of his mother's suffering, and his callous disregard for it over the years, tore at him. He still wasn't sleeping. Lying awake, thinking about being dead, about never being born, about being a foetus thrown in a dustbin by some overworked nurse in a Victorian hospital on the Whitechapel Road – this morning it had taken all his determination to get up, put on his work clothes and his work face, and claw his way back to some semblance of a normal life. Any kind of life, in fact. Being alive at all was something that he valued now, knowing how easily…

'Only if you think they're good ideas, of course,' said Eleni. I didn't mean to…'

He hoped she hadn't noticed that she'd lost his attention. She was waiting for his response, her face alive with pride at the trust he'd placed in her. He looked at her more closely than he'd ever done before. Not in the crude way that Gordon had done, but with a new interest in her as more than just a bright, young, smartly dressed assistant. Her olive skin, her long, almost black, corkscrew hair and her deep-brown eyes spoke of her Mediterranean origin. And how close in so many ways were those features to Deborah's, whose ancestors, like his own, had been near neighbours of those of Eleni before embarking on their centuries-long journeying. He'd never considered that before. Grandpa Ben's parents, his father's parents, Esther's parents – if they'd turned left instead of right or right instead of left when leaving the Old Country, or not gone at all, their families would have ended up in Auschwitz, or Treblinka, or Sobibor, or up some other crematorium chimney. And, once again, that would mean that Sam Shaykin would never have existed. God, when he considered all the pitfalls along the way, it was a miracle that he'd got to be born at all! The thought made him laugh out loud: a wild, nervous bark that took Eleni by surprise.

'Are you okay, Sam? Look, if you think I've been making too many…'

The last thing he wanted was to unload his misery on her. He shook himself and smiled at her. 'I'm fine. Sorry. I was just – thinking about something else. Your ideas are great.' He gazed around, forcing himself to look enthusiastic for her sake. 'And the shop looks terrific. I really like what you've done.'

She looked relieved. 'You really think so?'

'Of course.' A weariness had overtaken him. His pleasure at returning to work had lasted no time at all. 'Look, it'll take me a few days to get back into things, so why don't you carry on taking the lead for a while?'

'Sure, Sam. Glad to.'

'Good. I'm having a coffee. You want one?'

While the kettle boiled, he sat at the table with his head in his hands. At least he'd put an end to all the Esther crap. That was something, but he still felt like shit. He looked around at the tiny kitchen with its chipped sink, its electric kettle and orange wallpaper. His life had been saved, and for what? So he could piss it away here? He had to do something. Anything. Jack in the job, take out his savings and bugger off. Lie on a beach somewhere. Go to India, be a hippy. Drop acid. Sit at the feet of a guru and sing Hari Krishna. Swim. Stand on top of a mountain and look down. Get things in perspective. Forget this grandma stuff that had so completely fucked his life up. He took a piece of paper and started jotting down figures. How long could he get by without earning? Depended where he went, of course. Sell the car, that would help. Give up the flat, unless Deborah wanted to keep it on for herself. Assuming she ever came back, of course. Find a job when he got back? Maybe, maybe not. Right now, he didn't give a shit one way or the other.

He took Eleni her coffee and forced himself to focus on getting back into the job. Lunchtime came and went. He hadn't felt like eating. He dealt with the occasional customer while Eleni ate her salad in the kitchen. Just before closing time there was a rush, and for the first time that day they were both occupied. Finishing with a customer, Sam turned his attention to a slim woman in a calf-length navy-blue coat, a Doctor Zhivago-style hat and shiny black leather boots, standing with her back to him as she flicked through a brochure. 'Sorry to keep you waiting. How can I help?'

The woman put the brochure back in the rack. She spoke quietly, her face still turned away from him. 'I'm planning a trip home to St Lucia. To visit my family. Might you be able to assist me?'

'I'm sure we can…' He paused. The velvety voice was so familiar that for a moment he thought— But no, that wouldn't be possible. Not here. 'Yes, I'm sure we can help you.' She turned towards him. He could almost feel the hostility in Anna Bijou's eyes burning into him.

'Hello, Sam. It is Sam, isn't it? Sam Shaykin? Or is it Josh Silver? Or are you someone else today?'

He glanced across the shop at Eleni. She was busy and wouldn't have heard anything. He tried a smile but he was impaled on Anna's cold stare. He struggled to think of something friendly or witty to say. Nothing came to mind. 'Hello, Anna. It's good to see you again.'

'Is it really? You say that to me?' said Anna. She kept her voice low but he could feel its edge cutting into him. 'You disappear, I have to track you down, I find out who you really are, and then you tell me you're pleased to see me?'

He glanced around the busy shop. The customers' conversations were blended into a general hubbub so that their lips were moving without any distinguishable words emerging. Eleni was engrossed with a grey-bearded man in a turban. Three nuns were huddled over a Jerusalem pilgrimage brochure. A woman was shouting at a boy and a girl who were playing hide-and-seek amongst the racks. Maybe it was a momentary illusion – a customer who looked like her. Maybe the madness in his blood was beginning to assert itself and she was a spectre. He looked back. It was still Anna. He nodded towards the kitchen. 'We can talk in there.'

As soon as he'd closed the door she took off her hat, shook out her hair and turned on him, her eyes flashing. 'First off, this Josh Silver tomfoolery – what's it about?

Why are you going round making up silly names for yourself?'

She looked so fierce and disapproving that he could feel himself squirming like a naughty boy. He shrugged. 'It was necessary. At the time.'

'Hah! Necessary! What's up with you? This is a sick old lady, a person close to death, that you've been messing with. What kind of a person are you?'

He found it agonising that Anna should think so badly of him. And yet what she'd said was true. He'd put an end to her and to Esther without a word or a second thought, dissolved Josh Silver into thin air and retreated back into the skin of Sam Shaykin. He'd turned and run away without looking back. Surely, if she knew the whole story she'd understand and sympathise. The problem was, it was a story he'd promised himself no one else would never know. He sat at the kitchen table and pulled out a chair for her. She ignored the gesture and stood glaring down at him with folded arms. He had to try to make her understand. 'Anna, please. That's not fair. Things – a lot of things – have changed, that's all. It's hard to explain.'

She shook her head and wagged her index finger. 'Uh, uh! Don't bother to try. You dropped Esther cold, is all that matters. She's a hard person to get through to, and you did it. The Lord knows why she should like you, but she did. And then you go and disappear. Brush her off your hands and hide yourself away like she's nothing to you.'

'I'm not hiding,' said Sam. 'I wasn't that hard to find, was I?'

Anna took off her coat and folded it carefully over a chair. 'Not once I started listening to Esther. Listening properly, I mean. After you stopped showing up, she started asking me, "Where's Sam?" I thought she'd got mixed up. I told her, if she means you, it's Josh, not Sam. "Sam, Josh," she kept saying, "where is he?" So I called Hackney Jewish Aid. They said they didn't have a Josh on their books. Or a Sam. They said I should talk to this Ron Green, so they gave me his number and I called him.'

Sam risked a smile. 'And how did that go?'

He was rewarded with the ghost of a smile in return and she sat down opposite him. 'He told me I should go and see his brother who sells ladies' clothes. "For a friend of Sam's, the best wholesale prices," he said. "Just say Ron sent you."'

He ventured a laugh. 'That sounds like Ron. Did you go?'

She pursed her lips. 'I did not.' She seemed aware for the first time of her surroundings. She glanced around the kitchen and through the glass panel into the shop, where Eleni was busy tidying the display racks and arranging the piles of brochures as the working day neared its end. 'So, this is where you work.' She nodded towards Eleni. 'Just the two of you? You and that pretty lady?'

That's right,' said Sam, 'Just me and Eleni.'

'Is she your boss?'

Sam smiled. 'Yes.'

'I bet she keeps you on your toes.'

'She certainly does. So, Ron Green put you on to me, did he?'

Anna began turning her hat between her hands, smoothing down tufts of the fabric that had become ruffled. 'He explained it all. Which is when I realised.'

'Realised what?'

'That I'd made a mistake. I'd thought she was in her dream world again, when she told me she's your grandmother.'

Sam raised his eyebrows in feigned astonishment. 'She said that?'

'Don't—' Anna emphasised her words with a jabbing forefinger pointed at Sam's chest. 'Don't mess with me, Sam. Just tell me: is Esther your grandmother? Yes or no?'

'Yes.'

'And you'd never met her until now?'

'No. Never.'

'How come?'

He shrugged. 'I'm sorry, it's too much to go into. But I'll tell you why I – why I did what I did. I've found things out about her. Things she did. Bad things. Terrible things. Which is why now, I don't want anything more to do with her.'

Her eyes flashed at him again. 'Come on! How could anything be that bad? To make you walk away like that?'

'You've got no idea.'

'Try me!'

He shook his head. 'It's too complicated. You'll have to take my word for it.'

'No,' said Anna. 'Don't think you can take me for a fool. What could that woman have possibly done to you?'

Through the glass Sam could see Eleni starting to pull down the blinds and turn off the lights. It was time to bring this to an end. Anna would just have to go on thinking the worst of him. 'I told you, it's too complicated. You'll have to be satisfied with that. All you need to know is that the thought of ever seeing her again sickens me. And, believe me, I've got every right to feel like that. Is that clear enough for you?' He stood and opened the door. 'And that's all I've got to say. I'm sorry if you think badly of me, Anna, but—'

She stood up and pushed the door shut. 'You do realise the woman's mentally ill?'

The question made him bellow with laughter. Anna's offended expression made him laugh even harder. 'Oh yes, believe me, I know that only too well.'

'Oh, you do?' said Anna, her voice rising. 'Do you know how sick she is? She's psychotic. She's manic depressive. That's how bad she is.'

He had no interest in hearing this. 'You think I don't understand that? I do, and it makes no difference to me.'

'You're telling me you don't feel any sympathy at all for her? I can't believe that.'

'Whether you believe it or not,' said Sam, 'I don't.' He gave Anna her hat and held out her coat. 'I'll tell you this much, and after that we've got no more to say to each other. My mother suffered years of cruelty at that woman's hands. In the end things got so bad that she broke with her for good. That was even before I was born. And if that maniac had got her way, you and I wouldn't be—' He stopped in mid-sentence. His head had started aching. 'Never mind. All you need to know is that my parents had good reason to turn their backs on her. To them, Esther Symonds is evil through and through. And you know what? I feel the same. And if you knew why, so would you.' He sat at the table and turned his head away from Anna, hoping that she wouldn't see his tears.

She sat down next to him. 'Sam, I'm sorry. She was a bad mother? She gave your mum a hard time?'

'You've got no idea.'

'But she's dying. You don't think your mother would forgive her?'

He turned his head towards her. 'Before you found out about me, did you know Esther had a daughter? Did she ever mention that to you?'

'No, come to think of it, she said she—'

'She told you she couldn't have children, right? You told me that the first time we met.'

'That's right. But why—'

'Do you think she'd forgotten she had a daughter? Can anyone be as crazy as that?'

Anna thought for a moment. 'Yes, I think that's possible.'

The pain in his head was worse. He thought longingly of the bottle of pills at home in his bathroom cabinet. 'Don't give me that! She knows, all right. But she's still disowning her, just like she always did.'

'I can't believe that,' said Anna. 'Why on earth would she want do that? You're being very harsh. Heartless, even.' She took out a handkerchief. 'I have to tell you, you've disappointed me. I'd thought we were—' She stopped in mid-sentence, dabbed her eyes and cleared her throat. 'That was not polite. Not professional. I'm sorry. I just – I was vexed with you. It was not professional.'

She was sitting close enough for him to breathe in the flowery perfume that he'd smelled in Esther's grubby kitchen on his first visit. Not professional. An odd choice of words. He wanted to say something reassuring. 'Well, I can see it from your point of view. God knows what you must have thought of me, disappearing like that.'

She smiled at him. 'I'll admit I did feel uncharitable.' Her voice had regained its velvety gentleness. He was enjoying the closeness, the new absence of hostility, but he could tell that for her, this was still business. 'But now that we're having this talk,' she went on, 'I feel I know you a lot better. I can see there were things I didn't understand.'

He tentatively put his hand on hers. He felt no resistance. 'Anna, it's important to me that you know why Esther wants to forget she had a daughter. And why I feel as I do. Before I was born, she—'

'Oh, I'm sorry.' Eleni stood in the doorway holding a pile of papers. Sam drew his hand back, feeling an irrational need to explain himself. 'That's okay, Eleni. Come and meet Anna. She's – a friend of mine from – from a long time ago.'

The two women smiled at each other. Sam could see the curiosity in Eleni's face. 'I'm closing up now, Sam,' she said. 'Will you be—'

'We'll be staying here talking for a while, if that's okay with you,' said Anna. 'We've got a lot to catch up on.'

Eleni put the papers on the table. 'I'll leave you to it, then. I'll deal with these in the morning. So I can leave you to lock up, Sam?'

'Sure. See you tomorrow.'

'See you tomorrow. Pleased to meet you, Anna.'

They sat in silence while she turned off the remaining shop lights, put up the 'closed' sign and left.

As lightly as he could, Sam put his hand back on Anna's. She didn't seem to mind. She moved her face an inch closer to his. Her voice dropped to a whisper and acquired a tremor. 'Sam, after what you've told me I might be wasting my time, but – I need your help.'

As he'd thought. Strictly business. 'How come?'

'Esther's dying.' She was still whispering.

'I know that.'

'I mean, she's only got a few weeks left. Maybe less.'

'I'm sorry to hear that, but I've told you...'

She took her hand away but kept her face close to his. 'She's in pain, Sam. Suffering. She needs palliative care. Badly. The doctor wants her to go into a hospice. She'll be comfortable there, and looked after properly until the end.'

He pictured the emaciated woman besieged in her grim block of flats. He imagined the thugs closing in, adding to her fear and isolation. Even so, how could he feel sympathy for her, knowing what he knew? But how could he turn Anna down flat? And how could he possibly help, even if he wanted to?

'I understand that. But what do you think I could do?'

'She won't go.'

'Why not?'

Anna sat back and dabbed the corners of her eyes with her handkerchief. 'We've arranged a bed for her at the local hospice. St Jude's on Mare Street. It's a lovely place. Staffed by caring people.'

'Sounds ideal. So what's the problem?'

She folded the handkerchief and put it away. 'She's scared. It's run by nuns. She's got it in her head they'll convert her when she's too weak to stop them. Not let her have a Jewish funeral. Give her a Christian burial.'

Anna's expression made him cut his laugh short. 'Are you serious? That's ridiculous. Haven't you told her that?'

'Of course I have,' said Anna, 'but she doesn't trust me. She knows the history of the forced conversions of Jews. She talks about that, she talks about the Holocaust. She thinks I'm in on a plot to convert her.'

Despite his headache, it was another of those moments when he desperately wished for a cigarette. He had no idea what to do with the things Anna was telling him. He put his head in his hands and closed his eyes. He knew she was watching him, waiting. He was clutching onto the smell of her perfume. He opened his eyes. 'You said you need me? I don't see how—'

'She'll listen to you.'

He shook his head. 'Me, talk to her? I'm sorry. No.'

How could Anna's eyes be so gentle, yet capable of drilling into him like that? 'You can't just turn me down flat. She needs you. You're her grandson, no matter what.'

He felt as if he'd been slapped. 'Don't you ever call me that!'

'I'm sorry if it hurts you, but it's a fact. Whatever happened before, I know that means a lot to her now.' She hesitated. 'And besides, she'll listen to you because you're —'

He stiffened. 'Because I'm?'

For the first time Anna stumbled over her words. 'You know…you're…don't get me wrong… I'm not and you are, so—'

'Jewish?'

She nodded.

He laughed long and loud, not caring about Anna's disapproving look. He only stopped when he was almost out of breath. 'I get it,' he gasped. 'I go and see her and I say, "Look Esther, you're a Jew, I'm a Jew. So trust me. I swear on the Talmud and on the…the Torah, and on my mother's life, and – and —on this pot of chicken soup, that those nuns won't tie you down and christen you." And she'll say, "Okay, Sammy, if you say so. You've convinced me, let's go." Is that it?'

Anna stood unmoving, her lips pursed, her face otherwise expressionless. Another thought occurred to him. 'Come to think of it, maybe I shouldn't say "on my mother's life". Might give her ideas again.'

'What?' said Anna.

'Never mind. All you need to know is, no. Definitely no. I'm sorry. You're a really nice person. I-I really like you. A lot. And you probably think I'm a heartless bastard. But that's my answer. I can't help you. Or her.' He stood up and opened the door again. 'Now, if we're finished, I'm locking up and going home.'

Anna put on her hat and coat. Her voice was as calm as always, if a trifle huskier, and the tremor was still there. 'Sam, I know you're a good man. And I know now that Esther did great wrongs to your mother, and you take it personally, as any good son would. But…' She took a step closer to him. 'But, Sam, if you let hate get a hold of you and take you over, you'll lose your humanity. Did you think of that? The woman's suffering. She's frightened. She's sick in the head. She's alone. She's – she's your kin whether you like it or not.'

He gazed at her, thought hard about what might have been, sighed and turned away. 'I'm sorry, Anna. I can't help you.'

She dabbed at her eyes, muttered to herself again, 'I am not being professional,' and put out her hand as if ending a business meeting. 'Thank you for your time, Mr Shaykin,' she said, her voice firm and formal. 'I will find other ways to help my client.'

She turned back as she reached the door. 'Goodbye, Sam. God bless you.' And she was gone.

TWENTY-EIGHT

'This is not entirely professional, Sam,' said Anna, 'but I very much want to do it.' They were in an anteroom off the main atrium of the new wing of St Jude's Hospice in Mare Street. Sister Bridget – twenty years old at the most, in full nun's robe, copper-coloured hair peeping from a head-dress that framed a freckled face – looked on with a slightly reserved beam of approval as Anna folded Sam in a full-blooded hug and kissed him on each cheek in turn. Sam emerged from the embrace with his senses full of the fragrance of her perfume and the warmth of her body. 'Wow! Please feel free to be unprofessional as often as you like, Anna.' He looked surreptitiously at Sister Bridget for any sign that his joke might have offended her and was relieved when both women laughed.

He was making light of it for Anna's sake, but it had been hard. During another of his long sleepless nights he'd gone over and over her visit, thinking about what she'd asked him to do and coming more and more to regret his blunt refusal. Then, standing at Esther's door with his key in the lock, he'd sweated and trembled as he tried to decide whether to go in or to walk away. He'd had to bite back his revulsion at the idea of coming face to face with her, now that he could only think of her as the abuser, the woman who'd tried to deny him his life. And once inside, he'd had just seconds to decide whether he was capable of doing what Anna had asked, or whether he'd want to take this last opportunity to hurl in her face everything he knew about her, and unleash his fury on her.

He'd found her asleep in her chair and had sat waiting for her to wake. What he'd seen when she did, the spark of life lighting the dull eyes and the parchment hand lifting a fraction from her lap towards him, was enough to convince him that she recognised him. And when, after she'd sipped a little water, she'd managed to smile at him and croak his name – his real name – he knew that for him, for reasons he would never understand, it was over. The slate was wiped clean. He'd taken her fingers in his as gently as he could, and spoken to her quietly, until with as much of a smile and a nod as she could muster, she'd understood and agreed.

'I didn't think you'd mind, Sam,' said Anna, 'but I just wanted to thank you for the wonderful thing you did.'

Mind? Did she really not know what effect—? He'd enjoyed the close contact with her, and he felt genuine pleasure at knowing that what he'd done had pleased her. 'It wasn't as hard as I thought it would be. Once I'd managed to convince her that I wasn't in some sort of weird mass-conversion plot, along with you and the entire staff of this place, she started to come round.'

'We've made her comfortable in a little ward with three other Jewish ladies,' said Sister Bridget. 'It was touch and go for a few days, but now they're all getting on well.'

'Swapping recipes and finding out their parents all came from the same *shtetl*, I'll bet,' said Sam.

Sister Bridget laughed. 'We haven't got that far yet, but she's settling down nicely.' She handed Sam a leaflet and they sat at a table while she talked him through it. 'As Anna will have told you, here at St Jude's we welcome any local terminally ill person who needs our help, whatever their faith. For those who want it, ministers of their religions come here. If they don't, we respect that. Everyone here is trained to help people through their final days with dignity and make them as comfortable as possible. So your grandmother, Mr Shaykin, is in the best possible place. God will bless you for persuading her to come here.'

He wasn't at all sure about that. Which God would that be, he wondered, hers or Esther's? Sister Bridget took a file from a grey metal cabinet, laid it on the table and opened it at the first page. 'As your grandmother has named you her next of kin, there are some things I'm permitted to discuss with you.'

So he was her next of kin. That was news to him.

'Firstly, I understand that due to unusual circumstances you had no opportunity to meet your grandmother until a few months ago? Is that correct?'

'Yes, that's right. For reasons that I'd rather not talk about.'

'And we will respect that. Now…' She looked cautiously at him. 'I have your grandmother's medical history here. Can I please check this with you for accuracy? I understand that she has a long-standing history of mental illness? Diagnosed as, let's see, manic depressive psychosis?'

That was – what? – the third, maybe fourth time she'd said 'your grandmother', and he realised that he hadn't minded at all. In fact, he'd liked it. 'I believe that's the medical name for it. She's – she's had a lot of difficulties in her life.'

'So I understand.' Sister Bridget consulted her notes again. 'Also – please don't be offended – her notes say that she can be aggressive? Is excessively concerned about ageing, and unable to come to terms with her loss of physical attractiveness?'

'That sounds about right,' said Sam.

'And she has repetitive delusions of continued presence?'

'I don't—'

'Believes she sees and speaks to the departed?'

'Oh, yes. I see. Yes.'

She looked at the file again. 'When Mrs Symonds came to us a few days ago, it seems that she, in a manner of speaking, brought two brothers with her. Joel and, er, Nathan. Did you know of them?'

Sam nodded. 'Yes. They were killed in World War One.'

'I see. May God rest their souls.' She crossed herself with a rapid gesture and closed the file. 'Our Dr Michaels has examined your grandmother. I'm afraid he's confirmed that she has very little time left. Would you like me to take you to her? I can find you a visiting room where you won't be disturbed.'

Leaving Anna behind, Sam walked with Sister Bridget along a hushed corridor where the flooring absorbed the sound of their footsteps and the light from the weak autumn sun poured in from spacious windows and skylights. It was hard to believe that the traffic noise and smells of Mare Street were so close.

'She'll be happy to see you,' said Sister Bridget. 'And she's been asking when her daughter – your mother – will visit her.'

The thought of trying to explain was too much for him. 'I'm sorry, Sister, but I can tell you that won't happen. Whatever it makes you think of us.'

'You're sure of that?' asked Sister Bridget.

'Yes,' said Sam. 'I'm certain. There's been a broy— Please just take my word for it, my mother's got good reason to feel the way she does.'

'It pains me to hear that,' said Sister Bridget. 'Your mother must be carrying a great hurt indeed.' She showed him into the visitors' room and left him looking round while she went to fetch Esther. The room had two high-backed chairs and a table with a carafe of water, a glass and a vase of pleasant-smelling lavender. The pale-blue walls reminded him of the room in Kate's house. Here, though, in place of her Picasso prints, was a large plastic clock on one wall, and on another a framed poster of a forest with bluebells under giant trees. Shafts of sunlight shone down through their branches, and beneath was a quotation:

And this our life, exempt from public haunt,
Finds tongues in trees, books in the running brooks,
Sermons in stones, and good in everything.

'Here we are.' Sister Bridget skilfully held the door open with one hand while manoeuvring the wheelchair through with the other. She put on the brake and stood back. 'I'll leave you two together. I've put up the "Do not disturb" sign.' She indicated a green telephone by the window. 'Dial three when you want me to come back.' She beamed in turn at Sam and Esther and left.

Esther seemed to be dozing. Her head was slumped forward on her chest and a line of saliva ran down her chin from the corner of her mouth. Her knees were covered by a tartan rug, on which rested a claw-like hand holding a crumpled handkerchief. Sam sat and watched her. As her breathing rose and fell, she emitted a high-pitched rasping sound. A sour blend of bodily odours vied for dominance with the fragrance of the lavender. She seemed to have become even thinner than when he'd seen her a few days earlier. Her face was now a mask of shrivelled skin with no flesh at all, so that it resembled the face of a skull. What must it feel like, he thought, to be at this stage in life? How must it feel to know that all that remained was an undignified stretch of pain and decay, until in its own good time the body finally did its occupant the favour of permanently shutting down? What was the point of hanging on to those useless last weeks, days or minutes? And for those closest, looking on, how could they not wish for death to come as soon as possible, so as not to have to prolong the pointless agony of sitting it out together? He realised, suddenly, the irony of that thought. Here he was, wishing for her death just as she'd once shouted out her wish for his and his mother's. Except that he wanted it now, not from any urge to see her punished, but out of compassion. This emaciated skeleton had once been a beautiful, pampered girl, and a woman proud of her good looks. She had, for all her faults, been strong-willed and a force to be reckoned with, and had been exploited and abused. And just look at her now. He felt an agonising pity for the barely alive creature asleep in the wheelchair. He wondered if his mother would feel the same if she were here now, or if she'd feel that some kind of justice was being done – if she'd think it was right that the woman who'd caused her so much pain was now, in her turn, suffering. He hoped not.

The hand on the rug twitched. Just once, then in a spasm of repeated movements. He thought back to the late-night showings of old horror films at the decrepit Tatler cinema in Dalston. Sharing bags of crisps and peanuts with his school-friends. The moment when the Bride of Frankenstein shows the first sign of life and the crazed scientist shouts, 'She's alive!' Only now he was watching the last signs of life, not the first. She opened her eyes. They were watery and unfocused, just like the monster's bride at the moment of her re-birth.

He was trembling. He waited until he judged she was fully awake, but he still wasn't sure that she knew he was there, or even where she was. She lifted her head, blinked several times and starting coughing. He poured some water and held it to her lips. She drank a little and coughed again. Some spilled from her mouth and he dabbed her chin with his handkerchief. She turned her head slightly to look at him. He gave her an encouraging smile. Her mouth creased into a ghost of a returned smile. She tried to speak, croaked and coughed, and at the next attempt got the words out. 'Who are you?'

He crouched down beside the wheelchair so that his face was level with hers. 'I'm Sam, Esther. I'm your grandson.'

He wondered if she'd understood. There was no response. She closed her eyes again. He stayed quite still, crouched beside her, watching the red second hand go round on the wall-clock. After two minutes he unbent his legs and sat in one of the chairs. Two more minutes passed, then three, then ten. She opened her eyes and turned her head until she found him. 'Sam. Come here.' He resumed his crouching position and she stretched out her hand to him. He took it in his. It was icy and weightless. He held it with great care, imagining that the slightest pressure would make it crumble into pieces.

She cleared her throat with a painful-sounding rasp and spoke so quietly that he had to lean close to her. 'I knew.' He felt the slightest increase in the pressure of her fingers on his. 'First time,' she whispered. 'First time you came.'

Another long silence while he took that in, broken only by the rasping sound of her breathing.

'How old—'

'How old am I? I'm thirty.'

'May. Twenty-eighth.'

Another surprise. 'My birthday. That's right.'

'You know what I did?'

He nodded. 'Yes, I know now.'

'They left me after that. Sadie, Jack. Ben.'

'I know.'

Some tears came: small irregular drops as if her body lacked enough moisture to provide a decent flow.

'I didn't mean it. What I did. What I said. I told Josh I didn't mean it.'

She was getting confused. 'You mean my dad? Jack? You told that to Jack?'

'Jack, yes. Didn't mean—' Her voice trailed away.

'Why did you do it?'

No response. She closed her eyes and seemed to have dozed off. But after a minute or two her eyes fluttered open. 'I tried. To love her. I tried. I wanted – Ben – I tried—'

This time he was sure she'd fallen asleep. But after a while, 'Papa – did you get it?'

He was puzzled for a moment. 'You mean the photo of your father? And the one of—' He stopped himself just in time. 'I had it framed. I took it back to you. Do you remember?'

'Bring it.'

So she wanted to have Isaac's photo near her. A comforting link with her past, despite all his faults.

'I've still got your key. I'll bring it.'

With an effort she summoned up enough strength to open her eyes and smile weakly at him. 'Handsome boy. Like Jack. You know Jack?'

'Yes, I know him.'

Another silence. He'd been crouching down for as long as he could manage. He stood up and returned to watching the red second hand. Esther made a beckoning gesture and he moved closer to her. Her lips moved but no sound came out. He moved even closer and she tried again, but again there was nothing. He moistened his handkerchief in the water glass and dabbed her lips. She tried again. 'Sadie.'

'My mother. Yes?'

'Will she come?'

He hesitated. 'No. I'm sorry.'

'I hurt her.'

'I know.'

'Tell her. Tell her, come.'

'She won't come, Esther. I'm sorry.'

'You know what I did?'

Her eyes were drooping. Her head slumped again. Sam could barely make out her words.

'It wasn't always... Once I was... never dreamed... tried...temper...Ben...Sadie...I never meant ...tried...'

Her eyes shot open again and she stared at him. 'Who are you?' The sudden strength in her voice made Sam jerk back in alarm. It was a scraping, scratching effort at a scream, lacking in volume but terrifying in its intensity. 'Don't touch me! Help me! Papa!'

'It's all right, Esther,' said Sam. 'It's me. You're safe. Try to relax.'

He watched helplessly as she repeatedly ground out the painful notes of her distress. Then, thankfully, Sister Bridget was there. She must have been waiting nearby. She leaned over Esther and said soothing words. The sight of her seemed to agitate Esther even more. 'No! No! Don't do it! *Shemah! Shemah yisrael! Adonay elohaynu adonay echad! Adonay echad!* Ben! Joel! Papa!' Her breathing was fast and shallow, eyes bulging. She was staring at Sister Bridget as if terrified of her. Unable to manage Esther's terror, the young woman began to panic herself, until realisation seemed to dawn and she pulled off her nun's head-dress. Reddish-brown curls tumbled around her face. 'It's all right, my dear,' she murmured, 'I'm here.' The rug had fallen from Esther's knees. She grabbed both of Bridget's hands in hers and clung to them. Bridget gently freed one and stroked her hair. 'I think you'd like to go back to your room now, wouldn't you, my dear?'

Bridget released the wheelchair's brake and pushed her towards the door. Sam followed behind. 'Thank you,' he said. Sister Bridget smiled. With that lovely red hair around her face, he thought, she looked even younger. He wondered what made people like her want to devote their lives to this sort of work. He wished he knew how to put his admiration and respect into words without sounding clumsy.

'You're welcome,' she said, still smiling. She indicated her head-dress, still lying on the floor. 'Would you mind bringing that along with you? I'd better put it back on quick, before we all get into trouble.'

He followed as Sister Bridget pushed Esther back to her ward. It was another bright room, clean and orderly: four beds, each with a table, an armchair and a locker. Three women, similar in age and frailty to Esther, looked with curiosity at the arrival of the small procession. Sister

Bridget parked Esther's chair by her bed, took her head-dress from Sam with another smile of gratitude and put it on. 'Would you like to stay in your chair, Esther, or shall I help you into bed?'

'Chair.' There was no sign of her terror now. It had passed as quickly as it had come.

'Sam. The picture. Promise.'

'I promise.'

Esther raised a bony finger, pointed it at Sam and addressed the women:

'A *shayner mensch, kaynahora,* no?' she muttered. 'I'm his *bubbeh.* My Sadie, my daughter, she'll come. You'll see. She'll come.'

TWENTY-NINE

Sam didn't need the key. Esther's front door had been kicked to pieces. What was left of it swung uselessly on its hinges. The lock had been smashed away and was lying on the floor. Anger boiled up inside him. Whoever did this must have made a hell of a noise. How come no one heard anything? How come no one called the police? Maybe the neighbours were in on it. Or more likely, they just didn't care.

He kicked the remains of the door aside and stepped into the hall. He gagged as the stench reached his nostrils. With a handkerchief pressed to his mouth he found the source of the smell in Esther's room. There were pools of piss, piles of shit all around.

The room had been turned over, smashed, vandalised. The wardrobe had been emptied, her clothes thrown out and left in a tangled heap. Drawers had been upended and their contents scattered around. Her bedding had been thrown on the floor, the mattress and pillows slit open in several places and their innards scattered around the room. There was no sign of her TV and radio. Old and cheap as they were, they'd have been carried away and sold off for a few quid.

Broken glass crunched under his feet. Looking down, he saw the two photos that he'd had restored. The photo of Isaac Levinson's gravestone was ripped to pieces beyond repair, but his portrait, although crumpled and torn, was mainly intact. He'd take it to Mr Howarth, explain the urgency and get it fixed.

He thought about calling the police, but couldn't see much point. He'd better get the flat secured, though. Anna would know who to call to get that done. Meanwhile, the scumbags that did this were welcome to anything else they wanted to cart off or rip up. They'd be doing him a favour.

He was about to go when he thought of the album that Esther had shown him on his last visit, the one with the message from Elias Shapiro. He remembered leaving it beside her as she slept. Inured now to the stench of the place, he fumbled through her scattered clothes and muttered his relief when he found it. They'd shaken the pages loose, probably searching for money, then thrown them back down. He shuffled them together and closed them between their broken covers, together with Isaac's damaged photo. He checked the time. 3.30. He could still get to Mr Howarth before he closed for the day.

The landings and stairwells of Henderson House were deserted as he made his way down to ground level. No sign of Russell and his friends or anyone else, hostile or otherwise. Emerging into the relatively fresh air of Keir Hardie Street he leaned against a wall, closed his eyes and took several deep breaths. It was a cold day, and there was a wind that carried the rumbling of engines and the noises of falling masonry from the demolition of the disused canal-side timber-yards. Still trying to calm himself down, he heard a woman's voice shouting, 'Hey! Hello! Hey!' He ignored it. He badly needed to go home, wash off the stench of Esther's flat and get some rest.

'Hey! Over here!' He opened his eyes and saw the woman he'd spoken to on his first visit. 'I remember you,' she called, 'You're Esther's friend.'

He left the support of the wall and walked to the patch of weeds beside her balcony. 'Actually I'm…that's right. And you're…'

'Maisie.' She grasped the balcony's metal rail and leaned towards him. 'You've been up to Esther's? I saw them take her away. What's happened?'

'She's gone into a hospice. I'm afraid—'

'Hospice? Does that mean she's near the end?'

'I'm afraid so.' He glanced at his watch.

'The poor love,' said Maisie. 'She was a good friend to us when my Hayley was little, but we haven't seen so much of her these past couple of years.' She beckoned him to come closer. 'Anything I can do? I could go up to her flat and clean round if you like.'

He shook his head. 'Thanks, but no point. It's been broken into. Smashed up.'

'Them scumbags!' She clenched her fists. 'I know who they are. The same ones as have been making the woman's life a misery for years. Well, they better watch out. I'll have their guts. You mark my words!'

It was 4.30. If he left now he'd just make it. 'I'm sorry, Maisie, I've got to go. Thanks for asking about Esther. I'll come and let you know when there's—'

Maisie gave him a crumpled smile. 'Thanks. She was a nice woman before she started going strange in the head. She's lucky to have a friend like you.'

*

The phone was ringing as he put his key in the front door, but by the time he'd let himself in it had stopped. He felt relieved. He was itching all over and the smell of Esther's flat was clinging to his clothes and in his hair. He thought he could even taste it. Whoever it was, they'd have to wait until he'd cleaned up and changed.

He was on his way to the bathroom when the ringing started again. Muttering, he picked up the receiver.

'Son? Thank God! I've been ringing you for hours. Where've you been?'

He bit back his reply. 'What's up, Dad?'

'Up, he says? Nothing much. Your mother's gone *meshuggah*, is all! Can you come over?'

Sam sighed. 'What kind of *meshuggah*? What do you think I can do?'

'It's all to do with this Esther business you've dragged up. Your mother's in a terrible state and I'm sorry, God should forgive me, but this is all down to you.'

He was too exhausted to argue. He waited for Jack to go on. 'Son, I don't often say this, but I'm saying it now. Please get over here and help me.'

*

Sadie was lying on the sofa in her housecoat, hair in curlers, a handkerchief clutched in her fingers. She sat up, pulled Sam down into an embrace and kissed his cheeks. He chose his words as carefully as he could. 'What's the matter, Mum? Dad says you're upset about something.'

'Upset? Who's upset? What upset? I'm fine. What's your father been telling you?'

He groaned inwardly. 'He told me…' He was choosing every word with care. 'He said something's worrying you. That maybe I can help?'

'So tell him, Sadie!' said Jack. 'Tell him what *meshuggas* you've got in your head!'

Sadie blew her nose and pushed the handkerchief into the pocket of her housecoat. 'Jack, make me some tea. Strong. Lots of sugar.'

As soon as they were alone, Sadie beckoned to Sam to sit near her and whispered close to his ear. 'Listen, I want to see her. You know where she lives. Take me.' She was looking at him expectantly, nodding as if encouraging him to give the reply she wanted to hear. She'd caught him completely off guard. Did she really mean it? After all she'd said for all those years? He took both of her hands in his. 'Mum, are you serious? Is this what you really want?'

Sadie's expression changed. 'If I say it, I want it! Don't you treat your mother like an old woman who doesn't know her own mind!'

'Tea!' Jack was back with a tray and teacups. 'I made for you as well, Sammy.' He put the tray down and handed

Sadie her cup. 'Did you tell him? Tell him this crazy idea you've got?'

'Crazy!' said Sadie, 'Who says it's crazy?' She turned to Sam. 'She's going to die soon, you told me. Isn't that right?'

He nodded.

'So I want to see her!'

'What good do you think it would do? After all these years!' There was anger tempered with anxiety in Jack's voice. 'Look at you! All *verklempt*, and for what?' He calmed himself and spoke in an undertone: 'Sadie, why not take a couple of your pills?'

Sadie took the handkerchief from her pocket and twisted it with both hands. 'Pills! Please, *verdreh mir nisht in kop* with the pills! For years I dream of this. You know that?' She untwisted the handkerchief and put it back in her pocket. 'I dream I'm looking her in the eye, I'm telling her what she's done to me. And to my father, *olev hashalom*. And she's saying, "Sadie, I'm sorry, forgive me." *Feh*! A dream? A nightmare!'

Jack fetched a bottle of white pills, shook two out and offered them to Sadie on the palm of his hand. 'Here. Drink some tea.'

She did as he asked. 'So where does she live? I'll get dressed. You'll take me.'

Sam could see that he had no choice. 'If you really want to do this, you'll have to be quick. She's been taken to a hospice. She's got very little time left.' He watched Sadie's eyes drooping. He wasn't sure if she'd heard what he'd said. He took the cup from her hand.

'So, take me to this – hospice,' she mumbled. Her eyes closed and her head fell back.

'She'll sleep for a bit now,' whispered Jack. 'It's the best thing when she's like this.'

'What are those pills?' Sam whispered back.

'She's been having these turns ever since you started with this Esther business. The doctor says she's near to having a nervous breakdown. The pills help her nod off for a little while when she gets too upset.'

'I had no idea,' said Sam.

Jack shrugged. 'We tried hard enough to tell you.' He crept out of the room and came back with a blanket. He tucked it over Sadie and stood beside her. 'So, from what you're telling us, she's on her last legs now. God should forgive me, but I can't say I'm sorry.'

Sadie moaned and stirred. Sam tucked the ends of the blanket under her. A new thought was forming. An opportunity. He'd give it a try. 'So, this broygus between Mum and her, it's never going to end, is that right?'

'Never, Son. Not while she's alive.'

'What about after she's dead? Will the broygus carry on even then?'

'Why not?'

'Is that what you want? Is that what you want for Mum? For yourself? For me?'

Jack stroked Sadie's hair as he spoke. 'Son, a broygus isn't something you want. It's just – it just is.'

'Just is what, exactly?'

Jack eased himself into an armchair. 'Son,' he murmured, 'it feels like you're cross-examining me. Did you ever think of becoming a lawyer?'

Sam laughed. 'Sorry, Dad. But isn't it true that it's a sin to let a broygus go to the grave, and it's a *mitzvah* to settle one? To me that makes sense. Doesn't it to you?'

'Huh!' Jack waved his hands as if wanting to clear away Sam's words from the air between them. 'Hark at my son! One minute he throws his religion back in my face like it's a – a disease or something, and the next he's talking like a *tzadiker* rabbi all of a sudden! What, you've started studying Torah? You go to *yeshiva*? Sins, *mitzvahs*! Do me a favour! I've heard enough of your nonsense.'

Sam knew he was on dangerous ground. Push too hard, use the wrong words, and he'd never get his father to see things his way. 'Please, just give me a chance, Dad. Let me finish. I think it'll do Mum a lot of good if she can settle this broygus with her mother before she dies.'

Jack sat straight up and glowered at Sam. 'What are you saying? She should see that woman?'

Sam had to dredge up every shred of his courage to carry on pressing his point. 'I'm saying, maybe it would help her put everything behind her if she went to see her mother. Tell her how she's felt all these years. Even make some kind of peace.' He braced himself for the explosion.

'Now who's *meshuggah*?' said Jack. His voice had risen. He glanced at Sadie, whose eyelids were starting to flutter, and dropped it back to murmur. 'You mean it? Take her to see the old bitch in that – what did you call it?'

'Hospice.'

'Where is it?'

'Not far away. Mare Street.'

'What's it called?'

'St Jude's.

Jack's voice rose again. 'What? What's that? Some sort of *goyische* name?'

'It's run by nuns.'

Jack put his hands to his head. 'Oy vay! You're not serious!'

Sam found his father's reaction almost comical, but now wasn't the time to laugh. 'It's not like you think, Dad. It's really nice there. They respect all religions. They take in a lot of Jewish people.'

'Sure they do,' said Jack. 'But are they still Jews when they go out feet first? I've read about those places.'

Sam couldn't help laughing. 'Dad, I don't know where you get these ideas.'

Jack settled down into the armchair. 'No? Son, you never heard of Palestine Place? It was in Bethnal Green when we were kids. A big old house with grounds all round it. Everyone was scared stiff of the place. We wouldn't go near it, not even to peep through the railings. They had people there who went out every day to the slums looking for the poorest, hungriest Jews. They'd spin them some yarn about charity, bring them in, give them a bit of *pishachs* to eat, say a couple of prayers over them, turn them into Christians before they knew what was happening, then sling them back out. Saving their souls, they called it. Those bastards! They can take their saint this and saint that, and shove it up their arses!'

Sam felt as if he'd stepped on a landmine. Far from bringing his father round to his way of thinking, he'd triggered a childhood memory that had worked him up into a frenzy. Maybe he should drop the idea. Or perhaps it was worth just one more effort. 'I'm sorry, Dad. I didn't know anything about that. But that was back then. These things don't happen any more. This place is nothing like that. If you saw it you'd—'

Jack held up his hand. 'Stop! Enough! Not enough you bring all this trouble on us, now you tell me you stuck Esther Symonds in with nuns and *goyim*. Okay, that's what she deserves, and she should *geh in drerd arein*. But you're telling me your mother should go to that place? And you think I'd go there? So now, who's *meshuggah*? You or me?'

Jack had gone purple in the face and had let his voice rise to a shout. Sadie woke up and rubbed her eyes. 'You expect me to sleep with all that *geschrei* going on?'

Jack helped her to sit up and put a cushion behind her head. 'I'm sorry, *bubeleh*. Sorry we woke you. Me and Sam, we were just—'

'I heard you,' said Sadie. 'Sam, I want you should take me to that place. I want to speak to my mother before she dies.'

THIRTY

On the short drive through lashing rain to St Jude's Hospice, nobody spoke. Sam's mother sat straight-backed, her arms folded and her lips pressed tightly together, and his father stared morosely out of the window. Sam knew that they were steeling themselves for what was coming, and his own feelings of unease were bordering on panic.

He parked outside the hospice and led his parents inside, the repaired photo of Isaac Levinson in its brown paper wrapper tucked under his raincoat. His parents stood close together in the entrance hall, their arms linked for mutual support. Sadie's lips were still compressed and she was trembling slightly, but Sam was relieved to see her nod with grudging approval as she took in the tidiness, the spotless floors and the smart pine furniture upholstered in bright reds and blues. He went to the reception desk and banged twice on the brass service bell. No one appeared. He looked around for someone to help him but the place seemed deserted. He saw his mother clutch his father's sleeve and speak to him in an urgent undertone. Perhaps she'd changed her mind and was asking him to take her home. Maybe that would be for the best. He banged on the bell again and spoke with what he hoped was a light-hearted tone. 'Sunday afternoon. They must be short-staffed. We shouldn't really do this, but I suppose it'll be okay if we go straight to Esther's room. I know the way, and there's bound to be someone there.'

He was hoping to see Sister Bridget again. He'd liked her. He felt that their joint encounter with Esther had created a bond between them. The way she'd jumped in and handled Esther's meltdown had been – well, just fantastic.

'If you're sure that'll be all right, Son?' said Jack. He was wiping the rain from his glasses with a large white handkerchief. He put them back on, gently took Sadie's from her face and did the same for her.

'It'll be fine,' said Sam. He looked at his mother. She was gazing around, taking in her surroundings, her lips still pressed together as if she were forcing down a fierce internal struggle. He wondered what she was thinking. If she'd expected to be in alien territory, walking through a forest of crucifixes and religious icons, she'd be feeling reassured – or disappointed, depending on how she viewed it. Perhaps she was even now having second thoughts, or maybe she was concentrating on calling up reserves of courage. She took off her raincoat, shook it out and folded it over her arm. Under it, he saw, she'd made a real effort. She was wearing a smart dark-green dress with a cameo brooch and a gold necklace. Outwardly, except for an unusually frequent patting of her hair, she looked quite composed. He, on the other hand, was trying his best to control his hammering heartbeat.

Jack took both of Sadie's hands in his. 'Are you certain, *bubeleh*? Certain you want to do this? If you've changed your mind, Sam can—'

She took her hands from Jack's. 'No. We're here now, and I'm going to do it. I want to see her.' Her voice was calm, but Sam could see her anxiety. He looked at his father, who nodded his agreement. He drew a deep breath. 'Okay. Follow me.'

Three wraith-like women in floral housecoats looked up expectantly from their armchairs as Sam and his parents came into the room, then retreated back into themselves as it registered that they were someone else's visitors. Sadie managed a weak smile, and one woman smiled back at her. Sam was gazing with horror at Esther's bed. It had been stripped, leaving the mattress and pillows bare. Fresh linen and blankets were folded in a neat pile at its foot.

Unlike the other three lockers, there was no vase of flowers or jug of water on hers. He felt cold. His parents were looking confused, but he could see the understanding starting to dawn in their eyes.

'Can I help you?'

Sam had never before seen the tall, iron-grey-haired woman who stood in the doorway exuding authority. She was wearing a smart dark-blue medical worker's dress, high at the neck, low at the hemline, plain except for a silver fob-watch pinned to the lapel, and shiny black shoes. 'We came to see Esther Symonds, my grandmother,' he said. 'I'm Sam Shaykin. These are my parents.' He hesitated. 'But we seem to have—'

The woman's voice was business-like but not unfriendly. 'We do expect visitors to make themselves known at reception. It's a security matter, you understand.'

Jack was the first to reply. 'Yes, I'm sorry, Mrs—'

'It's Sister. Sister Bernadette. I'm a member of the Order, but I'm also a nursing Sister.'

'Yes, of course. Sister. I'm sorry, Sister, but nobody… This is my wife, Sadie. She's – was…'

Sister Bernadette smiled. 'I'm very pleased to see you here, Mrs Shaykin. I'm sure your mother will be, too. My colleague Sister Bridget has been taking special care of Mrs Symonds. I know she would have been happy to meet you, but she's away on a retreat until tomorrow.'

Sam felt a pang of disappointment. There was a silence while he, his parents and Sister Bernadette all nodded and smiled at each other and the three women looked on with renewed interest. No one seemed to know what to say next. Sam was unsure what to think. If his mother had come too late, was that a pity or was it for the best? In any event he felt the need to break the silence.

'So, Esther—'

Sister Bernadette indicated the room's occupants with her eyes and put a finger to her lips. 'We can talk outside.'

She ushered them into the corridor, closed the door and spoke in a hushed voice. 'Mrs Symonds is going fast, I'm afraid. We've moved her to a room of her own where she can be peaceful. Would you like to visit her to say your farewells?'

'That's what I'm here for,' said Sadie. So his mother was going to have her moment after all. He saw that a spot of colour had appeared on each of her pale cheeks. He knew she was screwing up her courage and he couldn't help feeling admiration for the effort she was making to maintain her determination.

'This way.' Sister Bernadette led them to a room a short distance along the corridor. She stood in front of the closed door and spoke in a low murmur. 'At this stage we keep the room warm and the lighting low. We're keeping Mrs Symonds comfortable with pain management, so she'll just be pleasantly floating in a dreamy state. She won't be feeling any discomfort at all.'

'I can talk to her?' said Sadie.

'Yes, but I'm afraid it's unlikely that she'll take in what you say. Of course we can never be sure how much or little our departing souls are aware of at this stage. One thing we do know, even when they're heavily sedated they still respond to their name. Would you like to go in now?'

Sam looked again at Sadie. Jack had his arm around her waist and she was leaning her weight against him. She nodded to Sister Bernadette, disengaged herself from Jack's support and took a firm step towards the door.

With its dim light and high temperature, the room's climate resembled a hothouse for exotic plants. The curtains were drawn across the window and a tang of disinfectant mingled with the odour of pine-scented air freshener. On one wall was a large picture of a group of solemn-looking white-bearded men dressed in hooded robes and carrying shepherds' crooks, standing in a green meadow against a background of snow-topped mountains, gazing up at golden shafts of sunlight shining down at them through dark clouds.

Esther was lying on her back with her head facing towards them. Sam was so shocked by what he saw that he had to look away, but he forced himself to look back. She was unrecognisable. Her face was a mask of dry, yellow, parchment-like skin stretched over an almost hairless skull. Her eyes were closed and one side of her mouth sagged half open. As far as he could tell, the shape beneath the bedclothes was completely inert. The sight made him feel a mixture of pity and revulsion. Was it his imagination, or could he taste the odours in the air from her dying body, that the chemicals and artificial scents couldn't conceal? Perhaps they really had come too late. Perhaps that was a blessing for his mother, who had turned her back on the bed and was staring fixedly at the shepherds. He was still carrying the framed photo that he'd gone to so much trouble for. She'd have no use for it now. He put his coat on a chair and laid the photo, still in its wrapper, on top of it.

'Come.' The Sister took Sadie's hand and drew her to the bedside. She followed meekly, but still kept her head turned away. Sam glanced at his father and saw the signs of strain on his face. He wished that he knew what to do or say to help him. He tried touching his father's hand, and was pleased when he felt him grasp his and hold on to it.

The Sister stood opposite Sadie, on the other side of the bed, and brought her mouth to within a few inches of Esther's ear.

'Esther.'

She was right. There was a thread of life still there. Sam had seen a tiny flutter of an eyelid. Sister Bernadette spoke again, in the same clear, quiet voice. 'Esther, your family is here for you.'

This time he saw no response. Perhaps he'd been fooling himself. Perhaps the Sister had been wrong after all. But she seemed so sure. She stood up and smoothed down the front of her dress. 'She knows you're here. It'll be a comfort to her. I'll leave you together now. I'll be nearby if you need me.' Her footsteps made no noise as she glided away.

The three of them stood without speaking for several minutes. Sam watched his mother force herself to look at Esther, while Jack stood close by. Two or three times Sam thought that she was about to speak, but each time she lapsed back into silence. He tried to guess what she was thinking, what words she was trying to form, but her expression gave him no clues. He caught his father's eye and with slight shrugs they exchanged an unspoken message of helplessness and concern.

Without warning, Sadie closed her eyes and began to sway. Sam feared that she was about to faint. He and his father moved at the same moment to steady her, and together they helped her to the chair beside the bed. Moments later, she opened her eyes to find herself looking into her mother's face. She jumped as if startled, shook her head and turned away, her tears streaming. Jack put his hands on her shoulders and spoke quietly to her. 'Sadie, what good is this? You've seen her. Now let's go.'

Sadie reached over her shoulder and patted Jack's hand. 'No.' She put her hands in her lap, clenched her fingers and straightened them out again. She shuddered, took a deep breath and leaned down close to her mother, staring at her closed eyes as though willing them to open.

'Mother.' There was no response.

'Mother!' She spoke again, her voice a trace louder and the tone a touch more cutting. Still nothing.

'Sadie,' said Jack, 'enough now. She's too far gone. You're wasting your time.'

Without taking her eyes from her mother, Sadie waved him away. Louder still, and with a sharp, incisive tone, she said, 'Esther!'

Sam drew in his breath as he saw Esther's eyelids flutter again. Sadie sat back and glanced at Jack with a look of grim satisfaction. Jack gazed upwards and shook his head in despair. Sadie turned back and bent towards Esther again, speaking without any sign of nervousness or even emotion, her voice clear and calm. 'I don't know if you can hear me. Please God you can, because I've got things to say.' With a steady hand she poured some water from a jug on the bedside locker, took a sip and continued. 'Every day, I don't make this up, every day of my life I think about you. Every day since you wished me dead. Thirty years ago now, that was. You remember that? You remember what you said to me? The last thing you ever said to me?'

To Sam's surprise, his mother had become calm, resolute, self-assured. She took another sip of water. 'Don't get me wrong, I want to be fair. You were nice to me sometimes, that I'll give you. When I was little you dressed me up nice, made me look pretty. And always in the house was good food to eat. You always kept a good table.'

Sadie paused. The rain, blown by the wind against the window, made tiny tapping sounds in the silence. Sam and his father exchanged another glance. She put the glass down and began again. 'You know what I remember? I was six, maybe seven, we went on holiday to the seaside. You, me and my father, rest his soul. We stayed in a nice guest house. In Cliftonville. A proper Jewish one with good *haimische* food. My father had this joke, you remember? He used to say, "Cliftonville, that's the Yiddishe word for Margate." We went on the beach every day. And every day my father, God rest his soul, he takes me in the sea and you, you stay with the deckchairs. So one day we come out from the sea, and you've got that broygus face. Seven years old, and already I know that face. You're doing the evil eye look, like only you can do. Whenever you do that look, I know it's because I did something wrong, but I never know what. And then you give my poor father the look. So I know you're broygus with him as well. You say something to him I don't understand, but I know it's something bad. I'm frightened. My father, like always, he just stays quiet. He takes my hand and he says to me, "Come for a little walk, *tatteleh*," in that quiet voice. And you say – no, you scream like a – like a madwoman, so the people on the beach near us, they turn round and look – you shout, "Take her! Good riddance! Don't bring her back! Give her away! She's filth! She's God's curse!" Do you remember that? The first time you called me filth?' Her voice cracked. 'I do. Every day of my life I remember that.'

Sadie poured more water and drank half a glassful. Sam found himself shivering despite the room's heat. How many more painful childhood memories had his mother held within herself for all those years? Did she hope that Esther, too, would remember that day? Was she honestly expecting that her mother, on the point of death and in a deep coma, would have enough life left in her to hear the bitterness in her words? Did she really believe that her mother would feel, or even manage to communicate in some way, the slightest degree of regret?

He inched towards the bed and stood near his mother's back, looking over her shoulder at Esther's face, trying to see if there were any signs that she even knew that her daughter was there, let alone know what she was saying or be able to react in any way. Sadie sensed his presence and glanced over her shoulder at him. He was looking into the face of a stranger. There was a part of his mother that she must have always kept to herself, never shared with him. He knew in that moment that he hadn't ever entirely known her; that after this, he was going to have to start getting to know her all over again.

Sadie turned back to her mother. She reached out instinctively to stroke her remaining strands of hair, but recoiled as she realised what she'd been about to do. She seemed to tense her body, then leaned close to her and spoke so softly that Sam had to strain to hear the words.

'A thing I want you should know right away is, I don't hate you. Not any more.'

She paused again, not taking her eyes from her mother. Was she waiting for a hint of consciousness, Sam wondered, or was she considering how to go on? The silence seemed to stretch out before she spoke again – in a matter-of-fact tone of voice now, as if having an everyday chat with an old friend.

'You look surprised. Why, you think I should hate you? You're right, I should. I did. I'll tell you a secret. You want to know my secret? Listen, I'll tell you. From when I was very young, I hated you. God should forgive me, every day I prayed for you to be dead. For you to have a heart attack, maybe, or to be run over. All my life I hated you. But now – no, I don't hate you.'

Sam watched as Sadie put her ear close to Esther's lips. 'What's that? How do I feel about you now? I'll tell you. Nothing. Nothing is what I feel about you. I'm looking in your face, and I know I'm finished with you once and for all. And what I'm feeling is, just, nothing. Can you hear me? Nothing.'

Sadie's composure cracked. She put her hands over her face and collapsed into tears. Sam rushed forward to comfort her, but his father got there first. 'Sadie, enough already! The woman can't hear you! She doesn't know you're there! You're making yourself ill. For what?' He put his arm round her shoulders and tried to draw her out of the chair. She pushed him away with her elbow. Her voice lost its control and became shrill and quavering. 'You go if you want, Jack. You too, Sam. But I'm staying until I've finished.'

Sam looked from his mother to the shrivelled, inert figure in the bed. Where, he wondered, should his sympathy be: with the dying mother or the distressed daughter? He was unable to disentangle his own feelings. His father took Sadie's hands from her face and gave her his handkerchief. 'Sadie, this isn't right. What, you want to torment the woman with her last breaths on earth? You want the last say in the broygus?' His voice rose. 'Sadie, this is wrong! Stop it! Now!'

She blew her nose and gave back the handkerchief. 'Didn't you say she can't hear me? So what difference if I talk?'

Jack shook his head in despair. 'Sadie, it's like you're someone I never knew before. So you tell me, what's the point of talking to the woman if she can't hear you?'

'*I* can hear me!' Sadie ground out each word in a shouted whisper of anger and pain. The points of red in her cheeks stood out even more clearly, and her eyes looked bloodshot. 'I'm saying this for me. It's my last chance. I don't care if she can't hear. And if she can, so better still!'

Jack and Sadie were locked in their drama. For the time being, Sam had no part to play. It was a strange, unreal feeling, like being a ghost with no substance walking amongst solid people, unseen, unheard and unable to participate in their lives. He stood back, observing and waiting.

The temperature in the over-heated room seemed to be affecting Jack. His face was turning a deep red. He loosened his tie and undid the top button of his shirt. Now there was less compassion, more firmness in his voice when he spoke to his wife. 'I'm sorry, I won't let you do this. You, of all people, talking to a dying woman like you want to punish her! No! This stops now! You hear me?'

Sadie smiled, kissed her husband's cheek and spoke to him in a reassuring tone. 'Punish? No. Just talk. I just want a little talk with my mother. We haven't had one for thirty years. Leave me be, Jack. Please.'

Jack sighed with exasperation and stood back. Sadie lowered her head and whispered to her mother in the same conversational voice as before. 'My father, *olev hashalom*, he knew I hated you, and he always told me not to. "Sadie," he used to say, "you must never hate. You never know what people have suffered. You must never hate anyone." It didn't make any difference. I hated you. But my father didn't. All those things you did to him, and to me, and still he loved you. You knew that. Didn't you?'

She waited, her eyebrows raised in anticipation. Sam was starting to feel revulsion at his mother's pretence of holding a two-way conversation. Or perhaps it wasn't a pretence. Was it possible that she believed she was hearing her mother's side of the conversation? He strained to hear as she began talking again.

'Did you love him? You can tell me. Did you?' She wagged her finger. 'No, don't bother. I know you didn't. You never did. He knew that. But he used to tell me, every time you did bad things, he used to say, "Your mother can't help it. Your mother's been through a lot. She doesn't mean to hurt you." That's what he always said.'

Sadie's face, too, was turning red. She drank some more water and signalled to Jack to re-fill the jug from the sink. 'And after what you did that time, when you wanted me and my baby dead, even then he didn't hate you. But I did. I hated you so much, it made me ill. It still makes me ill, did you know that? But my father always told me, right to the end, "You have to understand people," he used to say. "You have to understand people, not hate them."'

The rain had stopped and sunlight was trying to find its way in through the drawn curtains. Sam would have liked to open them and let the light into this dim, stuffy room with its fine dividing-line between life and death. He longed to be outside. He looked at the picture on the wall and imagined being one of the shepherds, holding up his face to the sun's rays as they burst through the clouds.

Sadie put down her glass and began again. 'So, I went on hating you. And I always loved my father. I still loved him, even after he told me the truth. About you and him, I mean. And about what happened to you. You think that made any difference, after he told me? You should know better.'

Sam stiffened. What was this? Even after her father had told her what, exactly? So she knew, after all? Still trying to remain unobtrusive, he redoubled his efforts not to miss a single one of his mother's whispered words.

'I know what you suffered, and I feel for you. What, that surprises you? I've got feelings for you, when you never had any for me? I told you, you can thank my father for that.' She cupped her ear, as if listening for Esther's reply. Sam had no more patience with his mother keeping up this charade. It struck him as tasteless and even cruel. He felt disappointed that she'd behave in this way. For whose benefit was she doing it? For her own? For his? For Jack's? What did she hope to gain by it?

Sadie widened her eyes in feigned surprise. 'What? He wasn't really my father? My father was one of those *mamzers*, a *missa meshuna* they should take, who did those terrible things to you? Oh, you're surprised? You didn't think I knew that? Well, I do! I've known it for more than thirty years. And you know what?' She stood up and walked stiffly away from the bedside. Her voice, steely and loud, rang across the room. 'Whatever happened to you – and God forbid such a thing should ever happen to anyone – Ben Symonds, your husband, *was my father.*' She emphasised the words by jabbing a forefinger at her own chest. 'He loved me. He taught me to love. I loved him. I still do, God rest his soul. But you?' She laughed. A sharp, humourless laugh. 'Bad things happened to you, so you made bad things happen to me. And to him. Is that your excuse? Well, if that's how it is, I should have made bad things happen to my Sam. Shouldn't I? But I never did. I love him. I always have. Like my father loved me.' She went back to the bedside and lowered her voice again. 'That's what I want to tell you. Nothing that happened to you forced you to be bad. You had a choice. I also had a choice. But I chose not to be bad. Thanks to what my father taught me, I chose love. You made your choice. You chose hate. You didn't have to. Your life could have been different.'

She leaned once more towards the motionless figure. 'My father was right. Look what hating you all these years has done to me! And to my Jack! And to my Sammy! So now, I'm not going to hate you any more. It finishes now!' She cupped her ear again. 'What, you want I should forgive you?' She shook her head violently from side to side. 'No, no! Never! But I feel for you. Yes, I feel for you. Even though you never felt for me.' She turned away, fixed her eyes for a moment on the shepherds still gazing up towards the sunlight, then turned back. 'Go to your end knowing that. And please God it should bring you a little bit of comfort!'

This time Sadie let Jack take her into his arms, sobbing. Sam had no idea what to do. He looked down at Esther, wondering but doubting if any of what his mother had said might have got through to her. Sadie's head was against Jack's chest and he was comforting her, so only Sam saw Esther's eyelids flutter and her eyes flicker open for a fraction of a second. In that moment he was sure that something – he couldn't say what, or how much – had registered with her. He felt a strong desire to be alone with her, to restore the atmosphere of calm to the room and to communicate to any remaining shreds of her understanding, that she was with a friend. 'Mum,' he said, 'I think you should let Dad take you out now. Go and find Sister Bernadette and see if she'll give you a cup of tea or something.'

Sadie was calm again. 'All right, Sam. I've had my say.'

'You go and get that tea,' said Sam, 'I'll join you in a minute.'

'What's the point, Son?' said Jack. 'Come with us now.'

Sam glanced at Esther. Her eyes were firmly shut and

there were no signs of consciousness. He couldn't be certain of what he thought he'd seen. 'Dad, please, no more arguments. I'll be a few minutes.'

Jack shrugged and nodded. Sam waited until his parents had left the room, then sat beside the bed. He pressed his lips to her forehead. It was ice-cold. Again, he thought that he saw a movement of her eyelids. 'I'll come back,' he whispered. 'I'll stay with you.' He kissed her again. 'I'm here, Grandma.'

THIRTY-ONE

Sam knew that he'd been dreaming, but as soon as he opened his eyes and saw Sister Bridget's face smiling down at him he couldn't remember what about. Every part of his body was complaining about the night spent in the chair beside Esther's bed. He moved his head carefully from side to side and tried stretching out his legs. He peered at the wall-clock: 6.30am.

'I've brought you some tea,' said Sister Bridget. 'Did you get any sleep at all?'

As she handed him the white china cup he could smell the washing powder freshness of her clothes and a hint of soap on her hands. He was conscious of being unshaven and bleary-eyed. He turned his face away to spare her the sour smell of his breath. 'Thanks. I think I got a few hours. I woke up a few times and checked her breathing. As far as I can tell, nothing's changed.'

Sister Bridget examined Esther, taking care to disturb her as little as possible. 'I'm glad I got back in time to see her through to the end. Her breathing's weaker but she's comfortable. Why don't you go home and get some proper sleep? It'll do you good.'

'I think I will. I could do with a clean-up and a change of clothes. You've got my number? You'll call me if anything happens?'

Sister Bridget folded her hands inside the sleeves of her robe. 'Of course. Would you like to join us for a simple breakfast before you go?'

He eased himself out of the chair. 'Thanks, no. I'll get off now and come back as soon as I can.'

*

He badly wanted some strong coffee and a bath, but amongst the junk-mail and bills was a letter with a Spanish stamp and his address in Deborah's handwriting. He sat at the kitchen table turning it over and over, hoping the news would be good and not knowing how he would cope, today of all days, if it wasn't. He tore open the first inch of the envelope with his thumb, then changed his mind and busied himself making the coffee. He couldn't remember whether he'd replied to her last letter or even the one before that. Time had been passing so quickly, what with everything going on. At that moment, missing her felt like a physical pain, a lump in his gut. And there was fear, too – fear that when he read the letter he'd know for sure that she wasn't coming back. And that would be exactly what he deserved.

The water had bubbled through the coffee maker and was starting to shoot out of the spout onto the top of the gas stove. He grabbed the metal handle and swore as the heat bit into his palm. With tears in his eyes he ran his hand under the cold tap until the pain subsided. He dried his hand and his eyes on a teacloth, poured a mugful, added milk and plenty of sugar and downed half of the syrupy liquid in one gulp.

Since being with Deborah he'd learned to trust again. But for her it had been all give, and he'd given her so little back. Worst of all, he'd kept on taking the piss out of her beliefs until he'd finally pushed her too far. He banged his mug down on the table. 'So, what exactly,' he said out loud, 'What the hell is my problem?' Hadn't she told him once – or was it Kate? – well, one or the other of them had told him the sad truth, that he was still blaming the entire Jewish religion for his parents' behaviour over Libby. He laughed out loud, a bitter laugh of self-recrimination and defeat. How fucking stupid was that! He could see it clearly now, but what use was it, now that he'd lost her for good? She had a great job in Barcelona. She'd made new friends. The world was opening up for her. Why would she want to come home to this grumpy, cynical atheist?

It was time to get back to St Jude's. He thought of yesterday's events, of the surprising new things he'd learned from his mother's visit to Esther. Would he write those into his journal, or was it time, now, to put an end to all that?

He took a bath and put on fresh clothes. He was halfway out of the door when he turned back and picked up Deborah's letter again. He studied the design on the stamp, turned the envelope over and read the return address in her handwriting, put it down, picked it up again, tore it open and flattened out the two closely written sheets.

His eyes skimmed down the first page. Usual stuff. *Lovely weather, work very busy. Getting to know the city. Nice Barceloneta clubs and bars. Found a place serves kosher tapas. Rented a car, travelled the countryside. Very beautiful.*

Second page. Better. *Haven't heard from you. Hope everything's okay. How are you getting on with Esther?*

Bottom of the second page. Yes! At last, there it was! *Missing you. Love you. Differences, yes, but hope you still feel we can—'*

Elation mixed with relief, mixed with hope, mixed with the anticipation of loss and the expectation of grief. So many emotions all at once, all racing around inside his head and coursing through his body. With a lighter heart he locked up, dropped in to touch base with Eleni, crossed the road for a breakfast of sausages and fried eggs on toast at Kelami's Café, and two hours later made his way back to St Jude's.

Sister Bridget was waiting for him. 'Oh, Mr Shaykin, thank goodness! I've been calling your home.'

It could only mean one thing. 'Esther? Is she?—'

Sister Bernadette appeared and took over. 'I'm afraid Mrs Symonds is very near the end now,' she murmured. 'Would you like to be with her, or would you prefer…'

'I-I don't know,' said Sam. 'I've never seen anyone…' But he had. He was five years old again, watching his grandfather's body floating to the floor in slow motion. 'I – yes, I want to be with her.'

'We'll come with you to make sure she's comfortable,' said Sister Bernadette.

He didn't know what to say. 'Thank you' sounded somehow too mundane.

When the two women had left Sam alone with Esther, he sat beside her bed. 'I'm here, Grandma.' He felt that whispering was appropriate, although he had no idea why. He kissed her forehead. 'It's me, Sam.'

There was no response, no movement. The only sign of life was a barely audible sound of clicking in her throat. He sat still and watched her, thinking of nothing in particular, every so often stroking her head or squeezing her hand. Once or twice he thought he felt a slight return pressure, and now and again he thought he saw her eyelids flicker. But he couldn't be sure. Eventually, when even the clicking had stopped and there was no sound at all, he went to find Sister Bernadette, who came and confirmed that Esther had died. 'My condolences, Mr Shaykin,' she said. 'God bless you. And – I wish you long life.'

'Thank you for that, Sister,' said Sam. 'And thanks to all of you for caring for my grandmother.'

He called Ron from Sister Bernadette's office.

'I wish you long life, boychick. You were with her?'

'Yes.'

'She was peaceful?'

'Yes, I think so.'

'Thank God. And the broygus?'

'I think it's over.'

'From your mouth to God's ears. Now, you want me to take care of things? Fix the *levoyah*? Make the arrangements?'

'Would you? I wouldn't know—'

'It'll be another *mitzvah,* boychick. Two days from now, Thursday. Okay for you?'

'Of course. Do I need to do anything?'

'No. I'll make some calls, then I'll let you know exactly where and when. Then you can let people know.'

'Okay. And Ron – thanks. For everything.'

'You're welcome, Son. How are you doing now? You feeling okay?'

'I'm fine.'

'Good. And boychick – just remember, you did a big mitzvah, believe me. A massive one. You helped the old lady. You were there till the end. You ended the broygus. It's what Hashem wanted of you. Now you can say the kaddish for her and your life will go on.'

Right then, Sam didn't have the heart to argue.

THIRTY-TWO

Thursday morning was cold, dull and rainy. During the hour-long drive round the North Circular to Stanbury, the silence in Sam's car was only broken by the slap of the wipers against the windscreen. Jack spent most of the journey gazing out at the traffic, occasionally using the cloth Sam had given him to stop his side window from misting up.

Leaving the North Circular at the Mulberry Hill Roundabout, they passed through the rain-sodden Stanbury Town Centre and followed the signposts to the Jewish cemetery. Sam turned in through the high wrought-iron gates and drove round the crowded car park.

'We're early,' said Jack. 'These'll be the people at the funeral before – before ours.'

Sam found a space, parked and glanced at his watch. '10.25. Let's sit here for a bit. No point waiting in the rain.' He undid his top shirt-button and loosened his tie. 'I'm glad you decided to come, Dad. I hoped you would.'

Jack shrugged. 'I don't suppose many people'll show up, so they might have a job scraping a *minyan* together. Which reminds me, I've got a spare *kappel* if you need it.'

He took a black skullcap from his pocket. Sam thought back to the night when he'd first told his parents about Esther. 'Thanks, Dad. I've forgotten mine as usual.' He hadn't, but taking the scrap of silk from his father felt like accepting a peace offering. He put it on. 'How's this? Do I look the part?'

Jack took his own skullcap from his pocket and fixed it in place. 'Yes. At least you look the part.'

Sam knew what his father meant. 'You know I'm just going through the motions, don't you, Dad?'

'But you're doing the right thing. You're showing respect. I'm proud of you for that.'

Sam felt his eyes prickling. He'd been determined not to let his emotions get the better of him today, and here he was, and the funeral hadn't even begun. 'Thanks, Dad. That means a lot. And by the way…' He leaned across and took a book with blue marbled covers from the glove compartment. 'You recognise this?'

Jack took it from him. 'Your *barmitzvah* gift from the *shul*? Of course I do.' He turned it over in his hands. 'It's in perfect condition.'

Sam took it back. 'Well, it's been a long time since I had any use for it.'

'So what's it doing here?'

Sam opened the book at a place he'd marked with a slip of paper. 'I'll be using it today. My Hebrew's a bit rusty, but I've been practising. Look.' He passed the book back to Jack.

'The *kaddish*? You're going to say the *kaddish*? For Esther?'

Sam nodded. 'It's part of the deal.'

'I don't understand, Son. What deal?'

He took the book from his father's hands and closed it. 'It's hard to explain. Let's just say it's something I want to do.'

Jack narrowed his eyes. 'You want to say a prayer – not just any old prayer, but that one – when you don't believe? You think that's right?'

Sam buttoned up his shirt and straightened his tie. 'Maybe, maybe not. But she was my grandmother, like it or not. And someone should say it. Do you want to?'

'Me?' laughed Jack. 'Do me a fav— I just meant, will it count for anything if you don't believe?'

'I think it'll do the job all right, Dad.' Sam put his hand on his father's arm. 'You know, I think I've forgotten what it felt like to believe. And what it felt like to know what you're believing in. If you can remind me, I'd really like you to.'

The rain had stopped and a pale sun had started to shine. The mourners from the earlier funeral were trickling back to their cars. Some held handkerchiefs and moved silently with downcast eyes. Others were laughing and chatting, relieved to be walking away from the inevitability of death, at least for the time being.

Sam checked the time again. 'This is it. Let's go.' They walked side by side along a paved drive towards the squat, flat-roofed funeral chapel.

'I thought maybe your mother might come,' said Jack. 'I asked her a couple of times but I could see how she was getting, so I didn't push it.'

Sam nodded. 'That's what I expected. But she got to say her piece to Esther before she died. I hope that did her some good.'

Jack stopped walking and Sam followed suit. They were looking into each other's eyes. 'You know, Son, it did. I think it was a bit like closing a book for her. I'm glad she did it.'

'So, does that mean I'm forgiven for starting this whole thing?' said Sam.

Jack put his hands on his son's shoulders. 'Son, what's to forgive? You don't always do what you're told, but you always do what you think is right. Believe me, I've also put a few noses out of joint in my time. You're a chip off the old block, you know that?'

*

The chapel's large double doors were open and bolted back. Looking inside, Sam took in a plain prayer-room lit only by four shaded bulbs hung on cords from the ceiling. It had white-plastered walls, two small windows and a green-tiled floor. There was a whiff of carbolic in the air. Apart from the few wooden folding chairs that were scattered around, there was no seating. In the centre of the room on a dais was a lectern draped with a red velvet cloth embroidered with a gold Star of David. Beyond the chapel the weak sunshine glinted on a landscape composed entirely of white headstones. Somewhere out there, thought Sam, his grandmother would soon lie buried.

'Boychick!' Sam recognised the voice before turning round. Ron Green, wearing a dark-blue suit and a matching trilby hat, had been walking behind them along the drive.

'Hello, Ron,' said Sam. 'Dad, this is my – my friend Ron Green.'

'Pleased to meet you, Mister Shaykin. I wish you long life,' said Ron, pumping Jack's hand with both of his. 'Quite a boy you've got here. You should be proud.'

'I am,' said Jack. 'Very proud.'

'Me and my wife Rachel, God bless her, we've got two,' said Ron. 'Leo, ten already. And Ella, *kaynahorah*, twelve in a month's time. You want to see a photo?'

Before Ron could get his wallet more than halfway out, their attention was drawn to the arrival of a grey Bentley limousine. The driver unloaded a wheelchair and opened the door to help Sam's great-aunts Eva and Sarah out. He hurried to greet them. 'Auntie Eva! Auntie Sarah! I wasn't sure if you could make it.'

'What, you thought we wouldn't come?' said Sarah. 'I said to Eva – what did I say, Eva?'

'You said we'll go and say our goodbyes and make a day of it,' said Eva, winking at Sam. 'You said your old boyfriend Micky Solomon's got a wedding car business in Portslade, you'll get him to send a driver.'

Sam took charge of the wheelchair and saw his great-aunts into the chapel, where Jack and Ron were chatting like old acquaintances. 'Eva! Sarah!' said Jack. 'A *mechayeh* to see you! I wish you both long life!' They exchanged embraces.

'And who's this?' said Sarah, scowling at Ron. He bowed and took her hand. 'Ron Green, Madam. An old friend of Sam's. By profession—'

'Aaron Greenbaum?' said Sarah.

Ron looked at her with new interest. 'Yes, that's what—'

'Mother, Julia, Father, Asher? Greenbaum the bootmaker's, Plumber's Row, Whitechapel?'

'Yes, but…' It was the first time Sam had known Ron lost for words.

'You haven't changed,' said Sarah. 'I was a friend of your mother's. You don't remember me?'

'Oh, yes,' Ron stammered, 'now that you mention it—'

'You should,' said Sarah, 'I used to give you tuppence for sweets when I took my shoes to be mended. You were just a little *pisher* then. You always had a runny nose. Your mother's still alive?'

'Thank God, yes.'

'Remember me to her. Tell her Sarah Markovitch. Symonds as was.'

Sam found Eva a chair, checked the time and drew Ron aside. 'It's almost eleven, Ron. Did you arrange everything like you said?'

Ron patted his hand. 'Don't you worry about a thing, boychick. Any moment now.'

Four bearded men in black suits and wide-brimmed felt hats appeared, each in turn shaking hands with Sam and Jack and wishing them long life, before standing together in a group, their heads bent together in murmured conversation.

'Do you know who they are?' said Sam.

Ron nodded. 'They're my mourners. I bought them in for the *mitzvah* and a couple of quid on top. In case we were short of a *minyan*.'

'Ron, you think of everything,' said Sam. 'Will we make it?'

Ron counted on his fingers. 'There's you and me, your dad, the rabbi, the cemetery foreman and his clerk, plus those four, that makes ten. Are you expecting any other men?'

Sam shook his head. 'We just made it, then,' said Ron.

A taxi pulled up and delivered its passengers. Anna Bijou was immaculate in a navy-blue outfit and a pill-box hat. It took Sam a few seconds to recognise the other smartly dressed woman as Maisie, Esther's ground-floor neighbour and friend.

'I hope you won't mind us coming,' said Anna. 'Maisie particularly wanted to pay her respects, especially when she found out Esther was your grandma. She asked me to bring her along.'

'Mind?' said Sam. I'm very grateful to you both for wanting to come. As you can see, not many people did.'

'That's a shame,' said Maisie. 'I know she had her ways, but she was a nice woman, was Esther.' She looked around nervously and lowered her voice. 'Sorry. Did I talk too loud? Tell you the truth, I'm a bit nervous. I've never been to a Jewish funeral. I don't want to show myself up.'

'You won't,' said Sam. 'Come and meet my family.'

*

Exactly on time the hearse arrived, a highly polished old black Rolls-Royce that drove slowly up to the chapel with two pallbearers in top hats walking beside it. Sam felt the emotion well up as he watched the men open the rear doors and lift the coffin, covered with a plain black drape, onto a small trolley and wheel it into the chapel. Leaving the drape in place they settled the coffin by the dais, closed the double doors and retreated to a discreet distance. Everyone fell silent. The coffin had become the focal point of the room. Sam stared at its outline, softened by the cloth covering. He tried to detach himself from the thought that a dead woman who had been his grandmother was lying just a few feet from him. Strange ideas came into his head. What if there had been a mistake of some kind – if it wasn't her in there at all? What if he could go back to Henderson House now and find her still there? In the silence that had settled on the room he kept his gaze fixed on the coffin, as if hoping that his eyes could drill through the wood and see the figure lying inside.

The rabbi, a gaunt man in his sixties wrapped in a blue and white prayer shawl, came in through a side door, accompanied by the cemetery foreman and his clerk, also in prayer shawls. He mounted the dais and ran his eyes over the meagre congregation. 'Good morning, everyone. If the ladies and gentlemen would please separate so that we may begin? Ladies on this side, gentlemen over there. Thank you.'

Sarah, who had been in conversation with Jack and Ron, uttered a snort of derision and locked down the brake on her wheelchair with an audible thunk. Eva stood resolutely beside her. The rabbi opened his mouth to remonstrate but caught Sarah's look before he could speak, and contented himself with a roll of his eyes. He polished his glasses and cleared his throat loudly as a sign that he was ready to begin. Everyone fell silent as he placed his hands on the lectern and began reciting the funeral service. In a pleasingly mellow tenor voice he half-sang, half-chanted a series of prayers in Hebrew, followed by some spoken ones in English. Sam automatically made the ritual responses at the appropriate moments, but his attention remained fixed on Esther's coffin. Deep feelings were stirring in him. The rabbi's voice receded into the background as he examined them one by one. What if Esther had been paid this much attention while she was still alive? What if someone had said to her, while she was still alive to hear it, that they thought she was a nice woman? Wouldn't that have made a difference? What if people had known what she'd suffered, had tried to understand, had tried to help her to heal? Was it right, what his mother had said in the hospice, that she'd had a choice and she'd chosen to be an abusive mother and wife – to be evil, as his parents called her? Did she really ever have a choice? Hadn't that been taken away from her, by her own father every bit as much as by those rapists? Had this woman really deserved to be shunned and hated all through her life?

The rabbi was speaking in Hebrew now, reciting David's Psalm 16. Sam remembered the musty room above the synagogue in Lea Bridge Road where another rabbi had taught the class the meaning of the line that he'd translated on the blackboard as *Yea, I have a delightsome heritage.* Was that in his parents' minds when they tried so hard to see Libby off? Did they believe they had a duty to save him from betraying his 'delightsome heritage'? Well, it was time to stop holding that against them. Time to let that hurt go too.

The rabbi began singing the closing portion of the service, with his father, Ron, the *mitzvah* mourners and the cemetery foreman and his clerk joining in. Never taking his eyes from Esther's coffin, Sam returned to his thoughts. What was disturbing him? Loss? Yes, certainly that, even though he'd known Esther for a very short time, and found her difficult, to say the least, for most of it. Grief? Possibly – no, definitely. Love? For Esther? How could that be? But yes, he had to admit to himself, he'd loved her. Pity? Without doubt. Self-pity? Yes again. But why? Fear of the thought of his own death? Ridiculous! Uncertainty? Ah, maybe that was it. For years now, he'd seen no sense in people being divided up into followers of different faiths and beliefs. He didn't believe in it, didn't need it. Nevertheless, a thought was beating into his brain, a simple sentence that threatened to give tongue, cutting across the rabbi's prayers. He had to force himself not to shout it out: 'Who will say *kaddish* for me?'

He jerked out of his reverie as his father dug him in the ribs. The rabbi's voice held a hint of irritation as he raised his voice and asked the question for the third time: 'Who will say *kaddish* for the departed' – he looked down at his notes – 'the departed Esther Symonds?'

'I will.' Sam stepped forward with his prayer-book open. He knew he wasn't just going through the motions.

*

'At least the rain held off,' said Anna, as Sam helped her over a patch of uneven ground on their way back to the chapel.

'Yes, it did,' said Sam. 'Thank goodness.'

'Looks like it might rain again,' said Maisie.

He was grateful to Anna for her thoughtfulness in starting this exchange of platitudes, which she doubtless understood was all he could cope with at the moment. Ahead of them, his father and Ron were sharing the task of pushing Sarah's wheelchair along the narrow gravelled path between two rows of tombstones. Eva walked a pace behind, placing her feet carefully and leaning on a walking stick. The rabbi was engrossed in a conversation with one of the *mitzvah* mourners. The other three had walked away from the graveside as soon as the final prayer had ended, and were now out of sight.

The burial of Esther's coffin had been without frills, but not lacking in dignity. The pallbearers had opened two doors at the rear of the chapel, identical to the two at the front, and wheeled the coffin between the rows of tombstones to the grave that had been prepared for Esther. Behind them walked the rabbi intoning prayers, and behind him everyone else. At the graveside the rabbi said the final prayer, two gravediggers lowered the coffin, and the rabbi invited *'the gentlemen'* each to throw shovelfuls of earth onto it. That had been the hardest part for Sam. He'd recoiled at every hollow thud of the clods of rain-soaked earth on the lid of the coffin. Relieved that the ritual was over, he'd turned his back on Esther's grave, unable to keep his emotions under control any longer. Moments later, the gravediggers had begun filling it in.

The space outside the chapel was now serving as a

dispersal area. Eva and Sarah's limousine was waiting for them. The chauffeur held the door open and Sam helped them in.

'Well, that's Esther,' said Sarah. 'So we live, so we die. That's life.' She gave Sam's cheek a hearty pinch – the Jewish Death Lock, he and his friends used to call it when they were kids – and a smacking kiss. 'Come and see your aunties. We'll visit Neptune again. He's been asking after you and your Deborah. Where is she, by the way?'

'Abroad,' said Sam. 'Working.' He hugged the thought of her letter to himself. 'Look, there's no need to rush away. It's a long drive back to Brighton and you must be hungry. Shall we get some lunch somewhere first?'

'You see that?' said Eva, pointing to a huge wicker hamper on the front passenger seat, 'I made us a little picnic for the way home.'

Sam laughed. It felt good to laugh. 'I bet there's some tasty stuff in there. Come to think of it, I'm a bit peckish myself.'

'There's plenty,' said Sarah. 'Jump in and come with us. Stay the night on the sofa.'

'It's tempting. Maybe another time.' He shut the car door and blew them a final kiss. 'Safe journey.'

Ron, Anna and Maisie joined him as he waved his great-aunts out of sight.

'I'll be off now, boychick,' said Ron. 'I've got two suits to finish off for Jeremy Thorpe, MP. Very particular, is our Jeremy. Can't afford any mistakes. I'm dropping off these two ladies on the way.'

'Just a minute, please.' Sam drew Ron aside. 'Ron, I can't thank you enough for organising all this. You'll need to let me know how much —'

Ron held up a hand. 'Plenty of time for that, boychick. We'll work something out.And, boychick, I'm proud of you. I mean that. Hashem's written this one up against your name, I guarantee you.'

‘I don’t—’ Sam stopped himself just in time.

THIRTY-THREE

Sam woke late from a deep, peaceful and dreamless sleep, the best he could remember having in years. He passed a relaxed morning playing his favourite LPs and tidying his flat. It was hard to believe that Esther's funeral was only yesterday. With the urgency, the conflicts and dilemmas of his quest suddenly at an end, he could feel time slowing down and stretching out. By midday he was finding it difficult to cope with having nothing in particular to do. He was surprised to realise that the habit of visiting Henderson House was still in his system, even though there was nothing now to draw him back there. Except that, for reasons he couldn't explain to himself, the thought of Esther's flat left wide open to intrusion and unprotected from further abuse disturbed him. It was as if this was the final thing he needed to do for her. Before he'd fully thought it through he was on his way, walking instead of driving, in an attempt to work off some of his restless energy.

Anna had been efficient as always. As he arrived, a workman was putting the finishing touches to a new door. Soon the Council would clear what remained in the flat and someone new would move in. He left, satisfied that he'd completed his last ever service for Esther.

Leaving Henderson House, he followed Keir Hardie Street down to where it ended at the old timber-yards beside the Lea Canal. Threading his way through a fenced-off demolition site he reached the towpath where, years before, he and his school friends used to come and watch the barges loaded with timber being towed to – come to think of it, until that moment he'd never thought to wonder where they were going. The towpath was rutted and muddy. In front of him, a long-dead barge was half-submerged in the canal's murky water. He could smell the decay of the rotting wood and the dead vegetation that had gathered around it. He stood there for a while, trying to decide whether to go back the way he'd come, or turn left or right and follow the towpath to wherever it led. He had a vague idea that turning right would take him to a bridge over the Lea Canal where it ran beside Lingfield Park, and he set off in that direction.

He walked along the towpath, hoping but not knowing for sure that he was going the right way, occasionally being passed by a cyclist barking instructions through a megaphone to the racing-boats skimming along on the scummy green water. For once, he'd chosen the right direction. He came to the bridge he'd hoped to find, and walked up the steep path through Lingfield Park to what he and his father had always called 'their' bench, which he was pleased to find unoccupied.

Of all the places he'd ever been in his entire thirty years, this spot was his unbeaten favourite. From this bench, perched on the top edge of the River Lea valley, he could see grassy meadows sloping steeply down to the Lea Canal itself, and beyond that the Lea Marshes stretching away in the distance, criss-crossed by silver train lines that glinted in the watery October sun. All this, just a twenty minute walk from his flat in Cliften Square, and not much further in the opposite direction from his parents' home on the Frobisher Estate. He'd sat here countless times over the years with his father, who would always indicate the view with a patrician sweep of his arm and say, 'Some day, my son and heir, all this will be yours!' Every time his father said it, they'd laugh as they remembered that as a small child he'd actually believed it was true.

The day was cold despite the sun, but the walk had made him warm. He was in no hurry to go anywhere.

Autumn had come to the park, and the landscape was turning to russet and gold. It was a perfect spot for him to sit and think until he was ready to move on, which he was in no particular hurry to do. When he'd rested here and gathered his thoughts for long enough, he'd go home and finish the letter to Deborah that he'd started last night but had been too exhausted to finish. He'd stick with it until he'd captured the words that always seemed to melt away whenever he tried to write them down. He'd tell her that he loved her, that he longed to be with her. He'd ask her if they could get married. He'd tell her that he'd willingly stand under the *chuppah* with her and stamp down on the glass to secure their happiness together.

He lay down on the bench and squinted up into the wan sun. Colours danced across his pupils and he squeezed his eyes shut. He saw nothing behind the lids except a field of reddish light. No hint of Libby there, or any other demons from his past.

He sat up and opened his eyes, watched a tiny toy train chug its way across the marshes, and thought back to the day just four or five months ago when Ron Green had come to his door and brought Esther into his life. What was it Ron had said when he'd first come calling? Something about maybe Hashem bringing them together for a reason? He'd laughed it off back then, dismissed it as part of Ron's sales pitch. But in the past few months he'd learned that it was unwise to be too certain of anything. After all, it was also Ron who'd advised him never to forget that in this world nothing is what it seems.

Another thought struck him. If he hadn't decided to put an end to the grudges that he'd held against his parents for so long, he'd have risked sowing the seeds of a new family broygus. And that, he was determined, was never going to happen again.

Now he needed to think about going back to work. He'd call Gordon later, then Eleni, and start again in a day or two. Go back to flogging package holidays for a living. Go home with a takeaway to an empty flat every night and live in limbo while waiting for Deborah's reply. The thought left him cold.

A noise caught his attention. Someone had walked up behind him while he he'd been looking into the distance, absorbed in his thoughts. He turned and saw an old woman dressed in an ill-fitting threadbare tracksuit and a Russian army-style fur hat with the ear flaps dangling, pushing a rusty pram piled high with bulging plastic sacks. She stopped the pram beside the bench by jamming a sandal-clad foot under one wheel, left the sandal there and sat down next to him. Her clothes were dirt-encrusted and from her body came a smell that reminded him of blocked drains. Her thin face was deeply lined and there was dirt in the crevices. She stretched an arthritic hand out to him. 'Fifty pence for a cup of tea, mate? Come on, give us it?'

His heart went out to her. Under the dirt it was Esther's face, pale, lined and pinched. And it was her voice, cracked, hoarse and ill. He took a five-pound note from his wallet and held it out to her. She stared at it, then at him. 'Gertcha!' she growled. 'I ain't no fucking prossie!'

He smiled. 'Just take it, please, and leave me alone. I'm busy.' The woman snatched the note from his fingers without any thanks, rescued her sandal and shambled off.

He'd been sitting long enough for the warmth of the walk to have worn off. He picked up his backpack, ready to move on. His notebook was still in it. He took it out and turned back to the first entry he'd made. *Sunday 11th July 1976. Another scorching hot day. A man called Ron Green came looking for me.* And now all that was over. He'd read it all again some time, maybe write it up properly into a story. Maybe one day even write a book about it. He turned to the last entry, that he'd written yesterday after getting home from the funeral. He didn't bother to read it, but turned over to a new blank page. A wind was getting up, blowing dead leaves around his feet as he took his pen out and wrote in capital letters across the top of the page, *WHERE DO I GO FROM HERE?*

The line below that was easy: *I WANT DEBORAH BACK IN MY LIFE.* The next one was more difficult. *I WANT HER TO KNOW HOW MUCH I LOVE HER.*

It was hopeless. He couldn't get any further than that. He closed the notebook, put it away and started on his walk home. He didn't need to pay attention to where he was going. He'd been walking this path since he was eleven years old. The forlorn, long-abandoned tramsheds; the synagogue on the corner of Lea Bridge Road where he'd gone to Hebrew classes and studied to prepare for his *barmitzvah;* the pond with its rustic bridge that must have stood, centuries earlier, beside what was then a village green; the secondhand furniture shops and pubs of Lower Cliften road, and finally the alley that led into Cliften Square. That was the problem, he now saw. It was all too familiar. It was time to let it all go and start afresh, if only he could find the courage to do it.

The absence of Deborah pervaded the flat. He dropped his coat and backpack in the hall and sank into the sofa, still lost in his thoughts. There was no doubt, his time with Esther had been like a thick line drawn under his life to date. He'd done things he'd never have imagined, learned things, understood things. And now, he knew, it was time to make sure that everything below that line would be better than what had been above it. There would be no more depression, no more dwelling on the past, no more blaming and resentment. No more taciturnity, self-centredness, belittling of beliefs. He'd wasted more than enough of the valuable time given to him on such things. If only Esther could have known it, at the very end of her life she'd done an enormous service to him in leading him towards those decisions. Against all odds, in the end she'd brought good into her grandson's life.

He decided to make the line even thicker and more permanent; to lay his past to rest and scatter its ashes, clearing the way for him to focus firmly on the future from then on. He gathered together his Esther Quest notebook, his mother's mutilated photos, Esther's album and her precious framed photo of Isaac, dropped them into a carrier bag and took them downstairs to where the block's large communal dustbins were kept. He opened the lid of the nearest one, lifted the bag to shoulder height and muttered a word of farewell. At the last second he paused, sighed, let the lid drop and carried the bag back upstairs. In his bedroom he tucked it into the bottom of a drawer where he kept some old clothes that he no longer wore but couldn't bear to part with. And there, he promised himself, it would stay undisturbed. Maybe one day his children, or even his grandchildren would find it, look inside and ask him to tell them its story. The thought made him laugh, but only for a moment. He had things to do. He wanted to finish his letter to Deborah in time to get it into the evening post. And he hadn't yet called Gordon about going back to work, and office hours were nearly over. He'd better get moving. He picked up the phone and started dialling the number of Head Office. Halfway through he stopped, replaced the receiver, lifted it and started dialling again. He drummed his fingers on the telephone table and whistled something without a tune as he waited for an answering voice.

'Good afternoon, SL Travel. Can I help you?'

'Hi, Eleni. It's Sam.'

'Sam! Great to hear from you. How are you?'

'Never better, thanks, Eleni. Listen, could you please get me a flight to Barcelona?'

ABOUT THE AUTHOR

Laurence Kershook grew up and went to school in Hackney, East London. His forbears, who settled in London's Whitechapel in the 1880s, were Jewish refugees from Smorgon in present-day Belarus, and from Wielun and Kielce in Southern Poland. He spent his working life as a teacher and a trainer of teachers. Post-retirement he has returned to live in Hackney and rekindled his early loves for listening to and performing jazz and writing fiction. His stories have been shortlisted in competitions mounted by London City University and Byte The Book. *The Broygus* is his first novel.

ACKNOWLEDGEMENTS

Thanks to the modern-day miracles of self-publishing, print-on-demand and e-book technology, *The Broygus* got there in the end. There are some people I particularly want to thank for helping me to make that possible.

First and always foremost there's my partner Frances Magee. The extent of her encouragement and the quality of her contributions defy my powers of description. Justine Solomons of Byte The Book provided unfailing support and invaluable advice. I also owe my thanks to Ingrid Charles, Leslie Mapp, Rebekah Lattin-Rawstrone and Caroline Goldsmith; to early readers Yvonne Birch, Chris Jude, Sara Magee, John McClafferty, Diane McLoughlin, Achim Schwenk and Gaby Weiner; to Jeremy Kershook for his work on the cover photo; and finally, to my friends from the 2018-19 Novel Studio group.

Printed in Great Britain
by Amazon

78376527R00189